A GRIFFON'S NEST

BETTY LEVIN
A GRIFFON'S NEST

MACMILLAN PUBLISHING CO., INC.
New York
COLLIER MACMILLAN PUBLISHERS
London

FOR ANNIE AND JAMES

Macmillan Publishing Co., Inc., 866 Third Avenue, New York, N.Y. 10022
Collier-Macmillan Canada Ltd.
Printed in the United States of America

1   2   3   4   5   6   7   8   9   10

Library of Congress Cataloging in Publication Data
Levin, Betty.
A griffon's nest.   Sequel to The sword of Culann.
[1.Space and time—Fiction. 2.Orkney Island—History—Fiction]
I.Title.
PZ7.L5759Gr   [Fic]   74-23497   ISBN 0-02-757350-8

Huginn and Muninn, Thought and Memory
Fly over the world each day.
I fear for Thought, lest he come not back,
But I fear yet more for Memory.

—From a poem in the Elder Edda
preserved in the *Codex Regius*
and translated by L. M. Hollander

PART ONE

ONE

"THERE, there it is," Evan shouted. He was standing on the cabin top, his arm around the mast. He peered into the haze as if sighting land after days at sea. The air was still and heavy with moisture. "There," cried Evan, pointing for Jon. "See it?"

Jon, a newcomer to Maine, commented that it looked like all the other islands around here.

"That," muttered Claudia, "is what I call a fresh way of looking at natural phenomena." She pronounced *natural phenomena* with heavy sarcasm.

"Claudia, that's enough," snapped her mother.

"I just don't see why we have to have those people on our island," Claudia whispered fiercely. She stared off. Susan, her mother, would be giving Claudia one of those looks that told her she was being unbearable again. Lately almost everyone had taken to moaning and groaning about this new stage they said she was going through.

"Remember," Phil, her stepfather, pointed out reasonably, "it was Sam Withorn's idea to cruise for the eclipse. To get a break from all the work he's put in cleaning out that old house they've bought. Thrumcap Island was your afterthought."

"Well, you can't make me like them."

"I can expect you to be civil," Susan responded.

Phil waved and called to Jon's father in the day-sailer behind them. Then he concentrated on leading the way

2

past the outlying rocks into the little cove. As they rounded the point, Claudia caught sight of Mr. Colman's double-ender lying slack to its mooring. Running forward to ready the anchor, she shot Evan a quick, gleeful grin. Mr. Colman was there on the island. Evan, staring, looked as if he was holding his breath.

As the boat circled and came to rest up-tide in the windless cove, Phil cut the engine and came to Claudia's side, then let her drop the anchor. It made a soft plop, barely disturbing the gray surface. The stillness all around them was profound. Something creaked and flapped on the Withorns' rented day-sailer not many yards off.

Claudia looked out toward the farther point. Their islet, their Other Place. She gauged the watermark against the shore. Half tide. They would not be able to cross over for a while yet.

Suddenly Jon's voice cut through the hush. "How many feet of tide here?"

Mr. Withorn answered from the other boat. "Nearly fourteen feet. You know what happens when the Bay of Fundy deepens. . . ."

Claudia felt Phil's hand on her shoulder. Was he warning her to behave? She looked up. "It's a good-sized island," he observed. "It would be hard for three kids to get in each other's way if they didn't want to."

She nodded. He wanted her to promise some kind of accommodation to this boy he'd foisted on them. "Don't spoil it for Evan," Phil continued quietly. "He seems to be making a new friend."

There were so many places to revisit that Evan was torn.

He wanted to show Jon the deep mossy woods with the orange mushrooms and the slimy swamp; he wanted to point out the place where the dead sheep had lain, to look down into the ravine where the live sheep sheltered; he wanted to search out the hidden raspberry patches beyond the old well and gaze out to the rocks on the far side, the unnavigable side of the island, where the seals basked on low-tide rocks; and of course he wanted to check out their unfinished stone hut, probably in ruins there on the windward beach after a winter of gales and tides. But above all, there was Colman, whose last name he could never remember, though he was Evan's special friend. First, Evan had to bring Jon to Colman's shack, the shack that was like a shell that fitted itself to the contours of that old man's strange and lonely existence.

"It stinks," was Jon's first comment. He said it as they halted before the granite step.

"It's all right," Claudia said. "It smells right."

Evan seemed suddenly tentative, possibly afraid that things would be different. "We call him Mr. Colman," he whispered.

Jon snickered. "It smells like he craps in here, if you ask me."

"Well, we didn't ask," muttered Claudia. She thrust past him into the darkness, then waited while her eyes grew accustomed to the closeness, the chaos, the filth and smoke.

Mr. Colman was in his usual place. At first she thought he was sleeping, but then in the dimness she began to see the eyes that peered out from under bristling brows. It was as if the year since they'd seen him had only been a day. Nothing was changed. He seemed to be wearing all

4

the shirts he would need for winter. The cap was on his head. The inscrutable, nearly vacant face slowly drew itself into a squint that might have passed for a smile.

"Two of 'em," rasped the old man, pointing past her. "Happen one's a shadow."

Jon giggled.

"You wait behind me," Evan directed. Then he said to Mr. Colman, "No, he's real, his name's Jon. He's older than me but younger than Claude. He came with his father. His mother decided to stay home. Our parents are here, too. We were afraid you might not be. We've wondered about your crow, but—" He looked toward the window where the crow dung had built up over the winter. "I guess you've got him all right," he finished, his eyes on the old man's face, his tone steady, the way it always was when the two of them carried on a conversation.

"He's hereabouts, all right, the bastard," Mr. Colman told Evan. "See he don't follow you." The old man set his watery eyes on Evan and Claudia. "You keep out of trouble now. Out of the sun burning through. See the crow don't get lost again." He paused. "Nor you."

"What's he mean?" Jon whispered from behind. "Ask him about the bronze man."

Evan shook his head. "Still lobstering?"

"Don't get around too good. A few pots off the island, the narrows."

"Do you still milk the sheep?" Claudia asked.

"Christ." He threw back his head and squeaked a kind of laugh. "Her and her baby both." He rocked back and forth. "Plenty of it." He pointed to the crate beside the door, and Claudia knew he was offering them some of the

5

special pudding he made from sheep's milk and a seaweed he picked at low tide.

"We'll be back," she told him. "We have to help set up camp. We want to sleep where we did last year, only the grownups want to stay on the boats. We have to show them we can make a decent camp so they'll let us stay ashore." Her glance fell to the hearth.

Mr. Colman, without shifting in the slightest way, seemed to sense what she was too afraid to ask. He nodded toward the loose stone. "Go on. Go on, the two of you."

Claudia knelt and dragged the flat stone to one side. Jon started forward. "Is that all?" he exclaimed, when he saw the dim, dull shape of the metal man. "You guys act like it's alive, or something. Like it's precious."

Claudia drew it from its hearthbed and held it up. She cast Evan an accusing look. That's what he got for bringing along this creep.

"Precious," Mr. Colman mouthed after Jon. "Precious."

Claudia couldn't tell whether the old man was laughing through his wheezing. "Is it all right?" she asked him. "I mean, in case later. . . ."

"Get on then, you two. You'll have no sun to fear this day."

Outside, even with the thick haze that hovered over the island, the brightness was nearly blinding.

"Let me see it," Jon demanded. "What was that old guy talking about in there?"

Claudia held the bronze man for Jon to see, but would not release it. Mr. Colman had specified the two of them.

"Let me hold it."

"It has to be given," Evan tried to explain. "Mr. Col-

6

man. . . . Once when it was whole, when it was a sword, there were marks on the blade, a kind of writing. It's Mr. Colman's now. I mean, this hilt is."

"It's too small for a sword hilt," Jon retorted. He dismissed the bronze man with a shrug. "I wouldn't believe anything that old guy said. He doesn't even make sense. All that about the sun and everything. He's crazy."

Claudia clutched the heavy man-shaped metal. Why bother with this kid? It wasn't even any of his business. She couldn't understand Evan wanting to share the wonder of the hilt with him. How could she convince someone like that of the bronze man's power? How could she explain what she didn't understand herself? Last summer, when the fog drifted in from the southeast or the morning mists rose from the land, she and Evan had followed the bronze man through the grayness, halfway between light and dark, into another time, another place. And when the sun had broken through, they had been trapped there across the ages.

While they had been in the Other Place, time had been different for them, reality altered. But now, even with the hilt right there in her hands, Mr. Colman's warning about the sun seemed remote, far-fetched. She had to force herself to recall that last summer she had very nearly been killed. Holding the man of bronze, she could think only of Fergus who had trusted her and let her serve him, of how for Fergus the hilt had been a burden as much as an object of enchantment.

Claudia's thoughts broke off as Jon shifted impatiently. "What Mr. Colman said," she began guardedly, "had to do with how this hilt leads . . . some people, but only . . . ." She saw Jon's look of contempt and stopped.

7

But Evan, though he sounded exasperated, wouldn't give up. "I told you," he reminded Jon. "I told you how the hilt was made for a burial, but you said it was impossible, so you didn't really listen. Marks were put on the blade by the people of the mounds and then it was supposed to lead a hero to the Land of Mists and—"

"Land of Mists. Come on, Evan. That's superstition."

"Okay," snapped Claudia. "Then don't worry about it. Just leave it alone."

"I'd just like a little demonstration of proof," Jon mumbled.

"We'll give it to you." Evan was ebullient, certain that what was for him a miracle must be a miracle for all. "See, this hilt's been passed on from one carrier to the next through hundreds of years, until finally Mr. Colman's father got hold of it before he came to this country, and Mr. Colman thinks it was trying to lead his father somewhere here, and it leads us, it leads some people like us who follow it, and we'll give you a demonstration just as soon as the tide's down. You'll see."

"Don't be so sure he will," Claudia cautioned.

Jon glared at her, then strode on ahead toward the sound of voices and someone chopping driftwood.

Evan reached over and touched the stern, wild face of the bronze man. "You know, Claude, it's not Jon's fault he's the way he is." Evan took the figure from Claudia, turned it, stared at the lines scratched into its back. "It's his parents. They're always making him learn. Making him work out demonstrations of proof."

"Tough," Claudia retorted. "I know kids with worse parents than that. Kids have to rise above their parents'

8

limitations. Otherwise people would never change. They'd go on being just as dumb as their ancestors."

"But Jon's folks aren't ancestors," Evan pointed out. "They're parents he has to live with, and they keep bugging him to be smart. Anyhow, he's no worse about the bronze man than the other kids were last summer."

Claudia thought about the "other kids," her own big brother and Evan's older sisters, her stepsisters. There had been a difference. They had teased and even been nasty at times, but that was because they had to fight against an inclination to believe at least some of what Claudia and Evan had recounted of their experiences with the bronze man. Jon wasn't like that at all. He was sure. He was beyond doubt, he was so sure of himself.

TWO

THEY could see the rocky bar that connected the islet to the main island; the water was deceptively clear. Plunging in, Evan found himself knee-deep. He yelped and clambered back. "I'm numb," he told Claudia, rubbing his legs. "We'd better wait till it's lower."

"Listen," Claudia said to him, "you heard Mr. Withorn. He knows all about weather patterns, and if he says it's clearing, we're finished. We won't see anything."

"If it doesn't clear," put in Jon, who was stooping at

the water's edge and reaching out for whelks and tiny star-fish to put in his specimen bucket, "then we won't get to see the eclipse. Which is what we came for."

What *you* came for, thought Claudia. "Or if it clears while we're there," she went on to Evan, "if we wait till it's really clearing. . . ." She let the threat hang unfinished between them.

Jon looked up. "What then? What if it does?"

Evan said, "I told you. You get caught then, in the Other Place. The sun locks you in."

"Or out," Claudia reminded Evan, and with that set off, stomping and splashing along the bar and clenching her teeth against the icy grip of the water. It was all she could do not to scream or quit, but she wouldn't even look back. She clutched the bronze man. She forced her-self to believe that if she kept going, Evan would follow. As for Jon, she didn't care what he did. Let him collect his tender living creatures on the ebb tide and watch them die in the lifeless water at the bottom of his bucket.

At last she heard the boys coming, heard their gasps, the breathlessness at the other side where all three of them paused before climbing the slope that broadened onto the green back of the islet. This part, which they called the tail of the turtle, joined the islet's main body; its carapace spread before them, ridging slightly at the center. The water that nearly surrounded the islet seemed to trap the haze.

"It's colder here," Jon observed. "Darker. I think it has to do with the contrast between the land temperature and the sea."

"Maybe it won't work any more," Evan whispered to Claudia.

That was what Claudia had been thinking. That was why she stood there instead of climbing onto the turtle's back and moving toward the seaward cliff. And if it did work, what would they find now that Fergus was dead, his story told? A barefoot scribe had taken the hilt from him. She couldn't imagine anything beyond the completion of Fergus's story. And yet it was impossible to resist the pull of the bronze man. Did Evan feel this too? Maybe he wasn't so sure he wanted it to work after all. She saw him lean back as though to brace against the force that had brought him this far. His hesitancy was like a goad. Never mind holding back and worrying. She extended the bronze man to him so that he could hold a leg. They started forward.

"Hey," called Jon, "wait for me. I don't know the way."

Evan slowed, then pulled back. "Here," he said, grabbing Jon's sleeve. "You take a leg too." He proffered the bronze man. When Jon stiffened, Evan changed his tack. "It'll keep you connected to us so you don't get lost or fall onto the rocks."

Jon took hold of the bronze man, and together, clumsily, the three of them edged forward.

"Where are the birds?" asked Jon.

"Shut up," said Claudia. She half hoped the terns, which regarded all people as invaders of their nesting ground, would zero in and dive bomb this seeker after birds. But it was too late in the day. There were no terns hurtling down on them, no guillemots fluttering low. Only a few languid gulls checked out their progress.

"When is whatever it is supposed to happen?" Jon wanted to know.

"Ssh," said Evan. "Listen."

They stood still, Claudia a little ahead of the two boys, straining into the whispery hush of the receding tide. Pebbles shifted on the beach below. The water surged from an unseen wave, then, hissing, sucked back into itself.

"It's a bell." Jon's voice filled the silence. "Must be some bell buoy around here. Sound carries more when the water vapor—"

"There's no bell buoy," Evan told him.

Claudia started toward the sound, a bell surely, clear and steady. Then through the haze she began to make out figures. At first they were like mist that is compressed until it becomes visible, white in the growing darkness. But slowly they stepped out of that darkness, each one more present than the one before. She could see no faces. A soft rain fell on them, but they seemed not to feel it. Their measured steps took them to a small stone building shaped like an upside-down boat. The belling ceased as the robed figures entered through a narrow opening; it was as if those steeply curving walls snuffed out sound.

Claudia was left in gray stillness. Where had the hilt led her? This place was nothing like before. Yet it wasn't the newness that gripped her; it was the feeling of being suspended in a world of silence where the fine rain washed away all color, all life.

A voice issued from the stone building. It was deep and slightly nasal. More voices responded all at once, dissonant and powerful. They broke off, and the single voice resumed its chant, rising like the ocean seeking some level determined by things unseen, by storms halfway around the world, by the moon itself.

Turning to make sure that Evan was seeing and hearing

12

all this, she found the boys were gone. So was the bronze man. She stared into the gray thickness, the chanting behind her and somehow muffled, as if she had already left it. "Evan," she whispered. Were they playing a joke on her? It was what you could expect from someone like Jon. She called again, more volume this time, and then moved slowly, blindly, in the direction she imagined them to be.

Maybe Evan was back there somewhere with those white figures; maybe he was searching for her. She could picture him casting about, one hand weaving a way through the fog, the other heavy with its burden of the bronze man. She couldn't picture Jon at all.

"Evan," she called, turning back. But once she'd looked that way again, she couldn't speak or move. The hull-shaped building was still there, its walls forming a continuous line from base to ridge, a solid grace in the fine dense rain. But it was distant now. From her new vantage point she could see that the building was ringed by a stone wall which was in turn enclosed by a larger circle of stone containing clusters of round stone huts. This encircled community was set on a grassy slope that seemed to be part of an islet. She could see how the land rose seaward, ending abruptly in precipitous cliffs. Toward her the islet fell away to a stony beach. She saw how the stones stretched out into a shallow channel to meet the point of land on which she stood.

"Then where am I?" she murmured to herself. This islet lying out before her was a place she had never seen until now. Still, she was certain that she was standing on the turtle's tail, really on the crossing between Thrumcap Island and its own islet. Only where was Evan? If this turned out to be the new place, wherever it was, whenever

13

it was, how could she ever return without the bronze man?

She didn't know which way to go. The faint chanting that sounded from the stone building was no longer compelling. The voices seemed almost sour. The place was bare, the fine rain relentless and cold.

The cold penetrated her damp dungarees, her light jacket; it gripped her throat. She hunched over to escape the falling droplets and heard again what the grownups had said when she and Evan had shown up with the bronze man. Jon's father had remarked that he hadn't realized that girls of Claudia's age still played with things like that. Susan, the mother and stepmother of enough children to take things in her stride, had shrugged and replied easily.

"Strange," Mr. Withorn had murmured. "Maybe part of a Victorian fire tool. Have you tried to identify it?" He'd given Claudia a nice encouraging smile, then turned to Susan and Phil. "Sometimes turning things into a mystery or puzzle will start them learning how to deal with facts, how to seek them out."

Susan had sighed. "Claudia goes about things her own way. It keeps her and Evan busy."

"But it's wasteful," Jon's father had pursued. "Now's the time for them to develop sound habits of thinking." He had laughed. "If only we could give some of Claudia's imagination to Jon and some of his methodology. . . ."

Methodology. Claudia had mentally filed that one away along with *natural phenomena.* She'd make a collection of hot-air words.

Phil had helped her out. "She soaks up a lot of history reading up on the background to her stories."

14

"Good," Mr. Withorn had declared. "That proves she can deal with facts."

"History isn't facts," Claudia had protested; "it's people." Then she had wandered off to sit alone on the great flat rock where last summer they had fished for mackerel and pollock. She'd sat on the rock and listened to Jon and Evan talking.

Thinking about how Evan had been with Jon then brought back to Claudia the possibility that he might be deliberately hiding or avoiding her. She decided not to call again. Hearing her own voice against the rustle of beach pebbles awash was bad enough. But hearing her unanswered call against the chanting voices entombed by stone and remoteness and age was unbearable.

She pressed her hands to her mouth and huddled into her jacket. Was she too far, or not far enough? If she was caught here between her world and the world inhabited by white-robed chanters, then where was Evan? Why wasn't he worried about her? Or scared. Or sorry. Why didn't Evan come?

Three

AFTER what seemed a long while, Claudia decided that going forward was better than staying put. Chilled and aching, she let her feet take her where they would. She looked down, not ahead, and concentrated on avoiding a piece of driftwood, the remnants of a nest still lined with traces of eiderdown.

When she reached the water, she hesitated, then sought out the rocks that formed an ocean paving. The flooded steppingstones must mean that she was on the bar, or anyhow some bar. Here was a mass of rockweed, slippery, but springy too. Hand over hand, she grabbed cold clumps of the rubbery green stuff fused to the rocky surface. Gradually each handhold became more familiar, each step almost automatic. There was a rock that she recognized, bare this time and offering itself like a step, but steeply set beside a giant boulder. Relief made her careless. She heaved herself onto it, forgetting that rocks that were covered at high tide usually supported one kind of slime or another. Her sneaker skidded sideways, thrusting her leg out and throwing her backward. She cried out, not from pain, but from exasperation.

The rockweed cushioned her fall. For an instant she sat wetly and held the leg bent to her chest. She barely heard the splashes behind her. Before she realized these were footsteps, she was knocked flat and pinned beneath a sodden weight. At first she could see nothing but her own hair. Then, as the weight shifted and she twisted beneath it, she saw the faded blue of dungarees, the heavy stitching of Jon's sweater. "Get off me." She punched at him.

"You're not Evan," gasped Jon.

She tried to heave the rest of him aside. "Stupid," she hissed. "Where is he? Where's Evan?"

Jon was sprawled at the edge of the water holding up dripping, sagging sleeves. "I thought . . . I thought he was here. He wanted to get you to see. . . ."

16

"See what?" she demanded.

Jon wrung out one elbow, then the other. "I don't know. Some . . . something he kept staring at."

"You left him?"

"What was there to stay for?"

"What direction?" She grabbed the sleeve of his sweater. "Show me. Does Evan have the bronze man?"

Jon started to laugh. "His dolly? Wouldn't let it out of his hands. Not that I wanted it. He sent me to find you, but I couldn't, and then I couldn't find him either." He wrenched himself free and got to his feet. "You're both crazy. I'm going back."

"You were the last to see him. If anything happens. . . ." She didn't know how to finish the threat. She was used to bullying Evan by appealing to his conscience, but she doubted that this kid had any conscience. She tore off across the rocks again. All at once she knew just where she was, where she had to go. She wasn't even scared any more, only determined. And relieved because Evan had been looking for her, had not betrayed her after all.

It was funny how easy it was to find him now that she was sure of her surroundings. Or maybe it was because she was sure of Evan, the doubts dissolved like the fog by the solid, known things around her, the sea blite at the edge of the high-water mark, the solitary iris stalk piercing the baffle of gray.

Evan was one of those solid things. He gazed off to the southeast, away from her, away from the cove and anchorage, away from old Mr. Colman's shack. He seemed to take a moment to recognize her. Then, sounding perfectly ordinary, he said, "How come you took so long, Claude? There's something funny with that little kid. I don't

17

think it can hear." He stepped aside as though he were standing in front of an invisible window. He pointed for her, but she might as well have been Jon. There was nothing out there but fog and the water slapping against the shingle.

"What is it?" she whispered.

"Sort of a tower," he said. "Like a giant hornet's nest with a wall around it. It's so . . . round. Can't you see it, Claudia? Jon couldn't see a thing. The whole time he just kept talking. So I sent him to find you."

"What kind of people? Are they wearing white robes?"

"White?" Evan sounded impatient. "Can't you see? Look, I think they're all women and kids down there on the beach. They must be picking mussels or something. Just like us at low water. See, the kids stop and eat some, and then the mothers slap them and point to the bags. Probably they're poor. They look pretty messy."

"I saw people in white," Claudia told him. "I saw a weird building too, only it wasn't round."

Evan turned his back on the scene he described. "Were we in two separate places?"

Claudia didn't know, but she thought they'd better stick closer together from now on.

Evan agreed. "I forgot about you because Jon was so nervous. When I began to see, I just dragged him with me, and that must be when you came apart from us. See, I was telling him to hold onto the man and—"

"And I let go," Claudia finished. "That's why I got so mixed up. I didn't have the man any more." She took hold of the knobby arm of the bronze man and turned back with Evan, and it was so evident, so immediate, that

18

she couldn't believe that only moments before none of it had been visible to her.

The building wasn't just tall and round. It belled out from a broad base, then narrowed and straightened as it rose. But the top of it looked broken off. People were all around the base of this conelike structure. The land where she stood was high enough to give her some view of the smaller buildings that clustered around the tower, but she couldn't make out details, couldn't tell more than that there was a lot of activity within the rampart wall.

"I was closer before," Evan whispered. "They didn't notice. They can't tell we're here. Come on. I want you to see this little kid."

The building dominated the area. At first Claudia thought all the people seemed unnaturally small because of its height, but as she approached the paved walkway that led to the entrance, she could tell that they really were small people.

Claudia wanted to work her way into the walled area so that she could see what everyone was up to, but Evan made her skirt the ditch and rampart and continue on to the beach where the women and children were gathering shellfish. Claudia noticed at once the harassed-looking woman who kept glancing out to sea and shouting and gesticulating.

Claudia watched the others, all small and agile. Shabby they might be, with their drab cloth tunics that had no more shape than burlap bags, but they worked with skill and urgency. The children climbed into crevices between rocks where the women could not reach. But one child was bobbing out in the water, and it was this one that had caught Evan's attention.

"She's driving her mother crazy," Evan confided. "At least I think it's a she. And I think that's her mother. They don't like her being out there."

A bell rang out suddenly, cutting through the chatter. Claudia and Evan wheeled around and stared up toward the massive tower. All the activity on the beach ceased. The women, even the children, stood as one, looking in silence toward the emerging procession.

There, taller than the drably covered people, was one of those white-robed figures Claudia had already seen. The figure followed a cluster of smaller men who bore something long that must be either heavy or precious. The bell clanged, a clear bitter note that sometimes went wrong, as if the clapper had hit something else by mistake.

Torches announced the coming of night, though the sky was not yet dark. The procession seemed to disappear at the perimeter of Claudia's vision. The women gathered up their loads of food and herded the children onto the path that wound up to the paving. As they came closer, Claudia could see that their faces were encrusted with dirt and their dark hair matted; weals of mud clung like leeches to their bare feet. The harassed woman shouted out to the water one more time, then flung her load onto her back and started off with the others.

Claudia turned to watch the nearly indistinct head in the water. The child was nearing the beach, but she seemed unhurried. From time to time she disappeared in a neat, silent dive that left only the smallest flick of a wave.

The women and other children reached the paved walkway before this loner stood dripping on the beach. She moved like the night, almost stealthily, until suddenly she was quite close to Claudia and Evan and they could see the sharp, pinched face, the too-large eyes, the underfed frame of a child of about six. Her scrap of tunic clung like an ill-fitting skin. Yet she didn't shiver, didn't hurry—in fact, stepped with a kind of assurance across the stony shingle and up onto the path.

Claudia shivered for her. The small feet trod the softer dirt where the embankment was eroded and the bulwark came to an end. High above rose the mysterious round building, darker than any night, huge and impenetrable.

Following the child, Claudia and Evan rounded the corner and saw a flat-topped stone beside the entrance. Two men with torches stood to the side of it, flanking the gateway through which the women and children hurried.

The small child coming behind hesitated at the stone. She stooped, as small children do when they examine something on the ground. It was like a deep, formal bow and seemed almost laughable in this little wet thing. Then she straightened and raised one leg in an exaggerated step and slowly, deliberately, placed her bare foot on the stone.

The torchbearers cried out. The torches dipped as they swooped down on the child. Then the women bringing up the rear of the group turned and gasped. The child moved quickly. In an instant she stood, legs slightly splayed, like a statue on a pedestal.

Claudia and Evan edged forward. Even in the flickering torchlight they could see that the small wet feet were set squarely in two great foot-shaped depressions on the stone's surface. Claudia could even see the water still dripping down the child's legs, could see two foot-shaped puddles forming on the stone. The child's face registered puzzlement at the stir she had caused, but her stance was triumphant, as if she had just learned how to play a new game and relished her remarkable achievement.

Then the mother shrieked and sprang toward the child. She was blocked by the torchbearers and thrust back against the other women and children, who dragged her backward through the gate. In another moment all were inside, even the torchbearers, all except the child. In the darkness Claudia and Evan could hear a bolt being driven into a socket. The light gone, they couldn't see the child any more. From above, the torchlight reappeared.

They waited a long time, until the returning procession appeared over the black rim of the land, first as diffused light, then as a series of lights, the figures last to be discerned. The gate was opened, and words, low but harsh, passed between those who waited inside and those who now entered. Claudia could not make out any white-robed figure, and whatever it was that the others had been carrying was no longer with them.

Once again Claudia and Evan could hear the gate rammed shut. They waited. Torches flickered above them. Claudia could see the yellow light reflected in the two foot-shaped puddles on the slab. There was no sign of the child. It was as if the night had swallowed every living thing shut out from the murmur of humanity within the great walled circle.

They started back in silence. Just where the pathway sloped down and seemed to become a part of the turtle's tail, Evan turned impulsively, jerking Claudia with him, since they both still clung to the bronze man.

"Look." His voice was reduced; it sounded as though it might belong to one of those small people.

The torches cast their demon reflections on a tiny figure huddled at the base of the tower.

"It's probably a dog or something. You can't really tell at this distance."

"It's not," he retorted.

Claudia tried again. "They're just teaching her a lesson. They'll let her in soon. She's not important enough. . . ." She wanted to say that the child couldn't be important enough to merit such extreme punishment, but she ended up trying to reassure Evan, declaring, "She's only a little girl. They'll let her in.

"It's almost dark," Claudia added, meaning, Here, here on Thrumcap Island where they really were, where supper was probably about ready, and the grownups who would never shut them out would begin wondering and calling and then worrying about them.

She led the way back across the bar at a run, slipping and stumbling but running on as though something were after her. Evan, usually faster, followed dispiritedly, lost in contemplations of a predicament he could do nothing about. But Claudia had to keep on running, had to get away from the image of that tiny solitary creature, perhaps still soaked, certainly cast out for some obscure but terrible deed connected with that stone she had stood upon like any ordinary kid proclaiming itself to be the king of the castle.

FOUR

CLAUDIA knew that her mother was trying to get her alone so they could have a private discussion. Private discussions were what Susan called appealing to reason and getting Claudia to make up her own mind; she would give Claudia a hug or a look that meant a hug; then Claudia would be left staring at the rug or the grass, and after a while she would go and do whatever it was that Susan had wanted in the first place.

So Claudia tried to stick close to Evan, but that was hard because of Jon, who kept getting in the way. Finally indignation undermined her vigilance; she went charging after Susan to complain about the way this guest was taking over. As soon as Susan turned and met her eye, Claudia knew she was caught, but she couldn't stop.

"If he doesn't like what we do, why doesn't he just leave us alone?"

"You could learn a lot from each other," came Susan's guarded answer.

"He wants Evan to sleep on the boat."

"Isn't that up to Evan?" Susan stacked some pine kindling in Claudia's extended arms.

"That's not the way we do it." Claudia's voice rose. "Just because he's afraid to spend the night—"

"Look, dear, he hasn't had a whole lot of brothers and sisters dragging him off to survive on islands the way you kids did last year."

24

"He's a baby." She choked. "Look at Evan. Two years younger and acts . . . acts. . . ."

"But you make allowances for Evan. And you're used to him." Susan smiled. "What Jon needs is encouragement. His parents, too. You should have seen them when I told them I wouldn't mind leaving you kids here on your own for a bit."

"What are they afraid of?" Claudia sneered. "Mr. Colman's sheep? The crow?" The crow had been in the shack when they had returned the bronze man, so they had introduced Jon to it. He had seemed almost intimidated, and the crow had looked as if it could tell. It had rattled its wings and lunged out with its beak, raking Jon's sleeve with that dry rasping sound. Evan had demonstrated how to feed the bird; he had rubbed his cheek against its shiny neck and grinned when it responded in the old way of last summer. "Anyway," she finished, "I'm not going to throw the whole day away because of the dumb eclipse. I'll stay here tomorrow."

"Oh, Claudia."

"Who wants to spend all day out at sea looking at the sky? Why doesn't Mr. Withorn just fly up to Nova Scotia or Quebec or wherever it is? He can afford to."

"He hasn't time. He has to get back promptly, especially since Ruth decided to stay home to finish getting ready for the auction. The only reason he came now was because of the eclipse."

Claudia waved her arms in frustrated abandon. All the twigs and dead moss and bark tumbled to the wet ground. She dropped to her knees and began to gather them up again.

Around the fire, everyone talked of tomorrow. Jon's

father had a special lens for taking pictures of something called a penumbra, which Claudia vaguely gathered had to do with the moon's shadow. Phil had seen the last total eclipse from Northeast Harbor; he told them how confused the birds had been at the sudden coming of night and then day again. That set Jon's father going about how the kids could keep a record of all the birds they saw and heard and try to observe their reactions.

Evan shook his head. "They don't stay in one place. And if you're anchored somewhere or just floating, you can't go after them."

But Claudia declared warmly, "That would be a perfect project for us."

Phil shot her an incredulous glance. She couldn't see Susan's face in the dark, had to guess at her mother's watchful skepticism.

"I mean," she amended, "that would solve the problem of overcrowding on the boat. And it would give us a . . . focus for the, uh, experience."

Mr. Withorn thought that was a splendid idea. Claudia's mother and stepfather said nothing.

Quickly Claudia added a few details. Old Mr. Colman had a new mooring over by the islet for protection from nor'easters. It would easily hold the day-sailer; the kids could spend the day moored out there where there were so many birds. They could observe, and if they had a dinghy tied on, they could always get ashore.

"Yes," said Evan, warming to the idea, "you could leave us lunch and everything and go wherever you want."

"You going to take the crow?" asked Jon.

"Oh no," said Evan and Claudia together. They had lost the crow last summer, and this time they didn't want to take any chances with it. They knew that if it got away from them, the black-backed gulls might kill it.

"You could tie it," Jon told them. "You know, with a string around its leg."

"Crow wouldn't like that," Evan pronounced.

"But what an ideal opportunity," declared Mr. Withorn, "to observe its behavior under conditions—"

"Right," Claudia joined in. "We wouldn't want to miss an opportunity like that. We'll ask Mr. Colman. We'll get his permission."

Evan started to protest, but she cut him off. Evan couldn't see what an advantage it was to have Mr. Withorn on their side. It would be all right if they used a string, Claudia agreed. She sank back, flushed with victory, while the parents launched into a boring session about safety and rules and promises, which covered everything from life jackets to lessons in indirect sunwatching.

Even though they were the only ones on the island for the night, Claudia and Evan didn't dare risk the parents' confidence by being caught with the bronze man. But at daybreak, when mist still clung to the coast, Evan couldn't resist the lure.

"I'm going to get the man. Just for a few minutes, Claude."

Claudia grunted and rolled away from him.

By the time Evan was back with the hilt, Claudia was sound asleep again. He had to pull and tug at her, coaxing all the while. Grudgingly she dressed and followed him to the cove, then dropped sleepily onto a rocky outcropping. She would keep watch for Evan while he tried for a quick glimpse into the Other Place.

She could barely make out the boat on which the others still slept. All was gray and still in the cove. "Hurry," she called to Evan, as he disappeared onto the tail of the islet and merged with the fog. "Tide's coming. Five minutes is all."

She wondered why she wasn't jealous of him now. Yesterday, coming to Thrumcap Island, she had felt almost bitterly possessive about the bronze man and its secret. Today she felt only resistance and resentment. Last summer it had led her into a world of danger and unimaginable beauty. She recalled her first sight of Fergus, splendid in his purple cloak, his wild hair blazing like the sun. She thought of the armlets and torcs of gold and burnished bronze, the sword itself like a thing alive, its scabbard seething with the scrolls and tendrils inscribed on it. But Fergus was dead, the Hound was dead, and yesterday the hilt had shown her a world without color, without beauty. Was Evan there now where everything and everyone was draped in gloom? And only that child. . . . No, she didn't want to think about the little girl, though she knew that was why Evan had felt so drawn.

Claudia tried to shake off the image of the child. It was pointless to hope to find her again. The hilt determined what they would see. Perhaps that one glimpse was all they would ever have of that small outcast. It was stupid to get caught up in the fate of one little girl, like caring about a single ant that was certain to be trampled under foot. She hoped Evan had found something more satisfy-

28

ing in the Other Place; she hoped it was bright and lovely where he was. Not that she wanted the sun to shine on him here. No, they were going to be careful this time. She wasn't about to be caught by the sun, at least not among those grim, ragged people or those faceless, hooded figures. And it was perfectly all right with her if Evan wanted to watch them some more. What she would really like, she thought to herself with an enormous yawn, would be to be back snug and dry in her sleeping bag.

Instead, she sat in the cold and watched the morning advance across the horizon, dim and chillingly flat, like inexpert scenery in a school play. Then she realized that she could see the boat. Many more than five minutes had come and gone. Trust Evan. The tide was rising, and if the light really broke while he was there, he might not be able to get back.

Forgetting the boat and its occupants, she rose to her feet and cupped her hands to her mouth.

"Evan. Evvvaaann."

She could tell when the first person in the boat rolled out of a bunk and stood up. Suddenly the sloop was rocking; the water plopped noisily against the hull. Damn Evan, she thought. Now she'd have to go after him.

She was halfway across the submerged bar when Evan appeared along the ridge of the turtle's back. He seemed preoccupied, in no hurry at all. As she stood knee-deep in the water that clenched her legs, she heard Phil calling, asking if everything was okay. She ran back ahead of Evan to forestall Phil's rowing ashore to check on them. Of course they were all right, she shouted back. They were just exploring. That is, they were bird watching.

"Seal watching," Evan amended, coming up behind her. "Dad, I saw the biggest seal out there. Not like the others."

"Start a fire," Phil told them. "We'll be over soon."

Claudia and Evan examined their soaking pant legs and sleeves. Relief that they had not been discovered dissolved Claudia's anger. One of the wild sheep looked out at them as they tramped back along the inland trail. Like a deer, it hovered in the undergrowth. They knew that eventually it would make its way to the shack, stand for Mr. Colman to milk it, and receive its daily portion of oatmeal.

"It was morning there too," Evan told Claudia. "Only I don't know what morning."

"Was the girl still there?"

"She was curled up against the wall. Like a mouse or something. Then she went down to the beach. I could see her picking things and eating them. But when people started coming out, she swam away. She still dives a lot, but I don't think it's for fun."

"Um," said Claudia, kicking aside last night's cinders and making a hole for dry firewood. She could stand wondering whether enough fog would remain to allow them to visit the Other Place later on, but she couldn't bear to think about the child.

"Say, Claude, did I mention this strange seal I saw?"

Claudia, her eyes on the gray horizon, nodded abstractedly. It wasn't as though she could do anything about the weather. If the fog closed in, then they would all spend the day together on the island. But if it cleared entirely, then even if she and Evan were left to themselves here, it would do no good. They might grip the

bronze man and walk dry-shod across to the islet without
ever seeing a thing or person in the Other Place. And now
that Evan had returned there in the mist and found the
child once again, Claudia knew they had to go back. They
had to follow the hilt wherever it led, even to that place
washed gray like its cold, hard stone.

"That seal," Evan went on, "was here on this side, I
think, but it was also on the other. Did you hear me,
Claude? Do you think the seal could have followed me
through?"

FIVE

THE day-sailer was a restless young animal held back
from a race or a hunt. Evan, astride the boom, clung as
to a bucking bronco, one hand on the saddle horn, the
other swinging the end of a rope. Jon, using both hands,
crouched amidships, his knuckles white. The crow, looking aggrieved, was gorging on the remnants of a leftover
breakfast doughnut. With each pitch of the boat it staggered, then righted itself.

Claudia hoped they wouldn't run out of morsels to
bribe the crow with. There were too many real problems.
The water was choppy and Phil had been concerned
about it. He had lashed the dinghy fore and aft so that
it wouldn't hang off and get caught by rocks on the
falling tide. She was glad he was waiting a while to be
sure they didn't change their minds. Of course she

wouldn't change her mind, but it was comforting to know that they weren't altogether on their own yet. Though there was the danger that if Jon were to quit, all three children would probably be hauled off to the bigger boat.

"Are you cold?"

Jon shook his head. He didn't seem able to open his mouth.

"Have you got the notebook ready?" A foolish question, but she wanted to keep him distracted. Of course everything was ready. You'd think they were setting out on a polar expedition. Jon's father had even provided them with those plastic chart covers so that they could keep their records from getting splashed.

She tried again. "We'll be glad of this splashing once the sun comes out."

Jon nodded. He was making an effort to respond. She felt sorry for him.

"If you ride with it like Evan," she suggested, "you'll find it easier to take."

His answer was to sink to his knees and lower his head.

She dropped down next to him. Immediately she knew this was the worst place to be. Once you lowered your head like this you smelled bilge water and outboard fuel and could see nothing but refuse from the last sail. There were sandwich crumbs down here, bits of Kleenex like stringy egg white. "Jon, let's keep a lookout for that seal." If she could get him to raise his head and focus on something beyond them, she knew he'd improve.

"The seal," he mumbled manfully, but could not open his eyes.

His father had galloped into their breakfast circle that

morning, upsetting coffee, then flipping over the milk carton so that it spilled into the doughnut box. "Two puffins," he'd exclaimed, extracting a drenched doughnut. "And the damnedest seal you ever saw. I'd swear it was an Atlantic gray."

"Maybe it was the one that followed me," Evan had said.

"Followed you?" Mr. Withorn was spreading the remaining doughnuts as though he really expected them to dry. "Sounds more like a common seal. Harbor seals are notoriously friendly."

"This," said Evan firmly, "was not a harbor seal."

Mr. Withorn had thought a moment. "Then it's probably sick. Or injured. Which might explain why it's around here. Except for a few in Frenchman's Bay, this isn't gray seal territory. You kids keep a sharp eye out for it, will you?"

Claudia had been quick to assure Mr. Withorn that they would. He was such a freaky man, she was half afraid he'd change his mind and stay to look for it.

Now she appealed to Jon, reminding him of their unique opportunity to observe this rare seal. Just as she was about to question Evan about the one he had seen early in the morning, a wave caught the boat on its rebound and slapped it so hard that Evan tumbled from his perch on the boom and rolled down beside them.

He laughed, oblivious to Jon's misery. Soft drink cans, released from their sodden carton, sloshed beside him.

"Let's dry out," Claudia told him in a no-nonsense tone. Since Jon couldn't play games, the only thing to do was to get Evan onto grownup things like making scientific observations. She reached for a sponge and thrust it at Evan. "Jon, you help me secure these drinks." There was nothing like a job to do to get a person out of himself.

"Where's the horn?" he mumbled.

"The horn?" She would play dumb. She'd stall as long as possible. "Come on, Ev," she snapped.

"What do you mean, come on? I'm sponging, aren't I?"

Hand over hand she made her way to where Evan was squeezing water over the side. "He's about to call the grownups. Distract him."

Evan turned and regarded Jon with astonishment. "Hey, Jon, help me feed the crow." He lunged toward the crow, which was so gorged that it was merely pecking at the shapeless mass that had once been a doughnut. Evan tried to untie the string from the cleat so that he could bring the crow to Jon, but the spray had soaked the knot tight. "Help me," Evan shouted back to him.

"Evan needs help," Claudia amplified, and pushed Jon in the direction of the crow and Evan. As Jon slid toward them, calling feebly for the horn again, the crow stepped to the limit of its tether, backed and lifted its tail. It seemed to take aim as it deposited its barely digested load into Jon's outstretched hand.

There was nothing they could do but spare the boat. Together they dragged Jon by the sleeves, his hands disappearing inside them. Claudia reached for his wrist, realizing that now the crow muck was inside his jacket. Never mind. The thing was to get him suspended over the side.

Claudia was beginning to feel a little queasy herself. The bird stench was getting to her now. Jon kept on heaving long after they'd brought the top part of him inboard again and Evan had gone to blow the horn. Claudia took off her foul-weather jacket and covered Jon. She was cold. And the motion, unlike the rhythmic soaring of an ongoing boat, was not something you adjusted to.

Phil, his dinghy bobbing madly beside the plunging day-sailer, took the situation in at a glance.

"What are you going to do with him?" Evan asked his father.

"Well, I'm not going to bury him at sea. He'll be all right," he went on. "There's just this funny bobble here where the land shelves off so fast. And I guess the current has something to do with it." He threw Claudia's jacket to her. "You guys want to come too?"

Claudia and Evan exchanged a quick look. Neither had expected a choice.

"How can we give up such a splendid opportunity?" Claudia responded before her stomach could make her give in.

Phil threw back his head and roared. "Push me off then. Don't stick it out if it gets miserable. With this onshore wind, the dinghy would take you right in. But steer for the shelf below the little cliff. Stay off these rocks."

They watched the family boat sailing out close-hauled. It was like a bird; the sea was its sky. In minutes the sail was just a speck, and then it was gone. They were really alone now, but they were fine, they would be all right, and Phil had made them safe and laughed with them and they were alone on a tumbling craft on a gray, white-flecked sea. Evan opened the first of the sandwiches.

The queasiness never left Claudia. She could drink

ginger ale but she couldn't eat. Smells bothered her, especially the tuna fish in Evan's sandwich, but when he obligingly changed to egg salad that was even worse. She turned her back on the lunch and gazed landward at the islet cliff she knew so well.

It looked steeper from out here. She had slid down it and clambered up it without much concern, but now the rocks that studded the shallows close to it were ranged like openings. She could imagine corridors of stone leading into the darkness at the cliff base.

The sky lightened, the wind and waves slackened. It was turning into an ordinary day. Well, they could always play horse or something the way Evan had started. Though it wouldn't be much fun if their mount grew docile and hung slackly from its hitching post.

"Look," shouted Evan.

"What?"

"Don't yell. The seal."

"You yelled first."

"Ssh. It's gone."

They waited in silence. The sun shone. The choppy waters were struck with rock shadows. Claudia could see no seal, and yet she could see seals everywhere a spot deepened and was ringed with white foam. "There's no seal."

But there was, a real one. She saw its back first, an arching streak, silver-black like a porpoise. She saw no face.

The children squinted into the brightness. A pair of guillemots whirred overhead and landed on a face of rock just showing. The crow stretched his wings and tugged at the string, hopping for a moment on one foot and losing his balance. Evan went back to work on the knot and soon had the crow up on the gunwale between them.

Gulls swooped close to inspect the remains of the crow's feast. Terns were everywhere, darting and gliding and plummeting headfirst into the water. There was probably something around stirring up the fish. The two guillemots were absolutely motionless. Did seals eat water birds? If so, what would happen to the eider ducks that fringed the island? If there was a seal out there, they didn't seem concerned.

The next time the children saw the seal, it was gazing intently at them, in the shadow of their boat. Claudia reached for the notebook. The seal slid under the water.

"Never mind the notebook," Evan said. "Just watch."

But Claudia thought they'd better justify being there. It would help for the next time. "We'll list all the things we've noticed," she began in a businesslike way, and then could think of nothing to write. She thought about the seal. Maybe it was looking for a mate that had been caught in a weir and killed, or searching for a pup that had been shot, or had been shot itself and left far behind its herd.

"What are you going to write down?" Evan asked.

Claudia began to list the kinds of birds they could see. "How many terns?"

Evan shrugged. "Say a thousand."

Claudia slapped the notebook shut. The water was so much quieter, the sun so warm, that suddenly she was hungry. "What if we rowed ashore and picked mussels out along these rocks? For supper. We could do it from the dinghy."

Evan passed her a peanut butter sandwich.

"I mean it," she pressed, munching. "We have to have something to show for today." She meant, since we can't go through the fog to the Other Place.

Evan stroked the crow. "You sorry we didn't go with them?"

She shook her head, then turned at the sounds of a sudden raucous squabble at the base of the cliff. The gulls were fighting over something. Claudia grabbed the field glasses. The thing was a piece of a huge fish, too big to have been killed by birds. While Evan tried to look through the glasses, she saw the seal again. It seemed to lack the kind of caution she was used to seeing. Perhaps it had been helped by someone and therefore trusted people. If that was the case, the next fisherman to come across it would finish it off. The seal wouldn't have a chance. Yet it had ducked when she moved before. She tried moving now. She reached out and touched Evan. The seal watched. When he shook her hand off, the seal rolled out of sight.

Maybe they could drive it ashore and then see if it was injured. Concentrating on the seal, she didn't notice the dimming of the sun. The birds were beginning to fly in a kind of aimless frenzy, first one way, then another. The crow strained at its string and hopped off the gunwale. It fluffed itself and hunched its wings, then shook itself and rejoined them. But the sky was sucking in the light, swallowing the day. Land birds joined the shrill cries of the gulls and terns. The false twilight sent shudders through this island universe. The crow, like a jack-in-the-box, raised its wing like a cover, flapped it closed over its own head, and put itself away for the night.

As if oblivious to all this commotion, the seal edged toward the remains of the abandoned fish. The children stared into the dimness. There was no sign of any ducks out where the sea darkened toward the sky. The guillemots, there on the rock a moment before, had taken off in the whirring dispersal. The silence was so abrupt and stark that they could hear nothing but the blowing gasps of the seal.

"Undo the dinghy," Claudia whispered. "Get the bronze man too. We can't let it out of our sight."

"We'll have to take the crow," Evan warned. "Otherwise he might try to follow and hurt himself." The crow looked incapable of any action, but they set it down in the dinghy. Claudia stuck the bronze man inside her belt.

They decided that the tide was low enough so that they could walk the dinghy in and avoid using the oars, which might scare the seal off.

Evan was over the side first. "Freezing," he breathed up at her, and hunched over the stern of the dinghy. She pushed the dinghy shoreward as she went in. Almost at once her foot touched something solid. Evan let out little wheezes. She was sure the seal would hear them. "You can get in the dinghy," she whispered to him. Her legs were numb, but she was so close now that it didn't matter.

Evan shook his head, then groaned. The seal whirled around and flopped toward the water. They tried to turn the boat broadside to block its escape. Claudia smelled raw fish and felt a blow against her frozen legs. Evan grabbed at her, one hand clutching at the bronze man in her belt. She stumbled, falling forward into the grip of the icy element that was the sea. Her gasp of surprise was really a gulp. Torrents of salt water filled her, and the ice clamped around her chest, her throat.

She was sick, sicker than Jon had been, sicker than she could ever have imagined. But the sea was no longer icy hard; it was gray and fluid and merely burning. Something strong had raised her up and now set her gently into a boat which had the most foul stench she had ever smelled. The bottom was slimy, animal-like. She could not raise her head.

The first thing she heard as the water ran out of her ears and nose and mouth was Evan, who was remarking on the fact that she was making an awful noise. Then she became aware of a second voice reassuring him. "She will revive. You will see, lad. Both maids are well enough."

"But the seal," Evan blurted. "What happened to the seal?"

The voice replied, "I've enough hauling three lost fishes from the sea without being after any seal."

Claudia felt herself being raised again. She tried to pull away, but the hands that drew her up were firm and steady. Besides, she realized it was too late to break free. They were caught. She was too dazed to comprehend more, could only sense that somehow the sun had come through and caught them. She recalled the dimming light. Then the water, pressure, the bursting sensation, pain, the absolute misery of her vomiting. They were caught, and Evan sounded unaware or anyhow uncaring, unafraid.

Moments later she was seated with her back against the deep side of a boat that seemed to be made of hide. It felt like her Indian moccasins when they got wet. She

40

rubbed the stuff; it was slippery but taut. Carefully she opened her smarting eyes, which felt as swollen and raw as her throat. A gray-robed figure was bent over a heap across from her. Evan was staring open-mouthed.

"This one is not unwell at all," said the voice from beneath the heavy gray hood. "She is only fearful like that crow of yours." He smiled at the bedraggled creature huddled against Evan, then drew back so that at last Claudia could see what Evan was gaping at. It was the child they had seen outside the strange tower. She looked much older, perhaps even older than Claudia, but she was certainly that same girl. Still small, her face appeared more fragile because of the enormous dark eyes that peered at all of them from under strings of black hair plastering her forehead and cheeks. Her spindly arms and legs, which seemed almost too long for her, were folded spiderlike about her body.

The man in the gray robe regarded all three children. "And so it seems," he murmured, "that I have traveled so far only to reach this tiny space on the vast seas where three small fishes would be taken." Reaching inside his robe, he pulled out a bronze man just like theirs, only not dull and marred and crusty, but smooth and gleaming. "And so must I follow."

He looked up thoughtfully until his eyes were level with Claudia's. His look held a deep and troubling inquiry that made Claudia want to hide, to turn from him. "It was as though I grasped its very shape when I plucked you from the wave. Its shape, its size." His voice was soft, his tone contemplative, yet she could feel a core as hard as metal inside that mild wonder.

Her answering look was blank. She let exhaustion

rescue her from his piercing scrutiny, but questions raced through her mind. Was this man the scribe to whom Fergus had given the hilt and its secret? Did he know its history, its power? Had his hands touched the hilt tucked into her belt and recognized it as his own? If he took it from her, how would they ever get home? Yet she almost felt like showing it to him, flinging it at him. She was swept with despair, not so much because they were caught, but because she felt tricked. It was as if the bronze man had betrayed them.

The man in gray began to speak of the cold and wet and hungry, of how they would land soon, though perhaps not soon enough. He knelt over a bundle and brought out a pasty substance which he rolled in his hands like clay. He passed the mushy ball to Claudia, who had taken the moment to slip the hilt from her belt and set it down behind her. The stuff smelled of rancid butter and her stomach heaved. She passed it on to Evan, who tasted it gingerly and made a face. The gray-robed man was rolling some more. He placed it in the other girl's lap. Her eyes followed every gesture, but it wasn't until he was rolling a third piece that she snatched at it and crammed it into her mouth.

Tentatively, as though approaching a wild thing, Evan extended the rest of his portion toward the girl. The man sat back on his heels, watching. Claudia leaned against the side of the boat and watched too. The girl sat perfectly still in the tumbling craft. Her great eyes followed the progress of Evan's offering. When she took it, her hand was so swift, the whole act completed with such speed, that it was like a strike.

Claudia saw Evan touch his hand with wonder, the

hand from which the girl had grabbed the ball of mush. Absently he extended it toward the crow. But the bird was beyond interest, its beak wide and empty and for once unmoving.

six

For a while the gray-robed man was intent on maneuvering the craft among the rocks. Then, swiftly and lightly, they were swept onto the shale. His first steps ashore were almost puppetlike; he seemed to move on stilts, his joints locked into place. As he pulled the craft clear of the water, a small group of white-robed figures were already descending the steep path to the shingle.

"God be with you," said a spokesman for the group.

"And in your house," replied the man in gray.

The group's spokesman added, "And God be with your poor crew." He paused. "You have our Nessa. It was not a day for her to be out, but she goes when the sea calls her."

The man in gray shook his head in wonderment. "She swam from here?"

The spokesman nodded. "She seems to seek the Vanishing Island. It is not far, but it disappears into the mists when anyone approaches. Only the seals may gain its shore."

A woman stepped forward to stand beside the spokesman. "Ours is a small community," she declared. "We tend our flocks and write our books and carry the Lord's message among the Pictish folk of these islands. And strike the hours on our sweet bell. Our guesthouse is ever ready, and we would make you welcome."

Without a sound, the dark-haired girl climbed out of the little boat and went to stand beside the woman, who bent to whisper to her, then looked long into her face.

"I believe that Nessa meant to guide you safely to us," said the woman. "There are few landing places here. Nessa has brought seafarers to us before. She even showed the way to the men of the north in their longboats. That is why the Pictish people blame her for their coming." She sighed. "They blame much on the child."

The man in gray looked from the woman to the first spokesman. Finally he said, "Abbot, if you are abbot, is this a wife who speaks at your side?"

The spokesman said, "Yes, I am abbot. I am called Colm for Columcille, who sent the founder of this settlement to these islands. This very islet was given in freedom till doomsday by Brude, king of the Picts, when Columcille taught him our faith. There have been monks here ever since. My wife, Fann, is abbess."

The man in gray declared, "But if you follow the rule of Columcille and serve the Lord of the Elements, you keep no women in your house. I am Baitan the scribe, from Erin, and though I have voyaged long, I must forgo the company of women."

Fann put her arm around Nessa. "The child and I will go from here rather than offend a guest. But know that I first served St. Gobnet, the nun of Ballyvourney, and that I love God as truly as any other." She turned away, leading Nessa with her. The others drew aside and held

44

themselves in attitudes of reverence until she had passed.

Baitan thrust out a stiff, crooked arm. "My voyage and solitude have made me cramped and stiff," he called after her, "in mind as well as body."

She turned then, but remained standing on the bank above him.

"I will speak no more of ways which differ," he went on, "but accept with gratitude what you and Colm offer. I'll be away before the light is gone." He pulled the bronze man from beneath his robe.

Seeing it, Colm frowned. "A sword hilt? A broken dagger? The monks of Deerness, not far from here, still go into battle, but we have renounced all weapons in this place."

"A hilt, yes. But fear it not, Colm the Abbot. It is no longer for smiting. This hilt is severed from its blade, though the words inscribed on the blade will ever rule the hilt. Whoever carries it must travel in distant places and across known bounds. I would end my voyage now and pass on this ancient treasure and its secret. I have followed it long."

"You followed a rule of an ancient sword?"

Baitan turned the bronze hilt over. "I have scratched this cross into the body of the man. His message is of a whole with the scripture most loved by our master Columcille: 'Leave your country and your land, and your neighbor in the flesh, and your own fatherland for My sake and get you into the country that I will show you.' I seek a place to end my days alone with God. A little island perhaps. Where is the one the child would swim to? Maybe our meeting will have led me to my final destination."

45

Colm shook his head. "No one has ever reached the Vanishing Island, though it is said that one day a man will come who will set his eyes straight toward that patch of green and, with steel in hand, cross the tide till he reaches it at last."

Just then Claudia coughed. Baitan turned. "This maid wants attention."

"I'll see to the child," said Fann. "And Nessa will look after the boy. Nessa, do take him to the fire." She held out her hand to Claudia. "Come."

Evan, starting forward, was stopped by the silent Nessa. Her gesture was abrupt and commanding. He followed her up the embankment without a word.

Claudia walked close to the woman for warmth. Even away from the beach the wind blew hard and wet. Fann's white robe was dark at the hemline from the soaking grass; the cloth smelled slightly sour and scratched against Claudia's cheek.

They had already passed between two upright slabs which marked the entry into the great wall. Now they entered the smaller circle of stone. When Fann stepped into the dark interior of the boat-shaped building, Claudia stood shivering under the lintel stone that spanned the narrow doorway. She saw Fann move from a stone table beneath a deeply recessed window. Suddenly a tiny flame lapped the darkness. Light trickled from a hanging bowl, casting shadows from two others, which looked like round boats afloat on a smoky sea. A silver cross below the one small window pulsed in the reflected glow. Fann seemed to hesitate. Then she turned to Claudia. "Let your master know that I have gone for oil. Then will I attend to your needs." She smiled and shook her head and hurried away up the path and out of sight.

Claudia waited, then entered the building. It seemed no warmer, but the metals gave off the impression of fire and the massive walls closed out the wind. Brighter than the cross was a kind of box that rested on the stone table; it was made of silver and gold, with stones banded in enamel bevels to form a flowing scroll pattern that reminded her of the scabbard Fergus had had when he carried the sword of Culann for his foster son. Yet this decoration was far more elaborate, richer and heavier. If the man who called himself Baitan was the scribe to whom Fergus had passed on the hilt, then this must be a much later time. Fergus and the Hound, the king and queen of Connaucht, even the Sidh maiden Fedelm, must already belong to the fabled past. Still, here was this box with its design echoing that past, connecting what was gone with what was happening at this very moment.

But what *was* happening? Bitter disappointment blocked Claudia's usual curiosity. Even her sense of danger was dulled by her feeling of loss. She should have left the bronze man under its stone in Mr. Colman's hut. She should have recognized what was finished; she should have refused temptation; she should have been guided by her uneasiness over the bronze man. It was almost as if she had suspected that it would lead her into this kind of gray and dreary world. She felt for the hilt. It wasn't in her belt. Then she remembered that she had left it in the smelly skin boat. She stood rooted, clammy with cold and confusion. She tried to tell herself that Evan

47

would think of a way to get it back. Evan would be full of ideas. She wondered where he was and what he was doing with that dark, silent swimmer who had led him off to some fire.

Claudia's teeth began to chatter. Fann certainly had a warped sense of priorities, going to get oil for the lamps when she was supposed to be taking care of a wet, shivering girl. Feeling injured and spiteful, Claudia thrust back the heavy, elegant cover from the box. It contained a book. Her sleeve caught one of its stiff leaves, flicking it over; another page followed. She tried to push it flat, then drew back, terrified as a drop fell from her cuff onto the waxy vellum. She held her breath; the fine writing did not blur. Slowly the page turned back. She began to reach, and again halted. A fantastic beast seemed to leap out of a tangle of sinuous bodies, its red mouth agape, its eye fixed golden on her intrusive hand.

She tried to shake herself free from its spell. It was only a picture, she told herself, an animal coiled round its seething young and twisted into the shape of a letter she could not decipher. It was only some imaginary monster, part lion perhaps, only with wings and raking talons, like some mythical griffon. Except it wasn't even recognizable as a griffon; it wasn't recognizable as anything at all.

But she couldn't touch the book. She backed away from it, then turned toward the little slanted doorway and caught sight of an object she hadn't noticed before. Hanging from an iron rod, it shone with the soft look of burnished bronze. She thought she recognized it as the square-sided bell she had seen in the procession. Maybe if she rang it something would happen. Anything happening in this place would dispel the gloom. Probably

Fann would come running and then recall contritely that Claudia was still waiting and might die of exposure.

She had to stand on tiptoe to free the bronze ringlet from the iron bracket. Carrying the bell in both her hands, she went outside. The air was clearer. She could see the contours of the outer wall, the round huts of stone set in clusters here and there. Close to her, like a tiny walled garden, was a graveyard. Stone slabs stood up from the close-cropped grass. Some were incised with simple crosses; others had curving designs, crosses enclosed in circles; one tall slab bore a cross with an elongated stem that ended in a curious boatlike foot. A few of the slabs had other kinds of figures on their opposite faces. There was a crescent moon filled with flowing spirals and pierced by what looked like a broken arrow, an object shaped like a hand mirror, a queer kind of animal with a longish snout, another that might have been a seal.

Claudia returned to the stone doorway and began to swing the heavy bell. She could feel the pull of it all the way to her shoulders, but nothing happened. It didn't clang or ring or peal or do any of the normal things bells are supposed to do, though it had a momentum from its weight that kept her arm swinging involuntarily. Finally, using both hands, she stopped it, turned it over, and stared into its deep rough hollow. There was no clapper, nothing at all to whack against the sides. She recalled the procession again and realized that someone must have struck the bell. Maybe if she looked in the church she would find whatever it was they struck it with.

She was so intent on looking that she failed to hear Fann returning with a vessel of oil.

49

Fann was aghast. "What have you?"

Claudia, still on her hands and knees, blurted, "I only wanted to call someone. I'm cold. I may get sick and die."

Fann reached down for her. "What else have you touched?"

Claudia was suffused with guilt.

"Though you wear no raiment of any monastery, surely your master has instructed you in the holiness of these things."

"He's not my master," Claudia mumbled. Now she was angry too. She had probably offended them all. Yet how could it really be her fault? No one had told her.

"Not your master." Fann seemed unable to grasp this. "Then how came you in his coracle?"

Colm's and Baitan's voices were heard just then. Fann half dragged Claudia out to meet them. Claudia stayed where Fann left her, dumped like a sack. She heard Fann cry, "Is she baptized?" Claudia could feel all those eyes focused on her. Out of the amazed silence Baitan's voice responded, "You ask me?"

"Is she not yours?"

"Why, I said. I picked up all three, just as I entered the shoals here. I thought—"

"Not this one," Fann explained. "Nor the boy. Only the Pictish girl is ours. We took her many years ago when her people shut her out and condemned her to solitude and starvation. We have no knowledge of the other two. I wondered, for they wear leg coverings like the men from the north who have settled near here."

"She was in the oratory?" Colm demanded.

"I thought she was his," Fann answered lamely.

"Are you baptized then?" asked Colm. "Speak, child."

Claudia could not speak. She shook her head. She knew they were exchanging looks. She had never felt so small.

Baitan said, "I have wondered as well." He reflected a moment. "Is this not the day we call the Feast of the Plowmen?"

The others told him that was so.

"It is a day from the ancient time," Baitan continued. "Columcille named this feast for the fullness of the crops and did sanctify it, but long before that, it was a time for the spirits of the earth. More than barley could issue from the ground this day."

All at once Colm stepped over to Claudia and made the sign of the cross. Then Fann pulled her to her feet, and she too made the sign of the cross. Claudia stood there as one after another, Baitan included, each robed monk stopped to make the sign of the cross over her.

"She has defiled the sanctuary as well as the oratory," Fann whispered.

Colm said, "We will use much holy water, for every place she has set foot must be purified."

"Go," Fann said to her.

"Where?" Claudia was shaking now, but not with cold.

"Wait for me outside the wall. This place is forbidden to all who are not baptized."

"What of the Pictish maid?" Baitan inquired as Claudia made for the gap in the wall.

"She has received instruction," Fann replied, "but cannot speak, cannot utter a single vow. She is no ordinary maid. She was considered an outcast by her people even before she stood upon the stone of succession and was banished."

"Is she deaf too?" asked Baitan.

"She hears, and often obeys. But she hears other things which we cannot hear. She hears voices in the sea and swims with the seals."

"But you do not banish her like her own people."

"We have raised her from a small child and—" Fann stopped. "What is it you ask?"

Baitan pointed to Claudia. "She too may hear other voices than ours. Consider the swallow that flies through a warmed and lighted hall, from dark cold to dark cold. So is this child like the swallow, for she is just come into sight and may know nothing of what shall follow or what may have preceded."

There was a brief silence. Then Colm said, "Our brother Baitan is right."

"But the oratory. The bell. She—"

"We will proceed to our prayers. See to that maid, Fann, and forget not the time when I carried Nessa to you." He turned to Baitan. "The child spent that first night in Fann's arms, the one clutching the other, as if each had been starved." He smiled at Fann. "That was many years ago. The child has often slipped away and caused grief and puzzlement among us. But Fann remembers. Fann will not forget that first night and the foster-age that came from it."

Fann had already begun to catch up with Claudia. "But forget not the purifying," she called back. She reached out, her grip gentler though still firm, and led Claudia along the path toward the round huts that nestled into the green windswept slope.

SEVEN

Claudia curled up on the pallet of dried grass. She could still taste the creamy soup; the globules of butter specked with green seemed to coat her tongue with a thick, acrid warmth. Her clothes were hung from stones projecting from the in-curving roof-wall of the round hut. "You know not right from wrong," Fann had remarked. "Remain here." The moisture from the drying things and the smoking peat were all too much for Claudia. She shut her eyes.

Later she had no idea whether she had just dozed off or had slept for a long time. She touched her clothes. Damp, but not sopping. Quickly she dressed. Where was Evan? Was he off somewhere like her, confined, surrounded by wind and stone?

She looked out, surprised at how much clearer everything was. Nearby there were paths and gardens, part of a flock of sheep blocked by the contour of the land as if tucked away in the folds of green. Farther off, she could make out people bent to some task, all absorbed, all alike in their whitish robes and total silence.

She felt not merely abandoned, but erased. When the bell began to clang its clear sour note and the white-robed figures set aside whatever they had been carrying or sorting, she was sure that someone would cross the dirt walkway to check on her. But not one person looked her way. Like sheep, she thought, as each fell into place along the path to the walled church. Then those figures were disappearing. The bell was suddenly still. There was only wind, the voice of a sheep carried on it.

She strained against the emptiness. Finally she stepped out onto a path which led to another cluster of domed cells. With an uneasy glance in the direction of the churchyard, she ducked low and entered a dark winding corridor. She heard a scream, a dozen screams, it seemed. She froze. A squawking rooster dashed blindly into the wall, then raced between her legs.

"What was that?" came Evan's voice.

Something stirred beyond, but no answer.

"A chicken? Just a chicken?"

There was a scratching, as if in response to his question.

Claudia followed the voice. Within the network of round cells there was a small courtyard full of shells and bits of clay pots. A line of slanting stones that formed a shallow ditch emerged from the foundation of one cell, crossed another, and disappeared under the wall. Into this ditch a small brown torrent gushed like a miniature tidal bore and ran out beneath the wall. Hoping that Evan was where that water had come from, she turned toward the cell and softly called his name.

Immediately he poked his head out through a low doorway, said, "Oh, it's Claudia. Claudia's up," and withdrew again into the darkness. Claudia heard him speaking some more. Then he called, "Just a minute, Claude. We're coming out. Can't see so good in here." He led the way. The dark girl, Nessa, followed with something like a smooth flat brick and some tools in her hand.

"She's an artist, Claude. You should see the way she

draws. She made so many pictures we had to heat up water and melt her wax thing to start all over. She's an artist, but she doesn't even know how good she is. They don't have any paper. They've got books, but there're no windows, so inside you can't see."

"Evan, you didn't look for me."

"What?"

"Didn't you wonder where I was?"

"They said you were sleeping. They don't talk much. You can hardly tell the difference between them and Nessa."

Nessa was scratching a picture onto the wax brick. She had already made a crescent like the one Claudia had seen on the grave slab. Now she was finishing a hump-backed creature that could be a pig or a bull. She looked up at Claudia, held out the wax tablet, and pointed.

Claudia, puzzled, said, "They're very nice. You . . . you've got talent." She wondered whether she should mention the bronze man now or wait until she could speak to Evan alone.

Nessa frowned and kept the tablet extended toward Claudia.

"She wants you to copy her," Evan explained.

Claudia blushed. "Tell her I'm not an artist like you and her. Tell her I can't draw."

"Tell her yourself. She's not deaf. She understands. Only what's hard sometimes is trying to figure what she wants."

"She wants," said Fann from behind them, "to find out whether you come from her father's tribe. She always hopes to find her people. To be found."

Fann and Colm and Baitan had entered the small

court so quietly that neither Claudia nor Evan had heard them.

"I thought she was teaching me," said Evan.

"Perhaps she was," Fann told him with a smile. "She may think you are too small to understand her question. She may hope that the maid is old enough to comprehend and answer."

Claudia turned to Fann. "But how can those pictures mean anything?"

"They stand for the clans and tribes of Pictavia. Nessa's emblem is that one over there." Fann pointed to a face of rock on which a graceful creature seemed to stand upright, as if from the water, with only its head and upper body and curious armlike appendages showing.

"Wings?" Evan wondered out loud.

"Flippers," Fann answered. "Nessa's father was Talorg of the seal-folk. Her mother and most of these islanders are the wild boar-folk. Across the water are the horn-folk and cat-folk and, south of those, the sheep-folk. Only Talorg's people are hard to find and harshly looked on by all the others."

Nessa turned from Claudia and drew Evan away with her.

"It may be," Colm supplied, "that they shun the seal-folk for being the only Pictish people who do not raise their children in their wives' clans."

Fann shrugged. "That, at least, is why Talorg never stayed. I think there is more, though, to have caused these Picts to look askance at Talorg's get." She regarded Claudia intently. "Have you come from these islands of the boars?"

"I . . . I don't think so," Claudia stammered. "We're

56

from . . . far away. We were on a boat." She didn't know how to go on.

"I would have thought from the leggings," Baitan remarked, "that she and the boy are from the northern sea. Only something . . . something keeps me from that belief."

Claudia's hands flew to her belt where the bronze man had been when he had lifted her into his coracle. She heard him asking Fann whether she had taken the clothes to dry. Fann was nodding.

"And was there . . . nothing strange?"

"The raiment was very strange," Fann responded.

"Besides the clothing?" Baitan pursued, but Fann only shook her head, puzzled by his urgency.

"If they belong to those tall farmers from the north," Colm declared, "we must treat them with care. Ours is an uneasy neighboring. They have built their steadings around the one fortress that still stands. They fish and farm and forge their tools and turn from us. But they prosper, while the Pictish folk have declined. The few Picts who remain blame Nessa, for since she was banished they have suffered losses of grain and flocks, and a weakness that carried off many of their young. Then came the tall farmers whose prospering has mocked them so."

"Why do they blame Nessa?" Claudia exclaimed.

The three adults regarded her and her outspoken question with some surprise, but Colm supplied an answer. "When the old chieftain was buried, in the leaderless time which is fraught with danger, she stood upon the stone which only chieftains' feet may tread, and since that time all that I have mentioned has come to pass."

"They scorned the child long before that," Fann put in. "For her swimming, for her picture-making, which no woman or child must do. And for her muteness."

Baitan shook his head.

"They scorned her," Fann repeated, "and then, long after we brought her here, when blame built upon blame, they decided to put her to death. I took her into hiding for many days, for she is careless and wanders. We sought refuge in an underground house made by her ancestors for keeping the grains. They never looked for us there, though they themselves have used such places to hide from their own enemies; these islands are riddled with secret passages in the earth."

Baitan said, "You were right to spare her life, and to keep it."

A look passed between Colm and Fann.

Baitan, noticing, said, "You believe other?"

"They took her mother," Fann retorted, her voice low and trembling. "I did not know. I could not know."

"It was not your fault," said Colm.

"It was not my fault," Fann repeated harshly. "Took her, they did, and cut off her hands and burned her body like heathens. They used the ancient coloring that causes the smoke to send blue into the sky. And they buried her hands within their wall to fend off all the evil they feared from her girl-child."

"And took the evil into the fortress with them," Colm added, "with their heathen slaughter."

Claudia, aghast, whispered, "Does she know? Does Nessa know?"

Fann spread her hands, examined them as if comparing them to those hands buried in the tower wall. "We told her nothing. But we never know what she learns and what she understands. In her simplicity there is wisdom, there is sight. . . ."

They stood quiet, only the wind speaking of sea and sky, of islands set between.

It was Colm who broke the silence. "Will you really set out this day?" he asked Baitan. "It is hard to believe that these strange encounters are not meant to make men pause and consider. In truth, this has been no ordinary day. Nessa was away early. She met you in your craft and must have come upon these lost children in the dark cold of the sea. Stay, Baitan, and wait for a day that breaks fair, especially if you mean to wrest the Vanishing Island from its mists."

Baitan brought out his man-hilt and held it up to them.

"That is bronze," Fann objected. "The Pictish folk believe that the man who reaches the Vanishing Island will carry steel and never look away."

"But here with my Psalter is the steel I will bear." He drew from beneath his robe a small leather bag, pulled from it a round bead and pointed to a tiny shaft of iron set inside it.

Claudia stared. The sunstone! There could be no doubt left. Of course Baitan possessed the secret of the sword. He had followed it just as she and Evan had. The bronze man had led all three of them in the sea to Nessa. And Baitan believed that the hilt might take him all the way to the island Nessa kept seeking.

Baitan set the bead into the hole in the center of the bronze man. "I have traveled far with this sunstone. This day, over a short stretch of sea—"

"Of treacherous sea," interjected Colm. "With the

worst riptides in these tide-locked islands. At least make certain you approach it on the flood. In the ebb you would not get near at all."

"Then I must leave soon."

Claudia felt vaguely disturbed. There was something she needed to do, something forgotten. But she was caught up now in his quiet determination, in the force beneath his mild tone. She couldn't be bothered with what she had forgotten. She had to listen to Baitan, who was insisting that although he craved solitude, he would never shun anyone who came to him in need.

"When I have brought this island out of the fogs of time," he told them, "it must stand ever after as a place of sanctuary. Let it be called Holy Island then."

"Brave words," muttered Fann. "You had best prepare your coracle well for its struggle through those currents. Come with me, Baitan, and take a gift of butter for the waterproofing. There is little more we can do."

"That will I take with thanks, lady, for the last of my butter was mixed with ground oats and fed to the ocean waifs. Only this one," he added, indicating Claudia, "took no food from me." He paused. "She is different, perhaps."

Fann rescued Claudia from his intense scrutiny by assuring Baitan that Claudia had been fed. Her manner was rough, direct. She was troubled over Baitan's insistence on seeking the Vanishing Island. "I'll not watch your progress," she grumbled. "Though I'll pray for your safety. I will pray for your landing."

Baitan laughed. "Send the children to watch," he suggested. "It will give them an occupation and keep the Pictish one from plunging seaward once more."

"A good thought," Fann responded. "I'll have Nessa take the newcomers across to the high cliff you pass on your way. Though it is within sight of the old fortress, which she usually shuns, it will offer a fair view of your progress." She called Nessa and told her that if she hurried, she might watch this monk's last journey and be the first to see any man set foot upon the Vanishing Island. "Be off now, all three of you, for you must return before the tide is too high to cross the strait."

eight

CROSSING over was like crossing onto Thrumcap Island from its own islet, except that the land they reached was much larger and perfectly treeless. The wind swept down from undulating hills; the turf was springy and very wet.

Nessa set a pace that kept Claudia breathless and increasingly resentful. The coastline, gentle at first, rose toward steep cliffs. Suddenly they were at the edge of a chasm where the ocean had eaten away great bites of the shore. Water churned and gushed around basking seals. Pointing at something, Nessa scrambled partway down. Evan crawled to the edge.

Claudia stood back. She could feel the ground shudder beneath her. The waves surging into the narrow gut seemed to gnaw at the root of the earth. As Evan wormed his way down toward Nessa, the seals all slid off their rocky shelves.

Evan, climbing back, said, "There's a cave down there."

Claudia said nothing. He hadn't noticed that he'd scared off the seals. They were gazing up from the water now like hundreds of spectators. Nessa, from whom the seals had not fled, dragged Evan on ahead to show him other sights. Claudia tried to keep up, but the distance between those two and Claudia seemed to stretch away like the blurred seascape.

Just when Claudia thought her lungs would burst, they reached the highest point of land, which looked out ahead to a little bay, its white sands curving to the fortress tower they had seen before. It was more ruinous now. Part of the bulwark had collapsed; the tide slid toward it in a pale green flood. Newer houses, long and curved at the ends, with low thatched roofing, were set in a cluster outside the crumbling wall. Nessa watched Evan and Claudia gaze at this scene, saw the look of recognition they exchanged, and beckoned them on.

When the children approached, women kneeling in enclosed gardens looked up, then went on with their chores. A yellow-haired child ran out of a house, chasing a baby pig. Another woman, standing in the doorway, her hands busy with a twirling object from which she drew a thread, glanced their way and paid no further heed.

Nessa advanced guardedly. They slid down a deep ditch, then climbed up to gain the broken paving. Nessa stopped. She seemed to be listening for sounds from within the tower.

From one of the gardens a woman called, "You, daughter of Talorg, it is open now and empty." The woman clambered over the earthen wall but came no closer than that. She wore a loose-fitting smock like the other women, but unlike them she was small and dark, and her black hair was so thick that even the head scarf she wore could not keep it from looking like charred thatching on a derelict house.

"You may as well go in," the woman shouted. "Drostan was here from Deerness to warn his people of the raiders. Or perhaps you saw him, for he was on his way to warn your monks as well. He took the inland track. Did you not meet him, his robe all torn and his sword covered with the blood of the foreigners?" The woman seemed enraged by Nessa's unchanging expression. "Well, go you in then. You have done your evil. All who remained are fled. Only my husband's people have no fear of those who come in longboats like their own. The boar-folk flee, and the men from the north go a-chasing the wild boar."

Nessa did not even turn. "Go you in," railed the woman, "but take care you are not buried there. We use the stones as they fall from the galleries. Get you into the stronghold if you can."

Not a flicker betrayed Nessa's reaction. It was as if she heard only the gulls laughing as they picked at the debris against the moldering walls.

"If someone went to warn those monks about some danger," Evan began hesitantly, but Nessa was moving on again and he never finished the thought.

They entered an area of shadowless gray, small dark chambers flanking their way through the double wall. In the circular courtyard upright stones from collapsed walls spread out like spokes of a wheel. At the center was a hearth, full of rubble. Huge stone querns lay putrid with standing water. Shells and bones were everywhere. The stench was frightful.

Nessa disappeared into a kind of tunnel. Evan stood at its mouth peering in. "Stairs," he told Claudia.

She said, "I don't think it's safe here." She glanced up. The circular walls looked as though they were leaning in on her. Level upon level, galleries opened to the court-yard.

Nessa appeared, her face wet, her black hair sticking to her cheeks. She gestured imperiously to the darkness below.

"Water," Evan declared. "Can we drink it?"

Nessa nodded curtly, but Claudia quickly disputed her. "Better not. God knows what's been in it."

Evan looked from Nessa to Claudia. Then, clinging to the slick walls of the narrow stairwell, he descended. He called up from below. "Tastes all right."

Claudia was furious. It was one thing to play favorites, but another to act like a fool and pay no attention to his own stepsister.

"Claude?" Evan sounded just a bit uncertain. "Nessa drank."

"Nessa's not my responsibility."

Nessa made for the stairs to the first gallery. Evan clattered up after her. Claudia took her time. Once she clutched at a protruding stone, only to discover that it was loose. Nothing held the stones together but the way they were set, and where one was gone, the others no longer held.

Closing her eyes didn't help. She could imagine the narrow steps, so steep and shallow that she had to climb

64

them sideways. She could imagine how the courtyard looked from every successive level—like a pit. And now she could imagine the way the wall fell apart in her hands when she tried to hold on for dear life.

As she reached the upper platform, she had to kneel, clutching at the rooted fringe of turf along the parapet. She thought the wind would blow her off.

"Look," breathed Evan, full of wonder.

Claudia wanted to gasp out her fear, her relief, her terror at the thought of going back down. But Evan and Nessa were gazing at the shimmering sea. The island Nessa pointed to was like a green boat edged in white. White dabs, like brush strokes, flecked the water. Baitan's coracle had the look of a little brown nut; it hugged the shore.

"Oh no," Claudia cried, suddenly realizing what this meant. "The bronze man. It's in the boat."

Evan turned in dismay. "And the crow. I . . . I just forgot."

"We can always get back without the crow." She couldn't bring herself to complete the other half of that statement. It was her fault. She had forgotten. It had been as though Baitan's bronze man had supplanted the one she and Evan had followed.

Evan appealed to Nessa. "There's this hilt. Not shiny like his. We have to have it."

"What do you expect her to do?"

But Nessa was already standing. She put out a hand, gesturing them to wait. Then she scrambled backward down the stairway as though it were a ladder she was used to running up and down all the time.

"Shouldn't we go down too?" asked Claudia, quaking.

"No," said Evan from the loftiness of his understanding. "We couldn't keep up. She'll get it."

One glance told Claudia that the tiny figure dashing across the white sand must be Nessa. Then she leaned her forehead against the damp turf and closed her eyes. Again she was aware of feeling betrayed somehow, as if the bronze man had distracted her and led her astray, as if it had tricked her into carelessness. Only now the sense of disappointment was displaced by a vague queasiness that might have stemmed from excitement and this awful height and the prospect of having to go down again. But it wasn't any of these, not really. It was fear. She knew that if the bronze man was restored to her, she would hold it tight and follow it as before. But for the first time she understood that it might be like that stone she had clutched at for support, the one that had come loose in her hand.

After a while Evan poked at her. "Look," he whispered.

She could see a dark speck in the water beside the small brown nut. Something moved atop the nut, and then something flashed for an instant. The speck was gone. No, it was replaced by a number of specks all about the little nut. Claudia shook her head. Maybe they were just spots from staring into the sun-reflected water. She heard Evan murmur, "Seals. It's like they're leading him, guiding him." The nut was turned from one of the white dabs that stretched across its bow like shirring on a black fabric. It turned once more, and the black specks hovered as it headed toward the gathering whiteness of the rip. Once there, the nut seemed to spin about and reverse its direction. Claudia had to close her eyes again. She could tell that Evan was holding his breath. Then at last she heard him sigh. "He's going to make it," he murmured. "He's almost there."

Nessa was with them again so suddenly that neither of them realized it till she was spraying them as she shook the water from her hair. She handed the bronze man to Evan and dropped once more to her knees beside him.

They watched Baitan beach the little craft, a tiny unreal figure. But Nessa was already staring off beyond the little island. She was so still that she seemed to be listening as well as watching.

The boats that slid into view from behind the cliffs of the high island to the north were no little nut shells bobbing on the water. They were three ships on a frieze of blue. Within moments they were strung out, ribbon-like, long and low and powerful. As they made for the shallows past the headland, the wind freshened, thrusting them forward with sudden violence. The air was full of screaming gulls and terns like white leaves torn and flung into the sky. A few black birds cast off from white ones like embodied shadows; one of these streaked toward the tower where the children knelt motionless, speechless.

The crow broke the spell they were under. Evan grabbed the string that was still attached to its leg. Other crows, having followed it, swooped and looked and shot off again toward the ships. The tethered crow was full of reproaches. The children, still staring at the ships, were just coming out of their trance.

Nessa acted first. Not with panic, but with a scowl of puzzlement and determination.

"What will we do?" Evan kept asking her as they clambered down the steps, half sliding from one level to the next.

Claudia grabbed at stones that seemed to offer themselves as handles. Sometimes they broke her fall; sometimes they clattered down with her and on top of her.

Back on the path, Nessa cut away from the coast and led them inland. They ran for a long time. Then they heard people running in their direction. Like wasting moths, the white-robed figures flapped toward them, Fann in the lead. She shouted, her voice shrill and pained, "This way, this way. As before."

Nessa stopped.

"Come," shouted Fann. "The raiders may follow us again. We must share your secret place. Besides, Drostan is with us. He knows of these places. Come, Nessa." The girl darted a look backward toward the fortress they had fled. "Come, child, inland. See, we have books, our bell here, and Colm's crozier." Fann turned from the irresolute child and spoke to a small dark monk, who took the lead with the sureness of a wild animal.

One aged monk carried something that seemed to drag him down. Finally Fann made him stop. She called for the sword of the Pictish monk and carved out a piece of the turf. Tenderly the old monk laid his box in its improvised grave. His stiff fingers touched the raised design that ran all around it. "All my tools," he whispered as another monk covered it.

"They will be safe." Fann was puffing; her face was blotchy, her gray hair wild beneath her hood. "Now you must make haste, Brother Crimthan, so that we may be safe as well."

Drostan pointed toward a small rise where the ground looked unnaturally swollen. Fann was the last to reach it. Her breathing was tortured. As they gathered there, Claudia realized that there was a concealed opening into the earth. The darkness from it seemed to envelop them.

"They say," rasped Fann, "that when a church and its servants are destroyed, the sky will cast out molten tears. But look now, it is flooding the day with early night. It is returning us to the void."

Screams rent the air. The Pictish woman was running toward them, waving her arms and shouting. "Talorg's daughter has brought this darkness on us," she howled. "Leave her to the raiders and the gods will return the sun. She is evil, the child of Talorg. Even my husband's people will suffer from this curse of night."

By now all the monks were cowering under the spreading blackness. Some of them eyed Nessa, whose wet hair still masked her face.

"Join us," Fann called back to the woman. "You may not be spared. We know what happened to St. Donnan of Eigg in the Southern Isles. Massacred, and with him all but those who were away to the fishing, women and children as well."

"I plead for my people," the woman retorted. "I have no fear of those from the north, for I am no slave, but wear the keys to my husband's house. It is the evil of that girl I dread. Heed me, Abbess."

The darkness cast a hush over the land. It swallowed the shadows, muffled the bird calls. Even the whispering sea, invisible now, seemed distant as the baffled sun. The Pictish woman sent forth one last wail before she disappeared.

Quickly Fann turned to the Pictish monk. "Leave your sword, Drostan. Haste. This sudden night may be a blessing, for none can see us here."

"Had I not this sword," Drostan protested, "I should not have hacked my way to you, and you would all be slain now, as at Deerness."

Fann was already gesturing monks into the hole in the hillock. "Your swords did not save Deerness," she pointed out. "Leave yours, Drostan."

Drostan leaned over to assist Fann, who was handing down an elderly monk. "Rather than give up this sword," he suggested in an undertone, "you would do well to heed the Pictish woman. It is true, you know; the child of Talorg has brought harm to all her people. And now," he added softly, "to you who fostered her."

"Those are heathen words," Fann snapped. "Cast aside your sword. If we are to die, it will be in prayer, not in slaughter. And you have much to pray for. Boy, get you down now. After Nessa. Then the maid."

Claudia heard the sword hurtling away from them. Then she was pushed into the blackness.

NINE

THE descent was steep, like the way to the well in the Pictish tower, only here there were no defined steps. Claudia had to lean against the sides as she felt her way down. She clutched at Fann's coarse, sour-smelling robe.

"Is this where you and Nessa hid before?"

Fann reached down to grasp Claudia's shoulder. "Don't slip. We've a way to go yet. There are many passages below," she went on. "Escape ways for the Pictish folk these hard years."

"And now," came a voice from below, "it seems we are driven to the ground and must end our mission like the creatures of the earth who burrow blindly in sunless caverns."

"No, Brother Cadoc," Fann called to him. "Now help this child. She cannot reach the bottom yet and is afraid."

Claudia began to protest. She wasn't afraid. Only she couldn't see where they'd all gone to.

"Down here," called Evan. "It's really neat, Claude. Sort of a room. It even has stone closets and shelves. You have to get down on your hands and knees to go into the hall. The crow thinks it's nighttime."

"That passage leads to the well," Fann told him. "Last time I could not fit there. Nessa had to fetch the water."

Claudia felt her legs being grasped. Only when Fann released her did she realize how strong had been that grip. She was eased down. A moment later she stood on rock-hard earth and was drawn backward, so that Fann could land there too.

Immediately Fann, quick to make room for Drostan, sought out the monk who had spoken those despondent words about burrowing into the earth. "Brother Cadoc," she said, "are we not one people, those of us here, those in the coracle with Colm, those already slain?"

Someone else said to her, "You should have gone with Colm."

"She would not leave without the Pictish child," declared Cadoc. "She had sent her across—"

"Ssh," warned Fann, but the statement was there before them. "There were but three coracles," Fann declared. "We could not all fit." She seemed to be thinking. "If Baitan reached the Vanishing Island, then Colm's craft may carry them safely there. Even if we die, the few who gain that island will keep our church alive. So be comforted. Our light will not be quenched by this or any other darkness. Besides," she added on a wry note, "it was fitting that I should not take a place in the coracle, if only to spare Baitan the presence of a woman."

"But the raiders from the north will pursue our brothers all the way to the island," Brother Cadoc responded. "Or will it vanish on the approach of the heathen?"

Fann answered, "Brother Drostan tells me that those longships may not land on steep or rocky shores, so there is no need for that island to vanish."

Another of the monks spoke of the books still hanging on the book cell wall. What would become of them?

Drostan described the burning of books at Deerness. "The raiders care only for the covers, for the stones and metals."

"We will arrange ourselves," Fann declared quickly, cutting the others off, "and then pray."

"We are too many. We are like a flock of sheep which consumes all the breath of a cave and is found huddled and dead in the deepest recess."

"We will arrange ourselves," Fann asserted more firmly, "and think not of books or burial. We will arrange ourselves; we will say the psalm for Compline, and then pray for our slain and our survivors. Lastly we will pray for ourselves."

"But Mother Fann, it is not yet time for Compline. The darkness is out of place and time."

"We will recite 'He that dwells in the secret place . . .' because the night has overcome our day. We will bow to the darkness, but we will 'not fear the terror of the night.' "

Claudia felt Fann's hand on her shoulder again. "You children can fit in the passages, so fetch water, for our running was hard and some of us had many years to carry in our flight." Claudia felt the woman turn. "How many of us are there? There is Drostan from Deerness and Brother Enda and Brother Cadoc. And who else? Brother Mongan? And Brother Gildas and Brother Ronan and—"

"Not Ronan. He stopped to bury some books before the raiders turned back to our church. He said—"

"But he followed," Fann protested.

"And fell," came the soft reply.

"He did not cry out," said Fann, her voice filled with sadness.

"He would not have you stop for him."

There was a long silence. Then Fann resumed the naming of the monks. "Brother Daire? Brother Crimthan?"

Each response came low. "Yes, Mother," they said to her, their voices barely audible.

"Any others?" she asked finally. The silence was long. It was as if they were listening for those who could not speak.

"There are many ways out," Drostan remarked. "If the children seek the openings where the air is fresher, they will leave more room for us here and fare better as well."

"Cannot you fit through those passages too, Brother Drostan?"

"I will stay and carry the water. I have much to redeem. Every minute the children remain shortens our time here. Bless them, Mother Fann, and send them off. Send them toward the light, and let them stay in safety. I will carry the water and ask forgiveness for wronging the child of Talorg. She is yours, Fann, and Colm's, and it is I who brought evil to this place."

Claudia felt a sudden stirring, a scuffling. Then Fann spoke, her voice muffled. "No, child, you cannot wait with me this time. Listen, I am old. I will know that you grow into a woman who loves the Lord and carries our word into the future. Listen, listen. Colm is there. Colm would always wonder. If we are to go out from here, why, I will tell him of your obedience and goodness. But if I do not, who will tell him of our peaceful end but you and these children who must speak for you?" Now Claudia felt Fann turn toward her. "You will tell him that the spirit of Columcille was with us in this place."

"But we'll find some way out," Claudia protested. "A passage you can get through."

"If you and Nessa and the boy will make haste and leave us, you will help us in our waiting and increase our chances for feeling the wind and the sun once more. We are without fear. You must settle where there is some small light, for there the air will improve, but avoid the brightness of day. Keep well inside and wait for us. Brother Drostan will crawl to you as soon as ever he can, so that we may climb out together. I will help you as before, child. Have no fear."

"How long—" Claudia began.

"We cannot tell." Fann was turning to Nessa again. "It is fitting that you move to the lighter places. We are not parting. Go now."

Claudia reached out tentatively toward Nessa and was nearly knocked off her feet. "What did you do that for?" Claudia gasped. She felt hands steady her.

"What did *you* do?" Evan demanded.

"I— Nothing," Claudia snapped. She would not admit the impulse to comfort Nessa.

"Let me take care of Nessa," he whispered to her. "She likes me. Here," he added, thrusting the bronze man into her hands. "I can't manage this and the crow too."

As usual Claudia brought up the rear. She could hear Fann's voice reciting, "He that dwells in the secret place of the most high shall abide under the shadow of the Lord." The voices responding were a muffled chorus. She gasped as her knee banged into a protruding stone. Faintly Fann's voice reached her; she heard, " . . . walk in darkness," and those were the last clear words.

The farther they crawled, the more certain Claudia became that she would miss a turning and be lost. It didn't help being bigger than the other two; it didn't help having to drag along the bronze man. Once when they had to turn back and she was in the lead for a while, she suddenly found herself alone. Nessa must have discovered the turning she was looking for and simply set off that way with Evan.

"Evan, Evan," she called.

He was just around the corner. He sounded half

amused, half irritated, as he directed her onto their trail.

Backing clumsily till she reached the branching tunnel, she found him at once and felt a fool for having called out like that. She thought of what Fann had said about the monk who had fallen and been left to the pursuing raiders: "He did not cry out."

On crawled the Pictish girl, and on scrambled Evan, and on groaned Claudia, who was on her stomach, stretched full length and squirming like a snake. A clumsy way to travel, but it gave her bruised knees a rest. Then the earthen walls seemed to expand. They were entering a chamber. Evan and Nessa had already drawn themselves up against the in-curving wall and were resting with their heads tipped forward.

How far had they come? There was no way to tell. Nor was there any way of gauging the distance to the opening, for the dim light was diffuse, nothing was clear.

After dozing awhile, the children tried to listen for voices from the chamber where the others were confined. No sound came to them. They were thirsty, but could find no well.

"You know that stuff Baitan gave us in the boat?" Evan remarked. "I heard him say it's good for thirst."

Recalling the rancid mush, Claudia's stomach lurched. "Maybe we shouldn't talk," she suggested weakly. "The more we talk, the drier we'll get."

There was nothing to mark time. Even the crow seemed resigned to a perpetual twilight. Finally Claudia suggested exploring toward the light. At first Evan agreed, but when Nessa refused, pointing back into the darkness from which they had crawled, he changed his mind.

After a longer sleep Claudia awoke to find the other

two curled in tight knots, like subterranean animals in hibernation. She tried waking Evan. He was groggy and slow to respond. She told him they'd better get closer to the opening. "Later," was all he could manage to say. She shook and prodded him, then Nessa. Nessa opened her eyes but wouldn't budge.

"It's Fann she's worried about," Evan guessed, and leaned back listlessly, his eyes half shut.

"What if I go ahead and see if there's a safe place a little farther out?"

Evan shrugged.

"Come with me."

"And leave her?"

Claudia looked at Nessa, who was perfectly still, her eyes set on them. Claudia thought of sentimental stories about dogs pining at their masters' graves. If Drostan never came for them, Nessa would remain there till she dropped. As long as Fann was imprisoned, Nessa would never stir. "What if they can't find us?" Claudia challenged. "What if they're already out?"

Evan glanced uneasily at Nessa. Nessa didn't move a muscle.

"What if they need us to help them out? We could go out this way and Nessa could take us to them. We could save them."

Evan, troubled, was nearly persuaded, but Nessa simply pointed back into the darkness, drew her knees up to her chin, and stared Claudia down.

"There's such a thing as stupid obedience," Claudia cried out. She couldn't stalk off, because almost immediately she had to drop to her knees again to reach the passageway. She was stiffer than she had been when she had first crawled here, but her knees were no longer sore. Realizing this, she was aware of the distortion of time. It made her shivery. Days might have passed in that dusky chamber.

When she first heard hissing, she froze. She strained to confirm that this must be water she heard. It was as if she had grown unfamiliar with waves and foam and was uncertain of their sound. It took a while to recognize the rhythm of the sucking in and gushing out.

She was torn between going on and returning for the others. Then she thought of the relief they'd feel and how Evan would have to admit that she'd been right to take things into her own hands.

Going backward was slow and painful. When the walls widened into the little chamber, she just managed to spin around to shout out the news to Evan.

Only he was asleep again, his arms cradling the crow. Nessa was seated against the curving wall; her eyes were closed too. When Claudia called, Evan stirred but would not raise his head. Nessa looked up at Claudia. Everything seemed darker after the brightness of the translucent water.

"You have to come," Claudia insisted.

Nessa shook her head.

"Just to see," Claudia pleaded.

This time Nessa didn't even bother to shake her head. She turned her face into the darkness.

Claudia waited a moment. She was still panting from the exertion of her backward crawl. "Then I'll go without you," she threw back angrily, as she pivoted on her knees and retraced her way out to the watery light.

She was nearly there when everything began to go

wrong. One minute she was plodding along like a puppy going home, and the next the light, which had been opening before her, began to go out. She couldn't understand. She had to race against the dimming, or she would be lost. What had been a quivering green sparked with yellow was now transformed into something dull and gray, an opacity without a trace of sun, lifeless as the stone through which she had been crawling.

She thrust herself out into that gray world, careless of any danger. She had no thought for lurking raiders from the north. She could think only that beyond this void must be the living ocean and the sun-filled sky.

She hit the water flatly, falling onto it more than into it, although seconds later she found herself submerged, grasping at rocks, at rockweed, at anything that presented itself to her hands. She came up spluttering, holding onto the gunwale of the dinghy, which bobbed and scraped and dragged her on her knees as it hit the beach. It slung off, hit bottom again, back and forth, back and forth. Her eyes stung from the salt. She was freezing, her clothes clinging and weighting her. But the cold and the salt felt good, sharp and clean and powerful.

She rubbed at her burning eyes and opened them painfully onto a miraculous dawning. Each second brought a quickening of life to the world around her. Birds muttered and chirruped and then laughed with the coming of the sun. An owl's hooting trembled on the brink of its lost night. Shore birds plunged and darted, ecstatic and complaining all at once.

Then she felt the warmth. It was all about her. The sea was blue-green, just as it had been before the eclipse, and the turf of Thrumcap Island glistened with leftover moisture refracting the sun's rays. Claudia picked a stalk of sea lavender growing in the shallows. She gazed at the delicate blossoms that tipped the woody stalks.

Clutching the sea lavender and the bronze man together in one hand, she dragged the dinghy onto the beach. The painter barely reached the rock she chose to tie it to, for the tide was dead low, lower than she had ever seen it.

"Wait for me," she called out to Evan, who must have scrambled on up the cliff, as usual way ahead of her. "Evan," she shouted, "did you hear all the birds?" At least he had the crow with him, and would be able to report to Mr. Withorn about its behavior. "Evan," she yelled, laughter bursting out as she struggled to catch up with him. She stumbled drunkenly in her wet, sloppy, freezing things. "Evan, you know I can't run as fast as you. Wait for me."

PART TWO

TEN

THE whole time she was drying off in front of Mr. Colman's stove, Claudia was able to believe that any minute now Evan and the crow would appear from somewhere or other, probably full of some solitary exploit, maybe even connected with that seal they'd been after. Evan would turn up all right. He'd been doing this lately, going off without a thought for her, taking up with Jon, then with the Pictish girl.

Only there couldn't really have been a Pictish girl. That wasn't real. They had plunged in the shallows after the strange gray seal, and then the sky had darkened and she had had this kind of shock from the cold, from having felt sick to her stomach, from all the tension that had been building up. She'd had a kind of dream; maybe she'd even lost consciousness for a minute. You could dream hours, even days, in a few seconds like that.

With Mr. Colman gone, it was possible to imagine that Evan might have just gone off with him in his boat for a little while. But she couldn't be sure of this, and she couldn't bear to wait. She would have to look for Evan.

As soon as she set off across the island she was knee-deep in moisture again. Her dungarees, stiffened and heavy, made her legs feel as though they were wrapped in wet concrete. Her knees were tender, as though they'd been bruised. Still looking for Evan, she slogged through the hidden marsh, green and gold in the late afternoon light.

The stench of rotting vegetation followed her out into the swale. It was like the dread that gnawed away at her beneath the bright simple assurances she kept piling around herself.

When the grownups finally arrived and everyone moved off together toward the campsite and began to talk about supper, the first question came and she could not avoid it.

"Where's Evan?"

The words slipped out unrehearsed. "I don't think he's back yet."

"Back from where?"

"I'm not sure." Then, quickly: "Mr. Colman had to go and check some of his traps. And Evan. . . ."

"He should have asked first. When will they be back?"

"You weren't here to be asked." She stopped. So far she hadn't actually lied.

Mr. Withorn said, "Lobstering? That's the kind of experience I'd like to see Jon get."

Jon came in on cue. "I wish they'd waited for me."

"You'd get seasick," Claudia told him.

"Not necessarily," Jon's father explained. "The motion of a moving boat is different. . . ."

They were off on a discussion, and Claudia was left to help gather driftwood. She made a separate pile. She stayed apart. She felt cut off by their acceptance of the ordinary unfrightening situation. For now that Evan's absence was established, his early return expected, she could not escape what she knew. Fear consumed and filled her.

They may have thought her sullen because she minded being left behind, first by them, then by Evan. She did nothing to encourage or dispel this impression. Their own viewing of the eclipse had been something of a bust because of the cloud cover, but they had made some useful observations. Claudia, unable to respond, simply shoved more beans into her mouth and chewed and chewed.

Evan's supper lay beside the fire, a silver bundle of foil-wrapped overcooked food. Phil walked up the path to see whether Colman's boat was back. Claudia was too afraid to go with him. She concentrated on willing that Colman would still be gone. Her ears hummed with the effort to shut out all the sounds of sleepy, comfortable campers.

Phil reported that the boat was not there. Claudia felt like shouting with relief. She began to concentrate on the next essential step: Let them get off the island and onto their boat with its padded bunks and its screens. But she needn't have wasted her energy. Phil and Susan had no intention of stepping off the island until Evan was back and accounted for.

"Sometimes Mr. Colman stays out all night," she declared.

They knew this to be true. They didn't think he'd be likely to do that with Evan along.

"If it was safer," Claudia pointed out, "he'd wait till morning."

They couldn't dispute her logic, so instead they berated her for letting Evan go off like that. In the future she was to get permission. Sam Withorn interjected something about seizing opportunities.

"Opportunities, hell," Phil retorted. He snapped at Susan when she tried to reassure him. And when Claudia opened her mouth, not at all sure of what would come out, he told her to shut up and go to bed.

She kept waking. The first two times she could hear her mother and Phil murmuring in the darkness not far from her. They were pretty sure that if Colman wasn't back by now, he wouldn't show up till morning. Their talk veered off onto other subjects, like whether the daysailer should be moved from that outlying point. Claudia held her breath. Susan and Phil listened to the breeze, the tranquil sea. They would not bother about the daysailer.

The third time Claudia woke she could hear her mother's breathing, a faint snoring from Phil. She probably had hours to go before the tide would be far enough down, but she got up anyway. Her clothes, still damp, felt awful, but she was comforted by this sign of moisture. It promised a semblance of fog, what Mr. Colman called early morning smoke. No stars showed; the moon, having played out its dramatic encounter with the sun, was itself blotted out by vapors. Cautiously she made her way toward the hut. The murkiness seemed to act as a baffle; no sound issued from the inland wood, and the shoreline slept like some huge beast, its heavy breathing absorbed by the night.

She could smell the sour smoke from the leaking stove. For a moment she let herself believe that she would find Evan inside along with Mr. Colman. It was a trick of fatigue perhaps, or else the habit of deception she had suddenly cultivated to shore up her swelling fear.

Mr. Colman, who slept through most of every day, was

easily awakened. Squatting down beside the stove, lifting the hearthstone aside to take up the bronze man, she gave him a brief account of the situation, then waited for him to tell her what she must do.

"The crow? Gone again?"

"Evan's got the crow. On a string. It's fine."

"Boy's fine?"

"Well, yes. No. I mean, where I left him . . ." She faltered. Colman was making it harder for her instead of easier. She had no idea how long they could survive under the ground where the stale air had put them into that deep sleep. "The thing is, I have to get back there. To that exact place. To that time." She studied the bronze man in the brownish light of the stove.

Colman shook his head. "It leads. You follow."

"I know." She waited. "I know, but I've got to get to Evan." Suddenly she thought of Phil and Susan. "They think he's out with you. I let them think that." She couldn't tell whether Mr. Colman had really absorbed this. Well, but that wasn't the crucial thing. "How can I get back?" she cried.

Mr. Colman was either thinking or sleeping. His shallow breathing was rough and high. He was old. Oh, she thought, he is so old. What can he do? What does he know?

Finally he spoke. "The boat."

"The one at the point?"

"Go in again."

"But we were picked up at sea. There's no one there now except those men from the north. They'd . . . kill me. I think."

"The boat," Mr. Colman repeated, and this time his silence seemed permanent.

The edges of the horizon were gray. The whole sky resembled something charred and smoking. It was if a whitened ash crept inward, curling on itself the way smoldering bark is consumed by an unseen fire.

There was just enough light to find a driftwood log to use for a roller. It felt good to be doing something purposeful. Claudia lifted the stern of the dinghy and shoved the roller underneath. She tugged, and the boat slid seaward till the log slipped out the uphill end. She dragged it around once more. This time when the dinghy fell off the roller, she was able to drag it the rest of the way.

She hardly needed to row before she was up against the day-sailer. She climbed aboard, felt around for two lengths of extra line, fastened an end to a cleat, its midsection to the thwart of the dinghy, and with the other end in her mouth, rowed back to shore. She brought the line around the same rock she had tied the dinghy to before, and finished arranging her outhaul so that the dinghy could be pulled either way.

Returning to the moored day-sailer, she shipped the oars neatly so that the dinghy would present a reassuring look of order, climbed into the day-sailer, and, feeding out one part of the line, pulled the dinghy gently off. She stood for a moment admiring her work. Phil would admire it too, she thought. He would find the dinghy, free of the rocks, hanging halfway between the boat and the beach. He would conclude that she and Evan had rigged this outhaul so that the dinghy would be both safe and easily accessible. And this setup would show him that the kids were safely ashore.

She knelt on the deck and looked at the water. On a bright night it would have been sparked with phosphorescence; under the sun it would be like smoked glass. But now it held no light. It was funny how different it was like this, but what was most different was being alone. Someone, even a younger stepbrother, somehow shared the danger.

She lowered one foot over the side and felt the clammy fingers of the sea reach up. She pulled back. Last time there had been the dinghy to hold onto. Maybe when there was more light, she would be able to go through with it. She scanned the horizon. The gray edges of the sky had curled back even farther. She noticed that the boat had shifted on its mooring. That meant the tide was beginning to change. Now was the time to make the plunge, or, as Mr. Withorn would say, to seize the opportunity. "The hell with opportunity," Phil had answered. Because he was thinking about Evan. It was necessary to think about Evan. Evan was the reason she was here all by herself, about to dive into the shallow water and head for shore. She closed her eyes, took a deep breath, and pitched forward.

Everything bubbled around her. She had to fight against the weight of pants and jacket that gurgled and sagged and then fanned out, everywhere in her way, everywhere dragging at her. The effort saved her from panic. This was more than boat busy work; it was life work. Slowly she discovered the rhythm that would make her strokes raise her and push her forward. The hand that clutched the bronze man was almost useless, but in a minute she was banging into the first rock and using it like a steppingstone. Then she broke through the surface.

Between gasps, she tried to open her eyes. She could not. Her hair was plastered all over her face and she needed her free hand to keep afloat. Half swimming, half treading water and walking, she forced herself on until, daring to open her eyes a little, she could discern through what seemed to be a film of green seaweed a wall of dry stone.

Then she lay exhausted, resting just inside that wall. She lay shivering with her face cushioned in her crossed arms on something that wasn't entirely dry and yet was nothing like the small beach with its salt and rockweed smell, with its hint of sea things left by the receding ocean.

ELEVEN

The first time she felt the touch on her shoulder, she ignored it. She was just considering raising her head to get her bearings when she became aware of a second touch, this time on her hair. She lay very still. If Evan was playing games with her, she wasn't having any. She had been through enough for his sake.

Suddenly, still half blind, she rolled over and lunged for the hand that had been at her head. "I've got you," she rasped. Her voice came out a grating whisper, but her hands felt another hand slipping through her fingers. Quickly she brushed back her hair just in time to see him fleeing into the darkness. "Evan," she called, "stop. Please."

He must have stopped running, because she couldn't hear his footsteps any more. Creeping, she was able to get close enough to see the boyish shape there inside the cave. He seemed smaller. A trick of the darkness? "I was so scared," she told him. "Never mind," she added when he failed to answer her, "what matters is, I've found you."

"But I'm the one who found you," he said in a voice that was all wrong.

Claudia froze. Evan playing tricks on her was one thing. But this was something else. She said finally, carefully, "I'm glad you decided to look for me."

"Grandmother said I might find a marvel on this day. That I was to bring it back." He was walking toward her. "Are you a marvel?"

She was rooted to the spot. This boy, smaller than Evan, was dressed like no one she had ever seen. "You're not Evan." Yet she was sure this was the right place.

"Who is Evan?"

"My brother. I think he's in there." She pointed past him. "I'm sorry. I'd like to talk to you. But I've got to find Evan first."

"You'd better not go around the corner in there. You'll not come out. Anyway, I have to bring you to my grandmother."

Claudia shook her head. "Not now." She crept forward and found him blocking her way. In the dim light she could make out a kind of tunic over leggings, turned up shoes, a knife at the wide belt. He deliberately prevented her going in. "It's all right," she said, "I've been in before. I know my way."

"No. You will have to obey me. My father is earl of these islands. My grandmother is a princess from Erin and knows many secrets of the dark. You will come with me."

"Now listen," Claudia burst out, "I don't care who you are. I'm not going anywhere till I get my brother. So out of my way. We can talk when I get back with him. Move."

"Your word is that you will return?"

"I have to, stupid. That's the whole point of coming here. Do you think I want to spend any more time than I have to in a creepy underground passage?" As she edged past him, it suddenly occurred to her to ask, "Is there any fighting out there?"

The boy shook his head soberly. "The fighting is where my father is, far from here. He and his hirdmen are still away to the summer harrying. When I am bigger I will go along and kill many men and bring home treasures and win lands. When I am grown I will have my own hirdmen pledged to fight for me, a warship of my own. When—"

"I mean, is it safe out there now? Is anything happening?"

"Nothing is happening," he replied with a touch of impatience. "That is why I had gone in search of marvels. My grandmother said it is the time for them if I but seek them in the dark places of the sea and earth. I waited for a while near the old pillar stone, for there are tales that at certain times it will walk to the loch for a drink. But it never budged. And then I found you, halfway between the sea and earth. I will certainly not let you go."

She felt like laughing at him. He was half her size. She crept away from him on her hands and knees.

She grew accustomed to the darkness. When she finally found herself in the little room, she had no trouble making out the sleeping figures of Evan and Nessa. But waking them was another matter. She called. She shouted. Then she reached out to shake Evan.

Touching him made her shriek with horror. His jacket was covered with a fuzzy coating that was both soft and gummy. She had to wait a moment before trying again. This time she aimed for his face, but what she touched was worse because it seemed as though he had no skin at all. Gathering courage, she tried brushing the stuff off. It clung to her hand. She leaned over him. He was breathing very slowly.

Next she tried to touch the crow, but recoiled at the feeling of its coated feathers. Nessa, who was lying on her side, her knees drawn up, was no more responsive than Evan.

Claudia sat back on her heels and contemplated this group. Then she dragged Evan into a sitting position. She was getting covered with the soft whitish stuff. It was like trying to work in a pudding, except that whatever it was that coated Evan was far from edible. It gave off a rank odor that reminded her of the island forest swamp. That was when it occurred to her that what was needed wasn't thumping and scraping, but more light and air.

Dragging Evan seemed to take hours, but all the whacking and bumping and the approach to the opening began to have an effect. He started to grumble. His eyes were still tight shut, but his complaints continued to grow in volume and coherence. At last he began to fight her, and then as she paused, panting, he twisted around on his stomach and opened his eyes on her.

"You're hurting me. What are you doing?"

"You need to get out. I couldn't wake you back in that room."

Evan yawned. "I was just having a nap."

"Look at that guck all over you."

Evan shifted onto an elbow and looked at himself. "What have you been dragging me through?"

"I found you that way. I think it's mildew or mold or something like that."

Evan scowled. It was obvious he didn't believe her.

"Listen, Evan, I was back. Phil's worried about you. You've been gone all night. We're in trouble, and I let them think you were out on Mr. Colman's boat. And he wants his crow back. So come on."

"What about Nessa?"

"Listen, you don't understand how serious this is. We've got to get back to Thrumcap Island."

"And leave her here?"

"She doesn't belong to us."

"Anyway, the crow's back there. Besides, we can't just go away and leave her."

Claudia was uneasy about going back for Nessa. Once awake, the Pictish girl would exert her influence on Evan again. But he insisted. He'd go no farther till they'd returned for Nessa and the crow.

Back in the chamber, Evan kept trying to peel the coating away from him. It smeared and stuck and seemed just like fake snow made out of detergent. He couldn't rid himself of it.

Hauling Nessa was easier than dragging Evan alone.

They put the crow on her stomach, and Evan took her hands, Claudia her legs. But once she began to awaken, the situation changed. One moment she was inert, light and supple and only slippery where they tried to grip her, and the next she was thrashing wildly, clawing at Evan and kicking at Claudia. Claudia yelled at her and Evan yelled at Claudia to be patient and understanding, and then the crow was waking and screeching forth a string of crow epithets that seemed intended for all three of them.

Finally Nessa pulled free, and Evan was able to get her to listen. He explained as much as he could there in the cramped corridor. He said that she could come with them if she wanted, or else go back to the place they had originally entered, back to Fann and the others, but what she could not do was remain in that little twilight cell any longer. "We would have slept forever," he told her. "No point being alive if you're asleep the whole time."

Nessa communicated with Evan in her silent penetrating way. Claudia, at Nessa's feet, was too far from her face or hands to intercept or interpret the girl's looks and gestures. After a while Evan sighed and said, "Uh, Claudia, I guess we'd better go back the other way first. To leave Nessa with her people."

"She can go by herself. She knows the way better than we do. We're near where we need to be and we're in a hurry."

Evan said, "She keeps making her hands like Fann blessing her. And shakes her head. Claudia, I'm going to take her back. To be sure she's all right. At least till we hear their voices."

"Till we can hear their voices then," Claudia assented

grudgingly. "But you've got to promise to let her go the rest of the way alone."

The journey was tortuous. They were tempted to rest in the little chamber, but by now even Nessa had no stomach for the sticky substance they had shed there; it was everywhere they touched or leaned.

From there on Nessa led the way. She was quicker than Evan, who was quicker than Claudia, even though he had the sleepy crow to contend with. Claudia, exhausted, kept calling ahead to him, "Don't forget. You've got to tell me as soon as you hear them."

Evan's grunt was the only answer she got. The tunnel became pitch black. All Claudia could really believe in were her knees, which felt as though she had baseballs tied on them. When she had gone what seemed miles, she stopped, rebelling. "Evan," she cried, "you ought to be able to hear them by now."

Evan called out to Fann. Then she added her voice to his. They waited for a reply. "But they'll be asleep too," Evan exclaimed. "It's stupid to expect them to be awake if we weren't."

Nessa was way ahead by now. When they arrived at the chamber, it was such a relief to stand that at first that was all Claudia was aware of. Next was Nessa's stillness. It wasn't her usual silence. Nessa was still in a way that made her seem one with the stone that surrounded her.

"They're gone," Evan whispered. "Left her."

Claudia began to feel around. She found an upright slab. She found a wall with one of those little shelves recessed in it. Then her foot met something that scraped along the floor and she knelt down. It had the consistency of waxy cardboard, stiff and unyielding to her fingers.

But the shape within it was unmistakable, a book. To try out her voice, she said, "They left this behind. Maybe there's something more." She swept her hand wide and felt something hard and loose, then more things, like pieces of wood jumbled together, and then like the branch of a tree that is perfectly curved, a set of arching stems. She rested her hand on those stems; she knew them to be ribs.

She could neither speak nor move. Then she had a vision of Nessa crouched among other bones, perhaps touching some object she could identify with the skeleton beside it. Claudia brushed her hand lightly across what must have been the skull, but she didn't let her fingers explore. She placed the book down beside it.

They had to lead Nessa away. For the first time the Pictish girl was docile. They took turns at the well, drinking and washing. Nessa did exactly what she was told, no more, no less. When she returned wet but cleansed of the remaining mold, Claudia, feeling her way through the blackness, discovered that Nessa was holding the square-sided bell. Tentatively she began to take it from her, but the grip the Pictish girl had on it was fixed as if the bell were an extension of her.

Now they struggled through the darkness, each with a separate burden, Nessa the tongueless bell, Evan the crow, Claudia the bronze man. Claudia was so dazed that it never occurred to her to warn Evan about the boy who was waiting at the opening.

She heard the boy and Evan all at once, Evan shouting, "Hey, we're home," the boy asking, "Are you a marvel too?" And Evan declaring, "You're not Jon. Who are you?"

"Come out here," the boy ordered, "where I can see you. How many? I want to see all of you. I will bring you straight to the bordland bu at Byrgisey and my grandmother will be proud of me. She will say, 'Well done, Hundi, son of the Orcadian earl who is son of an Erin princess. Well done!' Maybe she will be so proud she will give me a horse."

TWELVE

HUNDI led them along a path which kept to the gentle slopes looking out over the sea. They had no trouble recognizing their surroundings. Behind them was the tower with its curving double walls rising over the water. Though distant, it stood out solidly in the hazy light. The small island, set low between the shirred white of the riptides, looked placid and green. Claudia could make out the shadow of a great turf wall across that green expanse and a number of gray stone structures.

Trotting ahead to Hundi, she asked, "Are the monks on that island?"

"They live apart," he answered. "Grandmother says they starve for the pleasure of it. She says they are not fighters, are not men at all." He shrugged. "Once in a while you see one of them in those hide boats that can travel about the rocks. They are no threat to my father's earldom."

"Can you see Colm?" Evan asked Nessa, who was staring hard at the island.

She turned, looking at him, her expression blank, her thin face drawn.

Evan dropped back to whisper to Claudia, "She's not all right. Nessa's not all right."

"How could she possibly recognize anyone at this distance?" Claudia snapped. "Anyhow, she's not the only one who's not all right. How are we going to get home?" When Evan didn't reply, she went on. "If you hadn't been so wrapped up in that crazy kid, we'd be back now. You had to put on this protection act."

"You're mad because Nessa and I get along and she doesn't like you. You've been mad at me ever since I started being with other kids. You act as if you own me or something."

"I wouldn't want to own you. Only I could see she was making you do stupid things. So now here we are. And it's your fault, her fault."

They were so intent on their quarrel, they nearly bumped into Nessa, who was standing on the path, still gazing out at the green island.

"She's heard you," Evan whispered.

"She's not paying any attention to me. Or you," Claudia retorted.

Suddenly Nessa set off at a run, not along the coastal path, but down to the shore.

"Not that way," Hundi shouted. "That isn't the way to Byrgisey."

Calling shrilly, Evan started after her, but before he could reach the steep bank, Nessa, already far ahead, had dashed into the water. Evan cried out and stopped. Hundi made his way over to Evan. "She is like a seal," Hundi remarked. Ignoring him, Evan turned an anguished face to Claudia. "What will we do?"

"What can we do? Don't forget, Evan," she pronounced overclearly, "you can't own people."

Evan followed the swimming Nessa with his eyes. Claudia felt like screaming at him. He didn't give a damn about his own father, about Susan, who was like a mother to him. All he could think about was Nessa.

They turned finally and trudged on in silence. Evan kept his face averted from her. She hated his misery and her own cruelty, but would not give any ground. She had been right.

They passed the deep chasm where the sea fowl roosted and the seals sunned. "There," Hundi declared at last, "my father's bu. You can see it's much bigger and grander than any ordinary farm."

The islet he pointed to was transformed. What first struck Claudia and Evan was the massive stone wall that reared up like a fortress facing the land. They were still high enough to be able to see beyond that wall to the islet itself, crowded with people and animals. Long low houses made of turf and stone and thatching were everywhere. The green slope was segmented by small walled enclosures and a few turf dikes like the one on the little green island. Below them a kind of bridge had been built, a path through the channel that separated the islet from mid-tide to high tide. Hundi led them down and onto this walkway, onto paving stones wide enough to bear a cart.

They had almost reached the open gate of the fortified wall when something flashed in the water beside them.

Hundi leaped into the shallows and drew his knife, holding it poised above his head. Claudia thought it must be a seal or porpoise rolling, but it was Nessa's head that surfaced. She climbed out only a yard or two from Hundi, who slowly returned his knife to its sheath and beckoned the children on.

"I thought she was a seal," he told Claudia. "Sometimes, when they are hurt, they float in close, and then I can get them. It is a brave thing to kill one of the gray seals, for they usually keep to the open water and are fierce when they are attacked. My father says it is a sign of manhood to kill one with a knife, but my grandmother tells me to keep from them."

Nessa seemed surprised to have come across them. She must have been looking for Colm, but now as she gazed on the community that covered the small islet, she seemed to give up on her intense searching. Why not? said her look, when Evan pleaded with her to stay with them.

Claudia stared at the Pictish girl, who looked rattier than ever now that she was soaked. Even the girl's hands were like rodent paws, quick and sharp. Empty. Suddenly she realized what was missing. "Nessa, the bell. You lost it in the water?"

Nessa gave her that glance that discounted her, transformed her into something clumsy and dull.

"Where did you leave your bell?" Evan said to Nessa. Nessa pointed in an easterly direction, but seaward.

"On the island?" asked Evan. Nessa was looking at him, pointing. "With the monks?" Then Evan turned to Claudia. "And I guess Colm isn't there. She must have come here to look for him when she couldn't find him on the Vanishing Island."

"Holy Island," Claudia corrected.

"Eyin Helga is the name of the monks' island," said Hundi as he pushed them through a doorway of a house set apart from the main cluster of buildings.

Their first impression was of smoke and dimness, a hearth in the center that was long like the house, carved roof posts, red walls.

"There you are, there's my little Hundi," cried a voice from within.

"I have three marvels," Hundi declared. "And a raven."

"Come here," said the voice.

Claudia stumbled as she stepped forward. Her eyes were just growing used to the darkness. Embers glowed beneath a pot hung from a chain that descended from a roof beam; steam rose slowly straight up to a hole in the thatched roof. Except for the doorway, that hole was the only point through which light entered. She began to make out the carvings on the posts that formed a double column down the length of the house. There were serpents intertwined, bulging coils and heads disfigured by immense fangs. From the crossbeams hung herbs, fish, animal skins, even a headless rooster, all of them casting distorted shadows on walls already covered with pictures of huntsmen and boars, men and boys, islands and ships and rugged mountains with giants at their peaks. Metallic threads pierced the woven scenes of the tapestried walls like the phosphorescence of an ocean night.

Women came and went. One of them sat bent over a little loom in her lap. Another stood at a huge loom leaning against the gabled wall. Her gestures were vigorous and rhythmic as she shot the woof through the warp threads that hung taut, weighted near the floor by stones.

101

Other women crossing the doorway carried staffs of yarn on the crook of one arm, a spindle in the other. The spinning was constant. Conversation was intermittent, easy. Everyone was occupied.

Hundi led the children before an old woman who half sat, half reclined on a raised platform set back from the hearth. She was swathed in a voluminous shawl of brilliant colors, but beneath that a pleated, loose-fitting tunic fell back from brittle-looking arms as she plied her needle swiftly in and out of some heavy material. Something else showed when she raised her arms, a kind of jumper worn over the tunic and held at the shoulders by large oval brooches connected across the front by chains from which hung keys and scissors, needles and tweezers. As she worked, she would hang one needle on this chain and choose another of a different size. All these tools on her sunken chest made her seem burdened, dwarfed.

Looking at this array of metal made Claudia feel beneath her foul weather jacket; the hilt was there. Reassured, she went back to staring, taking in the crooked bony fingers nearly hidden by rings, the head covering tied back from the face, the bright darting eyes intent on her and on Nessa and Evan.

"One of the marvels seemed a seal," Hundi said to his grandmother. "The wet one."

"That is fitting." The old woman addressed Nessa: "Do you know this day, child of the sea?"

"She doesn't speak," Evan broke in. "She never has. Why were you expecting marvels?"

"In Erin, where I was born," she told him, "Midsummer Eve is the day for separating the lambs from the ewes. The priests there call it Lammas Day, but in the

102

ancient time when Erin was yet called Erenn, it was known as the Feast of Lugh of the Long Arm. Here on these islands, surrounded by unschooled Northmen, I strive to keep my heritage strong for the sake of those who come after. The Day of Lugh was a time for marvels." She leaned forward and whispered, "Here they call me Audna, but know you my real name?"

Evan shook his head. He seemed intimidated by the woman leaning over him, though she was tiny as a bird, sharp and fragile.

"My true name is Eithne. It was the name of Lugh's mother."

"You mean this Lugh is a relative?"

The woman drew back. "Lugh is the god of our ancient lore. All gifts and powers are his. I have raised my son, Sigurd, in his image," she added on a note of satisfaction. "And will do the same with Hundi if I live long enough." She pointed at Nessa. "It is fitting that this one came from the sea on this day."

Hundi looked pleased with himself and sank down to listen.

"Before Lugh was born," the old woman began, "it is told that Eithne's father learned that he was fated to be killed by his grandson. He kept Eithne in a tower on an island, so that none might get her with child. But a great warrior for whom a smith on the mainland was making arms was helped magically to the island. And there he found Eithne, and got her and all the women who attended her with child. When the women gave birth, Eithne's father took all the infants in a cloth and dropped them in the sea."

She paused; then, satisfied that the children were spellbound, she continued. "Of all those babies, one was saved by the same magic that had brought the warrior to the island, and that infant Lugh was carried to the smith to be reared. The other infants," she finished, eying Nessa, "are the ancestors of the seals."

Nessa met this look with her own level gaze. Water still dripped down her face and from her tunic. A puddle formed where she stood.

"Even the monks celebrate the Feast of Lugh," declared Audna, "though they call it the Feast of the Plowmen. In my land the assemblies of the kings are held on Lammas Day. That is," she added, "when the Northmen are not in power there."

"Did Lugh ever pay his grandfather back?" asked Evan.

"Pay him?"

"You know, what was fated. Did he kill Eithne's father?"

"Oh yes, but that is another tale," Audna replied, dismissing it with a wave of her tweezers. "We will have many tellings in my house, for we lack the company of skilled bards in this earldom. There is a poverty of song and word." She regarded them thoughtfully. "You must be clothed properly, so that none suspect what marvels you may be. We will bide our time till Sigurd returns. Now then, give me that crow, boy, and I'll have you all bathed and dressed and set to some useful tasks."

"No, he's mine," Evan objected. "I mean, he's not mine exactly, but—"

"I have need of just that bird, for my son's banner is ragged from his battles and was returned to me for repair, since I alone can craft its spell with threads of gold and jet. Come, Hundi, hold up this end to show what I have wrought." She lifted one corner of the material in her lap. It had the shape of an outstretched wing. Hundi took another corner and walked backward till the banner, somewhat lopsided, was nearly unfurled. It was a giant raven edged in gold, shredded, its gleaming eye torn and hanging, its beak agape as if poised to strike.

The crow started to squawk. It flapped its wings and tugged at its string and fell from Evan's shoulder in a flutter of feathers and excrement.

Audna snapped the raven banner to her. "Common beast." She glared with distaste at the frantic crow, which Evan was trying to soothe. "Still," she went on, "it is better than none. You know," she confided, "the Northmen look on my raven as one of Odin's." Her voice dropped conspiratorily. "But this is no servant of Odin; it is Badb, ancient war goddess of my people."

Evan drew back.

"Oh, come," she pressed irritably. "It is not forever, you may be sure. Give it to me."

Reluctant, but slightly reassured, Evan started to hand over the crow. It was dirty now as well as ruffled. Audna recoiled and had an attendant take the crow for her. "And find suitable clothing for these three," she ordered, then changed her mind. "Not that one. Not the Cruithne."

The attendant paused, confused.

Audna pointed to Nessa. "That one. The dark one. She is one of the Cruithne, the Pictish folk you sometimes see. Long ago Pictavia was a mighty kingdom. You Northmen think the world began with you, but it was already old when your gods brought forth your ancestors and your tree sprang to life. The greatest hero of ancient

Ulidia in the land of Erin is said to have been of the Cruithne. So that one," she finished, "will stay with me."

"What are you going to do with Nessa?" Evan demanded.

"Why, set her to her appointed task, serving Eithne. Why else was she sent to me out of the sea on the Feast of Lugh?"

Evan stood up to the old woman. "She's not a servant," he declared.

Audna gave a yelp of laughter. "Then she will be the keeper of the crow. For the moment."

"She's an artist," Evan asserted stiffly.

"Artist?" The old woman bent toward him.

"She . . . she makes pictures."

"Images," put in Claudia, conscious of Evan's grateful glance.

"Then she will assist me with the image of the raven." Chortling, Audna turned from them to instruct the attendant on the disposition of the crow. "I'll need him near me, but not on me," they heard as they were beckoned away to a chamber at the end of the house. "Yes, that is close enough for my purposes. Now fetch water to clean where he has fouled my matting. Water and herbs to scatter after. Common bird."

Thirteen

In spite of being Audna's marvels, Claudia and Evan were assigned the ordinary tasks of child thralls. One of these duties was to entertain the young Hundi, who was not quite old enough to be off with the haymakers. Audna was especially eager to have Hundi instructed in picture making, but his drawings were hopelessly crude.

Nessa's role was different, more slavelike. On the surface it seemed to be her Pictishness. But others about Byrgisey had her dark looks, though none were so small. The real difference was in the bond between Audna and Nessa, and it seemed to derive from Audna's identification with her namesake, Eithne, and those infants who became the ancestors of the seals. Somehow Nessa was never transformed, like Evan and Claudia, into acceptable copies of thrall children.

Though Claudia was aware that time passed differently whenever they crossed over into the Other Place, though she tried to reassure herself that they might yet get back to their parents on Thrumcap's next tide, still she chafed at the rhythm of life on Byrgisey. Evan's acceptance of everything, including the disappearance of the crow, and his concern for Nessa were like extensions of his long underground sleep. From time to time Claudia tried to shake him out of it, but more often she too was lulled into forgetfulness.

New sights and tastes and feelings began to claim her.

Cloud shadows stirred the muted greens and browns of the hills. The islands had a battered look, as though pounded and shaped by the ravening seas. On Byrgisey Claudia became used to the spray and the wind. She grew accustomed to light nights and dim houses, to sour milk and clotted cheese and stringy strips of dried fish. The simplest cloths woven at the looms were deeply textured and bore colors rich as the earth.

Claudia liked the loose, neat costume she was given. The smock was clean, the jumperlike apron, though patched and plain, a relief after her salt-stiffened dungarees and shirt. These things, the bronze man rolled inside them, the foul weather jacket wrapped around all, were safely packed away in a stone chest at the back of Audna's house. She had stuffed the bundle deep down beneath a pile of skins and folded cloth.

She was pleased with her hiding place, though once, when she was standing near that chest, she noticed Audna regarding her and the chest with a keen, though veiled, look. But Audna said nothing. Nor did she send a woman to keep track of Claudia, as she did of Nessa, who stole off whenever she could, searching, baffled by what was at once familiar to her and utterly changed.

"What's she looking for?" Evan whispered from the far side of a low wall over which Nessa had just clambered. The wall joined a house whose long stone and turf walls, bowed at the middle, gave it the look of something hunched under its burden of thick low thatching. Nessa was kneeling and rubbing some chicken dirt from a slab that was part of the paving. Then she rose and cleaned another with the side of her bare foot.

"Why don't you ask her?" Claudia suggested out loud. Goaded by her irritation with his single-minded concern for Nessa, Claudia couldn't keep from adding, "While you're at it, find out about the crow, too."

Nessa looked up, regarded the two of them without expression, then dropped to her hands and knees and crept toward the byre. Nearby, Audna's attendant gossiped idly with the woman of this steading. Hands cast off the twirling spindle and drew out one length of woolen thread after another, but eyes followed the strange gropings of the Pictish girl.

Now Hundi appeared. "You and Nessa give me another lesson," he demanded. "She's not doing anything. Only getting dirty."

Evan protested, and Hundi threatened. Finally Evan dragged himself off with Hundi in tow. Nessa glanced up, scraped dung from the sole of her foot, then resumed her quest.

As Claudia turned away, her eye caught something in the shade of the wall. She squinted to reduce the light some more. The marking she saw was the foot of a cross, a boat-shaped terminal like the one she had seen in the tiny graveyard. She didn't tell Nessa. It would only confirm what all these buildings and lanes and walls already told them. There was nothing left to mark the graves of the monks and the Pictish dead lying below this bustling community of seafarers and farmers. Grass sprouted from chinks in the wall; clumps of heather had taken hold in the turf that bound the stones into a baffle against the constant winds. Dense wiry stems sprang sunward from the top of the wall built of stones she had once defiled with her unbaptized presence. How long did it take to bury a graveyard? If Claudia couldn't reckon that time, what would Nessa make of it?

Claudia wandered back toward Audna's house. An attendant beckoned her to take up the distaff and spindle. Claudia was still struggling to master the spinning; usually her thread came out all lumpy or else it broke, but she kept trying so that she would not be set to the more boring task of picking the fleece for the carders. Dreamily she turned in the doorway, the low sun warm on her face and arms. She thought about Nessa, seeking and lost. Nessa was really a prisoner. But then so were Evan and she. They only crossed over to the main island when Hundi took them inland to his favorite lake in the shelter of a round hill. When Claudia pressed him to show her the spot where he had first come across them, he only shrugged her off. The ground was full of holes and tunnels, he declared, and they were not safe, for they were more likely to harbor monsters than marvels. He led her to the steep headland to prove his point, showing her all the mounds and rocky cairns that pushed up like fists out of the rolling land. Any of these might have harbored an entrance into the earthen darkness.

From the high headland Claudia could make out crumbled stumps of round fortresses all along the coast. She could see heaps of blackened stone beside the dark lakes. She could imagine hollows beneath the springy turf, but did not dare by herself to seek that underground passage that might return her and Evan to their own time and place. There were too many possibilities, and when the sun was banked by low clouds, the fists of turf

110

and stone, the cavernous eruptions, seemed to stretch before her eyes, their shadows reaching out as if to seize the winds that swept in from the encircling sea.

Evan and Hundi hurtled through the doorway like those very winds. The twirling coil of wool swung wide and dropped. "Can't you look where you're going?" she snapped, gathering up the lumpy thread.

The boys hadn't noticed her. It was Audna they sought. A viking had arrived from the distant land where Eirik the Red had settled. The ship was laden with skins and ivory tusks.

Audna's eyes sparkled. A feast would be prepared. The few men who were not away on the raids with Earl Sigurd would be called back from the fields to honor the visitor.

Hundi was dressed in fresh trousers, with red laces to bind his stockings and a newly woven ribbon to catch his hair. Audna would not fuss about her own garments. It was the men of this earldom the viking must respect, she declared, as she yanked Hundi's shirt beneath his belt and straightened his hair band.

Claudia and Evan were swept aside in the hurried preparations. When it became known that the viking was the son of Iceland's most honored lawmaker, a boar was taken from the home field where it had been fattening on the manured grass. It was slung out behind Audna's house, its squeals nearly drowning out the babble of excitement, the squawking of hens, the shouted orders. When the boar was stuck, Claudia sank down in Audna's closetlike chamber. She huddled into the linen to muffle the sounds of slaughter and waited there till she heard the old woman's shuffling footsteps. Out in the yard the blood was already carried away for the cooking. The flagstones were sloshed with water from wooden buckets hauled by strong laughing children.

Nessa came around the byre carrying a spray of angelica. She brushed aside the children as though they were weeds in her path. Her bare feet left small neat prints on the drying flags. Claudia thought of the stone of succession, Nessa's tiny feet set deliberately, firmly, in the footmarks reserved for Pictish chieftains. Nessa walked a different surface from any other being; she trod a way invisible to all but her.

Audna's house filled with the elders of the bu. Long low tables were carried in and set before them. Then the summer light was blotted out. The man in the doorway, tall and gaunt, paused.

Audna, seated before the fire, greeted him. Slaves and freemen alike shared the occasion with the mistress of the bu, though thralls like Claudia and Evan did not rank places at the tables or wooden bowls, but had to eat their slabs of dried fish smeared with butter with their fingers. Women whose husbands were important hirdmen of the earl had the honor of serving the food. It was clear from the manner of their serving that they were not overly impressed with this visitor.

Thorstein son of Hall of Side, though young, looked prematurely worn. He had neglected to change his shoes, which were caked with salt. His patched mantle, which fell to a point in front and back, seemed too small for him and failed to conceal his threadbare shirt. Still, he carried with him the most sumptuous bearskin these Orcadians had ever seen. It was thick and white with yellowed tips;

112

its raking claws rattled on the freshly strewn rushes as he laid it before Audna.

Audna declared that anything she could give him would be an insult in comparison. "When my son returns," she proclaimed, "he will present you with the treasure of your choice from his plunder. He is the champion of all looters."

Thorstein told her that the greatest gift she could make would be the promise of safe passage to the monks' island of an old monk he had rescued on his return from Greenland. The monk's needs were simple, some willow stems to make withies for his coracle, a skin that had not been cured, enough butter for the waterproofing.

Audna waved aside these trifles. Of course they would be available. Now what of the green land, she demanded, for reports so far were full of conflict. Was it truly fertile? How many had perished on their way?

Thorstein, seated at last, smiled. "Eirik has not the imagination of a poet, but he has the tongue of one who builds tales from the stolen runes of Odin. So he has called the new land green." Thorstein touched the bearskin with the tip of his stiffened boot. "Though most of what I've seen of it resembles more the white of this fur. Still, many men will seek it, and their belief that it is green may see them safely there." He shrugged off the mantle and rubbed his hands slowly before the bench of food.

Claudia saw Audna lean forward as though to prod him on. His slowness seemed to irritate her, but he set his own pace and would not be hurried.

"It may be better to begin there," he resumed thought-

113

fully, "even if grain will not grow, then to struggle at home where all the land has been taken." Thorstein took a long drink from the horn that was presented to him, then handed it back to the woman so that his aged hostess could complete the ceremony of sharing the ale. He appeared to measure his words as he spoke. "It is different for me. My father is honored in Iceland. So it was not want that drove me westward, though many good families have suffered bitterly since the famine."

"Then why did you go? To make a fortune? I am told your ship is brimming with skins and ivory. You must seek those treasures."

Thorstein smiled again. He seemed unaware of Audna's intensity. "What seem treasures to one man may be without worth to another."

Evan leaned close to Claudia. "She can't stand that man," he commented. "He's driving her crazy."

Claudia began to nod, then shook her head. "Or she can't understand him," she responded musingly. Suddenly she wanted to get closer to them. Something was happening between those two. She started to make her way toward the hearth, as though intent on poking at the turfs.

"The monk I carried all this way," Thorstein was saying, "has no use for skins and ivory. He wishes to return what he calls treasure to the little island known hereabouts as Eyin Helga."

"Treasure?" Audna's voice tightened. "We have long ignored the drab monks on that island. What treasure could they have?"

Thorstein spread his hands. "It is a thing of no great value, a man-hilt from an ancient sword. It is not set with stones, nor chased with silver or gold. But it has an enchantment known only to the monks. That is the only treasure of it."

"A hilt." Audna frowned. "Only a hilt? What is the nature of its enchantment? Is it useful?"

Thorstein shook his head. "Not for any man but one of those who wear the robes of white and walk barefoot on the ground. Which doesn't mean," he added, "that others might not value it. The monk I brought here was carried off by a man who believed that if he could discover the secret of the hilt he would be able to sail beyond all known bounds."

"How did he know that? Is it true? Who told him?"

Thorstein rubbed his chin before answering ruefully, "I fear he learned it from me."

Claudia froze at the look in Audna's eyes. For an instant there was a gleam, half triumphant, half savage. It flashed like a smile and was gone. "I am not fond of puzzles," she declared.

Thorstein seemed neither intimidated nor wary. Claudia felt an impulse to shout a warning and then felt foolish for it. What kind of protection did this tall Icelander need? His very simplicity and openness were a kind of protection. It was no puzzle, he was replying to Audna. "Though I regretted my ready telling of the marvel. It's why I was bound to rescue the monk when he was carried off by that ruthless robber."

Audna said quickly, "And are not all good vikings ruthless? And robbers?"

"This one," Thorstein informed her, "sacked the last remaining monastery off the coast of Iceland. I was raised in fosterage on that same island for some years. There was no gold there, nor silver, but only a few books and, for a while, that hilt with its sunstone."

Audna cut in sharply. "Sunstone? You mentioned no sunstone before."

Mild surprise showed in Thorstein's expression. "And should not have now, though I thought I had mentioned its enchantment. Well, but it will soon be back with the monks where it belongs."

"It would be strange indeed," Audna intoned, "if you put your trust in a . . . ruthless robber and kept it from an aged hostess who had welcomed you with honor."

Claudia crouched by the fire. She didn't dare look up or appear to be listening. She was drenched in sweat and could smell her jumper and hair being scorched. Yet she had to stay, for Thorstein, his voice tinged with reluctance but no more guarded than before, acknowledged Audna's hospitality and once again thanked her for the help she would provide so that the monk could complete the journey to Eyin Helga.

"And the sunstone," Audna prompted. "The monk will take the sunstone with the hilt as well?"

There was an almost imperceptible pause before Thorstein responded. "The monks I lived with used the sunstone bead in the hilt in their hard pursuit of greens among the rocky islets. Also—" He drew a small breath, then finished softly, "also I learned to voyage through the blind fogs of those waters."

She seemed ready to pounce on his words before he had finished speaking. "You learned the secret of the sunstone and the hilt?" Her voice was sharpened to a fine edge.

116

"It was the taste for it I learned," he replied bluntly, "not the power. No, Audna, I have no greater gifts than those of my fellows. I, too, head for the clouds, hoping there is land below, or follow in the wake of the geese during their spring flights. I carry crows as well, since they may fly upward and see land I cannot sight at sea level. And though I can read the sailing disk as well as any seafarer, I cannot penetrate the fogs as can those simple monks in their frail little boats. I have plowed many furrows in the ocean with my staunch vessel, but I am no match for those who yet eke out their island existence, chanting the hours."

Claudia drew back with relief. Somehow Thorstein's bluntness had redressed the balance. She covered her cheeks with her hands and let the soothing touch restore her own composure. Someone kneed her aside. She stumbled down onto Thorstein's mantle, still wet and rank from the sea. She sat there listening to Thorstein explain further that it was the monk he'd saved, once he was strong enough, who had directed this last sailing, though he had been close to death when Thorstein had rescued him.

"That was not clever of his captor," Audna remarked. "He would have needed the monk alive to use the power of the bead."

"Yes, but this monk had refused to eat. He would not have lasted till landfall."

"So what did you do?"

"I am afraid," said Thorstein mildly, "that I had to kill the robber and his followers. His ship sank."

"Well," said Audna, straightening, nodding her approval. "Well." Then she asked, "But why here? Why to the monks of Eyin Helga, who never set foot off that small island of theirs?"

"The tale is long and weaves back and forth, as these things do that have been handed down in scraps of legend and verse. The hilt belongs with those monks. It was far from my course."

"Your monk will find the currents treacherous, the channel strewn with hidden rocks. Perhaps if you approach and your monk shows himself, the others will venture forth and take him from you. You do not mind giving up the hilt?"

"It is not mine to give up," Thorstein said.

She drew in a breath. "It could be."

He did not respond. For a few minutes he consumed great portions of meat and cheese. A serving woman handed Claudia a board with crumbly remnants of a barley cake and sent her off to share it with the other thralls. Audna watched Thorstein closely. Finally she leaned toward the fire that separated them; her tiny face was orange in the glow. "Tell me, then," she pursued. "What is your course when you are not diverted by starving monks? Has Greenland other lures for you?"

"I am an Icelander, not a Greenlander," he answered finally. His hands were raised slightly, as if to keep them from soiling his well-worn shirt. His look was direct, earnest, as if he really strove to make himself clear. From the far end of the house, Claudia couldn't see his eyes, only his thick eyebrows bleached white like his long hair, but she could sense the intensity of his gaze. "But I am a voyager as well," he went on. "There is land beyond Greenland, and beyond even that. A certain Bjarni

118

sighted a wonderful coast, heavy with timber and edged with sand. Far to the west he saw this land."

"But why go so far from what is known, if not to conquer or settle?"

Thorstein scrubbed his hands in the bowl of water placed beside him. When he was finished, he accepted a cloth, dried his hands and wiped his mouth, drawing out his mustache between the folds. Then he dropped the cloth and answered Audna. "I seek the limits, the place where the sun goes when it sinks beneath the sea."

The old woman and the Icelander stared at each other through the hissing flame. Both were utterly still.

Then Audna pulled back. "I hope you will stay at least until my son returns. He is a fine man, great of size, for which he is known as Sigurd the Stout. The name reflects his stature and his heart as well. Some time ago country-men of yours, the sons of Njal and a noble youth named Kari, joined with Sigurd under the banner I have wrought with my special needlecraft. I would have you stay, Thorstein. Like Kari and the sons of Njal, you would be the richer for it. And I believe it would benefit Sigurd much to hear of some of these things you have mentioned. Also, there is the gift I have promised you from his loot."

"When I have seen the old monk safely settled, then will I rest in your welcome. My men and I will join these elders in the fields, for I can see that the grass ripens while your young men harry to the south."

"But listen, Thorstein, I am saying that you will gain from my son, who will not only buy your furs but may also ask your company among his hirdmen."

Thorstein shook his head and rose. He stood like a

tree accustomed to the wind. Across from him the princess was like a curled leaf that has dropped to the ground. He bent slightly. "I prefer to voyage. I have harried in my youth. I have seen much of Northumbria and enough of Mercia and Wessex, as well as the coast of the Frankish king. I would turn away from those lands, as from my own."

"And where?" asked Audna, her voice as dry and brittle as that shed leaf. "How?"

The Icelander pointed at the long tapestry, its colors glowing in the light of many lamps, its creatures seeming to leap in the flickering shadows and hills of smoke. "Like that," he answered softly, "like that one ship set all apart from the throng."

Everyone turned to look where he pointed and saw a solitary ship disappearing over the rim of a scalloped sea. The rippling waves were crowded with fishes and beasts, some with human faces startled or dumbfounded by the lone vessel in their midst.

"Look," Evan whispered to Claudia. "I never noticed that before. Do you see? They're like Nessa swimming, aren't they?"

"Westward," Thorstein finished.

Audna nodded slowly. "Yes." Her voice was barely audible. "The Land of Mists is westward. It is where the gods dwell, and all those who live on through time."

Thorstein said softly, "It is a place of mists, that is true, but also of ice and perhaps of white sands and green forests known to no people you have heard of, even in your ancient tales."

"If a man travels to the Land of Mists," Audna pursued, "he may not return."

Thorstein inclined his head. "Then, you see, he must go on from there. Ever to the west." He took his leave, striding abruptly out into the brightness of the midsummer night.

Claudia saw one of the women snatch up Thorstein's mantle from the floor and hold it out for another to examine. A look of distaste passed from one to the other, then a laugh.

Quick and birdlike, Audna snapped her fingers and waved the women silent. Let the mantle be washed now, she ordered, and with care, for on the morrow she would mend it herself.

FOURTEEN

THE children were drawn to the monk at his labor. He grumbled to himself, complaining over the quality of the willow he wove into supple gunwales, declaring the hazelwood of his youth far better. He grumbled at the stiffness of his crooked old fingers and their swollen joints. It was a struggle for him to bend the ribs for his coracle, but gradually the wickerwork assumed its walnut shape across the curving staves.

When he refused to be drawn into conversation with them, Claudia finally asked, "Are you under a vow of silence, or are you just being unfriendly?"

The old monk looked squarely at them for the first time and declared, "I may not enter into idle talk with any man." He nodded his bristly gray head in dismissal.

"Well, that's all right then," Evan quickly pointed out. "We're just children. As you can see."

The monk considered this. Then he nodded. Nessa stepped down the embankment and sat beside the other two, her knees drawn to her chin, her dark eyes marking every gesture of the weaving. Claudia watched her watching the monk. Those gestures must have been familiar to her from that other time when this islet belonged—in freedom and till doomsday—to the monks.

Till doomsday. Doomsday had passed Nessa by. The question forming in Claudia's mind burst out of its own accord. "Have you heard of a woman called Fann? Long ago. Fann, the wife of Colm?" Immediately she wished that she had waited till Nessa had left. It was too late now. The monk was shaking his head.

"Colm was abbot when the church was sacked," he said. "That was long ago, before the heathen swept south to Dalriada and Erin, Northumbria and Wessex. But it was well recorded, for on that day the sun died and was born once more out of the void. So say the annals. I think it was three hundred years and more, but Colm is still praised by the monks of the Holy Island."

"Three hundred years," whispered Evan with a gasp. "Maybe that was some other Colm."

Claudia glanced uneasily at Nessa's straining eyes and plunged on. "You must have heard of Fann, too."

"No abbot takes a wife," the monk asserted. "It is said that in the time of Columcille some churches allowed this, but Colm was a holy man, his saintliness unblemished—"

"But. . . ." Claudia was stumped. The monk's denial

122

obliterated everything, the sour wet smell of Fann's white habit, the firm warm embrace, the authority that had reduced Claudia to silence and shame, the love that had fiercely sent the Pictish girl into that twilight corridor between life and death. "But what if. . . ."

The monk saw Claudia's uncertainty and brought the matter to an end. "Scribes well taught set down in the annals what is true and does honor to the Church. The Abbot Colm was revered by those who followed. Except for Colm and an unnamed monk who first sought the little island in the tides, no one is remembered from that time." His hands pressed and pulled at the tough willow stems he was weaving.

Claudia couldn't bear to look at Nessa. A rustle like grass in a sudden wind informed her that the Pictish girl had risen and was off. Evan started to follow, then sank back. The monk grunted with the effort of his wickerwork.

"Why don't you let someone help you?" Claudia asked him.

"I have seen too much horror to take anything from the murderers and defilers of the Church."

"You take help from Thorstein," Evan said.

The monk looked up to where the children sat. "Thorstein is different. Like his father. Besides, this little craft must be of my own making."

"Because you want it to be all your own?" said Evan.

Claudia barely heard him. It had just occurred to her that this stubborn old man might be persuaded to take Nessa with him to Eyin Helga, the Holy Island. Now she listened. The monk was telling Evan that he could own nothing for himself.

"But you have the hilt and the sunstone," Claudia blurted, part of her mind still fixed on the possibility for Nessa.

The monk looked long and hard at her. She was reminded of another time, another look. She was unable to turn away. Then the monk resumed his wickerwork and said softly, "How come you to know of that hilt?"

"I heard Thorstein telling Audna."

"Then you must know that it is not mine either. The hilt is a gift and a burden, the stone and the secret as well. Our books tell us that it is from the sword of Culann and was given to the scribe who first wrote down the tales of our ancient heroes. Some think that scribe was the monk who came to the Holy Island yonder and rescued it from the fogs. But if he was, his name has been claimed by those same fogs."

Evan shot Claudia a glance of inquiry. He wanted to know whether Baitan was the scribe she had seen call Fergus from the Land of Mists to tell his story. If he was, how could she have failed to recognize him? But Claudia felt as though she and the Claudia who had known Fergus and seen that scribe were two different people. She'd had a kind of strength then, a strength made from trust and devotion, from a belief in Fergus and the sword of Culann. But now that sword's hilt was changed. And so was she.

She shook her head at her own thoughts. Evan would think she was shaking her head at his silent question. Well, let him think she didn't know. It was true. She shook her head again, this time at the impossibility of finding any answer. Evan turned from her in disgust to ask the monk what else he could tell them about Colm.

The monk sighed. "He was abbot. He fled the North-men. While the nameless monk lived out his remaining days apart and in a cave at the base of the island cliffs, Colm and his few survivors built an oratory and hung the bronze man on its wall. Over the years certain monks have been taught its secret and have carried it far to the west and north to build new monasteries. But the bronze hilt has always been returned to hang upon the oratory wall. Now," he declared, straightening, "it is time to attach the hide. My coracle is nearly finished."

The horse skin, which had been left to soak in a tidal pool, was heavy and slippery and far too cumbersome for one aged man to handle. Claudia and Evan begged to be allowed to help. Evan insisted that he was stronger than he looked now that he pumped the bellows for the blacksmith every day.

Doggedly the old monk tried to hoist the dripping hide onto his back. He staggered and fell. "Not one of you Northmen," he protested without actually consenting to be helped. "Where is the Pictish maid? I will allow her to drag the tail along and lift a little now and then."

When Evan flew after Nessa, Claudia followed. "Wait," she called. "Evan, listen. Don't you think he's the solu-tion for Nessa?"

"What do you mean?" Evan sounded suspicious.

"Well, we're going to have to find some way back. Nessa . . . Nessa needs somewhere to go, and. . . ." Claudia faltered, then tried a different tack. "You can't want to leave her here."

"But it's not up to us."

"You want to help her? You've got to plan."

"I don't know." Evan went on ahead to find her. "I

don't know," he flung back at Claudia. "I guess we have to figure out something."

Nessa's slight frame barely managed to carry its share of the load, but her face was animated, her eyes bright with pleasure.

The monk used sinew from the slaughtered horse to bind the skin to the wicker frame and he used a kind of twine made from rushes to lace the edges to the gunwales. Nessa seemed to know each step of the process, handing him lines, holding the skin taut, pushing at the right moment. Finally the monk placed flat stones over the bottom of the craft. He stood back. "Tomorrow," he declared, "if the sun comes, I will remove the stones."

"And sail?" asked Claudia. How much time would there be to plan?

"And cover the hide with butter."

"That will take a lot of butter," Evan observed.

"Thorstein will get it," the monk replied confidently, "and not old butter stored in the bog. There is much butter now where the cows are set to graze on the hills. Thorstein will send to the summer pasture for fresh butter from the shieling."

"And then you'll sail?"

"And then I'll set the stones upon it once more. After that, two full days of sun. I will make the oars and thole-pins while I wait."

"They don't have much wood here," Evan confided.

"Thorstein will bring me a plank of ash." The monk turned to Nessa and raised his calloused hands; then one blistered finger drew a cross over her. "Bless you," he murmured.

126

Nessa touched the hide once, then set off at a run for Audna's house.

Mulling the possibilities for Nessa, Claudia wandered back slowly. She found Audna boasting to Thorstein of Sigurd's prowess. Had Thorstein not heard of the victory at Skitten Moor which had brought vast holdings across the Pictland Firth into the Orcadian earldom?

"I had made my son a banner," Audna told Thorstein. "It was wrought with the finest needlecraft known. Like that," she added with an almost proprietary tweak at the mantle slung across Thorstein's arm.

Thorstein acknowledged her gesture with a stiff nod. His reserve seemed intended to remind Audna that he had not asked for the mending.

"But the banner," Audna went on, "had an enchantment threaded into its fabric so that it would bring victory to those before whom it was borne, though death to the bearer. Thus did my son, outnumbered seven to one, bring those bloodied lands into his possession."

"And the standard bearer?" asked Thorstein after a brief pause.

Audna answered curtly, "There were three for that battle. All fell."

Audna's chilling account of the raven banner brought Claudia's thoughts veering from plans for Nessa to fresh concern about the crow. She couldn't openly hunt for it in Audna's presence, and Evan was no help. When Audna shrugged off his inquiry by declaring the crow to be safe within her household, he didn't give it another thought. It was as though he was under some kind of spell.

But Claudia remained alert, waiting for a chance to look. Two days later the chance seemed to present itself. She had been spreading manure on the eastern field with some of the older women of the bu. When she returned for a bucket of fresh water, she found Audna's house completely deserted. Standing by the water barrel, wondering how to begin her search, she was startled by the silent arrival of Nessa from the other direction. Unnerved, Claudia wheeled and charged the Pictish girl with the loss of the crow. "You were the last to see it."

Nessa returned this outburst with a small frown.

"At least you could draw a picture to tell me something."

Nessa's frown settled into a look of bafflement.

"Draw," Claudia commanded.

Nessa dropped to her knees and reached for one of the stones kept for boiling water. Those that had broken over the heat had sharp edges, and it was one of these that Nessa selected. She scratched with it on the flagstone.

Claudia held her breath, determined to master whatever cryptic sign Nessa used. But the furred white lines had nothing to do with the crow. They presented an array of ships fanned out, one curving prow set off behind another. Nessa, hunched over the flagstone, formed a dragon head on one prow; then, with tiny lines, a weathervane filled with writhing beasts. Next she drew shields, one round overlapping the next like fish scales. The ships took on the appearance of living creatures plying the slatey waters.

Claudia was divided between frustration and wonderment.

Evan shouted from the lane, saw Nessa, and ran the rest

of the way. He took in the picture at a glance. "Oh, she came back to tell you. Good. I just couldn't leave while those ships were all still whooshing up. The men jump out while they're still moving. Horses too. Hundi's father. Claude, you've got to come see him." Evan stopped, stared down, and said, "It's five ships, Nessa. You've made six."

Nessa continued to scratch her soft white lines.

Claudia said, "I asked her to show me about the crow. We've got to find it."

Evan wasn't impressed with her urgency. How could she worry about the crow with this great spectacle down on the beach and everyone there? He dragged at her and babbled about the ships that had landed, about Hundi's father and all his hirdmen. Nessa, absorbed in her picture, never once looked up.

Grudgingly, Claudia went along with him. She felt defeated.

"Nessa didn't like me criticizing her sketch," Evan remarked as he hurried ahead of Claudia. "Later I'll tell her how good it is. Look." The minute they neared the beach he was off on his own to watch the unloading.

Claudia hung back. Men still struggled with lines to keep the ships from swinging broadside to the gently breaking seas. The ships seemed like the plunging horses, mad with excitement. Bundles were lifted down from the yellow and black hulls. Men splashed through the shallows under enormous loads.

Audna, tiny and splendid, stood supported by two of her women as treasure after treasure was set before her. But she seemed more concerned about Thorstein than attentive to those gorgeous offerings. Her bright, anxious glance darted from him to the hulking giant who was looking to the presentation of the treasures.

Claudia realized that the giant was Sigurd the Stout. He had nothing of the appearance Thorstein had presented on landing. If the water and sun and salt had faded his garments, he must have just changed them. His shirt was trimmed in metallic threads that matched the golden buckle on his enormous belt. His head was bare, thick yellow curls dressed with something that kept them springy and resplendent. He bellowed, first to a servant, then to one of his sons. He roared to Hundi, then swept him up, throwing him into the air, and placed him at Audna's feet. Her quick brittle hands clutched the boy's shoulders and drew him to her.

"What did I bring you?" Sigurd shouted. "What is the finest gift of all for the youngest son of a conqueror?"

Claudia couldn't hear Hundi's answer, but she heard Audna remind Sigurd that the first gift must be offered to Thorstein.

"And I brought you a bardic boy from Erin, Mother, since you are always bemoaning the lack of poetry here. But he will have to be tamed before he can be set loose in your house. He is a wild man, though he was already much taught in the court of King Brian. Perhaps he will be subdued more readily by women. We could but beat him, and that he seemed to ignore."

Sigurd lifted one object from the pile, then another. "Choose a brooch, a necklet, or this fine goblet. It is from a church that was very rich. We took linens, book covers, even the clothing of the bishop. I hope the blood can be removed."

A cluster of slaves was driven forward. Sigurd started

to wave them off, then raised a massive palm. "Let them stand before my mother, only back. Keep their shadow from my loot."

"Later," Audna told him. "I will look when I can be seated. It is more fitting in the house."

Sigurd couldn't stop. He picked out a house-shaped box set with stones, a silver cross.

"Yes, yes, I can see you have done well. But later, Sigurd. Just attend to the gift I promised this Icelander. I must go and prepare for the feasting."

Claudia edged forward as the throng closed in to watch the gift giving. She ducked low and came up near the front of the watchers. Sigurd was bellowing, "My mother wishes it. So look well, Thorstein son of Hall of Side. Don't bother with trinkets. How about this sword? You could tell friend and foe alike: 'This I received from the Orcadian earl.'"

While Thorstein stood awkwardly over the heaping treasures, Sigurd turned to Audna. "And speaking of swords, one of your people, the king of Meath it was, carried off the temple sword of Carlus and ring of Thor from Ath Cliath while the Northmen were disputing succession of their kingdom there. So when Sitric was finally named king of Ath Cliath, neither sword nor ring was available for the kingly investiture."

Audna smiled. "A brave deed. All the kings in Erin are brave. That is, the real kings."

"But the Northmen of Ath Cliath will recover those symbols of Thor. The men of Erin, Meathmen and Leinstermen alike, are in retreat along the eastern shore. We ourselves made river forays there and met little resistance. We found our rarest treasures along a curving river north of Ath Cliath. In an ancient burial mound. The bardic boy was hiding there with a small band of court folk. We would have brought them all, for none was without a fine honor price; but we had far to travel and had to sell them on our way." He swung his massive head like a bull about to charge. "Well?" he roared at Thorstein.

Thorstein shook his head. "I . . . cannot tell."

Sigurd picked out something golden, a neck ring with gorgeous animal heads for terminals, each head possessing eyes of red that shone softly. When Thorstein made no move toward it, Sigurd let it fall, lurched about, and made his way toward some of the horses. He pushed back, carrying a foal in his arms. When he set it down, it began to totter. "Sea legs," Sigurd declared with a laugh, gathering it up again. "A little stallion for Hundi. It will be a mighty steed."

Hundi flew at his father and clasped his arms about the staring colt.

"Take them," Sigurd directed one of his big sons. "They will share a bed of rushes this night, a bowl of mush as well. Hundi," he bawled after his son, "get the salt off him. He's black as Sleipnir beneath the white crust." Sigurd turned back to Thorstein. "Is my plunder not good enough for an Icelander? What is your choice?"

"This," said Thorstein. He had something in his hands, but Claudia couldn't make it out.

"What?" The earl checked his torrent of words long enough to examine what Thorstein held. He snorted. "It is only bronze. And badly marred."

"What is it?" asked Audna. "What have you chosen, Thorstein?"

132

"A scabbard." Thorstein started to show it to her when suddenly a boy leaped from the cluster of slaves. The boy moved so swiftly that not one hirdman realized what was happening before he had thrown himself at Thorstein and was clawing at him and kicking and beating all at the same time. Thorstein, looking slightly embarrassed, took the youth in one hand while he slipped the scabbard under his arm. Then he held the boy at arm's length; the boy continued to thrash and flail and even spit at the astounded Icelander.

Three hirdmen took the youth out of Thorstein's hands and bound him with rope.

"It is the thing he was hiding from us when we found him," Sigurd explained. "It was that metal that our torches found, for it sent back the light."

Thorstein looked at the boy, who glared at him with raging eyes. "Why cast yourself upon me, lad? Is this scabbard yours then?"

"Look inside it," the boy responded.

Thorstein said, "I have looked. The blade there is stuck."

"If you free that blade, you will find the message of the sword in oghams, which I can read for you if all in this gathering of robbers and murderers lack the ability to learn our ancient markings."

"His tongue is ever lashing out like that," Sigurd remarked to his mother. "Perhaps it would be best not to try to rear him. We could offer him to Odin when we make our thanksgiving."

"Wait," said Audna. "Hear him."

"And have you some idea of what those oghams say?" Thorstein asked mildly, ignoring all the boy's abuse.

133

"Blade and scabbard were placed in the grave with the Hound of Culann to lead him to the Land of Mists. The message on the blade was written by the Sidh-folk for him. It is worthless to you Northmen, but sacred to our ancient hero."

Audna addressed him now. "How do you know this is the sword of Culann?"

"A Sidh maiden told me. She came to me. There in the hiding place."

"A woman of the mounds? They seldom come these days. They are deep within the ground."

"And so was I then, lady, when I was hid in the tomb of the champion."

"What was the woman like?" Audna challenged.

"There was no light, but when she came, the gold of her hair lit up the chamber and showed me the object she said I must hide from the foreigners. I . . . it was burnished then. Not . . . not as it appears now." His voice was choked. Claudia could see tears stand out in his eyes. "She, the maiden of the Sidh, had shown herself to me before that when I fell into a sleep that would not end. She wore a gown of speckled green. Her name was Aibhall. She promised me safe journey to the Land of Mists if I would keep the sword from the foreigners, and I tried, but . . . but. . . ."

Sigurd said, "That scabbard led us straight to him. The maiden tricked him into capture."

Audna was plunged into thought. After a long silence she asked the boy's name.

He said he was called Dunlang. He glared at Thorstein, who was holding the scabbard across his hands and looking at it with puzzlement.

"Send the boy to my house," Audna told Sigurd. "I will see what can be done with him."

"Keep him in bonds," Sigurd warned her.

"I'll find a place for him," she replied, "but now I must rest and then give orders for the feasting."

"And I," declared Sigurd, his words rolling forth like thunder in what Claudia supposed was his conversational tone, "will attend to matters of payment and sorting."

Everyone was in motion again. Claudia was buffeted, pushed, then handed a slimy leathern sack to be carried to the earl's hall.

"And I have news of greater exploits than I have yet begun to tell," Sigurd roared after the departing old woman. "Listen, Mother."

Audna paused, leaning against one of her attendants.

"It is said," he shouted up to her, "that Olaf Tryggvason of the Northmen and Svein Forkbeard of the Danes were paid sixteen hundred pounds of silver by King Ethelred the Unready to give up ravaging Wessex and all the lands of the Saxons and Britons."

"It is a marvelous prize," returned his mother, "if true." Her women commenced to half carry her up to the roadway, but she was able to twist around and add as she went: "It is grander than the trick played in Erin on the Northmen of Ath Cliath by the king of Meath. But I am not sure that it can equal the possession of that dull scabbard with its blade of Culann which Thorstein has chosen. The Icelander is not an ordinary man. Have him beside you at the feast."

Claudia saw Sigurd glance incredulously at Thorstein, who was already making his way through the thronging hirdmen and women toward the place where the monk's coracle had been set aside. Except for his height, there was nothing in his bearing to suggest that he might be remarkable in any way. Sigurd shook his great head. "Yes, indeed, Mother," he shouted back to her, then shook his head once more before setting about the business of the homecoming. On his way he dealt the bardic boy a solid cuff across the head.

FiFCEEN

IT WAS Nessa who knew where to find a rare variety of butterbur that grew only in certain protected places around Byrgisey. Audna's wrinkled face puckered with thought as she watched Nessa begin to prepare the leaves for Dunlang. "Someday," she remarked to the bardic boy, "you will compose an epic honoring Sigurd the Stout. It will be worth your honor price and then some. Possibly a few cows, a ship of your own, silver, one or two slaves." All the time she was speaking her eyes were sharp with interest in Nessa's preparation. The hairy leaves were plastered to the abrasions and sores. Next came healing applications of cold sea wrack. Abruptly Audna recalled her own work for the Great Hall feast and quit the little byre.

Dunlang seemed weak, as if his attack on Thorstein had used all his remaining energy. Claudia helped Nessa carry in cheese and curdled milk to him. He ate without relish, though he looked starving, his limbs wasted and white but for the blue of new bruises, the yellow of old. His carrot-colored hair, tangled and bushy, gave him a top-heavy look. He sat against the wall with his head thrust back as if for support, but his eyes followed Nessa as she came and went.

"Can't she speak?" he finally asked Claudia.

"No." Then Claudia hastened to add, "But she under-stands."

Nessa thrust a wooden bucket at Claudia and jerked her head imperiously toward the drain outside. Claudia promptly emptied it and returned. Nessa was forcing Dunlang to shift his weight and change his position. Her touch on his flesh was firm and precise. He groaned but submitted to her dressings.

When the feasting began in the Great Hall, Evan wandered back to Audna's house and joined the others in the byre. There in the darkness of that hut, with a single soapstone lamp sputtering, they felt worlds away from the celebration, though once in a while the wind sent gusts of raucous laughter toward them, the voices filtered through sheaves of fine rain. Worlds away, closed in together.

When Dunlang grew restless and asked to go outside, Evan jumped up to accompany him. Without warning, Nessa dove at Evan and knocked him sprawling onto the rushes.

"I was going to take him," Evan explained. "He doesn't want to pee in front of a girl." But he didn't try to get up again.

At the doorway Nessa gestured to Dunlang. She escorted him, still bound, to the courtyard drain.

Returning, she gave Claudia one of those pushes she had begun to deal out.

Claudia supposed Nessa wanted her to fetch something; the curdled milk was gone. "The *skyr?*"

Nessa shook her head.

"To eat or for his sores?"

"She wants some fish," Evan interpreted. Tentatively he got to his feet. "I'll go," he declared with relief when Nessa did nothing to contradict him.

"Why doesn't she speak?" asked Dunlang after a while. "Is she half-witted?"

Claudia laughed. "I wouldn't talk like that if I were in her hands."

"She's . . . different," he commented.

"We all are," Claudia responded.

Dunlang seemed to digest this for a while. "And this place is different. No trees. Aren't there any trees? And everything made of stone. Everything." He sighed. "Nothing's been the same since that day."

"The day they found you?"

He shook his head. "Long before that. When they separated us. We were like brothers, Murchad and I. What days we spent together at Kincora. Even after Gormlath came to be King Brian's new queen, at least for a while we could still hunt, read. . . ."

Claudia could feel Nessa's attentiveness. Diffidently, she asked, "The new queen separated you?" She hoped he would tell them who Murchad was.

"Gormlath changed everything. I was sent to the court of Gormlath's brother in Leinster. Murchad went to live with the monks on Inis Cathaigh because, you see, when Brian drove the Northmen from that island, the monks of St. Senan's monastery, instead of being grateful, were so outraged because blood was shed on their holy ground that Brian had to give them his oldest son for a while, and then, then. . . ." Dunlang broke off.

"Then what happened?" Claudia prompted, for herself as much as for the mute Nessa.

"I told you. I was sent to study with the bard of the Leinster king, while Murchad was taken to the monks. After that, nothing went right. It wasn't surprising that those of us journeying north to Leinster found ourselves without shelter on the day of danger."

"You mean," Claudia asked gropingly, "when the earl's men found you?"

Dunlang gave an irritable sigh. "No. You must listen. I speak of the old danger, the Feast of Samain, when creatures emerge from wells and caves. That night we were on a windy moor halfway between the kingdoms of Munster and Leinster. We had no protection but our fire and a monk who said Mass to keep us safe." Dunlang uttered a bitter laugh. "One monk was not enough. Even he, with his relics from St. Senan to keep us from the spirits walking the earth, could not prevail, though he claimed the night was All Saints' Eve and declared the old danger finished. It would have taken many more voices chanting his Latin to drown out the omens we could hear in the darkness. And when Aibhall called me to her, I knew it to be Samain and could not refuse."

"You went with her?"

"She sang to me. A tune more lovely than any harp or bird. And she gave me an apple that became whole again after each bite."

Evan, in the doorway, said, "I wish you hadn't mentioned apples. We don't get fruit here at all." He handed the dried fish to Nessa.

Claudia said to Dunlang, "Is that when you were caught?"

Dunlang shook his head. "The music made me sleep. When I awoke, Aibhall was gone and the monk was praying for me. I was weak, weaker than I am now, and we could not travel that day or the next." He stopped to chew some of the dried fish. "No, it was long after, when I was at the rath of the Leinster king, that the earl of the Orcades came down into our valley, he and his band of robbers. We thought them avenging Northmen, because the Meathmen had stolen the ring and sword from the Northmen's temple at Ath Cliath. You see, the foreigners tend to regard all the men of Erin as one, be they Meathmen, Munstermen, or Leinstermen. I was sent into a mound to hide, along with many from the rath. It was night there for a long time before the light came and was Aibhall, and she charged me to keep the sword of Culann from the ravagers of our land." His voice dropped. "I failed. I shall not see that maiden again. Nor that land, nor my King Brian, nor his son Murchad who was like a brother to me."

"Why didn't the Sidh woman save you?" Evan asked him.

"The Sidh have not the power they once did. She tried to cover me with the *feth fiada*, which is a cloak of invisibility, but the scabbard shone through and brought the Orcadians to me."

"Well, anyway," Claudia told him, "you needn't be so gloomy about getting home and seeing everyone again.

They free most of their slaves here. You can earn your freedom. Audna even told you that."

"A lot of their slaves," Evan added, "stick around after they're free, because they're grateful for being taken care of so well, so it's hard to tell which are which."

"I'd never feel grateful," Dunlang declared heatedly.

Claudia laughed. "You'd better start acting that way, though, if you ever want to be free."

He drew himself back with contempt. "If it means composing an epic in praise of that murderer, never."

Claudia, tempted to share with him the secret of the monk's hilt, mulled his bravado and decided instead to caution Evan to be wary. And Nessa? Did Nessa grasp the significance of the hilt the monk would return to the Holy Island?

"If you work for Audna," Evan pointed out to the bardic boy, "it won't be exactly the same as working for Sigurd. And she's not bad. I mean, she hasn't been bad to us. Except," he added, "for stealing our crow."

"I'll have nothing to do with queens or princesses."

Claudia asked him which queen made him feel that way.

Dunlang's laugh was harsh and heavy with despair. "Take your choice. The queen I spoke of, though a northerner, has been wife to more than one king in Erin, sister of another, and she is mother of the new king in the Northmen's stronghold at Ath Cliath. I told you her name: Gormlath. It might as well be Cruelty. It was she who turned Murchad's father from his senses and parted Murchad and me." Dunlang smiled grimly. The flickering light dappled his bruised face, giving it a tortured look. "All men obey her. For her beauty. She drives them where she will."

"Audna's not like that," Claudia assured him. "At least, if she was ever beautiful, you'd never know it now. Besides, she comes from Erin."

Dunlang was silent. Then he spoke haltingly. "They are not to be trusted, though. Any of them." He fell silent again.

Hundi appeared and chattered about the feast that would last two more days, about his foal, named Sleipnir after the steed of the god Odin, about how Grandmother had sent him off to get some sleep, about Thorstein, who had just taken leave of the earl now that Grandmother was letting him go.

"What do you mean, 'letting him go'?" Evan retorted. "Thorstein's a free man and can do what he likes."

Dunlang snorted. His derision made Claudia repeat Evan's question.

Hundi shrugged. "I just heard a few words." He yawned. "I kept falling asleep. Everyone's lying on beds in the hall, but it's still noisy." He yawned again.

"Go to bed," said Claudia.

He shot her a look, but was too tired to complain about her tone. He turned away saying, "You're nothing but a creature from the earth. You aren't even much of a marvel. You're just like everyone else." With that he was gone.

Dunlang looked from one to another of them. "You're not Sidh-folk, are you?"

Claudia put on a yawn of her own. "We should all go to sleep." She nudged Evan.

He started to protest. "What about Nessa?"

Claudia didn't need to tell him that nothing would tear Nessa away from this carrot-topped boy whose livid skin she tended, whose every word she followed, whose weakness revealed a kind of wiry defiance she could understand and draw from as from strength.

SIXTEEN

At the gabled end of Audna's house nearest the byre the children found their bedding stored as usual on the raised earthen floor against the wall. Unrolling the skins, they transformed them from seat cushions into beds and lay down in the lonely darkness. They could hear Hundi stirring in the place beside his grandmother's bed closet. No one else was there.

Claudia propped herself up against the slab curbing that held the raised floor intact. She tried to recall the number of days—no, of sunny days—that had passed since the monk had replaced the stones on the hide-covered frame of his coracle. She tried to picture him lying there in the misting rain with only that coracle for protection. She thought of the hilt, hidden by his coarse white robe. She pushed herself all the way down onto the floor, then curled up to fit her bed skin. Suddenly she tensed. If the monk was lying on the bank with the hilt, then what was in the stone chest? If she dug down to her clothes, would she find the hilt she had secreted there? But confusion and sleepiness merged. She was too tired to try to figure it out.

She was nearly asleep when she heard Audna and someone else talking softly in the doorway.

"Too old," Audna was declaring of herself. "I cannot endure these ceaseless revels."

Thorstein's voice responded. "Should I call your women?"

"Not yet. I wished to speak to you alone."

Carefully, very slowly, Claudia rolled over. She watched the shadows of Thorstein and Audna, Thorstein's so tall that it bent at the roof beams and appeared to be doubled over the diminutive Audna. Audna's shadow was formless, it made her seem like a little shuffling animal that has risen onto its hind legs. A small paw reached out and was swallowed by an enormous hand. Thorstein was helping her up to her seat between the carved posts, then sinking down beside her.

"Thorstein son of Hall of Side, you know I would have you remain as hirdman to Sigurd. But I am no manager of men. Nor do I have the power of younger women. So I bid you listen well. What I have to say is hard; I betray my son."

Thorstein's shadow shot upward.

"No, be seated, Icelander, and hear me. For if I do not betray my son, then I will betray my hospitality and the guarantee I pledged to you. And you will betray that monk you have carried so far."

Slowly Thorstein's angled shadow straightened and lowered itself to her level. It looked ready to spring.

"My son would have the hilt."

"Who told him?"

144

"I did. I praised it too. Now Thorstein, before you judge me, know that so far I mention no deed worse than your own careless talk which caused the monk to be carried off."

The shadow of Thorstein's head nodded heavily like a lopsided pendulum.

"So. Sigurd wants the hilt. And will take it once you are gone." Again the small paw shot out. "Remember, it was not his pledge."

"Then I'll put off my leaving."

The little animal shadow rested its finger-claws on the shadow sleeve of Thorstein. "If you wait, he will find another way. Leave now, since you are determined not to remain, but let the monk take off as well."

"That means embarking at once to catch the falling tide. It is the dimmest hour of the night."

"Does the monk with his sunstone require more light?"

Thorstein considered this. Then he said, "Perhaps the earl would simply take back the scabbard."

Claudia shivered at the sound of Audna's laugh informing Thorstein that such a return would be an unforgivable insult. "I have wondered, though, at your choosing it," she added. "You must have known . . . something. . . ."

"I—" Thorstein seemed to change his mind about speaking.

Claudia held herself perfectly still so that she wouldn't miss a word. She wished she could find out how much Audna knew about the hilt and how much she only sensed. What was clear was that Audna intended to hold on, though whether to the hilt alone, or to the Icelander and his blade and scabbard as well, Claudia couldn't fathom.

Thorstein and Audna were silent, their shadows motionless against the somber red of the tapestry frieze. Then Thorstein's shadow slowly stretched until the roof received his head and shoulders. The beams stabbed through his neck.

"For this," whispered Audna, "I ask something in return. A promise. That when your seafaring is done, you will come to the side of this earl."

"How can I be but one more hirdman in his ranks?" asked Thorstein.

"I cannot tell. You'll know how to serve him then."

"And if I don't," said Thorstein with the hint of a smile in his tone, "you will no doubt show me."

The small head reflected on the wall jerked quickly from side to side. "I will not be there. It is for you to see, for you to carry out."

"My ship is ready, but I have men made drowsy by your hospitality. And I'll have to waken the old monk and prepare him." He paused. "I hope he'll not balk. His is no weak will."

"Tell him," Audna called as Thorstein reached the door, "that his mission is at stake. Let him refuse then."

Claudia couldn't see Thorstein's shadow or real self any more, but suddenly Audna raised her voice to catch him with a final word. "Safe journey to you, Icelander."

"And to my monk?" returned the voice from without.

"To all in your care," she rejoined, adding under her breath, "to all. . . ."

His steps could be heard on the flagstone walkway. Then there was no sound but windswept rain. Claudia's eyes closed. But a moment later Audna was calling for a woman to help her to bed.

Nessa slipped in so quietly she seemed to be skimming the surface of the rough central floor. Claudia, safe in her dark corner, raised herself on her elbow to watch. Nessa was everywhere at once, swift and sure. Claudia amended her judgment: nothing could tear Nessa from Dunlang except this old woman who relied on her.

"Take a message to Sigurd," Audna commanded sleepily as she tottered toward her bed closet. Then almost querulously, "Oh, you can't. Get someone."

Quickly Claudia lowered her head. She let Nessa shake her.

"Call Brusi, Sigurd's second son. No, wait; call Brusi's wife instead. Call her out of the hall," Audna directed. "Do you understand?"

Claudia looked down at the old woman bundled into her nest of feather cushions. She waited.

"She will let Sigurd know that everything is as planned. The small band that is to escort Thorstein's ship from here will turn back to head off the priest. Thorstein will see nothing for the rainy night. There will be no cry. Have Brusi's wife remind my son that the old man is to be left in his drifting craft. If he makes it to the island, so be it. I would not have Thorstein return to avenge any murder, even if it appears that the piracy was the work of a few drunken revelers. Be off now. Oh, and add this." The old woman sat up. A skeletal arm reached out, a bony finger pointed crookedly, more clawlike than the shadow had been. "Have them remind Sigurd to stay in the hall the whole time so that there will be witnesses to his innocence." She lowered her arm in jerking spasms and said to Claudia confidingly, "He is so fond of action, he would be tempted to take part in the spree. Especially for the hilt, which I think I have caused him to value. He lacks Thorstein's careful aspect."

Claudia nodded. At the door the Pictish girl sprang from the shadows. Together they moved out into the rain.

"I'll have to do what she says."

Nessa nodded.

"If we tell Thorstein, he can stay. I know he'd stay if I could make him listen to me." Nessa's eyes met hers. She said, "Do you want to go with the monk? To the island? If we could get you there, you'd be safe."

Nessa was caught up in the idea. Light from Audna's house fluttered across her face but didn't reach her eyes. Then she moved her head and her eyes picked up that light. Claudia saw her dart a glance down the length of the dwelling toward the byre where the bardic boy lay captive. Gravely Nessa shook her head.

"I'll deliver the message," Claudia said. "Can you get to Thorstein? He's seen you with Audna. He'd pay attention to you. If you could just keep him from going. I'll run as fast as I can from the hall to the beach."

Nessa turned and disappeared into the night.

Claudia delivered Audna's message to Gudrin, Brusi's wife, who had stepped outside the fire hall for fresh air. Claudia waited to see the pregnant young woman waddle back inside before she dashed off toward the beach. Twice she tripped; the second stumble sent her hurtling part way down the embankment. She sat winded, within earshot of the uproar of the earl's hall and the queries and orders from Thorstein's ship. Picking herself up, she made her way with some care; obstacles lay all about; the dismal rain shut out every torch like a screen.

Out of nowhere, Nessa clasped her shoulders, brusquely shook her.

"What is it? Did you speak to him? I don't mean speak. Where is he?"

Nessa led her over the shingle, then to the embankment where the coracle had been dragged out of the way of the homecoming fleet.

"Where is he? Where's the monk?" Blindly she began to grope. Nessa grasped her hand, tugging her away. Claudia resisted. "Help me find him." She could hear the ship afloat in the shallows, Thorstein underway. They couldn't see the little coracle, could only guess that while they had been struggling in the darkness, the sleepy old monk had pushed off in his untried craft, alone with hilt and sunstone on the rainswept sea.

Next she heard Sigurd's men laughing as they hauled down their graceful wooden rowing boats and clambered noisily in. "The tide seems yet high," one shouted to another. "Barely. But the Icelander completes the rigging underway. It is his custom."

"Then he'll be in no hurry," a third called to them.

"Nor need we be," the first responded with a laugh. "Remember, the one to reach that horse-skin basket will get a calf, says Sigurd. But he who reaches it too soon, before they're well off shore, gets nothing but the tongue and eyes."

There were splashes, then the sound of smooth oars cleaving the water.

Claudia sank down. "Too late. Nessa—" But Nessa was no longer at her side. Claudia called her softly, straining to see her. Here and there came low murmurs as the men who had pushed off Thorstein's ship and started the rowing boats into the sea coiled lines and dropped chains and headed back to the bright fire hall.

Numb with cold and misery, Claudia waited, curling herself on a heap of sails laid out for mending.

She was dozing when the first rowing boat slithered up onto the beach. The shoreline was farther away now, which meant the tide had been ebbing for a while. How long since the monk had gone? A second rowing boat scraped up beside the first, then another not far from those two. She couldn't see the men who pulled them up to higher ground; they blurred into one shifting person. The last of the boats returned. The group on shore waited for the rower; he trudged up to them in silence, his figure merging into the single whole.

"Well?" The voice was subdued.

"It was the seaweed, I think. Held me fast."

"It was basking sharks. There's no seaweed thereabouts."

"No," another argued. "Whatever it was had a hold on me like a monster trying to haul me down. I saw the eyes of it burning there, just below the surface. I've a fierce thirst from that struggle."

"It was seaweed."

"They say the seals guard that island and live off the flesh of men who stray near."

"Then his hilt will be at the bottom by now."

The men lapsed into silence.

"Is that what we'll say to Sigurd?"

Just then Claudia felt something wet and cold close to her. Nessa dropped down onto the sails. She was panting lightly, but not shivering, though her skin was icy.

"I'll not do that," said one, "for he's bound to find out

the truth of it in time. If the seals out in the sound eat men, it will be worshipers of Thor and Odin they prey upon, for all those monks husband the seals and harbor them. Besides, Sigurd can ill show displeasure if he must not own to his part in this."

Claudia, sitting there beside the dripping girl, heard one voice declare, "But I'll tell about the seaweed anyway, for that was what it seemed most like."

The girls waited till the voices and footsteps were gone. Claudia ached with cold and tension. Being close to Nessa made her shivery, as if it was she who had immersed herself in the sea. Nessa was still panting, but evenly, already recovering.

Halfway back to Audna's house, Claudia noticed a whiteness in the paling sky. She pointed. Together the girls stopped to watch the clouds tumbling headlong toward the new day. The rain had stopped.

SEVENTEEN

"Nessa's acting funny," Evan remarked as he raked the crushed shells through the grass.

Claudia hacked at a fresh heap. The cattle, back from the summer grasslands, had grazed on the stubble of the rich infields, while all the children had collected shells from along the coast. Now Claudia and Evan were supposed to spread the shells over the deep green slope. "It's having a purpose," Claudia finally answered. "Being needed."

"Well, she seems funny to me."

"If you ask me, she's never acted nicer." Claudia scraped her clogged fork along the stone wall.

"That's what I mean. Nice."

Claudia straightened. Her back ached. She wished they could go with the other kids who were out with most of Sigurd's household, harvesting the barley.

Hundi came to them over the rise, squinting into the sun. His grandmother had said that Evan could help him give a leading lesson to the foal Sleipnir.

Taking advantage of the break, Claudia dragged home the wooden rake and fork. Inside she found Dunlang seated at Audna's feet. Nessa waited on them both with fresh butter from the hills and strips of dried cod.

"Hundi wants learning," the old woman was saying. "Sigurd is still smarting over a trick played on him and must vent his irritation in plans for new raids, and so gives no thought to Hundi." She noticed Claudia and gestured toward her. "She knows what I mean."

It was the first open acknowledgment of what had happened on that rainy night. Thorstein's departure and the monk's disappearance had been submerged beneath the waves of celebration that had washed the islet of Byrgisey into a sea of stupefaction.

"Yes," Audna went on, "Loki cheated my son of his prize. Loki is never satisfied until he has upset the plans of those who plot."

Claudia looked about, expecting to be confronted with this Loki person against whom the old woman railed.

"What is it, child? Do you wonder that I speak of one

of the Northmen's gods, I who am named for the mother of Lugh?"

Nodding, Claudia marveled at the way Nessa went about her affairs, carding wool now that the dishes were set out before her mistress.

"Of all their gods, the one I am the readiest to see is that wrecker of plans, that little Loki who bedevils his betters wherever he can. For he was at work that night. You know which night I speak of."

Dunlang seemed to sense the current beneath her crossness. He was alert, cautious.

"They spoke of seaweed, those buffoons, of basking sharks and seals. Their senses befuddled by the feasting, they could not recognize Loki's mischief." Audna reflected, and when she spoke again, it was with half-closed eyes in a voice that seemed intended only for herself. "But Loki may have played into our hands this time, for now Sigurd's appetite is whetted. He chafes like the other Sleipnir carrying Odin to warfare in the sky. I have heard that Olaf Tryggvason's greatest victory came from raids he made in consolation for the death of his wife." She gave her short, dry laugh. "Sigurd will sail under my banner to the Southern Islands and return with twice the lands he now holds. And in time . . . in time. . . ." Her voice drifted into silence.

Nessa pulled at a piece of fleece and drew it onto a card. Deftly she plied one card against the other.

"I am old," Audna suddenly declared, her voice sharp, her attention returned to the bardic boy. "Eat your gruel, Dunlang. You must grow. Nessa, fetch honey for his bowl; it will quicken his appetite."

"But what can I teach the son of a Northman?" Dun-

153

lang asked. "I am trained in the verse of Erin. I dislike the poetry of the northern skalds; it is full of ornament that obscures the meaning. There was a skald in Brian's court for a while, so I know. I am against this mixing of our people."

"Tell me of Brian. Icelanders who served here praised him as their greatest adversary."

Claudia could tell that Audna had found the way to draw Dunlang out. He even began to eat now as he told her about Brian, the Munster king, who intended to become High King of all Erin.

Audna chose her words with the precision of a fisherman who feels a bite. "It is my hope that all the kingdoms of Erin will someday be held by my son."

Dunlang sprang back. The bowl was swept to the floor.

"Stay," Audna reproved with surprising mildness. "You must learn to temper your heat with some understanding. Nessa, clear away this mess before he flings himself after and cracks his head upon the hearth."

Nessa extracted a soft roll of wool from the card and laid it in the basket. Then she gathered up the rushes spattered with the gruel, retrieved the bowl, and carried it all out. Dunlang looked after her.

"Listen, bard," Audna resumed, her voice surprisingly gentle. "I know what you feel. I too was taken from my home and brought to live among a strange people."

"You were brought to be wife to the earl," Dunlang retorted. "I am a slave."

Audna smiled. "The difference—" She broke off, then began again. "A wife may have honor, Dunlang, but then so may you gain a position of respect, if you care to earn it."

"Why should I earn the respect of those who dishonor my ancestors?"

Audna shook her head at him. "Those might once have been my words. You will learn other. You'll have to, just as I did. Though I suppose you must first grieve. And lash out." Her smile seemed more reflective, her voice subdued as if she spoke now to herself. "The difference is not so great, the maid carried off to marry the earl, the youth taken from his people to live among—" She leaned toward him with a kind of urgency. "But we don't call the Northmen foreigners here, Dunlang, for we are in their lands now. We are the foreigners."

Dunlang glowered and did not respond.

"And now," said Audna in neutral tones, "tell me about the woman Gormlath. She is much married, is she not?"

"Three times," he mumbled, then added hotly, "She is not the mother of my foster brother, Murchad. She cares only for her own sons, especially Sitric of Ath Cliath, who is her first-born, though also for the son she had with Brian."

"Let me tell you, Dunlang, I am not surprised that this daughter of a king is ambitious for her son." She leaned over Dunlang and spoke very quietly. "I understand ambition. It is by design that my grandson is called Hundi. The day will come when he will take the kingdoms that his father and brothers win. He will bring glory to Erin and return it to itself."

Dunlang stiffened, but still did not speak.

"Why not?" cried the old woman. "Why should not he, son of a conqueror, grandson of the daughter of a king in Erin, reclaim those lands and these islands and all of what was Dalriada in the name of the champion, the Hound of Culann?" She let this sink in, then whispered, "It is all we can do, we who bear the sons of kings and wait at home while the spears are hurled, while axes split the skulls of foes, while ships are sunk. It is the only splendor we may have."

In the dim, cool house everything was quiet. Audna, poised over the young bard, was motionless.

Dunlang began to speak, but cut himself short.

"Say it," she commanded. "I would hear your thoughts."

His voice was low but taut as he said, "What if the men of Erin drive out your son and all the other Northmen?"

"That will not happen."

"Or," said Dunlang more boldly yet, "it might be Svein of the Danes or Olaf Tryggvason the Lochlanner instead of the Orcadian earl who prevails."

Shaking her head, she smiled. "With the raven banner before him, my son will march to victory. It can be no other way." She pulled back at the sound of footsteps running.

Brusi's wife lumbered through the door, gasping with momentous word. Olaf Tryggvason himself stood off the main island, awaiting the presence of Sigurd and all his hirdmen. Olaf was on his way to Lochlann to claim his kingship over all the Northern Way, and he would honor the Orcadian earl on his ship before completing his triumphant journey.

"And what says my son?" asked Audna.

"Why, he is making the quickest preparations to receive this honor. The barley will lie where it is, for all are in haste to launch the boats to take them to Olaf's mighty ship. They say it is greater than any other in the northern seas."

Audna frowned. "Tell Sigurd to see me first."

"If I can get to him. All are rushing about. He sent me to call for you. And to bring the boy."

"Send Sigurd to me," Audna said shortly.

After Brusi's wife had left, Audna made Nessa return Dunlang to the byre. Now, suddenly, she seemed to notice Claudia again. "And Sigurd will have the hilt as well," she declared. "Mark me." Claudia met her sharp gaze and felt her own eyes turn toward the stone chest.

"Do you know why?" Audna pursued.

Claudia snapped her head around.

"Does the Orcadian earl need the sword?" pressed Audna.

Claudia, still speechless, suddenly wondered whether Audna had looked in the stone chest and discovered the hidden hilt.

"Do you think he needs it?" she demanded.

"Well," Claudia began, "he has the, uh, banner. . . ."

Audna nodded. "That is for his living. The sword will be for his dying."

"But—" Claudia stopped, then gathered courage. "But Thorstein has the blade in that scabbard."

"Thorstein will return one day. Hilt and blade will be joined, for I believe they must be one. Whoever lies with them in the earth will find eternal life, not in the Hall of Odin, but with Donn, Lord of the Dead, on the Isle of Mists, with Manannan, god of the sea, and Lugh himself, Lugh of the Long Arm for whom all things are possible." She gave a short laugh. "They think that certain

157

swords are sacred, these Northmen. They hang the sword of Carlus beside the great ring of Thor on the temple wall and believe it carries the weight and thrust of Odin's powers. But only the sword of our long dead champion can lead a hero to the land where there is neither sickness nor death."

Claudia nodded. She was convinced now that the old woman sensed some connection between her and the hilt.

All the women vied for the privilege of boarding Olaf's ship with Hundi. "I wove this headband with silver threads," said one, smoothing back his hair. "And I tanned the skin of the kid for his boots. . . ." But it was Evan whom Hundi chose—and Claudia, when Evan insisted that it must be both together. He tried to include Nessa as well, but Audna would not hear of her leaving.

Sigurd had failed to appear. He had left orders for a rowing boat with cushions spread for his mother's comfort, but it was the children who were rowed out in the boat. Claudia was still troubled about the hilt, the more so now that Audna, who refused to budge, would be alone in the house.

The two oarsmen were silent and powerful. It was a long way south to the bay where Olaf's ship lay anchored. Each stroke of the oars seemed to lift the lovely boat from its ocean trough and thrust it into the shimmering mist that rode the surface of the water.

The same diffusion of light caught the great war ship of Olaf Tryggvason in a whitish vapor. From a distance, its shielded hull cast off a sullen glow. The tiny rowing craft all about it and the few ships anchored nearby looked somehow unreal, ineffectual satellites to its looming presence. Its grotesque prow reared toward the glowering clouds that gathered now, banking down the sky.

The ship was jammed, the smell of bilge and humanity almost overpowering. The exchange of gifts had already been made. Claudia was instantly caught up in the tension between the new king and Earl Sigurd. Craning, she watched them together and gradually learned that Olaf was describing his recent conversion to Christianity. "I even took the great gold ring from the temple," he concluded with a flourish, "and sent it to my new queen."

All the Orcadians were aghast. Sigurd's hirdmen watched the earl. Hands twitched at hilts. The gift exchange of minutes before might never have taken place.

"What does it mean?" Claudia murmured to Brusi's wife.

"It was the ring that is dipped in the blood of a sacrifice for the taking of an oath. Such rings are sacred."

"It will be all right," Claudia heard Brusi whisper. "They say Olaf has plundered churchmen as well as lords. The Christians do not approve of such acts. So it will be all right."

Olaf's voice broke through the whispers. "After twenty years, Earl Hakon's rule is at an end. I will be king and all who are my subjects will become Christians." Olaf Tryggvason stood regally upon a chest set beside the mast. "Does any man doubt that I will rule the whole of the Northern Way?"

Sigurd said, "You took the faith of those you conquered?"

Olaf Tryggvason laughed. "See no disgrace." His manner with Sigurd was almost genial. "We take what will make us stronger, do we not? What is wrong with seizing

159

that which will bind all of our people into fearing and obedient servants of Christ?"

"I serve Odin—" Sigurd began, but Olaf cut him short.

"Hear me out, Sigurd, for I will persuade you. Not perhaps as I have been convinced, but not all men come to the faith by the same means." Olaf smiled confidently. "You will be persuaded."

The two men stood face to face, unmoving.

Then Olaf spoke quietly. "The hermit who led me to the True King told me that I would win a kingdom and that I would show many men that faith." Olaf beckoned. Within seconds some of his men, clothed in bearskins and with the heads of bears like helmets over their heads, stood balanced on the gunwales.

The Orcadians, crammed below, turned one way, then another, in alarm.

"The berserks serve Odin," Sigurd challenged, his voice enormous in the still, tense atmosphere. Like a faint echo, distant thunder rolled across the sky. The air was heavy.

"Sigurd the Stout, you are brave before these madmen who in their frenzy are beyond harm." Olaf thrust out his arms, hands spread. At once two hirdmen placed spears on either side of him. "You know I cast two spears at once." He turned his wrists, and the spears flipped lightly, perfectly synchronized, and came to rest like staves at his side. "These spears serve Odin no longer. Nor do the berserks. They serve me. And I, the True King. And so, Sigurd, earl of the Orcades, you may choose between two courses that I offer you. One is that you ac-

160

cept the True Faith and my kingship. If you do, you will continue your earldom over these dominions, subject to my absolute worldly authority. And of course," he added, "you will reign in eternal joy in the kingdom of heaven."

Sigurd drew back in clear disdain. The berserks crooked their arms and spread their fingers as in a slow formal dance. Their fingers were tipped with gleaming claws; they bore no other weapons.

"I think," Olaf Tryggvason continued, "you can tell the remaining choice, but I will say it for the sake of those hirdmen and house carls in your company who might wish to show their loyalty to you."

Olaf's voice rose. "Know then, you Orcadians, you freemen of Caithness and Iceland and all other places from which stout fighters have journeyed to serve the stoutest of all, know that if Sigurd refuses baptism, he will be slain here and now, and all of you who have honored me with your hurried presence will never again set foot to land. And afterward I will send fire and sword through all your holdings so that your women and young will burn within your homesteads." His voice dropped. "Therefore, Sigurd, if you and your subjects do not renounce your idols at once and accept the True Faith, not only will you all perish, but you will be tormented in hellfire forever after."

Sigurd turned slowly from one to another of his most honored hirdmen. His look rested briefly on his three older sons and then moved anxiously through the throng, perhaps in search of Hundi. "I will not," declared Sigurd, his voice booming, "I dare not renounce the faith which my kinsmen and forefathers had before me, because I

161

know of no better counsels than they. I cannot know that the faith you preach is better than that which we have had and held all our lives."

Without a word Olaf flipped the spears and drove them before him into planks raised up from the bottom-boards. The shafts were still twanging as he stepped briskly between them. Like the spear shafts, the men about him seemed to vibrate with the force of his presence. They stepped back as if his powerful thrust had set them quivering to either side.

Claudia, seeing him bear down on her, could not move. She was blinded by the hard brilliance of his mail shirt, which even in the dull light of that overcast sky gleamed painfully. Just as he strode past her, the cloud broke open, lightning flashed. Olaf walked among them like a cold white flame.

It wasn't until the sky had closed once more that she was able to see what all the others were watching. Way up by the prow Olaf Tryggvason was standing, his sword drawn and raised in one hand. His other hand gripped Hundi, dangling him aloft like a little animal caught by the nape of its neck. Olaf's voice matched Sigurd's. "Now will I show you," he shouted back to the earl, "that I spare no man who will not serve Almighty God or listen to my preaching of the Blessed Message. Know this: I will kill your whelp before your eyes this instant unless you and your men serve me and my God. For I shall not leave these islands until I have fulfilled His blessed commission and you and this small son of yours and all your men have been baptized."

Olaf's last words were accompanied by a deep rumble and another flash of lightning that seemed to ignite the upraised blade. The sword shook and was a leaping flame, and then became again the color of night, cold and black. Darkness descended over the ship, over the entire bay. Everywhere winds sprang up, all fitful, powerless on this sea of chaos.

Slowly and not without grace, the enormous bulk of Sigurd lowered itself until the earl of the Orcades was on his knees. His subjects followed his gesture, some hastily, some with exaggerated awkwardness. Claudia felt herself being tugged. Down she went with them, and then could see nothing of the brief ceremony which followed.

Finally they were made to rise to witness the oath by which Sigurd swore allegiance to the man who would soon be king over all the Northern Way. Olaf's priest would remain in the Orcades to say Masses where the old gods had been worshiped and to see that idols were demolished. Claudia grew bored with these details. She looked around for Hundi.

As the arrangements were settled and the rowing boats loaded to return the baptized Orcadians to land, Evan pushed his way through to Claudia. "Boy," he chortled softly, "wait till that Thorstein's monk hears he's got all these murderers to look after, now that they're Christians like him."

"I'm not sure," Claudia answered in a hushed voice, "that this is the way it works. I mean, don't they have to *believe*?"

Brusi's wife overheard and said, "It will begin like this." She patted her huge stomach. "This one will be the believer. Where is Hundi?"

"That's what I was wondering," Claudia said to her.

Sigurd and Olaf were sharing a drinking horn. Gusts of laughter, like the spurts of wind, flew up and were snatched by the glowering sky. Suddenly everything was whipped taut, flattened. The ship strained back on its chain.

"Hundi," cried the wife of Brusi.

"Hundi," called Evan and Claudia in unison. All were bent and stricken, for the wind had collected from the hundred smaller winds and now had direction as well as force enough to drown them all. Men clung to rigging; others were jolted off their feet. Now that many were ashore, there was room to fall, room to be swept to the ribs of the hull.

Claudia hunched down, Evan with her, and looked up to see the king and his earl still standing against the gale. Olaf seemed to be making the sign of the cross, bidding Sigurd farewell. The priest, his arm around the mast step, looked on. And along the gunwales, like creatures from a scene in hell, the berserks stood up to the storm, legs spread wide for balance, arms locked in rigid frenzy. In the spasms of rain that coursed over them, they looked inhuman, vestiges from the carvings on roof posts and high seat pillars depicting beasts from another world.

"Where is Hundi?" shouted Brusi's wife from the side of the ship.

"Father," howled the voice of Hundi from down among the rowing benches.

Claudia couldn't hear the words exchanged between Olaf and Sigurd, but the intent was clear from the gestures. Hundi was to be taken as a hostage. Sigurd protested. He was on his knees again, pointing to the priest, flailing, describing in the rain the sign of a Sigurd-sized cross.

Olaf Tryggvason was unmoved. Hundi would remain with him, to make certain that Sigurd would stay true to his oaths.

"Father," wailed the boy.

And the wind wailed, and the ship creaked and moaned. Lightning pierced the pall of rain and showed once more the bestial figures, howling and crazed.

EIGHTEEN

W<small>HEN</small> Evan tried to tell Nessa about the conversion, she showed bafflement, then a kind of incredulity. She carried her wool bag over to Audna, who was dozing fitfully in the high seat, and there she remained like a dog that senses its mistress is not well. Audna, waking, noticed the children had returned and slipped off to sleep again.

Brusi's wife came in quietly, peeked about, and quickly withdrew. The rain drummed on the flags outside and thudded on the roof thatching. Inside it was very dark. No one lighted a lamp.

Sigurd came in like the storm. His first words about Hundi, uttered in a rush of defiance, jolted Audna upright. Nessa slipped away and returned moments later with a tankard which she held to the old woman's lips.

Sigurd flung his dripping mantle to the floor and

dropped down at Audna's feet. He sat that way for a long time, his face cupped in his huge hands.

Finally Audna spoke. "You blunder into things which take thought and cunning."

Sigurd did not speak. He didn't move.

"You knew that Olaf, next to Svein Forkbeard, is the most powerful chieftain of all."

"The message was that he would do me honor."

"In your own harbor? It was for you to call him to the Great Hall, to make a feast with wrestling and horse fighting and harps."

"The message was that he was speeding north to claim his kingdom. I could not refuse." Sigurd's words fell away.

"All . . . all is in that boy," she went on.

"I have three other sons," he answered, raising his head for the first time. "And Brusi's child coming."

Audna's response was an ugly sound. "Hundi is the one I hoped for. The others will go after you in one rash adventure after another. They will not last."

"Mother, it is you who have held up rashness to me as a virtue. Everything I am and do is of your making. Had I refused Olaf or stalled, you would have called me coward."

Audna uttered another exclamation of disgust. "You need a man by your side like that seafarer Thorstein who uses his head. He would have kept you from this trap."

"Let me remind you, Mother, I have not lacked wit in my lifetime. You think that when you made that raven banner you forced me to face every challenge. But when

166

you gave it to me, charging me with timorous hesitancy, I was not without my own plots and resources."

"You came to me then in great confusion, because the Scot-earl Finnleik had set the day for your battle on Skitten Moor."

"Not confusion, Mother. You misremember."

"Confusion and fear, for your forces were outnumbered seven to one, so you told me. You could not avoid defeat."

"I came for advice, but you gave me no chance to speak of my plot. Instead you charged me with weakness. You declared—and I will never forget this, my mother—that you would have brought me up in your wool basket all these long years if you had thought that I wanted to go on living forever and a day." His voice was choked. "In front of my hirdmen, and with the sons of Njal and those other Icelanders to hear you."

"It worked," she retorted. "It brought you to the battle furor—"

"Everything you have ever said to me has worked," he pronounced evenly. "I have always heeded you, just as on that day when you declared before me and my men that fate rules a man's life, not his comings and goings, and that it is better to die with honor than to live with shame. But you would not let me die. You would not have me join the warriors of Odin's Hall where the slain may spend eternity in battle. The raven banner was stitched to my fate. You would have me gain these lands and this power and that inheritance. So while you declared the one truth, you allowed me only a distant glimpse of it."

"Would you belittle a banner that brings victory to

all before whom it is borne, though death to those who bear it?"

"I belittle nothing about you. But I can harry without it, as I have recently done. Even for that battle against Finnleik I gathered forces about me by giving the Orcadians their land rights in return for war service. Was not that the work of a quick mind? You are disheartened by the taking of the smallest son, but we may yet benefit from the allegiance I have sworn to Olaf. Hundi might become a favorite of the new king; our realm may be enhanced. So charge me not with rashness as you have charged me with being faint-hearted. And," concluded the earl, rising to his feet, "prepare to have the faces on these pillars and posts cut away."

"No one," declared the old woman, also rising, "will touch a thing in this house of mine." She seemed doll-like beside her giant son. "I never thought that I would stand against you to defend your father's trust that the high seat pillars were the guardian tree of the family house. Is it all false then, the idea I honored for your sake and Hundi's, of the tree which joins the earth and sky? With your father I could but laugh. The roots of the tree he worshiped were said to reach all the way down into the spirit world of his gods. Yet not one tree could be seen on all these islands. His gods meant nothing to me. Only that wretch Loki, who makes his mischief everywhere. But this is my house and these are my storied pictures carven on the wood and stitched through the fabric, and no king of Lochlann or of all the Northern Way can order them effaced."

Sigurd threw up his hands. "We will make the barest signs of compliance for now. After the harvest, I told

168

Olaf's priest, we will see to the breaking of the idols. Only he must have something to report of our promise kept if we are to be assured of Hundi's well being."

"I will deal with the priest myself," she snapped. "And Olaf Tryggvason as well. I will have the young bard write a message to convey my warnings to that pirate."

"Mother, I have given my pledge—"

"I," she retorted, her voice rising, "have given nothing. Nothing but my chosen grandson, and that gift was not willing. Not willing, Sigurd," she croaked.

The earl was already retrieving his mantle from its pool of water. "Yet," he murmured as he made for the door, "any message for Olaf will have to be sent through my men or ships I grant free passage to. I will not have an old woman interfere with matters of this kind. It is enough that she has ruled my life."

"Sigurd," Audna shrieked after him, "when may we expect to have the boy returned?"

"In time," Sigurd responded sullenly. "In Olaf's time."

"Before I die?"

Sigurd gazed at her, but darkness held his look. "Why, Mother," he declared, his voice altogether different from before, "I had not thought you wished to live forever and a day."

Audna seemed unaware of Sigurd's departure. She sat in the high seat, muttering an occasional phrase or word as though in argument with herself. Nessa carried more turf to the fire and then draped a shawl about the old woman's tiny frame. Brusi's wife came to cook a stew. She sent Claudia to fetch a bit of the remaining barley from last year. Claudia hated to dig the wooden scoop into the stone container, for it sent the beetles scurrying in all directions, including up her arm. The rain thrummed and the ladle stirred in the small bronze cauldron that Brusi's wife decided to use because it came from Audna's native land and might bring some comfort to her.

The women of the household returned from the rain-soaked fields, saw and felt the atmosphere around Audna, and went quietly away. Brusi summoned his wife, and she left, too.

Then Audna was wide awake and commanding. She wanted mead. Never mind the stew. And she wanted the boy.

Claudia started to call for Evan. "Not him," cried the old woman irritably. "The other. The bardic boy." And she would have the others go away, then changed her mind, berating them for not surrounding her with silent, attentive obedience.

Finally they were all there, Evan and Claudia, Dunlang and Nessa. Audna refused Nessa's gestured offer of food. She wanted them to listen to her. She wanted Dunlang in particular to attend.

"Hundi," she began. "The little Hound. The whelp. One day he will be a great champion, like his namesake. Do you know how the Hound of Culann came to be?"

Dunlang nodded. "It is told that he was found among the leaves of the greenwood, that he was the son of a woman of the Sidh. Some say that the Druid Cathbad was his father. Others that it was the king of Ulidia, or else the warrior Fergus. A few believe that his father was Lugh himself."

Audna nodded curtly. "And do you know the parentage of the little Hundi?"

Dunlang shrugged, indicating unconcern as well as ignorance.

"He is my grandson," she snapped.

"Then I suppose he must be the son of Sigurd the Stout."

Suddenly Audna twisted about and darted a glance at Claudia. "Did he cry out?" she demanded.

Claudia was so startled, so transfixed by the eye of the old woman, that she could only sit open-mouthed, staring back.

"Did he cry, my little Hundi?"

Evan said, "He called for his father."

Now she eyed Evan. "Weeping?"

Evan stammered, "He . . . he just called him."

"He didn't weep before Olaf Tryggvason?"

Claudia realized what Audna wanted. "He was brave when Olaf held him up. He didn't make a sound. Everyone saw," she added. "Saw how brave he was." She could see the boy, white-faced and limp, hanging from the chieftain's fist. Well, if silence was a sign of courage, he had been brave. "He only called afterward," she added. "We . . . we were looking for him."

Audna turned back to Dunlang. "When he was born of a captive maid, I had Sigurd claim him for his son. Sigurd had taken the woman at the start of his spring raids. When she was brought to Byrgisey, she was already swollen with the child he had given her, worn and distracted by the life of the raiding ships, and close to death. I was sure that she was of my people. Her hair was like the berries of spring and her skin was like pure milk. They would have let the child die within her, but I was more vigorous then, for that was nearly eight years ago."

171

Claudia looked from the old woman to the bardic boy and wondered which was the weaver of words, the spell-binder.

"You will remember all of this," Audna directed, "and cast it into phrases that will be sung in every great hall, north and west."

Dunlang listened, rapt.

"When the maiden died in childbirth, Sigurd was plunged in grief. I had to place the ax in his hand and lead him to the bull. Three winters it was, a fine beast, though I could have wished for a red one with white ears in the manner of our ancient tales. It was felled with a single blow, and after that Sigurd was released from the grip of the dead maiden. He twisted the leg of the animal till it broke off in his hands; with his bare fingers he peeled back the skin for the making of the boot.

"At the ceremony, when the boot was placed before the image of Thor and Sigurd stepped into it with his right foot, it was I who carried the infant forward to set his tiny foot after his father's. Then I followed with my own right foot, Sigurd's three sons with theirs. So was Hundi received into the family of Earl Sigurd the Stout. He didn't cry then either, not even when his father held him naked for all to witness that there were no defects of limb or face to bar him from his place. I gave Sigurd the name for him. The water sprinkled on him must have been like ice, but my little Hundi never made a sound."

"He was baptized?" Claudia exclaimed.

Audna laughed with scorn. "It is the Northmen's custom, the sprinkling of water. They have many rituals like those of the priests. It will not be difficult for them to change to the new faith."

"But they won't have the old gods," Claudia pointed out. "Not even pictures of them."

"They won't allow sacrifices," Evan added.

"I have seen my own people carry the old practices and beliefs over into the new faith," said Audna. "It will be done. You, Dunlang, must know of these things. How is it with the Christian King Brian?"

Dunlang started to declare that Brian was perfect. Then he merely stated that the old could abide with the new without harm. Claudia supposed he was thinking of the Sidh maiden, Aibhall, who had sought him out and entrusted him with the ancient sword.

Audna was quick to seize the advantage of Dunlang's uncertainty. "You will recall my tale and transform it with your poet's wisdom and way. The Northmen believe that Odin stole the magic of runes from the source of life and that to be a poet is to possess a sacred gift. Not an unworthy thought. Dunlang, I would have you learn the language of the skalds as well. Do you understand?" She paused. "Did you not mention that Brian has kept a skald at Kincora?" She seemed to lapse into her half sleep. She might have been observing Dunlang's expression, or merely waiting for some sign of agreement from him.

The bardic boy rubbed his wrists thoughtfully. Finally he said, "Will you send me away to study in the courts of kings? That is what Brian intended."

"I may send you to the court of the new king of the Northern Way," she murmured drowsily, "since he who is dearest to me is already there." She sat up. "Hundi is favored, Dunlang, chosen and brought into fosterage. I think there can be no greater honor for my little Hundi

173

than that." She nodded, as if to herself, and a small smile crept across her features. She sank back and closed her eyes.

The rain, blown on a downdraft through the hole in the thatch, set the flames under the cauldron sputtering and hissing. Then the turf settled, the fire sighed like a thing content.

NINETEEN

Mass was celebrated on the main island beside a long lake. The place, to which even the children were brought, was on a tongue of marshland punctuated with rolling mounds that were said to be the graves of ancient kings. These were dominated by one huge barrow, steep and round, which the Orcadians made certain to avoid on their way to the vast circle of pillar stones. The stones had been raised by giants long before the Northmen or even the Picts had settled on the islands, but it was here that the Orcadians made their sacrifices and pledges, here that the new faith must eclipse the old.

Only Nessa refused to cross the ditch and earthen bank that surrounded the circle of stones. Silent and furtive, she slipped from the others, drifting through them like the troubled swans that retreated at their coming, gliding to precarious cover among the rushes.

Afterward Evan went to look for her along the coast across from Byrgisey.

"Oh, she's probably with the seals again," Dunlang observed. He didn't bother to follow Evan, but added to Claudia, "She's taken me there, deep inside the gut where the sea grows thick with foam. The seals go into the cave at high water. She's fearful for them. I keep telling her she'll lead people straight to them." He frowned. "She doesn't know how to stay away."

"Does she take you into the cave too?"

Dunlang looked away. "Sometimes." He walked off before she could ask anything else.

Later Claudia came across Evan and Nessa kneeling together over a red sandstone slab, scratching scenes. When they were alone like that, Nessa seemed to drop back into the childhood she had never really experienced. She didn't ever treat Evan like a little brother, but as an equal. It was only when Dunlang joined them that Nessa seemed to become someone older and nicer and more remote. And more and more often Dunlang did join them, composing verses to match their scenes. After a while the three of them worked out a method of illustration, words for pictures and pictures for words.

But as the days darkened and the winds increased, Dunlang grew restless. He would make his way out to the highest point of the cliffs and gaze off in search of a ship to carry him away. Nessa was apt to follow him then, always standing back a little, anxiously searching his face when he turned inland. Sometimes she brought him gifts, reminders of the care she had given him in the byre.

One time Claudia saw her carry up a spray of dried angelica. Claudia wondered if Dunlang would recall how Nessa had once drawn the sweetness from angelica stems to coax his appetite, how she had shaken the frail, scented blossoms over his bedding. Now as Nessa stood waiting, the wind, thick with froth from the sea, whipped the brittle stalks clean. When Dunlang finally turned, he found her bearing a dead branch stuck with blobs of spume.

They grew accustomed to seeing one of the monk's coracles skimming over the water to Byrgisey. Audna sent the moody bard off with a monk to spend some weeks on Eyin Helga to read Latin. Then she let the other children go a little more, farming them out around the main island.

Claudia was off on the eastern shore, helping to store butter in niches in the well hole of a ruined fortress, when word came that Hundi had sickened in the Northern Way and died. The news traveled like the stone casks, from person to person down the dark stairs. Unlike the casks, it had nowhere to go, and so reverberated, working up and back.

"Was he killed?"

"The king would not have killed him," said one of Audna's women. "Now he has lost his hold on Sigurd."

"Will we go to Audna?"

"It's the Pictish maid she'll want, not us."

Nessa was being used on a neighboring island to explore the passages of another underground storage chamber. She could not get back until the winds abated.

At Byrgisey, Claudia found that Brusi's wife, her new baby slung against her breast, had already put Audna to bed.

Audna clung to Claudia's hand. "Get them. Nessa. The boy." The bony fingers bit into Claudia's flesh.

Audna would allow no one but Claudia near. But Claudia was unable to raise and lift the old woman to the floor so that she could squat over the flagged drain. Soon the tiny chamber reeked of urine and excrement.

Sigurd came and went, disheveled, distracted, each time ready to announce his intentions, each time struck dumb at the sight of his wasting mother.

"Thorstein," she whispered to him one time. "Thorstein will return."

Sigurd, who couldn't fit inside her bed closet, bent awkwardly to catch her faint words.

"Have him serve you. Promise."

"Promise what, Mother?"

"Scabbard. Blade."

"I can't take it from him. I gave it to him. You know that."

"You," she rasped, "will have the hilt."

Straightening, Sigurd cracked his head against the wooden lintel carved with forbidden gods. He rubbed his head.

"That whoever dies. . . ."

He bent down again, still rubbing.

"Who dies first will give the other," she went on faintly. "For burial."

"I don't want it for my grave," he blurted, his voice an explosion in the hushed, cramped quarter. "I'm not old. I'm not about to die. I . . . I've just begun. I'll owe no more allegiance to that king. I'll take more lands than he will ever touch. I'll send my ships into every harbor south and west. . . ."

Audna shut her eyes. She wore a look of bliss upon her puckered features.

Another time when Sigurd went to her bed she opened her eyes suddenly and in a fully normal voice declared, "Marry the daughter of Malcolm the Scots king. She will bear you a son, Sigurd, who will be the most powerful ruler of all these lands. Do you hear me?"

Sigurd nodded, carefully avoiding the beam and also avoiding her bright, determined eyes.

"Sigurd," she added, "you know that no harm must be done to Thorstein's monk. Seize the hilt, but let no murder come between you and the Icelander. And where is the Pictish girl?" she demanded, her voice suddenly querulous and feeble.

"Coming. She has been sent for. The bardic boy as well."

"I want her to make the stone for Hundi." Tears suddenly engulfed her face.

By the time Nessa got there the stench in the chamber was unbearable. Nessa made Claudia assist her with the bathing and cleaning.

"I want you to make Hundi's stone," Audna kept telling her.

Nessa nodded, but busied herself with settling her mistress. She was quick and short-tempered, slapping Claudia for failing to provide sheepskin to put under the old woman.

"It's not my fault," Claudia snapped back. "It's all the women. They say you should use furs."

But Nessa ruled the bedchamber and had her way.

Observing at a safe distance, Evan commented, "The way Nessa's acting, you'd think she loved Audna."

Claudia said, "Well, she's . . . attached." She couldn't describe what she meant.

"Claude, you don't think Nessa's fallen for all that stuff about Lugh, do you?" He burst out laughing. "That would make Sigurd a sort of god. Can't she see it's all pretend?"

His laughter brought hissing from the women of the house and he was chased off.

That same day Nessa dragged Claudia across the causeway at low tide to show her plants to gather.

"But those are nettles," Claudia protested.

Nessa shoved her toward them.

"They sting," Claudia cried.

Nessa jerked a plant from the ground. Claudia watched tiny white bubbles erupt on the brown skin. Again Nessa faced her, gestured, indicating the protected growth that still contained some greenness. Under her gaze, Claudia wrapped her hand in her jumper and with gingerly caution set to gathering the nettles.

When she returned to Audna's house, Nessa was ready with a pot of melted butter. With her bare fingers she plucked the leaves, which shriveled and darkened in the bottom of the pot. Claudia rubbed her fingers and ankles where, despite her caution, she had been stung by the weed. But the only attention Nessa paid her was to send her to fetch ground barley and cream.

Claudia lingered beside the fire, drawn by the steam that rose from Nessa's brew. It had a thick green smell, full of warmth and strength. Nessa gave her some from the ladle before carrying the pot to Audna. The acrid aftertaste was that of the soup Fann had fed Claudia in the cramped beehive hut so long ago.

Claudia pondered Nessa's attachment to Audna. In Nessa's silence was stored all that had ever touched her.

Maybe it was the abbess she tended in her heart, or the mother before that, who had been sacrificed in her place.

Dunlang, returned from the monks, had one long visit with Audna which left him irritable, unnerved. She had kept talking to him as though he were someone else, he complained to Nessa and Claudia. Then he stalked off and stayed away from Audna's house.

The life of the bordland bu continued. It was time for the mead making. The barley was mashed and deposited in thick soapstone crocks. A bowl from each was brought to Audna so that her spittle could start the fermenting. The old woman was so dehydrated that they had to burn fresh seal fat beside her bed to make her choke and cough. Carefully they portioned out the saliva that dribbled down her chin so that each measure would be equal for the mead.

Claudia lost track of time. After a while Audna wouldn't swallow the nettle soup any more, but would only sip honey and water. A new sweetish smell took the place of the old sourness. Claudia would have kept away like Dunlang if Nessa hadn't needed her so often. Both girls were there when Audna called for Sigurd.

Audna's voice was like the breath of a dying bird. Sigurd, pulling away from the bed, told Nessa, "She says the boy knows the words that were marked on the blade. Does she mean Dunlang? She keeps speaking of the boy and of the children." He stared at Nessa. "Does she mean you? You're nothing but a Pictish slave. What children? Her thralls?" Enraged by Nessa's muteness, Sigurd stormed off to the shore, shouting orders as he went.

Claudia, looking for Evan, ran with those who followed. She couldn't fathom Audna's confused declaration. Did the dying woman imagine that the Sidh maiden had told Dunlang the blade's message? Or had Audna found the hidden hilt and guessed its connection with the blade and with them?

By the time Sigurd arrived at the beach a coracle was ready for him. The earl clapped his great hands, shouted for oars, and strode mightily into the craft as he would into one of his own sturdy rowing boats. The skin-covered shell slid out from beneath him, flipped, and shot into the air.

Claudia heard Evan's giggle and turned sharply. "Listen," she warned as men rushed to assist the spluttering earl, "he thinks Dunlang knows what's on the sword. We've got to get to Dunlang about it before he gets you involved. We've got to teach him the words."

Evan looked blankly at her.

"Don't you see? Audna's all mixed up. She must suspect . . . something about us. They'll find out the hilt brought us."

"Even if she does suspect something, what can she tell them?" Evan pointed out. "Anyhow, don't go telling Dunlang anything."

"Why not?"

"Because he's like Audna. They have these feelings about the sword. They're the ones to watch out for."

"You don't think Sigurd's got feelings about it?" she exclaimed.

"That's different. It's because she made him have them." Evan broke off as the men drained out the coracle and set it down for another try. This time they held it for Sigurd, who fitted himself into it and nodded curtly to be shoved off. His weight dragged the coracle down faster than it could be moved into deeper water. Sigurd set the oars between the tholepins and stroked futilely, as helpless as a flailing bug on its back.

Evan hooted. Claudia could feel the laughter seizing her, too, but she kept telling herself that Audna was dying and that they were all in peril. Meanwhile Sigurd's hirdmen were up to their chests in the water, trying to haul the coracle free. But the little craft, built to carry monks who lived on meager fare and pursued lives of self-denial, simply sank.

Sigurd chose, for the sake of his sodden dignity, to wade ashore and send Brusi to take his place. "Kill them or not, as you like," Sigurd bawled to his son, who crouched between the oars and grinned with pleasure at the task set for him. "Only not the monk of Thorstein," the earl amended. "That one must not be harmed." In his haste to get away from the eyes of his men and women, he was already striding up to the walkway.

"Which is the monk of Thorstein?" Brusi called to him, but Sigurd was already out of earshot.

Without turning, Claudia whispered to Evan, "We'd better get out of here. Not together. You first."

Then, as Claudia waited, she was grabbed by the hair and hauled back toward the shore. "Take this one," said the man who held her. "She knows the monk of Thorstein. I was mending nets when the old monk worked on his craft. All those child thralls of Audna watched. Spoke to him too."

Claudia was surrounded. Someone yanked her head back; she was looking up into piercing blue eyes. Questions were asked. The grip on her hair was eased enough to allow her to nod speechlessly. She was seized in powerful arms and carried out to the little craft.

Brusi laughed as the coracle shot across the water. "Riding a butterfly," he exclaimed. But when he approached the small green island backed by the russet hills of a larger island to the north, Brusi had to strain to keep the little boat under control. The water swirled and whipped it round on itself. Worse than the white foam were the dark patches that loomed beneath the surface or jutted out through the churning current. Claudia was breathless with fright and exhilaration. Twice they were swept onto rocks, but seaweed cushioned the impact and the light coracle bounced off, tilting dizzily until Brusi could right it with a mighty stroke of the oars.

They landed on a long, shelving rock. Brusi lifted the craft out of the water, turned it over onto its oars, and yanked Claudia after him along the stony beach. She trotted, stumbled, then tried running. She thought Brusi would pull her arm off.

The first monk to catch sight of them came to a standstill on the path and waited. Brusi brought Claudia to his side, then shoved her forward toward the astonished monk.

"Is this the one?" demanded Brusi.

Claudia, breathless, could only shake her head.

"It is not?"

"I can't tell . . . like this."

"Where is your temple?" Brusi asked the priest. Without waiting for an answer, he told the monk to gather all the community there. "If any one does not come, I will seek him out and kill him." Brusi looked around. "That one, with the steep roof, must be your temple."

The monk said, "I thought you were bringing us another youth for teaching. We had a lad here till lately."

"I bring you nothing, no one. I have come to take away."

"In the name of Christ, my son, you must be gentler with His servants."

"That is past. My father will show no more allegiance to the king of the Northern Way, nor obedience to your church. Get your brothers."

Claudia thought this was a fair imitation of Sigurd's manner, but Brusi didn't have Sigurd's size or voice. It was all the more unnerving, then, to see the white-clad man humble himself before the strident young Orcadian and go off to do his bidding.

Brusi swaggered into the church, then dropped Claudia's arm. He gazed at the luminous cup on the altar cloth, the objects that hung from the wall and from the stone beam above the door. For Claudia it was like returning to that small chapel on the islet; yet there were differences too. This small oratory was squared off, the ceiling peaked sharply; only the deep, curving recess of the single window opposite the door softened the angularity. The door was like the earlier one, narrow, the jambs sloping inward to a massive lintel.

The hilt hung above a great low chest of stone covered with carved figures and interlaced ribbon. Brusi slowly extended his hand, as though to touch the ornament, then pulled back, touched nothing.

The monks entered one by one, each hooded, faceless, like spectral figures. They formed two walls of white, six on one side of Brusi, five on the other. Not one of them uttered a sound.

184

When Brusi was certain that no more were coming, he declared that he would take with him the hilt and one monk who could carry the secret of its enchantment to his father. "Now," he ordered Claudia, "show me which is the monk of Thorstein, for I do not expect him to step forward on his own."

Claudia stared at the draped motionless figures. "I . . . can't remember. They're all alike." She noticed that her voice sounded odd, like that of a very young child.

"Throw back those hoods," Brusi directed. "Let the maid look."

First one, then the next in line, and the one after that slowly drew back the hoods. They stared ahead, their eyes on the cross at the center of the altar.

Cautiously, softly, Claudia made the rounds. No face turned to hers, no eyes registered recognition. She could hardly distinguish the old from the young. She would never know which of these was the one who had been willing to speak to her because she was neither man nor woman.

"Well?"

Claudia's eyes dropped to the long stone chest. She guessed that it was a tomb. Could it be Baitan's? Colm's? Overwhelmed with the thought, she pointed. All the bared heads turned toward her.

"Well?" demanded Brusi. "Do you see him?"

Claudia shook her head. "Dead," she whispered, thinking of Fann, of Colm and Baitan, of the terrified Hundi.

Shoving the monks aside, Brusi strode to the tomb and stared down at it. "It would take many years to carve that picture. The old monk was alive but a few months ago."

"Anyway," Claudia asserted boldly, turning and staring

Brusi right in the eye, "they'll never tell you if he's buried there, but I can't find him here, so you might as well tell your father you saw his tomb, because you won't be able to bring him."

"Then I'll bring another," blurted the youth. "It matters not so long as Thorstein's monk is unharmed and the secret is gained. The rest I will put to my sword." He reached out and tore the hilt from its leather binding. The sunstone bead rolled across the stone floor and came to rest at the feet of a young monk. "That one will come," Sigurd declared. "For you will be strong enough to work for your living while you attend the earl and show him the magic of the hilt. Pick up that bead."

Claudia said quickly, "What if you put them all to death and later learn that one was Thorstein's monk after all?"

"You just said—"

"What," Claudia pursued, "if Thorstein believes that Sigurd's son killed the monk he brought to this sanctuary? Then whether the monk is dead already in that tomb or whether he's thought to be one of these massacred monks will make little difference. No difference, I'd guess, to Thorstein," Claudia added slyly. "So not much more to your father."

Brusi, his sword already drawn, glared at the assembled monks. "Then I will take the one and leave the rest for now," he growled. He swept his sword across the altar before plunging it back into its scabbard. The chalice with its delicate silver figures, the reliquary shaped like this very church, the book were all dashed to the dark corners.

No monk moved but the one to whom Brusi gestured

commandingly. Claudia, behind him, glanced back once and caught sight of a familiar shape lying just inside the door. She stooped to look. It was a large bronze bell, square-sided like the one she had tried to ring, like the one Nessa had carried from under the ground.

Brusi made her hold the hilt and sunstone while he rowed back. The young monk, his face entirely hidden, sat low in the coracle like a white bundle. Claudia studied the hilt, traced with her finger the fine outline incised on the back of the bronze man. Against the burnished sheen, the marking was clear, a cross with curved terminals and an image at the base like the shape of a simple boat.

Brusi stood to row over the open rolling water. Claudia, lying low at his direction, murmured dreamily, "Gift and giver am I," and was suddenly aware of eyes staring out of the whiteness of the sheeted figure.

"Wield me who would follow," answered the monk in a whisper.

Claudia finished, "Fear me who would follow me not."

"What?" shouted the exultant Brusi, plying his new toy with skill and glee.

"I was just telling the monk to fear you," Claudia replied, squinting up at the laughing youth.

TWENTY

THE men and women of the bordland bu regarded the stone for Hundi with contempt and apprehension. Sigurd had his own carver prepare one side in the customary manner. But Nessa's designs reflected those discarded fragments seen in the unlikeliest places—in the muck of a byre, in a wall or shieling on a lonely windswept moor, or perhaps even in their own hearths where they set their cooking pots.

The horse Nessa had outlined trotted briskly forward, its head erect, its forelegs high. Evan's finger traced the inner lines depicting muscles that curved from the joints into those formal scrolls Nessa filled her symbols with.

"Will you make Hundi riding it?" he asked.

Nessa pointed to the figure lying below the horse.

"But it looks like the horse is walking on top of him."

Nessa nodded in agreement.

"I think maybe you should have him riding," Evan said uncomfortably. He seemed relieved to be called back to the smith, who was fashioning the blade for Sigurd's new hilt.

Nessa, worn out from all the nursing, seemed driven to complete the stonework before Audna died. The last figure in her design looked to Claudia as if it was going to be a mirror design, until Brusi's wife, stopping briefly, said, "That's from when Hundi was received into the family." She yanked the loop of her jumper up over her breast and closed it with the oval brooch at her shoulder. Then, covering the baby, she bent to the wind and made her way back to the Great Hall.

Claudia stayed. Nessa hadn't even looked up in response. Her face was drawn in concentration. She chipped at the outline she had scratched, cupping with the other hand to keep the light even on the face of the stone. Claudia stooped and saw what Brusi's wife had recognized—not a mirror, but the heel and ball of a small footprint. Claudia could think only of that other stone and the huge foot-shaped cavity, but nothing in Nessa's expression reflected any awareness that she was meticulously chipping away at the symbol of her own downfall.

Troubled, Claudia sought out Evan at the smithy halfway around the islet. Evan was already covered with ash, his face blackened. When he was at the bellows, he seemed to become someone else. Now he scarcely spoke to Claudia, except to inform her that the blade was being fashioned according to an ancient method. He pointed to the thin bars of iron packed in charcoal. He turned from her, tending this fire. His cheeks were flushed with heat under the black smudges, his hair was damp, his eyes charged with excitement.

"It belongs to the monks," she tried to remind him. His self-absorption made her angry; she couldn't talk to him about Nessa or anything else. "It's stolen."

Evan's look, brief and wild, showed how little she was getting through to him. He shifted the coals as soon as the iron bars began to fade. It was all he cared about, tending the fire to keep the iron glowing red.

Claudia returned later when the bars, cut into sections, were reforged and twisted together and then welded. The smith, huge as Sigurd but as silent as the earl was loud, worked in a rhythmic fusion of fire and hammer and tongs. Evan, at the bellows, didn't even know she was there. She had the feeling that if she could show him the way to return safely, at this very moment, to Thrumcap Island, he would ignore her. She watched him with growing resentment and some fright. Then she gave up. At least for now, Evan was lost to the sword.

Dunlang still had no suspicion that the monks' hilt or the words he had consented to memorize had any connection with the blade that had been wrested from his hands. Like everyone else in the bordland bu, he understood only that Sigurd considered the hilt vital because of its precious sunstone. Dunlang had been quite ready to believe that Audna, confused, had uttered the words to be inscribed on the blade to Evan instead of to him. It had been so easy to foster this impression that Claudia had rushed headlong into the arrangement, with Evan at first reluctant and then suddenly uncaring, himself plunged into the midst of what they had contrived.

Once again Claudia felt herself tricked by the bronze man, this time into the betrayal of its own message. Worse, she had helped to pass on this betrayal to Dunlang, who would never have knowingly divulged the words from the sword of Culann to the man who had stolen it from the grave.

Dunlang was with Nessa and Claudia when Evan came running to find him. Evan was breathless; he had no word or look for the girls, not a glance at the stone for Hundi.

Before he could speak a giant shadow fell across them. Sigurd, inspecting the carving, nudged Nessa with a leathered foot. "The horse," he declared, "should have eight legs. Sleipnir, the horse of Odin, has eight legs." With that, he strode away.

"The smith wants you," Evan told Dunlang. "Right away. It's for the quenching. Needs your hand to it, he says."

"Why me?" asked Dunlang.

"He's finished cutting the edge. The blade's all ground and filed. You've never seen such patterns. There in the middle where the strips used to be. It's . . . it's like roots. Or vines all tied together. He wants you now, Dunlang, because they've just killed the horse and the blood is ready."

"Did they have to kill a horse?" cried Claudia.

Evan gave her a blank look. "It's perfect, that blade. Perfect."

"But why did they kill a horse?" she insisted.

"For the blood," Evan told her. "If they use water, see, it steams, and that slows the cooling. So they stick the blade in blood."

Claudia said, "That's sick."

"It's not just because it's the honored way of the ages," put in Dunlang. "The earl wants the head of a horse to make a spite-pole. They say he'll stick the horse's skull on a shaft of hazelwood and write a curse in runes on it. You'll see." Then he asked again, "But why me? Why must I come?"

Evan shrugged. It was almost as if he had forgotten his own role in the baring of the words for the sword. It was enough that the smith had called for Dunlang, the wordsmith. It was enough that the ritual would be carried out.

"It's sick," Claudia repeated under her breath after they had gone.

Nessa was rubbing the horse's legs, still only four of them, with a round stone. She cast Claudia a weary look and went on with her polishing.

Claudia was full of dread, but couldn't keep away from the nighttime ritual of inscription. Even Brusi, who had argued that his father should use one of the Frankish blades they had carried home from last year's raids, was in awe of the finished sword, which was held up high for all to view. Dunlang, thoroughly rehearsed, repeated again and again, "Gift and giver am I. Wield me who would follow. Fear me who would follow me not." The young monk was brought to watch by torchlight as these words were wrought into heathen runes on the gleaming blade.

The young monk sent Claudia a look, searching and full of sorrow. Slowly she shook her head at him. But what could she have said? That what she knew of the sword was set into the years that stretched between this day and one he could not imagine?

Claudia was so deep in thought, so locked in the impossibility of righting herself with the monk, that she was the last to notice that a procession slowly descended to the landing beach. Seeing Nessa with the litter, she guessed that it carried Audna, but could see nothing of the tiny woman beneath the finery heaped upon her. Sigurd's voice thundered everywhere, first to ensure that the men who held the ship propped in readiness were prepared to bear the full weight of its cargo, then to fuss over his mother.

"It is fitting," Audna declared with surprising clarity.

"I thought it would be my funeral ship, but I take greater pleasure in this sailing."

"Mother, you will be too cold. And wet." He turned to her women. "Is this raving or sense? I thought her witless when she called for the bearers to bring her here. Yet she speaks as of old."

Audna strained to raise herself up. "I would see the stone of Hundi."

Sigurd seemed at a loss. Then he answered. "If you will return now, you will look on that stone, which has been set above the causeway near your house. We could not raise it by the loch and yet have the Pictish thrall serve you at the same time, but that loch and the land around it will ever bear his name."

Audna roused herself to reply. She seemed to be drawing on reserves of energy and wit that had lain deeply buried all these days. "I am no voyager or viking, but a princess of Erin who must enter the realm of the mounds. All that is left of me, of my power, is in the banner I made for you. Take the sunstone. Go. But heed me, return the monk when the learning is accomplished. For Thorstein will come again, and you must be ready." Audna paused before adding more faintly, "Care for the bard, Sigurd, and avoid dishonor. He will write words that will live longer than any man or woman."

After that, Audna began to ramble. The shift was so abrupt that all who listened were carried along for a moment before they realized what had happened. Claudia heard distinctly an admonition to Hundi, which made Sigurd draw back in horror. He studied the wizened face, then announced that he would sail at once so that they might test the marvelous sunstone while the cloudy night yet hid them from the figured sky. He peered up. Neither moon nor star of the north pierced the cover of darkness. He turned and issued hurried orders. As soon as the skull of the horse was brought to him, he climbed the embankment and was gone.

Moments later his voice rolled back to them like thunder from the high northern cliff. "Here I erect a spitepole," the voice proclaimed. Even Audna stirred and fell silent. "Here I swear by the sun and wind and all the elements, I turn dead eyes against the king of the Northern Way. May the power of this spite drive him out of the land which it faces. And may his grave be set into the north side of a hill where the sun never shines."

As soon as Sigurd reappeared, he sent men into action and took hasty leave of his mother. He would return, he promised her, with the secret mastered and the power his. Dunlang would be taken aboard with the monk to witness the taking of the secret. Audna muttered unintelligibly, belched softly, and closed her eyes. The earl signaled to the litter bearers to carry her off.

Nessa stood rooted until she heard the feeble voice of Audna utter syllables that might have been her name. Only then did she leave Dunlang's side to join the stumbling procession. Dunlang was whisked away into the darkness.

Claudia followed Nessa and the procession to the stone of Hundi. The smudged torchlight showed the little horse frozen in curves that seemed to draw their vitality from the living creature. The somber footprint below was shadowed, indistinct.

Claudia went around to look at the flowing serpent

Sigurd had had his own carver put upon the opposite face of the stone. The serpent's coiled body was gorged with runes as if it had devoured the boy whose name they spelled. Claudia was gazing at this serpent when she heard Brusi's wife sigh and whisper, "She breathes no more."

Nessa laid Audna's lolling head onto its crimson cushion. As she pulled her hands from underneath, Audna's head covering slipped off, revealing a skull with the yellow skin of a shriveled apple and a few wisps of dry hair.

The women gasped, for the dead were not to be exposed like that. They dashed into the windy darkness to retrieve the head scarf.

Nessa took no part in the scramble. Claudia saw one dark-skinned hand reach out, and with grave tenderness smooth back those sparse hairs blowing wild before the scandalized eyes of them all.

TWENTY-ONE

Even though everyone expected Sigurd to return triumphant before Audna was laid in her grave, they couldn't delay preparations for her funeral. While some of the women worked on the feast, most were sent along with the men to prepare her grave beside some ancient mounds on the main island. Hundreds of people labored at the digging. Then a few who had been Audna's personal attendants, freewomen and thralls alike, were released to carry Audna's goods to the sunken burial chamber that was being built of precious oak and ash. Craftsmen carved the corner posts that would support a wooden roof before the chamber was covered with earth. In Audna's house the great loom held cloth that was worked on day and night so that the coverlet would be finished in time.

It was while Claudia was helping to pack extra clothing into the recess of the higher earthen wall of the burial chamber that she found one hole that went much deeper than her arm could reach. When no one was looking, she had Nessa, with her longer arm, feel back beyond the linens that had already been stacked in the niche. Nessa couldn't get to the end either. The linens plugged a deeper hollow.

Carrying grave goods from the islet, Claudia mulled over that pocket in the wall of the grave. She remembered how Hundi had insisted that holes and caves were dangerous because they might lead to the secret tunnels under the ground. She found a willow stave to use as a poker, but the next time she went to the grave, the niche was so crammed with provisions that she couldn't probe beyond them.

When the funeral preparations were completed and there were still no signs of Sigurd, his sons gathered together in consternation. Olaf's priest reminded them that All Saints' Eve would be celebrated this night. He warned them that if Audna was not laid in her grave bed and covered, her soul might be carried off by the restless spirits that walked abroad, unable to find eternal rest. Brusi was quick to reply that none there held stock in those beliefs, but the other brothers chewed their lips and scowled and weren't sure that they should ignore such warnings.

All Saints' Eve. Claudia tried to remember why that day might be crucial to them. She wished she could talk to Evan. If this was All Saints' Eve, then it must also be the ancient Feast of Samain. It was a time of passage between worlds, a time of danger. What more could it mean? What was there about it that made her want to pause and collect her thoughts just now when she was swept by the current of excitement? There was no chance to be alone, to think. The pace of the preparation kept her moving, always moving.

The baking and roasting continued, the aroma of the cooking holding the stench of corruption at bay. The body of the princess of Erin, clothed in a fine pleated shift and draped with silk brought by a trader from the distant east, lay on its side, knees drawn up, in the position it would assume in the earth.

Claudia, shunted back and forth across the causeway whenever the tide allowed, was exhausted and dazed and almost constantly wet. She was stumbling off the pathway to make room for a cart when she heard Brusi's wife saying to another, "Someone should make the dark one ready. She will need fresh clothing for her journey with the mistress."

"They have begun," came the answer; and then to Claudia, "Move on, girl, we must hasten now that the sons of Sigurd have decided to heed that priest. The grave will be ready before nightfall, but the tide is rising."

Claudia did move on. She put on such a burst of speed she left the others way behind. Arriving at the grave chamber, she dropped the beautiful weaving comb beside the bronze cauldron from Audna's native land. Someone else would have to place it among the treasures. Claudia, who had begun to drape the chamber like a diminutive playhouse, taking pleasure in the festoons of color, forgot her artful housekeeping. Tripping over Audna's amber beads, she raced back to Byrgisey.

By the time she found Evan at the smithy, she was breathless and close to panic. Evan started to show Claudia how the smith was repairing the lock and ornate hinges on Audna's chest. The iron, worn from constant use, would need to be in perfect shape on the journey into death. Evan, with traces of the raptness that had possessed him since his involvement with the sword, insisted on showing her how beautifully the lock meshed.

Claudia tried to draw him away, but he put her off. The smith needed him at the bellows. Claudia, who could think only of Nessa, watched Evan pumping away. She saw that he used his back and shoulders with a new awareness; his arms had muscled. As soon as the smith turned to pound on the strapping over the anvil, she blurted, "Nessa's to be buried with Audna. To serve her."

Still, Evan was slow to come round. It was as if he had to find his way back from some distant place. But when at last he looked squarely at Claudia, he was the Evan she knew, eyes quick and vulnerable, the mouth working, but with no words.

They couldn't get to Nessa. She was being prepared in the byre where she had tended Dunlang for so many weeks. Claudia, who was allowed closer than Evan, was prevented from entering. Standing just outside, she heard the voices of women whose husbands were Sigurd's most trusted hirdmen. They sounded subdued, engaged. There was nothing to suggest that Nessa resisted their ministrations; there was no hint of struggle.

Claudia returned to Evan. When the funeral commenced, they would be surrounded by all the people of the bordland, they would be helpless.

Evan reminded her about the hilt. Whatever happened, they would have to get away from Byrgisey. They would need the bronze man.

"That's right. And, Evan, you know it's All Saints' Eve. Remember what Dunlang said about All Saints' Eve being instead of Samain?"

Evan's eyes widened. "You're thinking . . . not just of escaping from Byrgisey. You're thinking . . . home."

"I don't know. Yes. Yes, because it's one of the open seams of the year. Spirits walk. Things pass from one world to another."

"But, Claude, we can't even think about home till we get Nessa out of this. Nessa comes first."

Claudia couldn't answer. Relief welled up in her—relief that he talked to her and felt things, even if they were mostly about Nessa, that he seemed to have broken free of the smithy fire and its false blade. She could only nod her agreement that Nessa came first, but she knew that finding the hilt was vital now.

Rummaging in the crowded chamber, Claudia found that the stone chest had been cleaned out. Only a few remnants of twine remained.

"Where are the things?" she asked, desperation dividing her from caution.

A woman, preparing to help with the moving of the

corpse, stopped to see what Claudia meant. "Oh, they've been taken. Tell whoever sent you for them that they were long since packed away in the grave." She turned back to the bed. "Imagine sending the maid for Audna's furs at this hour."

Claudia quickly returned to Evan. The procession was forming. They saw Nessa walk serenely between a goat and a ewe. She was wearing a fresh jumper of rough brown weave, a clean white shift showing below, and she carried a spindle on the crook of her arm. She might have been on her way to pay a visit on the main island. Her hair, usually long and loose, was caught back in a twisted knot that lent her dignity. The small lost child atop the Pictish stone of succession came back to Claudia. She saw the wet hair, the spindly limbs, the face blank with the avoidance of all feeling. She clutched at Evan. "Nessa's scared," she whispered. "She's so scared."

"She's given up," he answered. "She does that, you know, gives up."

"We've got to think of some way to distract them," Claudia said.

The bed came next, the tiny corpse lost to sight beneath the gorgeous new coverlet. The bed had fit so snugly inside the closet that Claudia had never seen all of the headpiece before, with its winged serpent yawning, not horrifying at all, merely sleepy.

At the causeway Sigurd's three sons came forward to carry their grandmother to her chamber on the main island. They splashed and slipped and slithered, their pointed mantles dragging in the water. They had the priest with them, though Brusi's wife indicated that this was only a kind of insurance. Let him offer his blessing, just in case, and send Audna on her way to the gods.

An air of uneasiness hung over the throng. After all the elaborate preparation, the people of Byrgisey and the whole bordland felt that the procession was too rushed. Sigurd's name was on everyone's tongue. They feared his anger at their conducting the ceremony without him. Claudia and Evan, who hung back as much as they could without being noticed, saw another straggler catch up with the tail of the procession and shout his message. There seemed to be a gap in relaying it; the reaction was slow to catch hold.

"Sigurd has come," panted the runner. "Sigurd comes."

"Sigurd," answered one.

"Yes, Sigurd should have come," responded another. And, "Sigurd," and again, "Sigurd."

The name picked up like a starting flame, was extinguished, caught again, and then suddenly crackled through the crowd as though a wind had carried it. People were uncertain, directionless. Sigurd's sons were already laying their grandmother in her grave chamber. She was positioned with care, the entire bed moved so that her head was to the north.

The roof was held in readiness to one side. The grave posts, their figures carved in bold relief, reached up like arms to receive it. Tongues and wings, claws and talons and tails clasped each other and merged with their own dull shadows until Sigurd's sons stepped back. Then the animal shadows, blurred and distorted, fell to the coverlet.

Claudia recoiled. It was as if she was back in the gray

oratory with its decorated book, its capital animal snapping at her out of the vellum page. The carved beasts keeping their vigil at every corner of Audna's grave house seemed to have shed themselves from the wood. There they were, like so many nestlings, huddled with their dam on her deathbed.

One by one the women of rank who had attended Audna arranged the objects set around before. Once again she wore from her brooch the symbols of the mistress of the bu, keys and the equipment of her sewing. Lastly Nessa stepped forward. She held the goat while Brusi, with a sudden thrust, cut its throat and lifted it so that the blood ran down on one corner post after another. Next the ewe was raised, its strangled blat cut short as another son slit its gullet. Blood was still spurting into the cauldron as the third son commenced to skin it.

That was when Sigurd appeared. His clothes were in shreds, the barest remnant of his great mantle hanging like a bedraggled tail down his back. His eyes were dazed, his face slack. "The monks rescued us," he rasped. His powerful voice was gone. He drew the sword and held it up over his mother's burial chamber. "The monks." Then he started to laugh.

His sons dashed forward, but he waved them off.

"Dying, she sent me off to death." He brandished his sword, and all three sons ducked.

"Now," whispered Evan. "Get close to Nessa. Be ready to grab her."

Claudia said, "But we're surrounded. Wait. See what happens with Sigurd."

Sigurd was raving. His tale of mockery and wreckage was torn from his lips in hoarse babbling fragments. The sunstone had led them astray. The monk claimed that it was the heathen runes that spoiled the enchantment of the sunstone, that it was the runes on the iron blade that set it awry. It had spun the boat against the course of the sun and sent them onto the rocks instead of into safe water. Thus had Audna sent him on this infamous quest. "Gaelic bitch," he thundered, his voice cracking. Curses and recriminations scraped from his throat and left all who listened stunned and silent.

When finally Sigurd broke and was still, the sons asked whether the monk and Dunlang had been lost overboard.

"The bard and the monk were taken to Eyin Helga. Most of the others perished. It is to mock me that the monks carried me to safety hung like a boar between their boats of skin."

Then the priest spoke up. "The monks did not mock you, but spared you so that you might reform and spread goodness through your realm."

"Goodness," hissed the earl. He stared at the priest for a full minute. Suddenly he shrugged off his sons and his hirdmen and leaped down into the grave chamber. "Here then, my mother," he whispered, "is that which you sent me to claim." He pulled something from his neck and placed it around Audna's. "Let this sunstone lead you where no Northman may travel. You made me crave what could not be mine. Go, then, to your folk of old, your people under the ground."

He raised his sword high above his head. Still holding it, he climbed stiffly, groaning, out of the grave chamber and onto its wall. "But I will carry this sword as long as your banner flies before me. Stolen it may be," he croaked, "but mine as you wished. Lead me with that sunstone, for as I have followed you in life, so will I follow you with this sword in your wanderings of death."

"Better it would be to follow the cross that is drawn upon that hilt," said the priest, "than the heathen blade tainted with the runes of your false northern gods."

Again, though silently this time, Sigurd seemed to be laughing. He stood immense upon the low wall of the grave chamber and slashed through the darkening sky with his sword. "This is what I think of those who gave me back my life. This is the sign I would make over my mother's grave." He slashed once more, this time across the invisible gash he had described with his first downward thrust.

"The cross," cried the priest, dropping to his knees.

"The cross?" The ragged giant laughed. He looked over fishermen and freemen of the farms, over hirdmen and thralls, women and maids, smiths and carvers and workers of stone and metal. "What is this mark I have made?" he rumbled.

"The hammer of Thor," muttered one man near Claudia and Evan. "The hammer of Thor," said another standing off to one side. "The hammer of Thor," intoned the people of Sigurd's bordland as the earl strode into their midst. And while their shout was transformed into a continuous chant, Nessa was pushed forward to crouch beside her mistress. The woodworkers brought the gabled covering and began to peg it down over the posts.

Without realizing what she intended, Claudia pushed her way through the crowd, Evan in tow, and scrambled down the pile of peaty turf. "Wait," she yelled at the woodworkers. "We have to go with our mistress too. It is promised."

Evan screamed, though whether in protest or simple terror, Claudia could not tell. It didn't matter. Within seconds they were plunged in darkness, reaching for Nessa, each clutching the other. Then Claudia tore at the niche where the clothing was stuffed and threw things every which way until she could feel the hard object she sought burrowed deep within woolens and furs. She shook the hilt free, grabbing at her own clothes and scattering all those precious materials that had been stowed for Audna's funeral voyage.

Though Evan had screamed, it was he who had the quickness and courage to try the opening first. He un-stuck the linens and shimmied in. Claudia pushed Nessa after him. Above and around them were the voices of the celebrants of Audna's funeral, the pounding of wooden pegs and the clanging of bronze bindings at the corner posts. Briefly Claudia wondered about the priest, and shuddered at the thought of what was likely to become of him. Then she could feel Nessa disappearing into the niche and it was Claudia's turn to squirm through.

Just at this point, panic set in. She could imagine the slimmer Evan and Nessa barely making it through, leaving her stuck with the head of a sheep and the corpse of the old woman. She grew rigid with terror, but Nessa turned and there was space after all. Nessa and Evan, both facing her, were hauling her hands and dragging her toward them.

"Is it part of the same place?" she gasped as she dropped to her knees in a kind of underground passageway.

They couldn't know. Or even care. As if she could smell the sea ahead, Nessa led them toward it. The water shed a green light. Foam spurted partway into the opening; it gushed and gurgled as though beset by a consuming thirst for them. They were sucked outward.

The sea would have swallowed Claudia but for Nessa, who pushed her upward with a mighty shove and sent her crashing and gulping and blindingly happy onto the rough cold edge of their own islet on Thrumcap Island.

PART THREE

TWENTY-TWO

THEY made straight for the shack. Nessa, looking up at the trees emerging out of the fog, cowered and shrank from them. Boughs dripped moss and the moss dripped water like limp, tattered sponges. Nessa, who had never seemed to notice the cold, was seized by spasms of violent shivering.

Huddled around Mr. Colman's leaky stove, subdued by the reproach in the old man's eyes when he asked for the crow, they peeled off layer after layer of clothing. Nessa still wore the shift and jumper; she unfastened the oval brooches, letting the jumper drop to the floor, and raised her arms so that the shift hung shapeless. She looked like a child caught in a cloud of white dress-up stuff.

"What will you do with her?" Colman asked.

Claudia and Evan exchanged an appalled look. They were still mulling what Colman had told them he had said to Susan and Phil, that he supposed Evan was sleeping yet, that Claudia had insisted on going after him, that he'd taken his boat out again, and that he supposed the boy and girl would be ready to return after a bit. None of this had been a lie, they realized. Mr. Colman had somehow managed to cover for them with his enigmatic half-statements of fact. But it was up to Claudia and Evan to carry it from there.

Now this other and graver question about Nessa pushed all that aside.

"If we say we found her," Claudia considered, "they'll want to find her family."

"But if they can't, then we'll end up keeping her," Evan maintained. Claudia's silence forced him to retract. "I know, they've already got six of us." He looked at Nessa, then added, "Anyway, I don't think she likes it here."

"Well, she has to stay somewhere," Claudia declared. "Nessa," she said emphatically, "you know we can't choose, can't decide when or where we, you know, end up. . . ." Her words trailed off. How could she explain? She turned to Evan. "There's nothing left of where she was at the beginning. I mean," she added, faltering, conscious of the mute girl listening to her, "it was at the end . . . of things for Colm and Fann. And now, Audna. That's over, too," she finished lamely.

All they could do, they decided, was to show Nessa the parents and hope for the best. They agreed that the introduction should be as gradual as possible.

When they had pulled on their pants and jackets and started off with Nessa, they saw the four grownups and Jon lugging gear down to the cove. Claudia and Evan ducked back inside again and conferred. Claudia would go first, and then Evan and Nessa could slip out and find a good safe spot for Nessa to watch from, after which Evan would join the others.

The parents descended on Claudia like rapacious gulls. In an instant she was swept into her mother's arms, yelled at by at least three different voices, grabbed by Phil and spun around. It was at this moment that Evan made his appearance. The flock swerved and fell on Evan.

Claudia marveled at the way he fielded their questions and tirades. He was buoyant, even aggressive. How come they were loading up now? Were they going to do night sailing? He'd just had some experience being out on the bay at night and didn't recommend it. Unless, of course, there was a good reason, like seal-watching, where you couldn't afford to give up the opportunity, even if it meant getting stuck longer than you'd planned. Besides, wasn't it nearly suppertime? Without giving them time to reply, Evan finished off his nonstop assault by saying that he hoped they hadn't worried or anything, only he guessed Mr. Colman had set them straight, and it was the best adventure of his life.

"Mr. Colman does not set things straight," Phil answered tightly. "He sets things down, all right, but not straight, not even connected. We didn't know where the hell you were. I suppose there may be some excuse for your having indulged in your so-called adventure, but"— and here he turned back to Claudia—"I can see absolutely no excuse for Claudia, especially considering that she knew how upset we were in the first place."

"But she came to get me. Listen, Dad, Claudia was all for bringing me home." Evan gazed up at his father with a steady, earnest look.

"Then kindly tell me," said Phil between clenched teeth, "what possessed her to change her mind?"

"I did," said Evan stoutly. "I told her that Mr. Withorn would never forgive her if she dragged me away from this unique opportunity to observe the seal, and so we stayed for a while. We knew that Mr. Colman would tell you we were fine."

Phil took a deep breath and expelled it slowly.

Mr. Withorn said, "I can see how the whole thing happened. I'm only sorry you didn't think to include Jon."

Evan and Claudia turned to look at Jon, but he was gone.

"I think," Mr. Withorn continued, "it wasn't just missing the adventure. He felt shut out."

Claudia said, "We didn't do it on purpose."

"Maybe you could make that clear to Jon," Susan suggested. "Maybe invite him to stay on with us. You see, Sam has to get right back because of that auction. He only stayed this long in case he could be of help. It's going to be sheer chaos for Ruth with him getting home at the last minute."

Claudia hung her head. It gave her a chance to consider how they would deal with Nessa if they had Jon on their hands as well.

"How long are we staying?" asked Evan casually. "I mean, is it worth it for Jon to bother staying?"

"Well," Mr. Withorn said with a smile, "it might be nice to let him decide that for himself."

As if on cue, Jon came down from the direction of the shack. He avoided looking at the children. He announced to his father, "I said good-by to the old man. I'm ready now."

Claudia said, "At least you had a chance to get to know him. That's one good thing. Maybe we can all come back together sometime and go out with him and everything."

Evan came to her rescue. "If you stay with us now, we'll tell you all about what we were doing, which is almost as good as having been with us." He reached out toward Jon, an inviting gesture.

Jon sprang back as though Evan had taken a swing at him. His arms clutched protectively around himself. "No," he answered. "No, I don't think so. No."

The farewells seemed to take forever. Claudia was growing uneasy about Nessa. She signaled Evan, who directed her with a look to the low-growing brush just beyond the twisted fir tree at the edge of the embankment. She stepped back. The Withorns shouted from the day-sailer. When Phil responded, Claudia turned and ran.

She reached Nessa just as the outboard coughed and roared into life. Nessa whipped around, ready to dash, but Claudia blocked her and dragged her down onto the roots and fir needles. "It's all right," she gasped. "It's a machine that makes the boat go when there's no wind. It's instead of oars. It makes a lot of noise, but it won't hurt you." Nessa was still. "Only never swim near one," Claudia warned as an afterthought. "It has these blades that can cut you. And it stinks."

The outboard was set in gear; Nessa shuddered.

"Look at it," Claudia told her. "Then you won't be so scared."

Nessa looked, and looked away.

Hoping to distract her, Claudia led her back to camp, promising clothes and delicious things to eat. Hurriedly she rummaged through the stores and found a chocolate bar with raisins and nuts. With her own mouth watering, Claudia peeled back the paper. Nessa eyed it suspiciously. "Break off a piece and eat it," Claudia commanded. Nessa took the bar, handling it with a kind of fastidiousness. She smelled it, shook her head.

Claudia couldn't bear the waiting. She reached out to break off a section, but the wetness had made the chocolate slippery, rubbery, and it bent. Nessa looked on as though she were witnessing some kind of mutilation. Claudia crammed the chocolate into her mouth. It was wonderful and warming. She twisted off another piece for Nessa. "Open your mouth. Just let it melt on your tongue. You'll love it. Everyone loves it."

Nessa, still holding the bar, opened her mouth. Instinctively she shut her eyes as Claudia placed the section onto her tongue.

"Now taste," Claudia declared with triumph.

Gagging, Nessa doubled over and spat out the slithery mess. Tears ran down her cheeks. The look she gave Claudia was one of humiliation.

Sadly Claudia took back the chocolate. She scraped up some moss to cover what had been spat out. "Everyone I know likes it," she murmured, realizing that now, whatever she did next, she would have to overcome not only the horrors of the outboard but the hideousness of the chocolate as well. Maybe a Coke or ginger ale would settle Nessa's stomach. What she found was an orange soda. Well, that was more natural; it would be even better. She popped open the can, took a swig, then handed it over to Nessa, who was sitting back on her heels watching all of this with a reserved curiosity. "It's orange," said Claudia, pointing to the color. Then she realized that could make no sense to Nessa. She couldn't even say it was like the juice of berries. She said nothing.

Nessa sniffed through the hole in the top of the can.

Her nose wrinkled. To give her a good demonstration, Claudia took the can back for another swig. Claudia wiped her orangey lips with satisfaction and grinned at Nessa, who raised the can to her own mouth and tipped back her head. But she didn't know how to turn off the drink. It kept pouring. She clutched at her throat, letting the can drop, and kept on gulping air. Then she sneezed and coughed; sprays of orange shot forth.

Claudia lunged for the can and heard Evan's extra-loud conversation announcing that parents drew near. She whacked Nessa on the back, feeling the pathetic boniness of the girl inside the voluminous white shift and brown jumper, and then was sent sprawling by a stupefying blow. Nessa crouched over her, eyes bright with outrage.

"I wasn't hitting you," Claudia gasped. "I mean. . . ." She was too breathless to finish.

"When I get back," Evan was telling the parents, "I'll draw you a whole bunch of pictures of how that seal looked." His voice was ominously close.

Nessa, still poised over Claudia, hesitated.

"Wait for us in the shack," Claudia managed to whisper before the Pictish girl darted away between the rocks.

Later, when they were drowsily full, Evan was able to slip off in the darkness with some hot soup and bread for Nessa. He was gone a long time. Claudia, thinking that he might have brought Nessa near, did everything she could to be agreeable so that her mother and Phil would make a good impression, but the strain of the last couple of days told on them. They kept coming back to her thoughtlessness and carelessness, berating her for lousing up the excursion, for acting on impulse when she ought to be old enough to use judgment and self-discipline.

214

Claudia wondered how Evan could possibly convince Nessa to stay with them.

Long after the parents had fallen asleep, Claudia and Evan lay whispering. Nessa had rejected dry clothes. Now she lay rolled in Evan's sleeping bag not far from the camp. They knew she was too wary, too scared and untrusting, to allow herself to sleep. "We'll get you back, all right," Evan had promised with false heartiness. "You just warm up for a while and get some rest while we figure out the best time and all. We'll come for you before morning." Nessa had disappeared into the sleeping bag like a caterpillar, but they knew she was awake.

"If we showed her to them," Claudia whispered, thinking of those scolding grownups, "they'd put her in an institution. Probably think she was retarded."

"We could explain."

"That she's from another time and place and is really smart and can swim like a seal? What could we explain?"

"They might put her in a place for deaf and dumb people and teach her sign language."

"Can you see Nessa in an institution of any kind?"

"Is it worse than being in that monastery? Claudia, she's got to be somewhere."

They subsided into separate reflections. They couldn't find any solution to Nessa's predicament. They hadn't even started to deal with her recalcitrance at the notion of being shown to Susan and Phil. Even Mr. Colman drove her into her most awful stillness.

"This time, though, we'll leave a note for Mother and Phil," Claudia averred as she closed her eyes.

From a long distance Evan's response filtered through to her. "What will you write to them?"

215

It was like the question about Nessa, Claudia decided. Except it was easier. If they were going to be gone from one low tide to the next, some kind of reassurance and apology was in order. She slept for a while, then woke to feel Evan shaking her. Suddenly they were in a hurry. It never crossed her mind again, the note for her mother and Phil.

Nessa sniffed at the night air. She seemed more herself now that darkness blotted out the signs and reminders of this alien world. Her hair blew out from her face like smoke, tangling in her billowing shift.

Evan, who had ducked into the shack for the hilt, came crashing back to them. "It's gone. Gone."

"But I put it back."

"I know." Evan swallowed. "I woke Mr. Colman. Asked him. That . . . that kid, he took it. Jon. He told Mr. Colman we needed it." Evan's eyes filled with tears of rage. "He must have had it on him when I was inviting him to stay with us. He did it to get even."

The enormity of the loss struck them dumb. Only Nessa seemed remote from the paralyzing impact of the theft. She began to explore, feeling the soft needles of the stunted fir, sniffing the pungent resin.

In the end they decided to let her go. They explained that they would have to be away for a few days until they could bring the bronze man back. They explained that she should use the shack for shelter and that they would leave food there for her with the old man.

"Maybe," said Evan, "she'll try swimming away." He was torn about leaving her like that.

"I warned her," Claudia told him, gathering up instant cereal and powdered milk for the shack. "I told her the

216

water was full of those boats with cutting blades. She won't swim away from here."

"What if they won't bring us back?"

"They will," said Claudia grimly. "At least our parents have consciences. Just remember to build up our case slowly, so they don't get to Mr. Colman." Claudia was already rehearsing her brief. Beautiful, damning phrases came to her; she tried them out in a variety of sequences before she was satisfied with the power of her argument. "They will," she promised Evan, reaching for a box of graham crackers, "and if I get my hands on that kid. . . ."

"Never mind Jon," Evan interjected. "He doesn't understand how important the hilt is. Anyway, what matters is getting it back."

"Talk about getting even," Claudia muttered. She wanted vengeance as well as the bronze man.

"You sound like Audna."

"I don't care," Claudia answered, forgetting to keep her voice low. But she did. If she was going to pick someone to model herself after, Audna wasn't exactly at the top of her list.

The parents stirred. Claudia and Evan finished their preparations in silence, Claudia full of thoughts about Audna and how Nessa had somehow transferred her loyalty from Fann the good nun to Audna the ambitious princess. Claudia supposed that if you craved a mother badly enough, you'd settle for just about anything. She followed Evan along the path. She thought of Susan again and wondered whether, if Nessa were forced to, she might eventually take up with Susan in the same way. Only Susan would never exercise the kind of authority that would attract Nessa or make the kind of demands to which Nessa could respond. "It's funny," murmured Claudia, more to herself than to Evan, "but being wild isn't exactly the same as being free."

"What?" Evan turned, balancing the honey jar and the soup cans.

But Claudia didn't know how to go on. She was caught in the crosscurrents of her perception. Freedom might be terrifying. Captivity might be the dulling of a terror that was freedom. Nessa, shut out by her deafness and her difference, might swim with the seals and speak their language, but she would remain apart, even from them, separated always by her humanness.

TWENTY-THREE

NONE of Claudia's carefully rehearsed phrases panned out, but Evan helped by coming to Jon's defense. His generosity and understanding spurred on Phil's indignation, so that in the end the children managed to gain support and moral backing from both parents.

"Though how I'm going to get the time to bring it back," Phil muttered, "I can't imagine."

They were chugging along, the sails furled, the heat from the engine sending up a smelly warmth into the cockpit.

Susan emphasized the importance of tact. "After all, it was Jon, not his parents, who swiped your metal thing."

"Maybe they'll expiate for him by bringing the damn thing back," Phil suggested.

"No," cried Claudia and Evan together. "We've got to do it."

"In case Mr. Colman's not there," Evan continued.

"Because we know where it belongs," Claudia supplied.

"Well, if the Withorns offer to return it, you'll just have to pass along that precious information." Phil's sour mood spread over them like the chill southeast air.

By the time they made their home harbor and unloaded their gear, the Withorns' auction was well underway. Cars jammed the main street and filled the adjoining crossroads. Vernon's Variety Store was doing a brisk business in beer and tonic, potato chips and ice cream. A tent was set up at the back of the Withorns' house, and it wasn't big enough to shelter all the people.

The auctioneers acted as a pair, one holding up an item, unless it was too big or heavy, the other hawking its charm or value. "This is guaranteed to be one of the finest tavern tables we've ever had the opportunity to offer for sale. Turn around, boys," the auctioneer directed, "hold it up. Let the folks see the fine breadboard ends on that top."

Evan found Claudia staring at the decrepit table, its legs rotten, daylight showing through the split in the top. "I've looked all over for him," Evan panted.

Claudia felt a hand on her shoulder. It was Phil beckoning her to the back of the tent. The bids were climbing, sixty, seventy, seventy-five dollars for the tavern table. Claudia stumbled over feet, apologized, but was unnoticed. A few hands waved wildly. Dealers carried out their offers with a nod of the head or a flick of the wrist.

Once they were at the back of the tent, Phil didn't bother to whisper. "Jon's gone to visit a cousin. Some kind of trip, an unexpected opportunity. Sam says he was acting pretty upset, so they let him go."

"Where? Where's the cousin?"

"I don't know. Claudia, it's impossible out front. We just can't bug them now."

"I've got a mere one hundred and fifteen dollars on this rare primitive tavern table," shouted the auctioneer. "One hundred and fifteen looking for one hundred and twenty. Fair room and fair warning." His voice rang threateningly.

Susan appeared. "Phil," she whispered breathlessly, "they've got an old-fashioned ice-cream freezer. Good condition." Her eyes glowed.

"All in and all done," cried the auctioneer.

"Mother," Claudia wailed, "we're here to find the bronze man."

"Go ahead, bid on it," Phil responded. "Then we can get a cow to go with the freezer for the real old-fashioned cream."

"Mother," Claudia moaned.

"Oh yes," Susan told her, "and I got more out of Ruth Withorn while I was looking over the freezer. She thinks the metal thing was thrown in with all the miscellaneous junk."

"Where?" cried Claudia.

The cartons of junk were stacked beside some bedsprings. Evan made it all the way through the first box before they were stopped.

"Those are going to be sold as is, young man." The

auctioneer wagged a finger in their direction. "Those are surprise packages."

"We're looking for something that belongs to us," Claudia protested.

"Little lady, everything in those boxes is for sale. You bid on them and keep bidding and they're yours." He held a lamp up to the audience. "Now this fine Tiffany-type lamp has some age to it, but I reckon it'll shed some light on someone's subject, and with a coat of paint. . . ."

Claudia and Evan sought out their parents again. Phil said he'd speak to the Withorns. After what seemed a very long time he came back to report that Sam Withorn was sorry, but it seemed there was something in the contract about not withdrawing anything once the auction had begun. They'd just have to bid on whichever box it was in.

"But that awful lamp just sold for thirty dollars," Claudia protested.

"The boxes are only worth a few dollars. Look, Claude, Sam feels lousy about this. He realizes he should have kept that thing for you, but when Jon decided he didn't want it after all, they just tossed it on the heap. He's going to let you kids look through the boxes. Okay? Don't make any more of it now. Your mother and I are going home for hot showers. And a little peace."

"But are you sure—"

"Claudia, for God's sake, the whole thing has assumed preposterous proportions." Phil strode out of the tent.

"Run after him," Claudia told Evan. "Tell him we better have some money. Hurry." She pushed Evan off.

Evan came back with a five-dollar bill. "He says we

can get sandwiches or something and then keep the rest of it for bidding."

Claudia, who had just witnessed a wicker laundry basket going to the highest bidding of eleven dollars, thought they'd better forgo food. They argued, until Claudia caught sight of friends with a picnic lunch. Evan could go and cadge something from them. Only not till they had located the bronze man.

The cartons had been dragged aside for them. Claudia tried to be methodical, but it was hard, jammed in between a crib and a glass-covered bookcase. Evan was surrounded by choice items he couldn't live without, old egg beater gears and C clamps and hinges and canister latches that he could use if he made a box to put them on. Claudia had to keep reminding him that Nessa was waiting on Thrumcap Island. Evan wondered whether it would be cheating to put one or two of these items into the box that had the bronze man, so he could get them as well as the hilt.

Meanwhile the auctioneers changed places. The new one cajoled the bidders, who came to life again, the post-luncheon doldrums over. "Are you really going to let this choice hooked rug go for only twenty-five dollars?" he asked. "Why, I wish I was out there in front myself this very minute."

Claudia found the bronze man inside a big enamel steamer that clonked when she lifted it. It was there together with a funnel, two small colanders, and a jam pot. She showed Evan the hilt, its stern face gazing up at her from its unaccustomed place, the eyes slanted, the hair standing straight up, the knobbed hands and feet scarred and dented. Looking at the hole in its middle, Claudia

222

suddenly recalled that the sunstone bead had been buried with Audna. Then she thought of the iron blade that had been forged by Sigurd's smith and how the sword had rebuked the earl for taking it.

"Evan," she said, "you know what iron does to magnets?"

Evan said, "Don't forget to mark the box it's in."

"I wish we could just take it. It's ours."

"We promised Dad. Besides," Evan added, "if we get the box, maybe we can get a few of these things at the same time."

"You'd better put all that stuff back where you found it," she retorted.

Evan grinned at her. "Can you remember where they all came from?"

The auction seemed interminable. A butter churn went for fifty-five dollars; a pewter flagon brought one hundred. Claudia's heart sank. People spent so much.

The sun finally broke through and dried the tent. Claudia took off her gray sneakers and stretched her feet out into the warmth. She saw her mother, looking fresh and neat, weaving through the outskirts of the crowd. Dropping down beside Claudia, Susan said, "I hope I'm not too late for the ice-cream freezer. Did you kids get something to eat? Did you find that thing of yours?"

Susan's clean bright look, her aura of well-being, bore down on Claudia. She shook her head glumly. "I'm not hungry. The hilt's in that big steamer, the gray one."

"Well, let me know if you want any help bidding." Susan was greeted by a passerby and got up to chat. Claudia heard someone asking whether anything was wrong.

"Just moping a bit," Susan answered with a laugh. "Our cruise was something of a washout. She'll bounce back."

Claudia closed her eyes to shut her mother out. She thought briefly of making some retort about the difference between waiting for a freezer and waiting for the hilt of the sword of Culann. But here, surrounded by all these people looking for bargains, the little kids dodging in and out in endless games of tag, it was almost possible to forget that the man-shaped bronze hilt was anything more than just another oddity.

The first box that was put up for sale had a handleless skillet that would make a good planter and a bunch of *National Geographics* from the 1930s. The bidding leaped to four dollars, then advanced more slowly to seven-fifty, and the box was sold. After that, two more beds were auctioned, a commode that could be turned into a box for firewood, and a real sea chest. Then came the carton with the steamer.

"When's low tide?" the auctioneer asked genially. "Why, there's time yet to dig yourselves a mess of clams and get them on the fire for supper in this real genuine steamer like you can't get in any hardware store today."

Oh, shut up, Claudia told him silently. Why make such a fuss over an old steamer?

"And don't forget the corn," the auctioneer enjoined, launching into a recipe for melted butter.

Evan pulled at Claudia's arm. "Come on. Over here where he can see you bid."

The auctioneer was implying that there were some really fine bargains nestled inside this carton when the first bid was shouted from the rear. "Three dollars."

224

"Come on," Evan urged. "Aren't you going to bid?"

"Ssh. Not yet. It'll just force the price up."

When the bidding reached five, Claudia told Evan to go find Susan and get some more money.

"Well, don't let it go," he warned.

"Just get to her," Claudia told him. She was trembling. She raised her hand tentatively, but another bidder was seen by the auctioneer; her hand went unnoticed.

The bidding climbed. The auctioneer asked someone to guess how many lobsters could fit in that steamer. "Two-pounders, no shorts." Hands shot up all over the place. "Is that a bid? I have six here. Do I hear seven?"

Claudia was sweating. Someone down across the crowd, someone she couldn't see, was offering seven. Seven whole dollars. That seemed to check the bidding. The auctioneer looked satisfied. "Fair room and fair warning," he announced happily. "Do I hear eight?"

Claudia gulped. "Eight," she said hoarsely.

A man standing behind her yelled, "You've got eight over here." He pointed down at Claudia.

Claudia met the auctioneer's glance and nodded confirmation.

"Speak up," he chided. "You'll never get anywhere whispering."

"Nine," came a bid from across the tent. It was Susan's voice.

Claudia lost her head. Instead of just sitting tight and letting Susan get the thing, she jumped up and down and shouted, "No, Mother, it's me, it's me."

Everyone in the tent roared, then applauded. And in the midst of all the commotion, a man put in a bid of ten dollars and the carton was gaveled over to him.

225

Claudia tried to push through the rows, then changed her mind and ran around the back of the tent. Tears were streaming down her cheeks.

Evan ran to meet her. "Stupid," he railed. "How could you be so dumb?"

"Why didn't you just bring the money? How was I to know?"

"There wasn't time, so Susan said she'd just buy it."

Claudia shook her head from side to side. "I got all mixed up. Then everyone . . . they were making so much noise, and I couldn't see. . . ."

Susan caught up with Evan. "Oh, Claudia," she said. She was laughing, but she closed her arms tight around Claudia and held her for a moment, shaking them both with her laughter. Finally she was able to speak, to promise Claudia they'd find the person who had got the carton and buy the bronze hilt from him.

"Suppose he won't sell?" Claudia sobbed.

"Nonsense," Susan told her. "I'll take care of it."

They were locating the man with the carton when the ice-cream freezer went on sale. Susan gave Claudia another hug and asked her if she'd like to do the bidding. Claudia shook her head. She would never bid on anything again as long as she lived.

Just then Sam Withorn appeared to make sure Susan knew the thing she wanted was being sold. He was both amused and sympathetic over Claudia.

"She just got a little rattled," Susan told him. "I told her we'll have no trouble getting it back."

"I'm awfully sorry about the whole mess," Mr. Withorn said to Claudia. "As a matter of fact, if your parents will let me, I'll be glad to return it to the old man and even take you with me if you want. Maybe I can talk Ruth into coming this time. She knows I want to get back with some more film and see if I can catch that seal."

Susan, frowning with concentration as the bidding commenced, murmured that it was kind of him.

"We'll settle all our debts, won't we?" he said with a smile and a small pat on Claudia's back. "I'm only sorry Jon will miss this too."

The bidding on the freezer was up to fourteen dollars. There was a long pause. Then the auctioneer said, "I'm going to let this go now if I don't hear another bid, and you'll kick yourself because you won't get no ice cream to go with those clams you steam tonight." The man who had bought the box with the steamer bid fifteen, and quickly, almost before the bid could be recorded, Susan called out, "Sixteen."

"Now there's a woman who knows her own mind," the auctioneer declared. "And unless I hear to the contrary, I'm going to let her have it."

Claudia wondered what it was that came over her mother and made her flush with excitement over a ridiculous thing that probably wasn't worth four dollars.

Susan accepted the congratulations of friends and neighbors before seeking out the owner of the carton with the steamer. As soon as the man looked up, Claudia knew they were in for trouble. He didn't smile. He sprawled back, tipping the folding chair, and told them they'd have to wait till he was ready to look through the carton.

Susan was pleasantly firm. "It was a mistake, you see."

"Maybe," answered the man, "but I bought it."

"It can't mean anything to you," Susan pursued. "But these children. . . . Well, it's theirs."

"How do you know it's in there?" he wanted to know.

"Because of the mistake," Susan explained. "They had permission to look for it. It's in the steamer."

He wanted to see it. Not now. Later. Just to show them how disinclined he was, he shouted out a bid on a mirror, then let it go to someone else.

Susan waited a moment, then asked if Claudia could bring the bronze man over to show him. He gave a bored nod.

When Claudia held the bronze man out for his inspection, she did everything in her power to convey its worthlessness. Yet her hands shook a little. She tried not to look at his face.

"What's it for?" the man asked after a moment.

Susan gave a little laugh. "Search me. It's just something they picked up."

"How much you offering me?" he interrupted.

"Five?"

The question in her voice was a mistake. He shook his head.

"Well, how much do you want?"

The man reached for the hilt and removed it from Claudia's grasp. "Queer. Probably it's part of something that'll show up later in the auction. I'd better hold onto it."

"Oh no," Susan said with a rush. "I told you. It's here by mistake."

"I'll just wait," said the man.

"Now here's a piece of genuine import china," the auctioneer proclaimed, holding out a cracked ewer to the audience. "Just a few age lines to it. . . ."

"Down," whispered someone behind Susan and the children.

All three crouched and waited beside the man. The bidding was slow.

"I'll pay you exactly what you paid for the entire contents of that carton," Susan told him evenly, her voice low with contained anger.

The man looked down at them. People were turning from the import china ewer to watch this negotiation. Someone said, "Oh, what the hell, Al, let the kids have their thing."

The man said to Susan, "You the woman that got the ice-cream freezer?"

Susan nodded coldly.

A slow thin smile pulled at his mouth. "We'll swap," he told her. "The freezer for the . . . this." He dangled the bronze man in front of Claudia and Evan.

"Son of a bitch," someone muttered.

There were two tiny points of red on Susan's cheeks; otherwise her face was drained of color. Her gaze never left this man. She put out her hand as though to shake on the deal, then snatched the bronze man away from him. In another instant she was on her feet. "You'll find the freezer out by the cashier's table," she told him as she turned away. "I put it there for safekeeping."

Claudia and Evan scrambled to their feet and ran to catch up with her. She didn't say another word until they were well away from the tent. Then she came to a standstill and handed the bronze hilt over to Claudia.

"Now what?" said Evan, his eyes avoiding Susan's dead-white face.

"Now," Susan exclaimed roughly, "we're going down to Vernon's Variety Store and get three double peach ice-cream cones." She grabbed each of them by a hand and set off at an angry pace. She never slowed down till they were swinging through the screen door and making for the counter.

"Big day," said Vernon behind the counter. "Did you say double?"

"At least," Susan answered. And then, her tone almost back to normal, she added, "Yes, it's a big day all right. That's why we're celebrating."

TWENTY-FOUR

SAM WITHORN was charmed with the boat, charmed with himself as helmsman, charmed with the adventure he was seeking, and charmed with his righteous errand. It was even all right that his wife wasn't along, since she had promised to come the very next time. His cheerfulness was so open and honest that Claudia and Evan found themselves succumbing to it.

Claudia went forward to watch the waves. A little later Evan joined her. "I was thinking," he said. "Thorstein's someone we maybe could leave Nessa with. If we can find him."

"We can't choose. If we could, you know she'd want Dunlang. Anyway, first we've got to get there."

"Where?"

"Oh, I don't know, Evan. Byrgisey, I suppose."

"Maybe we could look at the place, the people and all, before we actually go there. In case there's someone . . . really mean, like that woman Dunlang talked about, that Gormlath."

"What I meant," Claudia told him, "is what if we can't get through at all?"

Evan stared at her, his mouth open, nothing coming out. Finally he said, "Well, there's always that early morning smoke. Just before the sun comes up."

"Tide's wrong."

Evan gazed off into the bay. Islands stood out on the slate-colored water, deep green mounds fringed with white and dotted about with black rocks jagged with the motionless forms of basking cormorants. Away downwind gulls spiraled toward a patch of silver that seethed with life. The gulls screamed, rising and plunging for the herring, shiny slivers caught in their beaks.

"We've got to get the crow back, too," Evan said.

"If there's no fog, no smoke, nothing to help us across, and if our time's up and Nessa still won't stay with us. . . ."

"Yes?"

"We'll have to leave the bronze man with her. So that she can go later by herself."

Evan started to nod, then abruptly checked himself. "That means we'll never have it again."

"Otherwise," Claudia went on, fingering the bronze hilt thoughtfully, "she'll be stuck. She'll be nowhere."

"But she'll be nowhere no matter what happens," Evan responded. "She's already lost. There's no place for her to go, no one to go back to who can take care of her."

"Still, she doesn't want to stay here."

After another long pause, Evan asked, "Do you mind, Claude?"

Claudia shrugged. She felt resigned, that was all. They had some kind of obligation to Nessa. Claudia wasn't sure how it had happened or when it had begun. Maybe it started the first time they had seen the small, miserable, defiant child and had minded leaving her to her fate. Maybe it was because they had stayed with her under the ground, or perhaps only because in saving her later at Audna's burial, they had wrenched her still further out of her own time. What else could they do but let her have the hilt to take her back?

But Evan kept struggling with the idea. "Claudia," he finally declared, "we can't just let her go without knowing where she's going to land."

Claudia didn't bother to answer. Evan would have to discover for himself that they had no choice.

"Claudia," he said, "it could be worse than anything we've known about. And there's no one to speak for her but us. She's so. . . ." He didn't know how to finish.

Claudia was thinking about this too. If they had to teach Nessa to trust the bronze man, to follow it, how could she also be made to understand that it was . . . not safe? Evan was right. They couldn't just leave her like that.

Suddenly an idea struck Claudia with such force that she burst out laughing. She grabbed the hatch rail and swung back into the cockpit. "Mr. Withorn," she began, "how will you work out observing the seals without being seen?"

He smiled at her. "I'll have to figure out a way. And hope for good luck."

"What would be the best approach?" she asked, her face drawn into an earnest frown.

"Actually, a small boat. If I had the right craft and enough local knowledge. . . ."

"Like Mr. Colman?"

"Who? Oh yes. Exactly."

"Why don't you ask him to take you out?"

"That's a good idea, Claudia. Only it's not that easy to communicate with that old man. I tried when you and Evan were gone and your parents were so worried."

"Evan gets along with him like anything," Claudia replied. "I bet Evan could explain what you want. I mean, maybe you'd have to pay him something, but he's got an awful lot of local knowledge."

Evan, clambering aft, assured Mr. Withorn that such an expedition with Mr. Colman could be arranged. "Only you might have to stay out for two low tides, the way I did, to be sure of seeing anything."

"Yes, and I suppose that would be rather hard on two active kids."

"Oh," Evan offered casually, "we wouldn't mind staying on the island this time. Just leave us some food and stuff—"

"I couldn't do that without your parents' permission."

"Don't forget," Claudia reminded him, "we've stayed on Thrumcap a week. It's like a second home for us. Mother even told you before that they'd think nothing of leaving us for a couple of days. If it was convenient."

Mr. Withorn was convinced. He beamed at them.

"I'm glad I brought all that extra film. Of course, if the weather turns, I'll come right back to you. Your parents are right. What could happen to you on an island?"

"Yes," said Evan.

"Yes," said Claudia.

But Mr. Colman proved nearly immovable. They had to threaten him with the permanent loss of his crow before he would yield to their plotting and agree to take Mr. Withorn away.

Mr. Colman was out of sorts because of Nessa. "Had to set the food outdoors, for her fearing." His tone was aggrieved.

"She's not used to being here," Evan told him. "She's scared of outboards and engines and things. Listen, she's never even seen trees before."

Mr. Colman scratched at his stubbly cheek. "Take those sheep," he went on. "Some of them never touched by any man, but you can get to them if you wait long enough. Now there's some animals won't ever let you near." He tipped back till his chair creaked ominously. "Not worth the bother," he concluded, dismissing the untamable.

They found Nessa on the outskirts of the little flock. As they approached, the sheep got wind of them, scurried up the rocky ravine to the grassy tableland, stared briefly, and fled. Nessa waited for them to run up to her. They had refrained from calling to her because Mr. Withorn and Mr. Colman weren't yet on their way, but now Evan grew careless with excitement and relief. Ebullience replaced his usual awareness of Nessa's limits. He spoke of ice-cream freezers and auctioneers, dollars and antiques. He waved the bronze man excitedly and told her how Mr. Withorn was going off to photograph seals.

Nessa wore the hint of a smile, a kind of tentative pleasure at being sought and found, and with it a reserve born of something close to hopelessness. No, she tried to tell them with her gestures, her eyes, she would not live here with those dung-matted sheep, nor with the smelly old man who made his boat roar like a chained beast, nor with the scolding parents with drinking vessels that popped and smoked, though they held no visible fire. She stood before them with her partial smile and let them know that she would return to that other place beyond the water and the mist.

"Maybe we'll find Dunlang," Evan declared, now launched into the various possibilities he and Claudia had considered.

Nessa was transformed. Her smile left her face, but her eyes grew large and bright, the taut skin straining over the cheekbones, paling at the forehead. Dunlang, sang her silent, yearning expression: Dunlang, yes.

Once the seal photographing expedition was underway, they had nothing to do but wait for the next low tide and to will a change in the weather. The change came with a rapid massing of black clouds out of the northeast, a sudden diminishing of light. Evan was delighted, but Claudia cautioned him; if it got bad enough, Mr. Withorn might come back. And if there was a chance of lightning, they'd have to stay off the islet. Evan started to argue, but Claudia stayed firm. It was as if having to come to grips with the possibility of giving up the hilt had removed her somewhat from its enchantment. It was clear to her that they couldn't take foolish risks for the sake of returning Nessa to some questionable place in some questionable time.

Nessa wouldn't accept the extra rain gear they offered her. They kept to the shack, where a steady rain beat on the roof and drummed against the stove stack. Rivulets coursed down the pipe and settled on the uneven floor in darkened depressions already rotted by innumerable downpours.

When it was time to try for the islet, the rocks that usually showed at this stage of the tide were barely visible in the churning bay. They joined hands, Evan in the lead, Nessa following, Claudia bringing up the rear. It was slow going. The waves that pounded the nearly bare mussel beds had a force that could throw Claudia to her knees. Nessa was the firmest of the three, the fulcrum from which they took their bearings and gained their balance.

Claudia was grateful for the rain now. It meant she was safe. No light could possibly catch them in the Other Place. She began to feel the old eagerness to see whatever it was that awaited them. Once she had climbed the turtle's tail, she surged ahead, drenched and confident, dragging the others after her. On they went, until suddenly there was no rain, though they themselves were sodden and water dribbled from their faces and hair and sleeves and pants. It was as though they had stepped across an invisible line.

Their sopping wetness was reassuring; Claudia felt no impulse to step back. Only Nessa might not understand that while they stood upon the islet of Byrgisey, they weren't really there. Claudia turned to her. She pointed to the men and women swinging the flails. "Nessa, those people can't see us."

Nessa was too intent on one of the threshers to respond. The youth's back was to them, but as he swung the flail he raised his head enough to show his bushy red hair. Nessa stepped closer to him. All about her, workers laid sheaves of barley on clean flagstones or drew off the grain into winnowing baskets or bundled the stalks. Nessa moved through and around them until she stood opposite the red-haired youth. Then she stooped and peered up at him. She turned on her heel.

She continued her search, stopping wherever she saw a boy or youth with a certain look. Finally she stared off beyond the partly submerged causeway where carts rattled down with the sun-browned barley and splashed across to Byrgisey.

Reapers were still cutting the low fields of the main island. Along the coastal path to the southeast, others lifted and turned the heavy-headed swathes. Sigurd's voice carried across from there. When Claudia and Evan finally made him out, he seemed different somehow. They exchanged an uneasy glance, then went back to watching. Probably it was seeing Sigurd with his kirtle open and torn that made the difference, Claudia decided. Except for his size, he looked like any other farmer, streaked with sweat and straining to hold the laden cart from tipping as it descended to the causeway. Then they heard his voice, ranting now at the teetering load of barley, now at the waves that sprayed it.

"Let's go," Evan called to Nessa, who was running from one youth to another, even to the older men and smaller boys, to those who could not possibly be the one she sought.

"If only we could leave her," Claudia said. "Dunlang's got to be somewhere around here. I know she'd find him."

"But we can't. None of us can get through now." He called to Nessa again, but when she came, she looked so anxious, so desperate that he faltered.

Claudia could see Nessa sizing up Evan's indecision. "Tell her," Claudia told him. Nessa was about to dash off again. "Tell her," Claudia insisted. She knew that if Nessa left them now, if she plunged into the sea around this Byrgisey, she would never really get there, would always be on the outside. Evan seemed paralyzed by Nessa's anguish. "Explain," Claudia commanded.

"We'll try later," Evan mumbled. "We'll come back."

Nessa flung herself off, but Claudia grabbed her and pulled her away from the threshers. "It's because the weather's wrong," Claudia shouted to break through the wall of pain that held Nessa rigid and unyielding. "It's nighttime," Claudia cried into the sun and wind of Byrgisey, and then, helplessly, began to laugh at this absurdity.

Evan was infected by her laughter. He took hold of Nessa, and with his free hand clutching the bronze man, pointed into the sun-filled sky. As they all looked up, they found themselves once more on the ridge of the islet of Thrumcap. The rain droned down, black and cold. All they could do was head for the shack, grateful for its fetid warmth, for sleeping bags already wet in spots so that it didn't matter that they snuggled down inside them without waiting to get all dry.

TWENTY-FIVE

In the morning the island was steaming as the sun pressed down through the cloud cover. Nessa was restless. She kept going to the door to look out. Twice she set off toward the bar, the second time returning with such a look of urgency that Evan was moved to go for a look. The steam was thinning as it rose. Everything dripped like a rain forest, but there was a brightness high above the island.

"Either we swim," said Evan, "or it'll be too late."

Claudia dreaded getting soaked again. She'd had enough water to last a lifetime. But Evan insisted that it was now or never. The sun was drawing up the wetness from last night's downpour and the steam would dissipate before the tide fell.

"Maybe," suggested Claudia, "we should just let Nessa go. She's such a good swimmer, and she doesn't mind—"

"You can stay here. I'll go with her." Evan's voice shook. "We can get along without you."

Sullenly Claudia followed, waded after the other two, gasped at the clamp of icy water, then forced herself forward, deeper and deeper, till she was sobbing with the misery of it, the pointlessness, the fright of being so utterly at the mercy of her own clumsiness. Here and there she made contact with a boulder. She clutched at rockweed and allowed herself to rest, babbling her wretchedness under her breath. Evan and Nessa were far ahead.

They might not even remember that she was there. The water made her joints ache, it squeezed the breath out of her.

Halfway up the turtle's tail, she found the bronze man, either flung back into her path deliberately, or else dropped in a moment of confusion. Panic gripped her just as the water had done. She took the bronze man, which Evan had been carrying, and let the shielded sun bring her out of her numbness. Evan had been right about the steamy ground mist; it was burning off in shimmering patches, bright and silvery and elusive.

When she first caught sight of Evan and Nessa in one of those patches, she didn't realize that she was already separated from them. "Wait for me," she called. "Evan, wait. Nessa." But they didn't even turn. Then she stepped from blotted sunniness into refrigerated air, and Evan and Nessa seemed to be flying out of the water toward the steep shoreline of Byrgisey. The shallow harbor was teeming with small boats and beached ships, with people running everywhere.

Claudia was blocked from Evan and Nessa by a busy group from Sigurd's household. She ducked around them, but they paid no attention to her. The people were so real, the cold so penetrating, and the familiar smells and sights so palpable that it was hard to realize that the patch of sun that had caught Evan and Nessa had carried them through without her and had sunk back into vapors.

She drew up not far from Sigurd and Thorstein, who were looking down at Evan and Nessa in astonishment.

Nessa stared at a young man who waded ashore, laughing and totally unconcerned with the soaking of his tunic and trousers. He leaned to retrieve a cloak he must have thrown aside before plunging in and draped it around the narrow shoulders of the dazed Pictish girl. Still laughing, he declared to Sigurd, "See, I told you that was no seal cavorting in the shallows. I thought you told me you had buried this maid with Audna."

Nessa continued to stare at the young man. He was dressed for winter, his tunic of woolen cloth sagging now with water, his hands reddened by the weather, but his face stark white beneath his carrot-colored hair.

"Speak," commanded Sigurd, who was fatter than ever. "Has my mother sent you to me?" When Evan failed to respond, Sigurd turned to Thorstein. "I recall that the Pictish maid was voiceless. I don't know the matter with the other. Were there not two?"

Claudia tried to clear her throat. She stepped closer. She was unseen.

Thorstein scratched his beard in puzzlement. "It was many years ago." Claudia could see more than the passage of time in him. He was not just bonier, but also more angular and off balance, tilted like a ship on a falling tide. "Perhaps Dunlang will know," he said.

Dunlang prodded Nessa, who still could not take her eyes from him. She looked stricken. "She was my companion then," he volunteered. He touched Nessa's cheek with a wind-roughened finger. "Do you know, I thought of her as Sitric's ship brought me within sight of these islands again. With the monks for so long and then sent forth to practice my craft at one court after another, I had not thought of her for many years. There was a time when she was my shadow, and I her other self." He smiled at Nessa, who stood unmoving, staring at this man she knew and did not know. "She is like the Sidh maiden Aibhall, who never changes. The lad as well. They have not aged as we have."

"Why?" intoned Sigurd, turning his anguished gaze on Thorstein. "Why has my mother sent them at this time when the bard has also just returned. And you too, Thorstein. All of you at once. What does it mean?"

Thorstein said, "Perhaps she sent them—us—to you to make you mindful of her scheme. I have heard the old people from my land speak of the eve of Yule as the Night of the Mothers. If she would keep you mindful—"

"I have ever been so," answered the huge man. "I even married the daughter of the Scots king, and our little son is already called King of the Scots. It has worked out well, the mother of that boy well dead, the alliance well established. I had finished, I thought, with making my earldom. Lately I have turned my efforts to cultivating this bordland. The barley yield this year exceeded all others; we have killed more pigs than ever before and yet have twice the number to carry through till spring. Now comes Sitric, king of Ath Cliath. Surely he did not come all this way merely to return the bard. King, bard, you, Thorstein, and these thralls of my mother. What more will I be compelled to do?"

"You need not be compelled. Let your sons carry on for you."

"What kind of advice is that from an Icelandic hero? My mother held you up to me as the most valiant and trustworthy—"

"Your mother knew me briefly. She honored me, though I made no viking claims and spoke only of my longing for the unknown lands to the west. Since then I have traveled far and seen much. New lands have been found; my countrymen have taken the Christian faith. But nothing is greatly changed. When I returned to Iceland, I found my people torn apart by dreadful quarrels that have led to killings and vengeance. Even my father has been caught up in the struggle, his son, my brother, killed."

"To lose a son," answered Sigurd slowly, "is the very worst that can befall a man. Had Olaf Tryggvason lived, this sword of mine would have gone through him right down to the hilt." He thrust aside his mantle to show his sword.

Thorstein regarded the hilt that stood out from Sigurd's scabbard. "How is it that you wear that bronze man?"

"It was her wish," Sigurd answered, quickly adding, "but not one drop of blood was shed for it. Listen, Thorstein," he continued, casting his words like pebbles at the Icelander's shield of silent scrutiny. "Listen. Though I care little for the monks of Eyin Helga, I have been faithful to my mother's pledge to you. Even after her death, when I had cause for vengeance, I spared them."

Dunlang laughed.

"This you know, bard." The earl swung his pendulous torso from Thorstein to Dunlang and back again. "I left the bard in the care of those monks for his safety and learning. He is witness to my restraint. I have not violated their sanctuary."

Again Dunlang laughed.

"That is the truth," Sigurd bawled.

Dunlang spoke through his laughter. "That is so, Sigurd. You are in fair security. If you are ever convinced of their God, you will not be altogether lost."

"That is not why—"

"Do not," the bard retorted, all traces of laughter stripped from his words, "press me with your version of the why."

Abruptly Sigurd lurched around, turning his back on Dunlang. "Thorstein, tell me the rest of the news. How does your father fare now? Does he seek vengeance?"

Thorstein shook his head. "The wrongs pile up, one upon the other. When the families on both sides brought their grievances and demands to the Althing for settlement, it was my father, who is chief lawmaker, who set the tone for peace. He gave up honor price and blood."

Sigurd scowled. "Unnatural. What kind of man would yield up his son like that?"

"The kind of man my father is," Thorstein replied. "A maker of peace."

"Maybe he cared little for that son. Perhaps he felt that one son like you sufficed."

Thorstein's face was taut, but he kept his voice level. "When my father stood on the Hill of Laws at the Althing, he spoke of the grief he had suffered. It was his task to set a price on the fallen, and he knew many would expect him to place the greatest value on his own son. But having taken sides like all the others there, he would only atone for his part in the killings and grant both pledges and peace to his adversaries. He put no price at all on his son. He begged all men to follow his course."

Subdued, Sigurd remarked, "It is a different way, to beg, to yield."

"It is the way of the new faith," answered Thorstein.

Sigurd stiffened. "I have seen other in the name of that god."

"Still," pursued Thorstein, his eye once more on the bronze hilt at Sigurd's side, "it is the way of my father and is what I heard as a boy when I was with the monks."

Sigurd was silent awhile. Then suddenly he declared, "You are here, and yet you claim ignorance." He indicated Evan and Nessa. "Those two thralls may be Norns come from the spring of fate to foretell my destiny. I dislike the convergence of their coming and yours, and Dunlang's, and King Sitric's—all on the eve of Yule. You speak to me of things I cannot grasp, but explain not what troubles me."

Thorstein spread his hands in a gesture of futility. "These children are from a time I barely recall. Why not ask Dunlang, who knew them then?"

Dunlang stood aloof from Thorstein as he spoke. "I know only that before your people ever filled the Yule Eve with the clanging of spears on shields, the folk of my land looked on this day as fraught with unnatural things. They yet wear masks and skin and horn and hunt the smallest birds—the wren, the swallow, or robin. Some folk kill the little birds and bear them on branches of holly; others only pull out their tails and afterward let them go."

"What has this foolish talk of birds to do with what we see before us?" Sigurd demanded.

Dunlang shrugged. "Audna may have played like that when she was a maid in Erin. And may yet do so." He made a show of examining Evan; his mock gestures proclaimed Evan to be tailless.

"Speak sensibly," the earl roared at him. "Thorstein asked—"

"I cannot," Dunlang retorted harshly, his face set in

245

bitterness, "nor would I address myself to any man who carries the stolen blade and scabbard of Culann."

"So that is why you would not greet me," Thorstein declared. He caught Sigurd's eye. "Let us speak no more of this."

But Sigurd ignored him. "You have always been head-strong, Dunlang. And now you charge this seafarer with crimes he never made. The scabbard was a gift to him. Yet, after all these years, he would make payment for it. To you, Dunlang. The first thing Thorstein asked in return for the service he will bear me was ownership of you, that he might return you to your homeland and grant you freedom. This he requested before you came ashore from Sitric's ship."

Dunlang started to retort, defiance in every feature. "It is to have advantage over me," he finally uttered. "To have my gratitude." He turned, his eyes blazing. "Never will I make a poem or chant a song for you, Thorstein son of Hall of Side. I could not praise what I detest, and all I have just heard from you about the bloodless yielding betokens a world I would not enter were there nothing left but cruel death."

"You have no care for those monks who taught you?" Thorstein asked, his voice conveying genuine curiosity.

"They are not of this world," Dunlang retorted. "But you . . . you are supposed to be a man."

"Fool," shouted Sigurd. "Only a man of valor could prevail against so great a battle wound." Sigurd pointed to Thorstein's leg, which hung as though loose in its socket, the heel drawn up and useless.

Thorstein attempted to stop Sigurd, but the earl charged on. "Carry your limping leg with pride," he

246

roared at Thorstein, who merely shook his head and looked embarrassed. Finally the Icelander managed to slip in a quiet phrase. The huge Orcadian continued his harangue; it was moments before Thorstein's words caught up with him. "What did you say? Not a battle wound?"

Thorstein nodded. "There was sickness in the new land I found. I was spared far worse crippling than many."

Dunlang laughed, grabbed hold of Nessa's hand, and yanked her after him.

"Wait," shouted the earl. "Where are you taking the Pictish maid?"

"Out of harm's way," the bard called back. "She is but a wild thing that would be helpless before the likes of you or even the other, that blunderer who has come to serve you. And own me. I will see her to safety for the sake of old carings."

"What about me?" blurted Evan, suddenly come to life and near panic. "She needs me. I understand her."

"Oh yes. The swallow. Come along then," answered Dunlang. "We will leave the lords to their plotting, for it is they who determine what shall fall upon the quaking and the dumb."

"I'm not a swallow," Evan retorted as he ran to catch up with Nessa and Dunlang.

Dunlang drew up and waited. "Seal or swallow," he returned, "it matters little which."

Evan tried to take Nessa's free hand, but it was limp. It dropped away from him like something dead.

"It was not the time to speak of my plan," Thorstein said to Sigurd, his reproof mild enough, but his face drawn into a deep frown.

"Well, I have no patience with that one. Were it not for my mother, I would have sold him long ago. As it is, I kept him from Byrgisey as much as I could. But then I heard he was a fair poet, and thought it time to bring him back. I am not one for words myself and can be no judge. Sitric's ship brought another poet as well, a skald who is going to the Northern Way. I will let skald and bard vie for a prize at the feast this night. Make Dunlang work a little for his keep." Sigurd glanced at Thorstein's shrunken leg, and looked quickly away.

Claudia watched the two men walk up from the beach. She could see how Thorstein's leg swung out at every step, the toe scraping in an arc that barely touched the ground. His whole body seemed altered, lopsided. Still, he kept up with Sigurd. Claudia, trying to follow, had to duck around the men and women intent on preparations for the Yule feast in honor of Sitric, king of Ath Cliath.

She clutched the bronze man and made her way along the paving to Audna's house. Listening to shouts and commands, she learned that this was where the honored guest, King Sitric Silkenbeard, was to reside. The sacks and bundles carried up were his, and some of these men were slaves and house carls from his ship. She turned away, setting off for the barns and byres attached to the earl's Great Hall. "Excuse me," she murmured as she plowed into a woman carrying an enormous board set with cakes.

The woman, thrown off balance, cried out as the cakes went flying to the turf. Instantly dogs set onto the cakes and another woman set onto the poor carrier. "It wasn't me," wailed the woman, as the other flailed at her with a broom and struck her briskly about the head. "Loki himself must have been after the cakes, for it was he who upset the tray and pushed me down."

Claudia ducked behind a wall, her heart pounding. If she could have this effect on that poor woman, then maybe she could be seen after all. Waiting, she heard Evan's voice beyond her in one of the byres. Hushed, hesitant, she called his name. Again she called, louder this time. She could hear him perfectly clearly now as she crept along the wall, huddling into its shadow. He was insisting on an explanation for being called a swallow.

"Once when Ath Cliath was under siege," came Dunlang's terse reply, "swallows were caught, twigs attached to their wings. Then all the twigs were set afire, the swallows released. They flew burning to their nests, falling on the thatched roofs of the defenders' houses. While the warriors ran to save their flaming homes, Ath Cliath fell to the enemy."

Silence followed. The story made Claudia's skin crawl. Finally Evan's voice, small and uncertain, came through. "You said swallows and seals alike."

"Yes. Fodder for the griffon. It's always that way. Since the earliest time when Balor cast the children of Eithne's attendants from the cliff and left them to become the sea folk, those who belong to the land but cannot survive on it. Since then, the dumb, the helpless, the harmless are used and then cast aside or fed to the griffon. Even the beasts of burden. The horse, for instance; the griffon becomes crazed for the flesh of horse."

"What exactly is a griffon?" said Evan.

There was an uncomfortable silence before the bard spoke. "How can you be ignorant of griffons?"

Evan declared quickly, "I . . . used to know, but I've

forgotten. Nessa knows probably. Only it's too dark in here for her to draw me one. Maybe outside with the moon—"

"No, stay here out of Sigurd's sight. Do not venture beyond the drain outside."

"Will Sigurd do anything to us?"

"Not if he is reminded that you serve his mother. Sigurd is not unlike his guest, Sitric. Both are in thralldom to their mothers. I know, for Gormlath, who once was wife to Brian and is mother of King Sitric, stays with her son Sitric at Ath Cliath these days. And plots against Brian."

"Why does Gormlath hate Brian?" asked Evan.

At first there was no answer. Then Claudia heard Dunlang say, "Maybe because they are so different. Though of course she claims it is to honor the spirit of her ancestors who would never have submitted to a High King of Erin over them."

"From the way you used to talk about Brian," Evan went on, "he seemed a little like Thorstein."

There was a sound like a hiss.

"I mean," said Evan quickly, "in the way they look at some things."

"Brian," declared Dunlang, "is the greatest warrior in Erin. That his goal is to rule over that land in peace and justice does not weaken his strength as a fighter and a dealer of justice."

"I suppose you mean punishment," Evan ventured. Claudia marveled at his boldness.

"Of course that's what I mean," Dunlang retorted. "What other kind of justice is there?"

"Still, you told us Brian was a Christian too."

250

"You remember many things through these eighteen years in service to the dead mother of the earl. What sight had you from the grave?"

"Not much," Evan told him. "Which is why I asked about griffons." He paused, clearly waiting for Dunlang to fill him in.

Dunlang said, "Oh, they're creatures to be feared, more fierce than any other. The griffon has the head and wings of a monstrous eagle and the body of a beast not known to you. It is called a lion."

"I do so know about lions," Evan retorted.

"Well, think of a lion then. Or a she-lion like Gormlath. You know, it was Gormlath who sent Sitric on this mission. She hopes to get the Orcadians to join Sitric in crushing Brian. If Sigurd goes," added Dunlang, "he will be a fool."

"Will you warn him?"

"I have no love for Earl Sigurd the Stout."

"But he's taken care of you—" Evan began.

"For Audna. And only so that I should carve his name on the stone of history. I intend to see Sigurd fall at the hands of Brian and Brian's sons." Dunlang cut himself off. His voice tight with suspicion, he demanded, "Why do you ask? You come from Audna's grave. Will you carry this word to Sigurd?"

Evan's protests and breathless yelps gave Claudia some idea of what Dunlang was up to. "No," Evan cried. "I only care about Nessa. Really."

The sounds of skirmishing changed. Claudia heard Dunlang exclaim, his tone surprised, angry, "Now what? You too?" Then he began to laugh. "Call her off. I'll believe you. So you attack me, Nessa, you who brought me out of misery. What a strength she has for one so slight. The seal has jaws like a trap."

Claudia clung to the cold stone of the wall. She wished she could see through it. If Nessa had attacked Dunlang for Evan's sake, then she must be recovering from her paralyzing shock.

Dunlang sounded as though he was pulling himself away from them. "We have talked enough. With you two, I forget to have care. Though I believe you will not betray me."

"It means so much to you to see Sigurd beaten?"

"To see them all go down." His voice lower, he said, "I have already written it that way. I have written what my heart has allowed me to see, and that is Brian triumphant over all the Northmen who still hold out against him on the eastern coast of Erin."

"But that's crazy," blurted Evan. "That's not history."

"It will be." The poet laughed. "It will yet be, for I have had that vision."

Claudia thought he sounded deranged. She was tense with cold and dread.

In a small voice Evan answered him once more. "If you're so sure it's right, why don't you wait to see how it all comes out?"

Dunlang uttered another harsh laugh. "Remember when I told you of the Sidh maiden Aibhall who came to me and came again in the grave of the ancient hero?" There was a pause, and then Dunlang continued. "She has been with me since. At Ath Cliath in Erin she pleaded with me to go with her to the Land of Mists. She is as gentle as Gormlath is harsh, as sweet as Gormlath is false. Yet it gives me some sense of the power of that queen when I feel the force of the Sidh maiden compelling me to follow her into the earth." There was a stirring. "Will you be warm enough, Nessa? Or shall I have them send you a shawl?"

Claudia strained to hear something that would indicate a response from Nessa.

There was a smile in Dunlang's voice when he spoke next, but he sounded farther away. "Well, though you have left your mark on me, dark one, I shall not forget your hand from that time when I was half grown. Just carve not your Pictish signs on my poor skin. I'll see to your safety." His voice dropped. "I'll not forget. That you healed me. That you drew your pictures so that I should want to put words to them. And made me smell the angelica and touch the hair of the seal and lean upon the sun-drenched weed above the sea and feel the pungent air, sharp with salt and dank with cow droppings and sweet, sweeter than all the angelica you picked for me."

Claudia heard his steps fade away on the flags across the wall from her. For a long time after that there was silence. At last, just as she was beginning to sink into sleep, Claudia heard Evan speak to Nessa.

"Later we can go and look at your stone, the one you made for Hundi."

Claudia imagined Nessa listening, staring.

"We can look for new lambs or calves. Do you think they'd have any? I guess it's too early. That would be in the spring. Well, we could cross to the main island to the . . . well, to the loch. . . ."

Still she must have stared, unresponding.

"Well, what do you want to do then?" Evan suddenly sounded like a bored host beset by a visiting child who didn't know how to play. He sighed. "Seems to me," Claudia heard, "that if Dunlang's seeing to your safety, our safety, he might just give a thought to how hungry people can get when they've come as far as us. Nessa? Nessa, aren't you beginning to get hungry?" After a moment Claudia heard Evan driving on, filling the darkness of that byre with his bright, confident words. "You were great before. Great the way you went at him. Nessa, don't feel bad. At least you're here. I mean, even if we've lost Claudia, the main thing was to get you back here. I'm not worried about the bronze man either. I mean, dropping it like that was terrible, but at least it gives us . . . her a chance. See, Claudia knows. . . ." Evan faltered, then resumed brightly, "She knows I can't get back without it. So she'll come. As soon as she can. . . ."

Huddled against the wall, Claudia listened to Evan plowing forward, spreading the comfort of his inadequate words wherever he could, doing double duty since he was alone now, but refusing to admit any worry or fear. She wished she could tell him how near she was. She wished she could tell him she was proud of him. She wished she had a cloak like Nessa's, or anything warm. Nevertheless, she felt herself drooping. She closed her eyes.

TWENTY-SIX

THE cold finally raised Claudia from her miserable dozing beside the wall and drove her to the doorway of Sigurd's Great Hall. There she shrank from every comer. She didn't understand how she could have made that woman with the cakes stumble and scatter her precious burden. She didn't want to take any chances with anyone.

The hall was magnificent. Burnished shields mounted along the walls distorted images and repeated them, each surface reflecting the light of countless lamps and the huge fire in the center. Arms reaching for tankards and drinking horns flashed over and over again as the shields caught the light from armlets of silver and gold.

King Sitric Silkenbeard was seated in the place of honor. He had a haughty bearing and beautiful hair; he stroked his yellow beard almost continuously. Beside him, the aging earl, elevated in his booth of oversized dimensions, introduced the next entertainment. There was already talk of a horse fight on the morrow when daylight would let the spectators watch every strike and bite of the goaded stallions. But now two poets would be set against each other in a battle of words. The hirdmen roared their approval.

"You know," shouted the king, "I knew nothing of poets till one stopped at Ath Cliath and offered me a poem about myself. Well, Sigurd, I was taken aback. No one had done this for me before. I had been moving about too fast from one battlefield to the next to stand still long enough for a poet to catch up with me." Sitric poked his knife into the platter set before him. He tugged and chewed at the dripping meat and continued with his mouth full. "And while the poem praised me mightily, it also mentioned the gifts great kings bestow on poets who praise them. So," the king went on, washing down the meat with a long drink from his silver tankard, "I called the man who keeps my treasury and asked what I should give the poet. 'How about two merchant ships?' I asked. Would that be enough?"

Claudia edged her way closer to the high seat.

"My treasurer then informed me that a sword or a bracelet would be more in the order of proper payment. Sigurd, you know what I did?" The king stood up and fumbled with the brooch that held the cloak he wore thrown back from his shoulders. He had trouble, because his elegantly combed beard got caught in the latchet at his throat, but finally he was able to swing the cloak high above the fire. It was scarlet on the outside and lined with silver fur. "I gave that poet my newest raiment," Sitric declared, "and so will I now. To the winner." He slung the cloak to the floor, where hands immediately caught it up and pulled it back from the hearth.

Claudia heard Dunlang speak in an undertone to Brusi and Hrafn, one of Sigurd's hirdmen. "That same poet did as much for Sigurd, who was at least as ignorant of payment as Sitric."

Hrafn the Red laughed. "I was there. It was a Yule Eve feast like this one."

"How will you do, Dunlang?" asked Brusi. "Will you wear King Sitric's cloak?"

Dunlang shrugged. "I care less for gifts than for truth."

"But what sort is the skald?"

"His rhymes are where they ought to be and his images are rank with Odin's tongue and Thor's hammer and all the phrases of his art."

Sigurd called his hirdmen to him. Claudia guessed that he was trying to figure out what gift might match but not insult the gift of his guest. She saw one of the men point to his sword. Sigurd clapped his hand to the hilt, but Thorstein, standing at his left shoulder, spoke a word, a single word, and Sigurd's hand lifted.

Finally Sigurd's eye lit up. "I have it," he bawled. "My gift to the winner shall be the winning horse in the Yule Day fight. I shall place in that battle my old stallion Sleipnir, who has never lost a fight and may yet sire a hundred champions, though he is aging like his master and slowed in that age."

Sigurd's hirdmen drank to the horses, to the vikings, to the women, and to the poets whose contest was about to start.

"You will let the skald win the stallion?" asked Hrafn, returning to his seat.

Dunlang's white face was whiter than ever. "It is the foal of my captivity," he muttered. "That foal shipped here, like me, in bonds." Then he leaned back and listened to the rambling, amiable dispute about which poet should say his poem first. Those who were too drunk to argue enjoyed the arguing of others. Threats were bandied back and forth, and then suddenly the matter was settled with an understanding nod passed between Sigurd and Sitric.

The older poet, the skald, stood before the host and

guests and declaimed one verse upon another. The rhyming phrases were short enough to follow, but each seemed oddly disconnected. All Claudia could tell was that it was about a king. She couldn't make any sense out of phrases like wolf-steed and Odin's mead-drink, but she grasped one or two. Warrior's marrow and eagle's-meat must be the fallen in battle. She was proud of being able to decipher this much, but then she got hopelessly tangled in something about the slinger of the fire of the storm of the troll, and she gave up trying to follow.

The poem was received with noisy acclaim. Some of the king's hirdmen even stood and rattled spears or slapped their scabbards.

Claudia saw Sigurd beckon to Thorstein. She edged her way around the hearth and over to the platform on which Sigurd was spread. She arrived in the middle of his whispered comment to Thorstein, and heard only, "He asked for all our forces to join with his in crushing the High King of Erin, who has only drawn back from Ath Cliath because the Yule approached. Brian's people are Christian; they wished to spend what they call the feast of Christ with their families. But Sitric says Brian will return, that only with our help can he defeat Brian's armies." Sigurd paused and wiped a pulpy hand across his sweating face. "He praised my warrior prowess, my command over men in the field of battle." Sigurd paused again. "Why do you not speak?"

"It is far from here, Ath Cliath."

"I have traveled farther and dealt the blow of our Orcadian might to the south and east and west."

Thorstein seemed reluctant to comment. Compliments were still being shouted back and forth across the fire and the skald remained at the central hearth, flushed with heat and praise.

"What?" said Sigurd, leaning back to catch Thorstein's unspoken word.

Thorstein shook his head, then spoke. "You may as well finish telling me."

"Telling you what?"

"What powerful inducement he has offered to bring you to such serious consideration."

Sigurd's face broke into a smile. It was the smile of a child, utterly open. It lasted only a second. Claudia thought Thorstein, too, must have caught a glimpse of it, though he was kneeling on his good knee, leaning awkwardly to the earl's side. "His mother Gormlath for my queen," said Sigurd. "The kingdom of Munster and all of Brian's other holdings to the south."

Thorstein was speechless.

Again that smile crossed Sigurd's face. "It is everything she intended for me."

"You mean Audna?"

"Of course. Who else?"

"I have heard that Gormlath also rides the steed of destiny. She may be as ambitious for her son Sitric as Audna was for you."

"But it would have pleased my mother. It will please her. Now I see why those thralls appeared this day. To prepare me for this challenge, that I might not relax my warlike countenance and let it pass from my grasp."

Thorstein said nothing.

"You have other views?"

"I have no view as yet. I cannot shape my views with haste."

"But I am to answer tonight. If I refuse his offer, Sitric will go to others, to Cnut and his Danes. He will not lose what he has set out to win. Only I will lose."

"That is one view."

Sigurd uttered an exclamation of disgust. "How came my mother to saddle me with so stiff-legged a beast as you? Not only your body is twisted and weak. Yours is the plodding nature of a cart horse." Sigurd scowled when this outburst brought no response from Thorstein. "If it was only for the scabbard which you carried away these many years ago, why, then, am I a fool to stick with you now and heed your cautious ways?"

"I have said my regrets for not returning with the scabbard. It was my intention to do so, but events ruled against me." Thorstein spread his hands as if to show their emptiness. "Perhaps I have nothing to offer you, Sigurd."

Sigurd shoved the open hands away from him. "She saw in you what I should need. And I did promise." He turned as far as his folds of fat allowed. His voice was suddenly pleading. "If you could give me reason for refusing Sitric Silkenbeard, I should do so promptly. Oh, promptly. I had such plans for early sowing this year."

"Wait," advised Thorstein.

Sigurd nodded, then twisted partway around again. "Thorstein." He grabbed Thorstein's lean arm. "Thorstein, I have heard there is no lovelier woman in all the world than Gormlath. Her beauty is celebrated everywhere."

Thorstein looked grimly at the fat hand that had clutched at him. "She's run through husbands at the rate some swords, also celebrated, run through foes." Gently he disengaged the heavy fingers. "Consider this, Sigurd: Who will gain and what is at stake?"

"I don't know what you mean," Sigurd insisted petulantly.

"If those child thralls have come from your mother's grave, Sigurd, to guide you or to bear witness to your acts, consider what rules your decisions now. Consider whether the real contenders are the king and earl, or whether they are those women of whom we speak, directing events from the confines of the homestead and the grave."

Sigurd's shoulders sagged. He waved automatically as one of his men called on him to acknowledge the final bow of the skald. His smile was detached and dispirited and soon drooped into the creases of his cheeks and chins.

Dunlang stood beside the roof post near the hearth. He was so still and straight that he seemed to be carved of wood.

"Show yourself," the king demanded.

"Yes, of course," mumbled Sigurd, trying to rouse himself to interest in the recitation. "Come forward, Dunlang."

"It is a different poem than I had prepared," Dunlang said in a dry voice.

"You'll be lost already," Brusi interrupted, "if you do not fill your chest with air and strain your heart at the saying of it."

Without responding, Dunlang launched into his poem. Because his voice didn't change, few realized that the recitation had actually begun. Gradually the noise in the

261

hall diminished until there was only the clattering of knives dropped on platters, the resounding thud of tankards set onto table boards, and the crackling and hissing of the enormous fire. And Dunlang's tight, hard voice uttered its swift, cutting phrases.

The poem was about a horse fight. Yet, as it progressed, Claudia realized it was not only about horses, but about men who set the field for their game of blood and set their finest stallions to maim and blind and perhaps destroy each other. A savage joy burst through the hideous details. Everyone listened. When Dunlang came to describe the mares in heat brought alongside the stallions to sting them into frenzied attack, Sigurd's face darkened as he leaned forward to catch each phrase. The fire seemed to wrench his flesh out of shape; the deep furrows of his skin oozed sweat.

Each line seemed like a dagger thrust into Sigurd's dreams. The dying stallions were stripped of their grandeur, their masters exultant with the sacrifice. Now almost all the guests were beginning to squirm. Who were the winners of this bloodstained contest? asked Dunlang, evoking the pitiful image of beasts torn apart by the craving of men for bloody splendor. The field of grass became a field of gore, he finished. To send the horses there into that gap of danger was to plunge a naked hand into a griffon's nest. The blood of those harmless steeds overspread the green of the land.

There was no applause when Dunlang finished. Men who had laughed and shouted before, who had eaten of the meat and loaves with lusty appetite and downed one tankard of ale after another, now sat as though oppressed by the heat and smoke and closeness of the feasting hall, each unwilling to meet the eyes of his companion.

The first sounds uttered were not in words but in a mounting growl of indignation. These vikings felt offended and couldn't tell why. They were challenged, but their challenger was the tersely spoken word, already thinning like the smoke that rose toward the roof hole.

Thorstein murmured something to the earl. Sigurd roused himself from his deep gloom and shouted for the tankards and horns to be filled once more. "We will hear the verdict," he proclaimed.

But the men were unwilling to pass judgment on Dunlang's poem. In the end, amid the blustering of Sigurd and the disdain of Sitric, the prizes were divided, the scarlet, fur-lined cloak to be given to the skald, the winning horse to be given to Dunlang.

The guests were growing restive, excitement already building in them toward the climax of the celebration that would usher in the Yule. Quarrels and cross-quarrels sprang up. Mead and ale sloshed and spattered as the gestures grew wilder, voices rose. Sigurd called for the harpers, but their music could scarcely be heard, and so he proposed another entertainment, a storytelling. He called for someone who could recount the burning of Njal and his sons in Iceland. The roar of countless voices was stilled, anticipation and tension replacing the excitement.

Thorstein told Sigurd he already knew more than he wanted to of the burning and would take his leave before the telling of that story. Sigurd didn't want him to go. He mentioned Dunlang's poem and shook his head like a bewildered ox that has been struck and prodded into confusion. "Do you think the bard intended to speak insultingly of my mother, who saved his life and gave him his learning?"

Thorstein shrugged. He seemed anxious to get away.

"He could not have meant Gormlath," Sigurd went on, "for he has seen her at Ath Cliath. He knows she is beautiful."

Thorstein said, "He served Brian once, and I believe he does so in his heart to this day."

Sigurd drew himself up. "Then it was of Brian's fall that he composed his tragic lay. Not of mine. Not of Sitric's. Don't you see, Thorstein, that it is Brian he sees entering that gap of danger, Brian the old warrior horse, with Gormlath, who was once his wife, driving on the opponents in the heat of battle."

Thorstein said, "There may be other reasons why those child thralls appeared just now. Remember, Sigurd, it is the eve of Yule."

"It is a dangerous time, yes. But if all our spears are rattled and all our shields beaten at the appointed hour, then how can harm come from those grave-children?"

Thorstein said only, "It might be well to move toward commitment with caution."

"Do you expect me to fail?"

Thorstein started to speak, but said nothing.

"Would you fight by my side?"

"I would. But I would also advise you to consider avoiding it."

Sigurd smiled. "Many years before you came here, when I and my men were badly outnumbered, I sought my mother's advice. She never heard me out. Her tongue was a lashing wave, full of salt and sting. She mocked me, said I wished to live forever." Sigurd's voice trembled. "Never will I forget that, Thorstein, nor will she let me. In truth, I do relish this life. I— But she will not allow me to turn my back on her vision of my destiny. Listen, I'll go. I'll tell King Sitric that I will meet him there at the time of the planting. For I have that raven banner she made me, and cannot fail. What do you say to that?"

"That I will accompany you." Thorstein stooped down to his twisted foot to tighten the lacing of his boot.

Sigurd suddenly blurted, "You should not be unwilling to let others look on your crippling as a battle wound."

Thorstein replied, "I see no honor in being crippled by the hand of man. My deformity is an act of God."

"Well, if I were you—" Sigurd broke off. "Look, Thorstein, get those thralls of hers away from my sight. I cannot"—he stumbled over his words—"cannot abide their presence. It . . . it's like that stinging wave poised to break over my head."

"What shall I do with them?" asked Thorstein, adding, "Dunlang has sworn to see to their protection."

"Let them be sent away. With Sitric. He leaves with the afternoon tide this Yule Day. Let them be a gift. No, no, not a gift, but a proof of trust. Yes, trust. I don't suppose my mother would stand for my giving them away altogether."

Thorstein limped past Claudia. She followed him at a distance. He set off toward the byre at the back of the Great Hall. The wind was shrill and biting. The gaunt Icelander stopped for a while, then abruptly changed his mind and direction. He turned down to the barn and home field where the stallion grazed beside Sigurd's best boar and bull. There he came to a halt. Claudia stopped too. Gradually she was able to make out a figure of a man beside the stone wall. As soon as he moved, she could tell by his quick, tense manner that it was Dunlang.

"What will you do?" asked Thorstein.

Dunlang whirled around at the sound of his voice. Then he sprang over the wall and approached the horse. "I will claim my prize in advance." His voice held defiance and desperation.

Very softly Thorstein replied, "The tide is high. You cannot get the beast away from Byrgisey. And if you do. . . ." He didn't finish. His tone conveyed the futility of Dunlang's gesture. "He will die soon anyway."

"Blinded?" rasped Dunlang. "Mangled and crippled?"

"If that is his fate. . . ." Thorstein dragged himself to the wall.

"I have given them his death already in my poem. Let them make a spectacle of themselves instead of howling over the ruin of this animal." Dunlang ran his hand up the side of the stallion's neck. The graceful head went down to rub against his side.

"Was it the horse only?" asked Thorstein wonderingly.

After a pause, Dunlang answered him. "It was the horse as well."

"And do you know that Brian will soon face all these Orcadians as well as the Northmen of Ath Cliath?"

"I know," said Dunlang bitterly, "that even some men of Erin will join them against the High King."

"And will Brian go to meet them," Thorstein pressed softly, "as if he had reached into a griffon's nest?"

Dunlang gave a short derisive laugh. "You have heard me, Icelander."

Thorstein turned into the wind, which now carried tiny beads of ice in its wake. Snow whirled up as though springing from the earth, intense and sudden.

"You'll miss the heathen celebration," taunted Dunlang as a great clamor issued from the hall. "The Yule beating is a good time to settle old debts and finish old battles." Dunlang uttered a short laugh. "The men who make that din are not like those meek Icelanders who followed your father, Hall of Side." Dunlang was still laughing as Thorstein, bent and slow, merged into the thickness of the night.

Moments later Dunlang leaped the wall and ran along the paving toward the entrance of the Great Hall. Claudia, who was freezing, started along the same way, then saw Dunlang reappear. He stood at the threshold, framed in the smoky light from within. In his arms he carried a bundle. As he raced past her, part of it was flung against her arm; it felt soft and supple, like fur. She almost turned to follow him, but she was tired as well as cold, and it was all she could do to make her way to the dank warmth of a cattle byre, where all storms were shut out by the turf-lined walls of stone.

TWENTY-SEVEN

Yule Day broke under squalls. What had promised to be a continuing feast began without celebration. King Sitric's navigator urged an earlier departure, and Sigurd's hirdmen, quick to express misgivings, arose to confront their earl's commitment to the king of Ath Cliath.

Claudia didn't see Evan and Nessa until they were brought down to the water. Evan, swathed in bulky leggings, was squirming and generally making a nuisance of himself, but no one bothered about his protests. When one large Orcadian picked him up and tucked him under his arm to carry him out to the loading boats, the yelling Evan made no more impression than the squealing pigs and squawking chickens that were being carried aboard and tied down deep within the ships.

Nessa was prodded along and then given baskets to carry and left to her own devices. Claudia saw her dawdle and cast glances this way and that and guessed that she was looking for Dunlang. Meanwhile Evan howled about how his sister was coming and he couldn't leave without her. All that showed of him were his hands clutching the gunwales and the tight-fitting cap that someone had given him, a helmetlike thing of wool that bobbed as the boat lurched and tripped over the steep chop.

Claudia started toward the loading boats, then shrank back to avoid contact with the milling people. She wanted to shout something reassuring to Evan, but she couldn't even see him any more, let alone be heard by him. The confusion and crowding bewildered her; the boisterous leave-taking of hirdmen and carls was distracting. In their heavy woolen mantles it was hard to tell one viking from another. Only Sigurd stood out because of his bulk, and Thorstein because of his height and limp.

In the midst of the leave-taking a messenger darted up to the earl, hesitated, then delivered his word to Brusi, who frowned, looked quickly at his father, and then away. Thorstein noticed the exchange and sent Brusi a questioning look. Claudia saw gestures, shrugs passing back and forth. Finally King Sitric grew curious and demanded an explanation.

"An accident," declared Brusi. "Word has just come. It is good that you did not wait for the horse fight."

Sitric scowled. "An accident? And did you know that the skald could not find my cloak this morning? Strange omens on the Yule Day."

"It is found," Brusi responded shortly.

"The cloak? Then have it brought to the skald."

Brusi cast Thorstein a look, and the Icelander started up the path.

"What is this?" Sigurd exclaimed. "Thorstein is not a carrier of cloaks." He set off after Thorstein, Sitric following.

Thorstein stopped, as if to protest, then shrugged and went on. His dragging foot scraped scallops in the thin covering of snow. He paused finally when they had all crossed the meadowland beyond the home field. A small gathering already fringed the edge of the cliff. Men and women huddled in the wind, all silently staring below to the rocky beach.

Claudia pushed her way through, then squatted down. She sank back. On the rocks, his legs thrust out as though he were still leaping, lay the stallion Sleipnir. Tied over his head was the scarlet cloak of King Sitric, its fur lining thrown back in a tangle, so that at first the cloak itself seemed a part of the horse, the scarlet its torn flesh.

Those huddling at the edge of the cliff backed away as Sigurd and Sitric drew near. Only Thorstein remained. A figure out of proportion, like a spear impaled in the trampled turf, he leaned into the gusts that whipped and shook all the others. Sigurd lurched around, casting a look of blunt horror at all those who stood watching him. He seemed ready to charge them like a bull. They cowered together.

"Who . . . ?" he rasped. "Who?"

"My cloak," said Sitric. "Ruined."

Sigurd caught sight of Nessa, who had followed them. "Fetch the cloak," he ordered, his anger lashing out at her. She could not have seen Sleipnir yet. She had not seen the cloak. He pointed. Without hesitation, Nessa stooped to leave the baskets she had carried so far, and then she made straight for the cliff.

"She is too agile," muttered the swollen-faced earl.

Claudia looked over the edge. The steep drop made her queasy. She shifted around till she was stretched out on her stomach. She saw Nessa peel back the cloak as though it were skin. Sleipnir's mouth was horribly open, as if he had died in mid-cry or gasping for a breath. She thought of Dunlang goading him into a gallop and driving him blind to his death. The bard would have told the horse he was setting him free. That would be like Dunlang.

Tears stung Claudia's eyes. He had used the animal to get back at the master.

Nessa struggled with the heavy cloak, but it was so soft and supple that it kept collapsing and falling from her arms. As she gathered it together again, she stopped suddenly and seemed to stare into the face of the cliff. Her expression was swept for one fleeting second with the look Claudia remembered from long before, and Claudia knew that Dunlang must be there. Hiding? It was a ridiculous place to hide. Nessa, after that brief glance, paid no more attention to the place under the cliff, but struggled up with the cumbersome cloak.

Claudia heard Sigurd whisper to Thorstein, "I suppose I'll have to think of another gift for the bard."

"I wouldn't worry about Dunlang," Thorstein replied. "He has yet to learn how to receive gifts with grace."

This made Sigurd laugh and helped to restore a semblance of good humor to these last important minutes.

Everyone started back toward the ships. The wind was at their backs now and bowled them headlong across the meadowland.

Claudia heard more laughter as the men strode off on the wind, but she didn't follow, didn't even get up off her stomach. She wanted to see what Dunlang would do once the others were gone.

She didn't have long to wait. Within minutes, Dunlang stepped out onto the rocks where the horse lay. He was not alone.

Claudia gasped at the sight of the woman who accompanied him. She was fair, with braids like ears of wheat, and she was wearing a faintly green, speckled gown, with sandals to match. Her gown looked flimsy, but she didn't seem cold.

"You mustn't count on me to cloak you in invisibility out here, Dunlang. It is not like home. If Sigurd had found you keeping your stubborn vigil, he would have torn you limb from limb."

"I had to stay with Sleipnir," Dunlang answered, "so that no one would think of eating him."

"You are behind the times. The Church has banned the eating of horseflesh because of the heathen ceremonies attached to that eating."

"You are the ignorant one, Aibhall. Firstly, most here are still heathen. And secondly, even in Iceland, where all are supposedly Christian, there are allowances for the eating of horses."

"Well, let us not bicker about such things. The point, Dunlang, is that my powers are feeble here. I know, for the Pictish girl saw right through the cloak of invisibility. She is not like the others."

Dunlang squatted down on his heels beside the dead horse. He flattened the forelock for a moment between the rigid ears, then let the wind blow it wild. Claudia's stomach lurched. She hugged the turf. The wind was bitter, but the sun was forcing itself through the scudding clouds. There were blotches of brightness that flared like flames and were snuffed out again. One of those flames licked at her back, a fleeting stroke of warmth. Aibhall looked searchingly all about them, then pointed to the ships setting sail, fighting the wind, the oars plying the waves like running legs on waterborne insects. Claudia thought of Evan, bundled and helpless. Had he given up struggling? Had he given up hope?

"I must go," Aibhall told Dunlang, "or I will miss Sitric's ship. See, the others are already underway."

"The Pictish girl will be on the ship with you," Dunlang warned. "You will need to be sly to conceal yourself."

Aibhall tossed her head. "I will manage. After all, I kept hidden even from you on the way out." She turned again, this time inland, and stared at Claudia full in the face.

Aibhall pointed again, but Dunlang wasn't following her gesture. Aibhall spoke quietly. "You have another visitor."

Now he looked up too. "Oh yes." He shrugged. "It is the other one from Audna's grave. The boy said she would come."

Claudia assumed they were looking across a gap in time, just as she did. She made no attempt to speak to them.

"She is bigger than the Pictish maid, but younger." Aibhall said this in a dismissive tone.

Suddenly Dunlang recovered himself. "She is left behind. Her brother and the Pictish girl are gone with Sitric." He gestured to Claudia, pointing to the small fleet that glinted now and then under the open and shut sky. "They're gone to Erin," he shouted up to her. "You may follow when we join them in the spring. Only Aibhall can make it to that ship now."

It never occurred to Claudia to try to answer. She had become, like Nessa, a silent witness. She was already unused to being accepted and dealt with.

"Don't worry," Dunlang called again. "They will be cared for. Don't fear for them."

Still Claudia made no response.

Dunlang sighed irritably. "She has caught the silence of the tongueless girl."

"Or else is only partway here with us," mused Aibhall. "After all, only she and the Pictish thrall could see me." Then she shrugged. "It matters not. She is so young. . . . She is nothing."

Discounted, Claudia felt herself to be nothing. She remained there, silent, dazed, and only heard the people returning when they were almost upon her. Sigurd led the way, spewing forth a stream of abuse at all or any who might have dealt him such a humiliating blow before Sitric. When he saw Claudia, still lying, but now half turned and staring up at him, he came to a full stop. Then he moaned.

"Thorstein, Thorstein. What is she doing here?"

Thorstein limped through the ranks of followers to stand beside the earl.

"What is my mother trying to do?" whispered Sigurd.

Thorstein shook his head in wonderment. He rubbed his wind-reddened ear and shook his head again.

"Well, girl," shouted Sigurd, "your brother and the Pictish one are sent away. I suppose you know that."

Claudia nodded.

Thorstein said, "She is not deaf, Sigurd."

"Where are they gone to?" The storm of Sigurd's voice moderated slightly. Aside, to Thorstein, he added, "I forgot. It's the Pictish thrall who cannot hear."

"Erin," whispered Claudia, wondering if she should correct Sigurd's mistake about Nessa.

"See?" hissed Sigurd. "She knows. She knows."

"The child seems to know, yes," answered Thorstein.

"Do you doubt that she has been sent here as the other two were sent?" He turned away, refusing to look on her any more, forgetting that he had returned to the cliff to begin the hunt for the killer of the stallion. "Look to her, Thorstein. I cannot. Cannot." He stumbled away with all the others but Thorstein in his wake.

After a minute Thorstein asked Claudia if she was cold. She nodded, but then he seemed to forget all about her. He moved into the wind and peered down from the cliff. Claudia looked where he was looking. She saw Aibhall reach down to Dunlang's forehead and brush back his wild red hair. Aibhall looked up slowly and smiled at Thorstein, then stepped under the cliff edge out of sight. Dunlang looked up to Thorstein and their eyes met. Hatred and confusion sprang from Dunlang's look. Claudia couldn't see Thorstein's eyes.

"Tell him then,'" shouted Dunlang. "Tell Sigurd."

"I tell him what I think will help him," Thorstein answered mildly. "What can only rile or chafe is not worth speaking of."

"He serves both mares, the dead one and the living. And will go to his death in their service."

"Be careful, Dunlang," Thorstein said, "that you do not yourself land in that nest you spoke of."

Dunlang, still seated beside the dead horse, began to laugh. "You and your warnings. You talk like a woman."

"I am surprised to hear that from you, for all the women I have ever heard you describe were drivers of men, not protectors."

"There are women who drive and women who are fair in all their deeds as well as in their looks. I have known both." He threw back his head in angry mirth. Crashing waves and spray bursting about him drowned out his derisive laughter. Only the sea roared and hissed, while Dunlang bared his teeth in grotesque imitation of the stallion's death throe.

Claudia, staring in pity and horror, felt something heavy and coarse spread across her shoulders. She huddled, shivering, under Thorstein's mantle. High up a gull laughed. The sea hurled itself onto the rocks below and splintered its frothy shards over Dunlang and the wet, dead horse.

TWENTY-EIGHT

THE days were wet and dark and similar. It had never occurred to Claudia that if the summer sun barely sank to the horizon, there would be a winter balancing of that condition. Darkness made up that balance—darkness, wind, and rain.

Only preparations for the foray to Erin kept the men and women of the bordland bu from retreating into that darkness and living quietly off dried meat and fish and stored grains. There were ships to be repaired, weapons to be forged, the vests of mail, so tedious to contrive, to be worked during long hours beside the sputtering fires.

Often Claudia was sent out into the windy darkness, even as far as the tower where she had first seen Nessa. Sometimes, to avoid the stinging waves that lashed the coast, she followed the inland path that Hundi had shown her. She would dig the roots of the hawkweed and heather, and return, drenched and freezing, stooping to the salt-struck wind, until finally she reached the stone that marked the causeway to Byrgisey. It had been raised by the earl in memory of his mother and stood facing Hundi's stone at the base of the islet. Her arms would ache with their burden. She would only glance at the ribbons of runes that covered the face of Audna's monument. She would hurry across, careless of waves splashing about her numb ankles, for there would be no place for her at the fire until she had soaked the roots and brought them to the shore.

If Thorstein himself happened to be at work on his ship, she would stand by, rigid with cold, to watch him pull the softened roots around cleats in the planks, then through holes for fastening. But usually she would steal off before she could be caught and sent out again.

She was given these miserable jobs because she had no mistress. Brusi's wife was too alarmed by her reappearance to tolerate her. She clothed Claudia; that was all. Claudia would not risk the loss of the hilt again and so wore her dungarees rolled up beneath her shift. She wouldn't stir without the bronze man tucked under her belt and hidden by the shapeless jumper that fell from her shoulders. Not that anyone paid much attention to her. Claudia was like one of those bordland dogs that was owned by no one, though occasionally noticed and fed.

Only Thorstein, with absent-minded kindness, and Dunlang, who seemed drawn by some compelling curiosity about her origin, ever bothered to talk with her. Once she felt bold enough to raise the subject of Nessa with Dunlang. He was squatting on his heels inside the Great Hall, at work on the straight blade of a new sword. When Claudia ventured to ask him how he would feel if Nessa stayed, he rubbed with the stone in long, even strokes along the blade and took his time before replying.

"She is not like the others," he said finally, using Aibhall's words.

"Would you feel that you owed her . . . anything?" Claudia was plucking bits of chaff from a pile of wool. It was hard to find the specks in the fleece with such poor light. "If she were alone?"

Dunlang shrugged irritably. "I suppose. Yes." Then he snapped, "But I cannot let a Pictish thrall determine my fate."

"What . . . ," answered Claudia faintly, "what will you let determine it?"

Dunlang rose. "You are sent to harry Sigurd like this. I have no connection with that Audna." Then he composed himself. "Who determines my fate? Not that old princess of Erin, your mistress. Not she. But others, those who commanded my earliest loyalty."

"Like Brian?"

"Yes."

"And Aibhall?"

"Leave Aibhall out of this," he flung at her. Driving his blade violently into its scabbard, he stalked away.

After weeks of loneliness, of jarring encounters with Dunlang and cryptic remarks from Thorstein, always in passing, she finally met Thorstein alone. She had been sent to fetch more oil for the lamps and found him packing oil-soaked reeds for the voyage. He greeted her there in the ill-lit shed, then seemed to pay no further attention to her, till suddenly, when she was completely off guard, he accosted her with a searching question about Audna's grave.

She was tempted to lead him on, to encourage him to believe that she was sent to bear witness for Audna. She understood that as long as Sigurd believed this to be true, she and Evan and Nessa were safe. But looking into the light blue eyes of the bony Icelander, she couldn't utter the embellishments to that lie.

"I don't really know why I'm here," she blurted. She was holding the vessel of whale oil. Some of the oil dribbled down the sides onto her hands. She set the vessel down, looking for something to wipe her hands on.

"Your mistress knew more than she said." Thorstein handed her a rag from his box. "I have long wondered."

Claudia gave back the rag.

"Do you know how Sigurd got the hilt from the monks?"

Claudia nodded, then answered with a small, "Yes."

"Though there was no killing, I have heard that it was taken by force." He leaned down to her. "Child, the monks have told me that it was returned to them in the keeping of a seal, which guided the coracle of the helpless monk to their shore. Did you know of this?"

"No," Claudia answered him. "I mean, it's probably a story to explain something that may have happened," she finished lamely.

Thorstein was searching her with those mild, light eyes. Now he dropped down onto his knee, creaking slightly, and told her, "But you know that Audna believed . . . believed herself to be like the mother of an ancient god of Erin."

Claudia shook her head. "Audna used to speak like that, but it was like a wish, to make herself believe." She stopped. She was on the wrong tack. Somehow she had lost the thread of Thorstein's query about the hilt and Audna. She said, "It isn't fair to expect me to understand."

Thorstein laughed. "Never mind understanding. Tell me of Audna's grave and where you have been with her."

Claudia shook her head. "I can't. It was dark. But you know she has the sunstone."

Thorstein nodded slowly. "I heard that it drew Sigurd to the rocks. I knew then that the hilt had been taken. Did not Audna understand it had to be a gift to grant the carrier its power?"

"She knew only what you told her," Claudia reminded him.

"And never mentioned the blade together with the man-hilt?"

Claudia started. It was the first time anyone but Audna had suggested a connection between the two. She didn't dare to look at him. "I don't think so. I mean," she stammered, "yes, she wanted Sigurd to have both. She made him promise to receive you well. . . ." She could feel Thorstein's eyes on her. She faltered.

"So you know," Thorstein said to her, "what I have long wondered." She felt his grip on her arm. Bony fingers clasped her chin and raised her face to his. "The hilt belongs to that blade and scabbard."

She was forced to look at him. She wanted to beg for time. She wanted him to promise that she wouldn't lose Evan or be lost to him. She wanted to beg for mercy. But she found herself pleading for Nessa, as she had with Dunlang, as if she knew that time was running out.

For a long moment he held her face tightly in one hand, her arm in the other. She felt in the grip of a skeleton, but his eyes were as soft as his hold was hard, and she could tell that they saw into her confusion. "Do you trust me?" he asked her.

She indicated that she did, but she trembled.

"Then I will share my secret with you. And then you will tell me all you know." He waited a moment, then began again. "I have not the blade and scabbard, but I know where they lie. It was my intent to return them to the grave of the dead champion from which they were stolen. But when I learned that Sigurd had the hilt—"

Claudia found that she could look at him again. She saw him struggle to put his thoughts into words.

"It came to me that Audna must have seen a connection between the blade and the monk's hilt and that I should not move rashly. Then it was taken."

"Stolen?"

He seemed to be musing. Then he roused himself. "Not long after I left Audna and Sigurd, I stayed awhile in Greenland. From there many set forth in search of land to the west. My ship was one of the few that made its landfall. The survivors wintered on a grassy coastland, but there were too many there. We had heard of sightings of forests thick with game on land farther west, but we had also heard that the skralings dealt slaughter on any who ventured beyond those shores."

"What are skralings?" Claudia asked.

"People who live by their wits and strength off that

wild land. Their ways were known to us, their arrows felt like their fierce intent. Alone, I had met with one or two, also alone, and discovered that for all their forest ways of stealth and cunning, they were men like myself. They had a look as dark and wild as that of the Pictish maid, but they would share a kill or a shelter from some storm with me, and I with them. So I thought. . . ." Thorstein shook his head as if to discount what he had thought.

"That you could live together?" Claudia supplied.

Thorstein nodded. "In a new place. Each to share what the other lacked. They with their forest skills, we with our knowledge of the seas. So did I begin, first with a tiny settlement, but returning afterward to Greenland to fill my ship with more who sought new lands to cultivate, new worlds." Thorstein stopped. When he resumed his account, all life seemed drained from his voice. "A flourishing little settlement. Every day some exchange with the skralings, whose chieftain met with me in trust. Then, soon after I had brought the new settlers, sickness descended like an evil cloud. Crippling and death rained down on us. First to fall were our women with child, then, like a mockery of all our sharing, so did those skraling women who carried unborn babies. Then the children. Running one moment, unmoving the next. Some would open their mouths like fledglings fallen from the nest, but could not swallow what was given them for nourishment, and so starved. Skralings and Northmen alike lost most of their children to this curse." Thorstein ran his hand across his face. "The skralings turned on us then."

"They blamed you? But how could they, when you were all going through the same thing?"

"They sought to drive us off our island and away from their coast. And their chieftain, who had been as a brother to me, drew back into the forest to plan each assault on our weakened people. I . . . I was helpless, myself struck down by the sickness. In my fever I raved much about the blade, for I could not help thinking that the ancient god of another people wreaked vengeance on those who had carried it so far from its appointed place. So at least did I convey this notion to my people, for they took the scabbard with its blade and offered it back to the spirits that had seized their children. I had some sense of their design and struggled to stop them. I begged to return it instead, but if they thought me right, they did not think that I would live to carry out my resolution."

Again Thorstein came to a halt. Then his voice grew firm, almost matter-of-fact. "The scabbard and hilt lie there still. The dead were placed within a cave at the bottom of our island cliff, and I was carried, senseless, to my ship. For days then we were lost in dense fogs, and I was lost to the world of light and reason. I could scarcely breathe or move or even swallow. Till finally my crow, left behind, found its way to our floundering ship. It brought hope to the despairing and bereaved. And on that same day the sun broke through, and I opened my eyes and raised my head and could recognize all that had been distant from me. And found that I could breathe once more. So. . . ." He gave a long sigh, as if expelling all that life-giving air that had filled his lungs at last. "So," he finished, "I have not the scabbard and blade, but I know where they lie." He hesitated, pondering what he could not easily articulate. "Only now I cannot tell whether I am to return the hilt to the monks or its blade and scabbard—if they are its blade and scabbard."

"Don't," she whispered. "Don't bring the scabbard back where Sigurd can get it."

"And Dunlang?"

"I don't know. How can I tell? Oh, why must you act as though you're in Audna's power?"

"I made her a promise in return for the safeguard of that monk."

"But that was long ago. She's dead."

"A promise is like memory. It may be buried, but it will not die. And look, she has sent your brother and the Pictish maid. And when we shipped them off, you in their stead. And all of this just now when Sitric's offer holds out to Sigurd the glory of which she dreamed. Can you question the power of that woman?"

"But you can't believe— I mean, aren't you a Christian? How can you believe all that?"

Thorstein smiled thinly. "I owe allegiance to the gentle Christ, but when I am swept by ocean storms or lost among the mountains of ice, it is often Thor and Odin I call on. I cannot help it. Does that seem strange?"

When she made no answer, he went on. "I never sail without my crow; for if I am lost, that bird will fly up and show me to land. The one I mentioned came to me out of the wooded depths of that island; it was as wild as the skralings and just as knowing of the elements. Even now, though it is old, it never fails to show me my way. Odin possessed not one but two ravens, whose names were Thought and Memory. I have given one of those names to my crow. Can you guess which?"

284

Thinking of Thorstein's thoughtfulness, she said, "Thought."

Thorstein shook his head. "It is Memory I chose, for what is thought without memory, or my belief without knowledge of that which my father and his father first believed? We do not blot out what we have been, even when we go forward with what we are becoming."

"But you don't believe that Audna is a sort of goddess, do you? I must say, you have a very flexible kind of belief."

"Have you seen where the planks of my ship are pulled back to cut away the rot?" Thorstein placed one hand above and overlapping the other. "So are the planks lashed one at a time to the ribs. A rigid ship would break up in the rips of the Pictland Firth and in the storms off Greenland and beyond. My ship is strong because it is flexible. It takes each blow and bends to the contour of the sea." Thorstein picked something off the floor and held it out to her.

"What is it?" She could see a small stone of the kind that was often hollowed into cooking pots. Two shapes were dug into the stone, one a hammer, the other a cross.

"It is the mold of a metalworker who has no time at present for casting charms to be worn, but is no doubt busy making mail shirts for the battle. See," Thorstein said with a smile, "he serves all. There is the cross of our Lord, and there beside it, Thor's hammer. He will do a brisk trade wherever he may be."

Thorstein's laughter made Claudia flinch, but she answered him. "When you spoke to Sigurd about your father's speech on the Hill of Laws, you didn't sound like that. You talked about peace and forgiveness." Suddenly she noticed a change in Thorstein's expression. Unable to imagaine what wrong thing she might have said, she plunged on. "You were talking about what you believed in. And when Dunlang—" Then she stopped. She realized that as far as Thorstein could tell, she had not been present when he had made those statements.

He was staring at her, not in fear, but with something like dread. "And when Dunlang . . . ," he prompted, his voice low and even.

Claudia covered her face with her hands and began to cry. "I don't know. I can't remember. It's not my fault. Please, please don't look at me that way. I want my brother. I want Nessa. I don't know what to do." She felt him take her grubby hands in his great bony fingers. She looked up.

He was shaking his head slowly, bewilderment and kindness together in his expression. "It may be that you are faultless. You are only a child. I am not clear about fault in children of your size. Among my people, a youth of twelve may bear the fault of a man my age. We will deal only with those things we can see together. It may have been wrong for me to attempt to see more deeply and further than I can, especially through the eyes of a child."

His tone said one thing, his words another. It made no sense at all that he was comforting her, yet speaking in terms she couldn't grasp. She rubbed her nose with her sleeve and seized the moment of sympathy. "Also, we have a crow too, and we can't leave without it."

Thorstein pretended to scowl. "You have the other crow of Odin?"

"Actually," said Claudia with a sniff, "Audna thought it belonged to her. Anyhow, she borrowed it. She called it Badb."

"Not Thought?"

Claudia blinked back tears and grinned. "No, not Thought."

"A pity. Our crows might have joined forces." He offered the rag for her nose.

She took the rag, nearly gagging on its rancid filth. "Our crow doesn't have a name," she told him. "I suppose I could call it Thought."

"Good," he exclaimed, releasing her at last. "I'll tell my Memory to keep a lookout for your Thought, and if the gods—I mean, if the good Lord wills, we will have the pair of them before too long."

TWENTY-NINE

THE broad moldshare used by the Orcadians for their early plowing left furrows that filled with water; the furrows gleamed like a craftsman's inlay, silver strips in the deep brown. Ewes brought down from the inland hills began to drop their lambs in the home fields. But the winds were still fierce, and sails were reinforced for the voyage to Erin.

Thorstein summoned Dunlang to him to ask whether the bard had been fitted for a vest of mail. Claudia, who had brought Dunlang at Thorstein's bidding, stood by while the two men faced each other.

"Warriors of Erin do not dress themselves in the viking fashion. Leather will suffice."

Thorstein said, "Then carry my shield." He sounded weary, though whether at the prospect of combat or with Dunlang's tiresome contempt, Claudia couldn't tell.

"What care have you for my life?" asked Dunlang in a tone that conveyed, What right have you to care?

Thorstein said, "You are yet young and well taught. The earl has the raven banner, and though it may bring victory to those before whom it is borne, you will not be among them."

Dunlang eyed him hostilely. "Why do you say that?"

"Because once we set foot on your native land, I will set you free to serve where your heart leads you."

Dunlang stared at him. "Does Sigurd know?"

"Sigurd cares for Sigurd," Thorstein answered. "He cannot imagine that you might make a difference on the battlefield."

Dunlang flushed. "I could make a great difference with my writing."

Thorstein said nothing.

"Listen, do you know why Sigurd spared those monks? You suppose, of course, that he fears being caught outside that faith. Oh, he may, but what he feared still more was me. You do not know that he took all the annals from the monastery at Eyin Helga and told the monks that their new history would come from me. And of course I was to witness his mercy, Icelander. I would record how he spared them. I would not send him through history with the violation of that holy sanctuary. There does my difference weigh."

"I have no doubt of it, Dunlang. But if you choose to go unprotected into battle against those who have been your masters and your benefactors, there will not be writing from you ever again."

Dunlang started to speak, then stopped himself. His voice was choked with misery and hatred. "You play with me."

Thorstein shook his head. "I have no time for play. What lies ahead is no game, bard, but a deadly struggle I barely understand. I am uncertain whether your poetry will honor that design, but—"

"It will honor truth," Dunlang blurted. "I have not learned the art of your skalds over all these years without absorbing the lore of their gods. I know that Odin is said to have stolen the word, which is the source of all poetry. And hanged himself in punishment from the tree of knowledge, sacrificed himself to himself for the theft of the runes and all their power."

"Are you Odin then?" asked Thorstein. "Do you possess his sight and insight?"

"All real poets possess that gift," Dunlang responded hotly. He gazed at Thorstein, as if he suspected him of irony.

Thorstein rubbed his chin, scratched through his thin white hair. He looked like a naked tree, twisted, riven by time. Dunlang was firm, bearing himself with assurance, his feet set slightly apart, his head held with pride. Thorstein's head jutted forward from outsized shoulders like one bent with age.

"Still," said Thorstein evenly, "it would be foolhardy to squander that gift in unnecessary sacrifice."

"What makes you stay with the old earl?" Dunlang demanded boldly.

"A promise."

"What makes you keep a promise?" Dunlang strained toward Thorstein. "Honor? If there is honor in the commitment of a crippled Icelander, why should there not be honor in the act of a bard of Erin?" Suddenly Dunlang seemed to notice Claudia. "He cannot answer that. It is because these men have the souls of thralls. Remember, he could not answer me on that."

Claudia wondered whether Dunlang regarded her as some kind of judge from the grave, or its messenger.

"Tell me, then," taunted Dunlang, "what binds you to that service for which you clearly have no heart?"

"I suppose," said Thorstein with slow deliberation, "it is that of which you spoke before, the thing that is at the source of what we are. It is the Word."

"Games," muttered Dunlang, striding off.

"All the same," Thorstein called after him, "you will have to weigh your life against the death of what you possess." He turned to Claudia. "When the time comes, you may take him my shield. I will not pursue him now. Like Sleipnir, he gallops full tilt toward the abyss. I only push him on." He let his hands drop heavily to his sides. "Have you fear of the crossing?"

His abrupt shift caught Claudia in the midst of her own reflections. She stared at him.

"We will make our landfall," he told her, but his tone conveyed something closer to regret than reassurance.

They left under a blustery sky that sharpened every rock along the shore. Miraculously Claudia wasn't sick. But many of the younger passengers, huddled together like livestock and each one setting off a reaction in the next, made steady use of the bailing buckets. Thorstein's men rowed two to an oar to keep the ship under absolute control through the rips and turbulence of the firth. Then Sigurd's ship appeared to alter its course; Thorstein conferred with his men and turned in after Sigurd toward the shore of Caithness.

Claudia wasn't sorry when they made their way into the protected water. Thorstein rowed off to Sigurd's ship. His men pulled up their oars, lolled in the sun, and teased the youngsters who had been sick. When a call came for some of Thorstein's special caulking, Claudia knew where the bag of woven hair and wool and stripped roots had been stowed, and then found herself being let down with the pouch into the rowing boat. She crouched low, bemused by the brilliance of the afternoon, the salt caking her hair around her face, the pitching sensation from the crossing still with her as she was rowed shoreward.

Sigurd's ship was still beached when darkness began to fall. First the sun blazed like an enormous shield of bronze. The shields along the slanted ship were suns too, each of them mirroring the sinking disk. Gold was reflected on skin and hair. Each man and woman seemed cast in precious metal. Even when the light had dimmed, the dull glow, like that from a flame, adhered to the faces and hands of the people on the beach.

The few women who had been brought in Sigurd's ship started fires and set up tripods from which cauldrons were soon hung. The fires replaced the sun, mottling each presence with an orange warmth. But in between spread great patches of fluid blackness. The moon had not yet risen. The stars, cold and distant, blinked at the sea of night.

The women gathering fuel were reluctant to travel far. Even the men stayed close to the fires, their voices fanned into gusts of laughter by Sigurd, who tramped from one boisterous group to another, until he paused to make fun of the silent Icelander.

"Thorstein is gloomy," yelped Sigurd. "He would wrap his oiled batting round hearts bursting like barley for the great encounter."

Thorstein stretched a tongue of caulking between the shrunken boards of the earl's ship. He seemed deaf to Sigurd's taunting.

Dunlang brushed past Claudia with a fresh torch for one of the carls lighting Thorstein's work. "It's true," muttered the bard. "The Icelander has no stomach for combat."

"Why should he?" Claudia shot back. "His leg—"

Thorstein glanced up and she fell silent. Whatever she said would only add to Dunlang's ridicule. She couldn't reconcile Dunlang's contempt for Thorstein with his railing against the callousness of kings and earls leading men to slaughter. It was as though the bard was divided by what he both loved and hated. For a moment she was tempted to confront him with his inconsistency. But he was beyond her, just as Evan had been at the forge, his laughter too quick, too bitter, and his eyes burning with a kind of rapture that made her afraid and cold.

A scream cut through the blustery voices. Then a

woman appeared, waving her meager sticks of firewood and shrieking hysterically. As Sigurd and Brusi and Hrafn and other hirdmen gathered around her, she gestured into the darkness, babbling and sobbing. Thorstein splashed out of the shallows and dragged himself up to the men, who stood irresolute, glancing where the woman pointed. Then he set down his tools and limped off into the night.

Claudia ducked around the others. She heard her own footsteps thudding on the beach, then muffled on the turf. She heard his lumbering tread. Then she couldn't hear him any more. She panicked, ran harder, and slammed full tilt into him.

"Oof," he said.

Claudia's ears hummed from the running and from the impact. "I was afraid—" she said, panting, meaning she was afraid of being left behind.

Thorstein thought she spoke of a different fear and took her hand as though she were a very small child.

She could only keep up with him by jogging at his side. His lurching pace kept yanking her, till quite suddenly he slowed, proceeding more cautiously toward a house that loomed in the darkness. There were no signs of life around this steading. She felt a wall, but the grass alongside was high and coarse, last summer's growth. No animals had trod this lane through the winter. None of the customary smells of a farmstead greeted her. She waded through more grass and weeds, and then they were at a single small window.

She could hear her own harsh breath. Thorstein made no sound at all. He looked in. He remained looking for a long time. She felt his grip on her hand harden. Then he leaned down to her. "Return to the beach. Bring Sigurd."

She was terrified of setting out through this night. She dreaded wading through the unused paths. The neglected walls seemed like a maze to her; they could send her off in the wrong direction. "I can't see," she whispered.

He turned her part way round. "Listen," he commanded.

Obeying, she heard the surf. It had been so much a part of her world that she hadn't realized it was there. "Then how will I get back here?"

"Bring Dunlang too. He listened to the woman. He heard the directions."

She started off slowly, carefully.

"Run," he called to her.

She broke into a trot, tracing her hands along the wall to remember how many turns to avoid when she came back.

Dunlang came to her first. "Thorstein?" He sounded gloating. Did he think Thorstein was in trouble?

"He sent me for you," she gasped. "And Sigurd."

It wasn't so easy returning. Twice she faltered, the second time nearly immobilized by Sigurd's wrathful impatience with her.

"If you have lost my second in command—" he intoned threateningly.

"He's not lost," she protested, close to tears. "We are."

But then Dunlang coolly reminded her that she might retrace her steps by orienting herself toward the sound of the surf.

She didn't know which was worse, Dunlang's indifference or Sigurd's rage. She imagined arriving at the wrong wall. She imagined leading them into some death trap, a ruin perhaps. She ran her hand along the wall. Some of the weeds were up to her chin. Sigurd kicked at something; Dunlang pushed past him. They were there.

Thorstein stepped aside without a word and Sigurd took his place at the window. He reeled, uttering a whispered curse. Dunlang started to look, but Sigurd thrust him back and returned to the window again. When he came away, he was muttering senseless phrases. Claudia heard, "No. Mother, no."

When Thorstein went to him, Dunlang and Claudia together took a turn. Claudia could barely see anything, even on tiptoe. She struggled to grab hold of the sill, reaching inside. Her hands slid back. She could grasp nothing, because the stone was slimy and cold, as if no fire had warmed that house for a long time.

Dunlang stared silently, then gave a hollow laugh and went to join the others. Claudia tried to find a niche in the wall for a toe hold. She clawed at the stone. Behind her the three men were having some kind of argument, but their tones were so hushed, she couldn't make out what they were saying. Finally Sigurd's voice broke through. "Ask the maid. She would know, for she comes from that place."

A moment later Thorstein was beside her. Quietly, easily, he held her up so that her legs hung straight down. She reached for the sill, but Thorstein pulled her away. "No," he whispered. "Touch nothing from that room. Only look."

At first she tried to tell herself that this was merely a weaving house, that the women at the enormous loom were as ordinary as those she had seen at Audna's loom.

But though they dressed in the usual manner and walked to and fro with their weaving, and though the huge frame that leaned against the inner wall seemed no different from those on which great cloaks and mantles were woven, nothing was the same, nothing ordinary. The weights that held the warp taut were not stones, but the heads of men. Both weft and warp appeared to be slimy. She could make out the heddle rods more easily, because their metallic outline glinted coldly and showed them to be spears. Each woman plied a shuttle and each shuttle was tipped with blood, dripping. But what held Claudia transfixed was the beater itself, gleaming at the hilt and dead black in the long straight blade. It was Sigurd's sword.

She lost all sense of time. She gazed at the weaving, the women stepping across the loom as she had seen so often in Audna's house. It was like a dance, a pair of women starting at each end and joining at the center, then crossing and plying the weft toward the opposite ends, while another pair of women commenced the pattern. In and out, crossing each other, meeting, joining, separating, they paused only to raise the beater which was Sigurd's sword. The warp weights, human heads, dangled at their ankles.

It was a while before Claudia became aware of their singing. Their voices were not hushed, but were caught inside the house and seemed to emanate from its airless essence. She couldn't make out any words nor anything remotely like a tune, but she knew that the weavers were chanting to the dance of their grisly loom. In matronly tread, they carried out their pattern, as if the stuff they wove was simply yarn, though the threads they unraveled before her eyes she knew finally to be the entrails of animals or men.

In the course of this dance of the loom, one of the women seemed to run short of intestines for her shuttle. Without interrupting the flow of the dance, she gestured commandingly toward a dark corner. Out of that corner stepped a servile figure with a skein-winding reel and what must have been fresh supplies for the weft. The slave was so dark and dressed so darkly that Claudia couldn't at first make out any features. Then, as the skein of intestines was handed over and as the bronze sword hilt flashed in the dim light, Claudia caught a glimpse of the face. It was Nessa's. Immediately the slave turned and disappeared into the corner darkness.

"Nessa," Claudia cried out. "Don't stay in there. Nessa, it's me." She felt Thorstein pull her away from the window. "No, no," she shouted, kicking and thrashing.

"Hush," he whispered. He set her down in the long weeds and held her.

"It's not Nessa," came Dunlang's mocking voice. "How can you think it's Nessa? No one could be more opposite. It was Aibhall at the loom. The whole thing's a joke."

Claudia strained to pull herself away. She had to free Nessa from that ghastly servitude. "Nessa," she tried to shout, and Thorstein's hand was clapped over her mouth.

"What is she talking about?" Sigurd demanded.

"She thinks," Dunlang told him with a laugh, "that Aibhall is Nessa."

"Aibhall?"

Dunlang turned to the earl. "As I have been trying to tell you, the weaver, the one who turned to look at me, is a Sidh maiden called Aibhall. You must have seen her, for she was the only one of the lot who was young and fair. Her hair is the color of corn at the harvest and her gown is not plain like the others, but mottled like the willows in first leaf."

"But there was no maiden—"

"Of course there was," Dunlang retorted, his voice rising. "Aibhall is responsible for this vision. She wishes to prevent me from going into battle." He laughed again. "She tried to frighten me with her song about the web of battle they weave."

Thorstein said, "Sigurd saw no maiden. The woman who chilled his blood was not young, not fair."

"I suppose," Dunlang shot back, "he also thinks it was the Pictish maid."

"It was the face of my mother," Sigurd declared with a shudder, "and yet not a face. She turned and looked at me. It was my mother in death." He moaned and sank onto the ground, a shapeless heap, his flesh aquiver, his will cowed by the vision he had seen. "My mother with a crimson weft, the warp bloodied." Slowly he raised his head until he was eying Claudia with dread. "That maid knows. She brought us to this place. She knows it was her mistress at the loom of war."

"It was Nessa," Claudia maintained in a small voice.

Thorstein said, "We have all seen the heads of the slain. We have seen the bowels that will be strewn across the field of war."

Sigurd heaved himself up. "I'll show you then. Come back to the window."

Dunlang pushed past Sigurd to get there first.

Thorstein made no move to follow them. After a moment he relaxed his grip on Claudia.

"What else did you see?" she asked.

They heard an exclamation from Sigurd, a laugh from Dunlang.

Thorstein spoke in a low voice. "I saw no face of Audna, no Sidh maiden, no Pictish thrall from the grave. I saw only what the Norns know will be, the blood of men and the weapons that will draw that blood."

"The weapons," Claudia repeated, thinking of the sword. Then she asked, "How can Norns know . . . all that?"

Thorstein studied her before answering flatly, "You must know. They are said to dwell near the springs of fate from which Odin drinks."

She would have asked more, but Dunlang and Thorstein were returning. The weaving house, they said, was empty now. Sigurd wondered how that could be possible, but Dunlang was not surprised. It was just like Aibhall to contrive that, in the hope that the wet black emptiness of that interior would be as unnerving as the vision she had delivered into it.

Sigurd kept shaking his head. "Keep that thrall maid away from me," he instructed Thorstein. "She might bring us to them again. Make her walk behind."

Thorstein dropped back with Claudia. She did her best to keep up with him, aware that he was trying to gauge his great dragging strides to her short ones. Twice he stumbled, righted himself, appeared surprised to find that he had still this small companion at his side.

Up ahead they could hear Sigurd muttering to himself

and Dunlang trying out phrases that seemed to echo the song of the weavers. "The war-woof weave we," he chanted, and repeated the line once again. "Death-dealing daggers, sorrow's sharp sword; wind we, wind swiftly our war-winning word." Suddenly Dunlang stopped. "There was death for all in that song." He turned about, facing Thorstein, who also came to a standstill. "For all who rule. Did you hear that too?"

"I saw the blood of the fallen," Thorstein answered. "I saw all the gruesome remains, but I did not recognize which head was which, nor did I know whose corpses spilled into that weaving."

Dunlang started to protest, to explain what he had meant. But something in Thorstein's bearing kept him from speaking. He turned back to the muttering earl and began walking toward the sound of the surf, which washed now in rising crescendo all along the coast.

Thirty

As they headed into the great crescent bay, Dunlang pointed to the bold cliff at its entrance. It was called Ben Edar by his people, though the Northmen knew it only as Hovud, or Headland. There beyond the ancient wall that tracked the edge of the mountain was the Hill of the Sidh, where Aibhall might be waiting, this very moment watching the red and white sail being furled, the anchor readied.

The ship rounded a little island that seemed set like an eye beneath the glowering brow of Ben Edar. Dunlang gripped Claudia's shoulder. "There," he told her, pointing, his voice low and tight, "there where the rivers meet is the Dubhlinn, the black pool of Ath Cliath."

Claudia looked southward at the river snaking its way in silver coils across a green plain. Farther still, a solid range of peaks stretched to the horizon.

"The river Dothra," Dunlang said, then turned her until she was facing the other, its broad peaty mouth full of the marsh through which it wallowed. "That one is the great river Liffe," he told her, "and there crossing it is the Slighe Cualann, the road from Tara that reaches all the way beyond the mountains to the coast."

Claudia heard his eagerness and pride. Her shoulder burned from the fierce grip of his hand. She thought of Evan and Nessa and wondered if anyone had brought word to them that she was here, waiting for her turn to disembark.

"The two of you," said Thorstein, as he gestured Claudia away from those being lowered into rowing boats, "are of a kind. There are things to be done before you may be reunited with your people. Also," he added, "some discretion will be needed if Dunlang is to reach his chosen place."

The harbor was teeming with all kinds of craft. Thorstein was gone a long time. Dunlang paced the ship. Claudia scanned what she could see of the fortified hill of Ath Cliath that rose from the marsh like the immense hull of a grounded ship. Buildings of timber and mud-packed basketry were crammed together inside the walls. Bridges and roadways showed here and there; they were

301

made of timbers bound together, and the carts bumping and rattling over them provided a percussive background to the clamor that was everywhere.

When Thorstein reappeared, he told Dunlang that the High King Brian and his men were camped on a greensward just north of the river Liffe. The Meathmen were separated from Brian's Munstermen by one plowed field. Thorstein had learned from Sitric that both armies had been harrying together, plundering all the way to Hovud.

"Then why are the Meathmen apart?" Dunlang wanted to know.

"There has been some kind of dispute between them," Thorstein told him. "While I was with Sitric, a messenger from his uncle, the Leinster king, arrived with advice to attack at once to take advantage of the rift."

"And will Sitric attack? Why do you not release me?"

"I waited because I couldn't tell what would follow. Now I know. There will be fighting on the morrow. Sigurd has agreed to that. Only Brian will not wield a sword nor break his fast, for that is the day on which our Lord was crucified."

"Treachery," whispered Dunlang.

Thorstein set his level gaze on the bard. "War," he answered. Then he turned to Claudia. "I have seen your brother and the Pictish maid but could not speak with them. I'll try to get you safely inside the ramparts before the fighting commences, but first I must deliver Dunlang over to the king he has chosen to defend. There is little time. Sigurd expects me." Thorstein sounded as though he had already dragged himself through a dozen battles.

As soon as night fell, he rowed them ashore. The bay

was still. The oars dipped soundlessly into the water. Lights flickered on anchored ships and inland where the armies camped. From many fires came the sound of clinking metal as last-minute repairs were hammered into shields and axes and coats of mail.

"I know my way," Dunlang insisted.

"I will go with you," Thorstein told him firmly. "If you are seen alone advancing toward the greensward, you will be killed." Thorstein handed Claudia ashore and said to her, "I cannot leave you, so you must come too. When we return, I'll see whether you and the others can remain inside Ath Cliath with Sitric's family."

Dunlang uttered a soft laugh. "I'd sooner face the battle to come than Sitric's mother."

"The two children have survived some months there. Do not alarm this maid, Dunlang. Nor make me regret more than I already do that I am sending you into . . . what was it? . . . a griffon's nest."

But Dunlang couldn't help rejoining, "Gormlath is more dangerous than any griffon."

They slogged through the sticky marshland. "Soon," Thorstein said to encourage Claudia, "we will begin to climb the ridge beyond Ath Cliath and the footing will be better."

"Then you will have only the hazelwood to contend with," Dunlang jibed. "In places it is impenetrable."

Thorstein hauled his useless leg from the sucking mire, staggered, and led the way in silence. When they drew near to Brian's camp, Thorstein made them move more cautiously under cover of the trees that rimmed the sward.

"I'll leave now," Dunlang declared.

Thorstein was deep in thought. He didn't seem to hear.

Then he stopped abruptly, shook his head, and whispered, "The children. Of course Gormlath was willing to keep those two. She would use them like swallows." He shook his head again. "I will not leave any more children to the schemes of men . . . and women." He looked at Dunlang and Claudia. "I'll go back."

"Good," Dunlang asserted. "There was no need to come so far with me."

"You will wait," Thorstein ordered, his tone suddenly hard as the blade he carried. "You will wait with this maid and see that no harm comes to her, else you will serve not the king you love, but only the scavengers of the field."

Claudia gasped.

Dunlang believed the threat. "How long?" he mumbled sullenly.

"I don't know," said Thorstein. "I don't know how I can bring them out of there. But you watch over this one till I'm back."

"I can't," whispered Dunlang, his words clotted with humiliation. "You would treat me like a woman to fend for this thrall maid when I am set to offer myself into battle for my king."

"Is it so great an indignity to watch over a child?"

"It is not why I am here."

"Then you are clear as to why you are here," Thorstein countered grimly. "I'm glad. I envy your certainty." He turned and disappeared into the thick wood below them.

At first Dunlang waited in lofty silence, ignoring Claudia entirely. But when nothing happened, when the sounds of preparation died out, lights were extinguished, and sleep seemed to descend on the encampment, Dunlang could not resist moving closer. "It's dark enough," he whispered to Claudia, yanking her after him. "I will find the tent of my king and of my foster brother Murchad."

"Thorstein said—"

"I will not reveal myself. I will only be readier." He stepped stealthily from tree to tree. He looked back from time to time, sometimes grabbing her and then shaking her off as soon as she was at his side.

The tents of Brian's men were cruder than Sigurd's and badly worn. Instead of elaborately carved posts and ridgepoles, most of them were supported by newly cut trees. The king's tent, though mud spattered and patched as the others, had some semblance of ragged grandeur. It was round and raised to a point from which a standard stood out stiffly, lighted from the lamp that burned inside.

Claudia thought Dunlang was about to forget Thorstein's warning, forget all caution, and fling himself at the feet of his beloved Brian. But just as the bard seemed ready to plunge forward, a figure from within appeared, turned back the flap, which cast a triangle of light onto the ground beside them, and Aibhall stood framed in that yellow triangle. She hesitated, then stepped sideways into the shadow of the tent. The flap dropped.

"Aibhall," Dunlang whispered, "I thought you would be inside the Hill of the Sidh."

"Hush," she cautioned, pulling Dunlang and Claudia into the shadow with her, for another figure darkened the filmed light and pulled back the tent flap. She pointed to the figure that slipped into the night. "He summons Murchad. St. Senan's monks came in a vision to Brian's chief warrior; they came singing psalms and chanting and demanding payment for what Brian still owed them for shedding blood on the holy island of Cathaigh. The warrior protested at their coming on the eve of battle, but the monks declared that they had to, for tomorrow would be too late."

"Is that what the monks said?" asked Dunlang.

"Yes."

"And then?"

"And then disappeared. The vision faded. Brian rejected this message. That is why I came." She held Dunlang with her soft gaze. "Since he had not heard the monks himself, nor seen them, there was room for doubt. And so I came and confirmed what they had told Brian's chief warrior."

Dunlang uttered a strangled sound, but no words came.

"Brian did not wish to hear me either," Aibhall went on. Her voice was cool and limpid like the still water of the bay. "I cannot be blamed for what I see. When I told him he would fall on the morrow, he asked me which of his sons would be king after him. So I told him it would be the son on whom he next set eyes. That is why he sent that fellow, who has just gone out, to fetch Murchad."

"I don't blame you," Dunlang told Aibhall, "but are you certain? I cannot help wondering how much you contrive in order to keep me from this danger you dread."

"Only this," she answered, removing her mantle, which was pale and delicate as the fine-veined hazel in new leaf. "I would have you dwell forever in my realm, where there is life without death, without aging and decay. But if you must press on to the side of those you love, at least wear the *feth fiada* so that you will not be seen by any mortal."

"How can I be safe when those by my side face danger?"

"You are their hope. Fall beside them, and all that might make their names live forever will be lost."

"But that isn't so," Dunlang argued. "I have written the epic already. Not the one for which I was stolen and trained. I have written of all contained in this struggle between Brian the Good and Sigurd the Stout and Sitric Silkenbeard of the Northmen."

"Have you?" said Aibhall. "Then you must know which men will fall."

Dunlang stiffened, started to retort, but was stopped by the sound of footsteps. A man entered the tent, a voice spoke.

"I heard you talking just now," said the voice, "and I thought I would stop by for instructions. Father, my men and I are ready for the battle. Shall we continue our forays out toward Ben Edar?"

There was a stirring, as of someone heaving himself up in bed. "Donnchad! You!" The voice speaking now was cracked and thin. "I do not care which you do," it snapped with petulance. "It was not you I sent for."

The man whirled to leave. At the same time another approached and met him at the entrance. .

"Well, brother," declared the newcomer, "did our father send for you as well?"

But the first one pushed past in silent anger and strode off. The newcomer entered the tent and was instantly berated for having taken so long to come.

Claudia heard his yawn. "I understood no urgency, father. I had to dress. And so, now that I am here, what do you wish?"

"It is Murchad," whispered Dunlang, his voice filled with delight. Then he realized the meaning of what he had witnessed. He grabbed Aibhall and shook her. "You knew," he charged. "Even when you told the king it would be the son on whom he next set eyes, you knew."

"I cannot be blamed for what I see," she retorted, tossing back her disheveled hair. Then she put her arms around him and drew him to her. "I cannot be blamed," she murmured, rocking him as he bent to her shoulder.

While Dunlang stood in her embrace, Murchad also left the tent. Then Dunlang broke away. "I will show myself to Brian. At least that will raise his spirits."

"You can't yet," Claudia burst out. "Anyhow," she went on, grasping at the first argument that came to her, "one more fighting man can't make that much difference to him any more than it does to Sigurd. Your value to Brian is as a poet," she told him. "Otherwise it will be Sitric's skald that tells what happened."

"You have sight, girl," Aibhall remarked with approval. She turned to Dunlang. "But you may look upon the king. Only wear the *feth fiada.*" She spread the mantle over his shoulders, and he became a shadow of the shadow in which they stood.

Claudia saw the tent flap fold back of its own accord. She peeked in. In a tangle of twisted covers lay a frail, white-haired man. She could see folds of skin around his eyes, the protruding belly showing under the night tunic. She stared, and then something like a gust of wind forced her backward into the shadow. Dunlang was with them again, the pale green mantle lying in a heap on the ground.

Dunlang shaded his eyes with his hand as though he had been blinded. "He's old," he whispered incredulously. "He's . . . just an old man."

Aibhall nodded. "It is what happens to all mortals who live long on this earth."

Dunlang muttered brief, perfect phrases about the fair, noble brow of the good King Brian, the bravest king ever known to Erin. Then he stopped and stared at the closed tent. "But he's so old," he repeated tonelessly. Slowly he turned back to Aibhall. "All during my captivity," he said brokenly, "I have looked forward to this moment. If my stay at Sitric's court had not been cut short, I would have managed to get to him. . . ."

Aibhall gazed at Dunlang with pleading eyes.

He turned on his heel. "Come along," he ordered, "or else there will be trouble from the crippled Icelander."

They met with Thorstein and Evan and Nessa in a thicket at the edge of the sward. Greetings had to be muted. But relief poured out of Evan in a flood of disjointed whisperings. He and Nessa had been watching the fires set by Brian's men. Everyone within the walls of Ath Cliath could see the burning of the strongholds high on Hovud.

"Not Hovud," Dunlang corrected. "Ben Edar."

"Anyway," Evan chattered on, "it was a sight. Like hundreds of bonfires. Claude, I couldn't believe it when Thorstein said you were here. I was watching the fires across the bay. . . ."

Thorstein conferred with Aibhall and Dunlang in a low voice, while Nessa looked at Dunlang, her gaze never wavering. Dunlang asked if he could go now, chafing when Thorstein detained him, incensed when Thorstein spoke once more of the three children, the thralls from Audna's grave.

Evan continued to jabber at Claudia. He wanted to know who Aibhall was, but didn't stop for an answer. He wanted to know how come Claudia was here, and did she have the . . . you know what? If only she'd been with him from the start, especially when Sitric's mother, Gormlath, met their returning ship in the bay and sent Sitric right off again. "Nothing from the Orcades was unloaded," Evan exclaimed, "not even us. She insisted he had to hurry and catch this viking named Brodir who was anchored off some island. She said Sitric had to have Brodir on his side against Brian. You should've seen Brodir. He has the longest and blackest hair, longer than—" Evan shot a look at Thorstein, and then stopped. They were all listening to him now.

"Speak on," said Thorstein, "only softly."

Evan's tale held them all spellbound. Sitric had won Brodir's allegiance as he had Sigurd's—with the pledge of Gormlath in marriage and the kingdom of Munster after Brian's defeat. Later, when Brodir arrived at Ath Cliath, he had described three terrible nights following that agreement. On the first night boiling blood had poured from the sky; he and his men had covered themselves with shields to keep from being scalded, but one man had died on each of his ships. The second night the men's weapons had jumped into the air over their heads, and again one man had died on each ship.

Evan was growing uncomfortable under the intensity of their listening. "Of course I didn't believe any of that stuff," he assured them. "Especially when Brodir told them that on the third night he and his men were attacked by ravens with beaks and claws of iron, and men died the same way. Brodir said these omens were the blood of battle and the crack of doom. Gormlath told him not to worry. She said that with Sitric and her brother the king of Leinster, with the Orcadian earl and, best of all, Brodir himself, they couldn't possibly lose."

Aibhall murmured, "The ravens were the gods that would drag the Northmen down into the pit of the ocean."

Evan turned to Dunlang. "And you were right about Gormlath. She was awful to Nessa. And she almost didn't let Thorstein take us away. We were lucky to have Brian's daughter on our side."

"Brian's daughter?" exclaimed Dunlang. "At Ath Cliath?"

"Yes, Sitric's wife," Thorstein supplied from where he now sat on a tree stump, his chin in his hand.

"But I was recently there," Dunlang argued. "She wasn't—"

"You were not long enough at Sitric's court," said Aibhall. "But did you not know that Brian makes alliances with the Northmen when it suits him? Once it was to his advantage to give his daughter in marriage to Sitric. And these thralls were fortunate indeed; for Brian's daughter is seldom with her husband."

Dunlang had the look of a cornered animal. "Brian was always determined to break the back of the foreigners in Erin."

Thorstein said dryly, "Perhaps you will write over what you have already seen fit to narrate."

"Oh, Dunlang," Aibhall begged in her sweetest tones,

311

"do not squander the poems that may yet be written on ugly, ignoble death."

"Noble," he retorted. "At least I will not desert Murchad in his last battle."

Thorstein shrugged. "It is time I returned to Sigurd. The day is nearly on us. I'm not cast in your glorious fire, Dunlang."

"But you will not abandon Sigurd," Dunlang answered with a sneer.

"I am still bound. Had I choice, I would shatter the illusion of Audna's vision and set him free from its fetters. Maybe, Dunlang, that is why I tried to free you."

"You have done that," Dunlang reminded him.

Thorstein's hand fell to Nessa's head. He pulled back her hair and turned her face to Dunlang. "She is truly like the seal, coursing an element all other animals have shunned. Free? Captive? Do you not wonder about this Pictish maid from the grave, who speaks through images on stone? Can you name the beasts she draws?" He let Nessa's hair drop over her shoulders. "What will happen to her?" Thorstein asked softly. "The battle will sweep all the way to the sea like a fire driven by two winds of death. Dunlang, what will happen to this Pictish maid? She will never be heard. She will utter no cry at all."

Dunlang shrugged as if to dislodge the image Thorstein forced him to consider.

"The seal," Evan blurted. "Dunlang, the swallow and the seal."

Claudia pushed her way to Dunlang and spoke to his back. "You told me you'd care for her."

Dunlang wheeled around, grabbed at Aibhall's mantle,

and threw it at Claudia. "Put that on her, then, on all of you. That will keep you through the battle."

Aibhall started forward, her eyes flashing. "You must share it with them. Only then will I allow them to remain in its protection."

"From one captivity to another?" Dunlang cried. He glared at Thorstein. "So you knew what you were speaking of."

Thorstein ignored him. "I will return for them when the battle is finished," he said to Aibhall. "If I live."

Aibhall nodded grimly. "It is not the prize I set out to win." She gestured the three children to draw close. She waved off Thorstein, who dragged himself from tree to tree and was soon lost to sight.

Dunlang started to laugh. "So Gormlath will watch the slaughter from within the stout walls of Ath Cliath as her two intended husbands go to their deaths for her sake. She draws them in," Dunlang continued, his laughter breaking off. "All, on every side, to her very nest."

The sky grew pale and was without color. Northward in the distance Ben Edar loomed like an island pinnacle.

Brian's army marched down into the lowland, crossed a river, and pushed out onto a wide, grassy plain. Claudia, under cover of Aibhall's mantle, saw every kind of man and boy, and women as well, trudging earnestly after the leaders. She saw tall vikings with black hair and white skin, blond giants, red-headed folk like Dunlang, and even some of the small darker people whose ancestors may have been the same as Nessa's. Each went forward without complaint, though they grumbled about other things and spoke readily enough of the holes in their leather shoes,

the flies that assaulted them here at the marsh, the belly-
aches that came from being rushed through their meal or
from having had no decent meal at all for many days.

On they went, while down on the central lowland the
enemy forces gathered under the softly tinted sky. Claudia
could see a splendid line of warriors amassed. At their
center, amid banners of every shape and color, Sigurd's
black raven soared on outstretched wings.

Thirty-one

Aibhall argued that Dunlang could not fight under the
feth fiada without drawing the children of Audna into the
thick of the battle.

"Then let me go," he shouted at her.

"You choose the cause of Brian, who is too infirm to
join in combat and will spend the day in the tent they
have raised for him. See?" She pointed to the edge of the
wood where Brian's banner hung limp in the airless
morning.

"Brian stays from the battle because he will not defame
this holy day."

"You saw for yourself what he is," Aibhall charged.

Dunlang said, "I was not expecting. . . . Of course he is
old, and age may erode the spirit as well as the body. But
Murchad is still my foster brother, and I will stand beside
him."

"Stand or fall?"

"It is the standing that counts."

Now Aibhall chose a different, desperate tack. "Is it possible that you choose to stand and fall in this cause so that you need not face the truth that this is no clear struggle between good and evil or even between the men of Erin and the Northmen?" Her arm swept the wide plain below them. "There are Northmen who will fight with Brian's army; there are men of Erin, like the Leinstermen, who will face them on the battlefield of Clontarf."

Dunlang followed the sweep of Aibhall's arm and only muttered, "What a view will Gormlath have." Then he turned. "So will you from this place. Release me for a while. The children will be safe enough, and I will wear the *feth fiada*."

"And return to us?"

"Aibhall, the tide is high. In the hours to come the waters will recede and leave in their wake the great sands. I don't think the combat will end before the tide has drained that battlefield. I will come to you with the returning tide."

Already the Northmen marched across the bridge that spanned the tidal river. They spread out once again in battle formation, a wall of shields turned from the sea. Some stragglers were leaping from boats. Splashing, laughing, they waded ashore. The rowing boats returned to the ships, and the ships returned to deeper water where they would not be caught on the falling tide. Weapons and mail shirts glinted somberly at the edge of the gray water.

While the forces from Ath Cliath advanced inland, the different segments of Brian's army spread out to meet them. The men formed a solid line that had the look of a living breakwater thrown up to stop a surging tide that threatened to flood the entire land.

Only Aibhall knew where Dunlang had gone. The children had to guess which was Murchad's section by watching Aibhall. She stood rapt, unable to turn away from the spectacle of slaughter already begun.

Washed by the shrinking tide, the battleground unrolled like an enormous carpet. Aibhall told them it was named Clontarf, the bull's meadow, for the way the surf roared when the sand bar was exposed at low water. Even on a quiet day the sea would surge against the shifting barricade, churning sand and water, though now the bellowing of the bull would not be heard until the screams and howling of the battle were done.

Claudia and Evan kept track of Sigurd's banner. They were too far off to recognize individuals, especially when men encountered other men at every hand. Claudia wondered how they could tell which was friend and which was foe. Once or twice she thought she saw Sigurd's mighty bulk, but every time she tried to point him out to Evan, the earl was caught in a knot of fighting men and lost to view.

Twice during the long morning they saw the raven banner fall and disappear briefly into the fray. But each time, within minutes, it was raised and carried high above the heads of warriors, sometimes landward, sometimes seaward, over the reddening sands of Clontarf.

Impatient, Aibhall decided to take them down as far as the well; that way, sooner or later they would catch a glimpse of Dunlang. Evan didn't want to go any closer to the fighting. "Then stay," Aibhall told him, her eyes flashing. "I did not ask for your company."

Claudia preferred to be with Aibhall at the well than alone in a no-man's-land between the enemy forces. But she knew how the reluctant Evan felt. As they followed Aibhall along one rough pathway after another until they had skirted Thor's Wood, the sounds of the battle seemed to come from every side. Sheltered by the trees, they saw only those wounded who had the strength to drag themselves inland.

The well was on a rising slope back from the battleground. Warriors craving clean water pressed around it. Guards drove off the mangled and bleeding. Occasionally one of them would pour a bucket over a wounded warrior, but usually they cast them off with brutal urgency. The children saw one guard pull his sword on a man whose face was smeared with blood and vomit. The man stumbled blindly, persistently, toward the smell of water. "Back," warned the guard. "Away." He slapped the warrior with the flat of his sword and sent him reeling backward down the hill.

"Why? How . . . ," spluttered Evan. "How could he?"

"They must keep the well pure," Aibhall retorted. "If the water runs red, it will be over."

When Murchad approached, the guards drew up a whole bucketful of water for him. While he slaked his thirst and sloshed his face, the well guards reported to him the progress and condition of other segments of the army.

Dunlang appeared just after Murchad had returned to the battle. Aibhall, who could see him, called softly from behind the tall furze where she and the children stood waiting. He slung the *feth fiada* over his arm and dropped down beside them. His color was high, his orange curls wild, his eyes feverish.

"I have slain many." He wiped the dribble of water from his chin. "It's hard. Some have deserted us. Murchad has sent for Donnchad, who was leading a force into Leinster. Every man is needed right here."

"You said you would return to me with the incoming tide. You cannot keep Murchad from his fate."

"I'm accomplishing much, I tell you. We will drive all the way to the walls of Ath Cliath, where Sitric stands to defend that fortress with only a handful of men. Word has come to us that Brian's daughter mocks him now that we are pushing the Northmen to the sea."

"You push, and they push, and men are falling on every side. You would all be heroes. Oh, Dunlang, resist the mortal lure. Stay now. Even the High King will not fight."

"Since the tide was full this morning Brian has been on his knees in prayer," said Dunlang. "They have surrounded him with a wall of shields to keep him from harm." Dunlang's voice shook. "Can harm come to him while he prays?"

"That depends," said Aibhall shortly, "on what you believe harm to be."

"Well, it makes me hate this mantle of invisibility," Dunlang blurted.

Claudia couldn't bear Nessa's mute witness to this outburst. "Can't you see," she whispered, "he isn't worth. . . ."

Nessa turned her anguished gaze on Claudia.

318

Claudia plunged on. "He believes in all that junk, Nessa, in all those stupid things even Sigurd, way down, must know are pointless. He—" She could never explain what she meant, how Dunlang seemed to love, not Brian, but his notion of what Brian was. Even Dunlang's loyalty to Murchad was part of that notion, while Nessa, silent and bereft, merely put him on edge.

"Why do you make it worse?" Evan demanded.

Claudia tried to shake off tears of anger and hurt. "He drags everyone down with him."

"He's fighting for Murchad," Evan countered. "For his king."

"It's stupid. It's all stupid," was all she could reply. How could anyone make sense in all this chaos? She was engulfed by the shouts and cries of killers and their dying, by the stench of countless mutilations. For a long time she sat huddled, her face squashed against her knees, unable to blot out the sickening awareness of the slaughter.

When Murchad next returned to the well, Claudia looked up. The guards had fallen or fled. Murchad staggered past warriors who informed him that the well had failed. He pushed on, gasping, his tunic rent, part of his leathern vest gashed and caked with blood. Dunlang sprang toward him.

"No," whispered Aibhall. "Only with the *feth fiada*." She cast it over him.

Murchad leaned, then sank to the stones that banked the well. The wooden bucket lay unused. He rested a moment, then, groaning, drew some water. He sat staring at it for a while. Then slowly he poured it onto the ground. All the warriors who stood about, unready to return to battle, watched in dread as the murky red water spilled out at Murchad's feet. He said dully, "The bottom of the well is at the top. The source is overturned." Groaning again, he staggered to his feet. "I knew. There was a change this last hour. Until then I had felt a presence beside me. Now I am alone."

Instantly Dunlang was with him, supporting him. The leafy mantle floated down at the feet of the children and Aibhall, snagged on the spiny bush.

Dazed, Murchad stared. "Dunlang? Dunlang, is it you?"

"It is," declared Dunlang with joy, "and has been since the fighting started. Till this last hour."

"You beside me?" Murchad managed a pained, lopsided grin.

As soon as they set off together toward the battle, Nessa darted after them. Aibhall caught her, then beckoned the others. "One dying gesture is enough," Aibhall told Nessa. "Besides," she added, covering the three of them with the *feth fiada*, "I will not have Dunlang's final hours filled with the image of a Pictish slave."

The ranks were thinning, the fighting more desperate and frenzied. Aibhall led them in and out of battles to which Claudia had to stop her ears and close her eyes. Stumbling sometimes, she would be forced to look around to gain her bearings, only to catch sight of a slashing sword or an ax falling onto a tangle of bodies. She couldn't bear to look down, because it was human slime on which she kept slipping.

Once they had to pause while Evan was sick. Claudia couldn't bring herself to go to him. It was Nessa who held him doubled over, Nessa in whom not a trace of the child companion remained, Nessa like a mother, her dark

320

fingers shadow bars against his blanched skin. When he finally straightened, Aibhall, with a look of revulsion on her lovely face, yanked Claudia and Nessa along once more, leaving Nessa to cope with Evan whatever way she could manage with one arm tightly held.

After a while Aibhall stopped short. Claudia opened her eyes on a small force of Northmen regrouping and bearing down on Murchad's diminished band. A wall of shields faced them, not the burnished disks of the long-ships, but stout and solid wood. There was something more awful in their workmanlike simplicity than in all the decorations that showed beneath the gore on swords and axes which flashed in every direction, even hacking at the fallen. Claudia's eye was caught by the glint of one of those axes descending in a mighty arc. A hand appeared behind the wall of shields, a powerful hand that seemed to seek the axhead, as if to thrust it back. Nessa pivoted, facing Evan, so that she blocked his view. But Claudia watched the axhead rise and fall and rise once more, until the hand came free, just a hand and some wrist along with something trailing like a whitish tail. The ax was so deeply embedded in the grasp of the hand that it seemed amazing when the fingers opened and let go.

Claudia managed a kind of half blindness. Her dry mouth was putrid with the reek of bodies and pulp. She couldn't make a sound.

"Look," came Aibhall's sharp command. Claudia felt her face being snatched and turned toward the blurred forms along the wall of shields. The wall had caved in.

She focused where Aibhall directed and saw the banner above the Northmen waver and begin to fall. The black raven edged in gold plunged behind the wall of shields.

"That was my sling," came the laughing shout of Dunlang, "that felled Sigurd's banner bearer."

"Thorstein," roared the voice of Sigurd. "Where is Thorstein son of Hall of Side?"

"I am with you," they heard.

Sigurd's voice rolled forth again. "Thorstein, bear the banner for me. I will take the king's son."

Claudia yelled, "No, Thorstein, no," but no sound came from her. She was drawn back with Evan into Aibhall's clutches just as Nessa slipped free and disappeared through a break in the shield wall.

A voice shouted from Sigurd's ranks. "Take it not, Thorstein. All who bear that raven get their death."

"Hrafn the Red," bawled Sigurd, "you bear it then."

"Bear it yourself," declared the voice that had warned Thorstein. "It is your war devil that brought us here."

"I cannot . . . cannot raise it," Sigurd gasped. "Help me."

Claudia couldn't see what was happening. She only knew that Murchad's men were pushing the remnants of the wall into the sea even while Sigurd floundered, struggling to raise the banner his mother had made for him. She could hear wood splintering. Someone screamed and was suddenly silent.

"No, Sigurd," came Thorstein's voice.

"Yes. It is fitting. Help me."

Then the raven, hideously mutilated, flapped upward as though a current of air had seized it. Its dangling claws raked the sky. Then it lurched forward and was aloft.

At this moment Murchad and his men penetrated what remained of the wall of shields.

"Oh, look," shouted Evan.

Murchad's men turned to see a tall viking dash past them toward Thor's Wood; his tangled hair, black and shiny, was partly caught in his belt; the rest of it streamed behind.

Evan clutched at the *feth fiada*. "It's Brodir." But the viking was already out of sight.

Claudia stared at the banner that dipped suddenly when Murchad drove his sword into the falling earl. Black wings flailed. The dying sun, a clot of red over the bay, stained the metallic threads that edged the plumage. The raven's beak was wrenched in a piercing scream. As the attackers thrust the Northmen deeper into the bay, Sigurd was left lying at the edge of the water, a shred of black with threads of gold still grasped in his fingers. Overhead the screeching raven, devoid of golden outline, plummeted toward Aibhall and the children.

Still in Aibhall's grip, Evan held out both his arms to the bird, which landed with a thud and a squawk right through the mantle.

Some of the retreating Northmen struck out for the anchored ships, but the tide had risen swiftly and water covered most of what had been battleground hours before. The warriors of Brian's army had every advantage. They splashed from one Northman to another, each viking hopelessly trapped by his heavy vest of mail. Claudia could see Murchad gleefully pursuing them, his sword cutting right and left. She caught a glimpse of Dunlang, laughing, still at the side of his foster brother, wading in blood, dealing his blows wherever a floundering Northman showed life.

"Look to the Pictish maid," called Thorstein.

Startled, Claudia realized that he was speaking to Aibhall, who held the mantle of invisibility over Claudia and Evan while she herself was revealed. Thorstein was supporting the head of the dying earl.

"I will not," the Sidh maiden retorted. "I'll not step in that fouled bay."

"Sword," whispered Sigurd. His voice, high and hollow and air-bound, was barely audible. He struggled to speak, and Claudia heard a kind of fluting wheeze.

Thorstein bent over him, listened, and then said, "You may be buried with the blade you had fashioned. It has the runes you set upon it. But the hilt belongs to Eyin Helga."

Sigurd whispered something else, and when Thorstein nodded, the earl seemed to fall into deep contemplation.

Claudia heard Evan giggle. "Sigurd's whistling," Evan told her. "Why's he doing that?"

Claudia's mouth was too parched to utter anything. She shook her head.

All around them the embattled armies sloshed through water clogged with corpses. Unarmed men, suddenly spent, came to a standstill and dropped without a word.

"Thorstein?" Sigurd sounded as though he were calling from far away. "I was baptized once. Maybe. . . ."

"Whistling," Evan insisted, his voice rising, convulsed.

Claudia moved her tongue to her lips, found them wet, tasted the clean salt of her tears. Her voice came unstuck. "Shut up," she rasped at Evan.

"There are no grave goods at a Christian burial," Thorstein was explaining to Sigurd. "Not even swords. But if you wish to be carried to the monks. . . ."

Sigurd shook his head. "Cannot . . . cannot tell." He

324

opened his eyes wide, as if just waking. "Fancy you with your shriveled leg and me . . . in . . . prime. . . ." His mouth drooped and a long whistling sigh issued from it.

Evan's giggling was out of control. He staggered wildly until Aibhall slapped him silent.

A cry broke out from the wooded place where Brian prayed in his tent. A youth came running. "Killed," he screamed. Brodir pursued the youth, his dripping ax upraised in both his hands. "Yes," he proclaimed, gaining on the boy, "and henceforth let man tell man that Brodir felled Brian the High King." Before he had finished speaking, the wounded, armed only with branches, had dragged themselves into a circle around him. He tried hacking away at this motley band. He laughed at them. "I nearly missed your king. I couldn't believe that shabby old man on his knees was not a penitential monk. Where was his guard?"

"The guard left to hunt the Northern wolves," replied one man hoarsely. He coughed and faltered. "We will finish off this last one."

The wounded and dying were closing in on Brodir of the black hair. Slowly, step by step, they forced him back toward the darkness of the trees. When his screams issued from the Wood of Thor, Sigurd grew rigid as if he had uttered the cry in his own agony. And when the screams died away, the huge body of the earl was still.

Thorstein drew Sigurd's sword across his knee. "He would have had me carry him with the hilt to Eyin Helga," he said in a low voice.

Aibhall smiled grimly. "A sudden faith."

Thorstein shook his head. "He was caught between two faiths; he himself had not enough for either." Thorstein

325

pressed down, pressed harder still, and suddenly, with a sharp snap, the blade and hilt were parted.

Claudia's hand flew to the hilt concealed beneath her jumper; she drew it out. Under cover of Aibhall's mantle, she gazed at each hilt in turn, the bright bronze in Thorstein's hands, the dull encrusted metal in her own.

Thorstein glanced up at Aibhall. Hurriedly, guiltily, Claudia returned the hilt to her dungarees. "Look to the children," Thorstein said to Aibhall.

"Why leave them to me? I owe them nothing."

"They kept your bard when he might have perished. Look to them, Aibhall." Suddenly he broke off and gestured her away. Aibhall retreated under the mantle just as the wounded and dying avengers of Brian's murderer came down to deal with this last Northman kneeling in the blood-soaked sand. By the time they reached him, Thorstein had concealed the hilt and was tightening the thong lacings around his leather bootlet.

"Why don't you flee like the others?" asked the hoarse warrior.

"I cannot run." Thorstein thrust his leg out and lurched upright. "Besides, I could not reach my home. For though I come from Iceland, my place of rest lies far to the west."

The pursuers looked at each other. Their spokesman shook his head in astonishment. Then he shrugged. "Oh. You may as well go in peace." As they turned away from Thorstein, the wounded Murchad was borne out of the bay and carried toward the wood.

"Fetch Dunlang," Claudia heard Murchad command weakly as he was carried past. "He was caught on the flooding sand bar. Fighting so fiercely, he failed to note the tide and was swept with the Northmen to the fish weir at the river mouth. Find him."

But it was Nessa, not Murchad's men, who retrieved Dunlang's drowned body. She dragged it face down to the edge of the beach, then squatted there as if she might watch over him forever. Bits of netting clung to his arms and swathed his upper body. His hair was dulled by the water and debris, by the fishnet trapping his head. Nessa picked at this shroud of woven horsehair as she might have picked at wool for carding. Her eyes were liquid brown, but no tears fell.

Aibhall muttered bitterly, "So he has returned with the tide. One promise kept." Abruptly, harshly, she addressed Thorstein. "I will not touch that blood-drenched Pict, but will get the other two on your ship. I'll set them aboard covered by the *feth fiada* so they will come to no harm till you sail." She stared down at the dead bard. "And I will leave the body of my love to the fishes."

"I'll have a slab raised for him. At Kincora where he longed to be."

Aibhall sighed. "A stone, yes."

Thorstein stopped the man who had spared him and inquired about a stone, a cross-shaped stone, for Dunlang. The man was amazed that this crippled Icelander who had fought with Sigurd the Stout should wish to raise a slab for a bard who had fought beside Murchad, son of the High King. Thorstein was quietly insistent. Claudia saw him count out pieces of silver from his pouch. Then he limped over to Nessa and told her he was taking her, with the hilt, to the monks on Eyin Helga. Nessa tried to spring away from him, but he reached out with his long arm and caught her easily. She struggled briefly, straining

327

toward Aibhall and the children, and then went still. He led her by the hand just as he had once done with Claudia.

The man with whom he had left the order called after Thorstein, but his shout was drowned in the flood of the dying. "What name did he say?" he wondered to himself.

"It was Dunlang the bard," his companion supplied.

"No, I mean the Icelander."

"Oh, Thorstein, I think," said the other.

"Yes, that's it. Or was it Thorgrim?" Puzzled, he concluded, "I'll tell the carver to write: 'Thorgrim raised this cross,' in runes, for that is the way of these foreigners, and then, since he was overgenerous with the silver, I'll have the carver add, 'A blessing on Thorgrim,' in proper oghams."

"Thorstein, I think it was," corrected his friend.

"Oh yes. I hope I remember."

"And he won't, of course," muttered Aibhall, as she hauled the children after her and kept them going at a brisk pace. "That Icelander could not get his intent carried out decisively if his life depended on it. He's that kind."

"But it's all written down in Dunlang's epic," Claudia reminded her.

"We won't speak of Dunlang any more," Aibhall retorted. "And leave the crow, boy. It has no place in the mound."

Evan clutched the crow. "We brought him and we're leaving with him," he declared. "Besides, we're not going to any mound. We're going with Thorstein."

Aibhall strode on in silence.

Thirty-two

Claudia was beginning to wonder why Aibhall was leading them so far. She was about to question her, when Evan asked suddenly, "Who won the battle?"

"That depends," snapped Aibhall, "on which verses you chant or which song you sing. Or, if you are one of the newer kind, which writing you read. That is," she added after a moment, "if there are any writings left after the slaughter."

"But who really did win?" Evan persisted.

"Look around," Aibhall told him. They were trudging along a winding path that seemed to climb toward the summit of Ben Edar. Aibhall pointed back toward the Wood of Thor, where daylight had already departed from the trees. A long stream of torches lit the path along which Brian's body and his fallen son were borne.

Next Aibhall pointed to the scourged sands and swales of Clontarf. There the dying light was still reflected from the bay. Everything was tinged with red. Sitric's banner fluttered from the ramparts of Ath Cliath, while far below, caught in the swollen bay, thousands of dead men sank or floated or were dragged out by survivors. It was like looking down at night and day all at the same time.

"Some might say the living are the winners," Aibhall said. "Others will weep and envy those who met their glorious death on the sands of Clontarf. Sitric did not

329

enter the battle at all. He still rules over Ath Cliath, though he is ringed by the armies of the High King." She gestured, as though counting off the candidates on her fingers. "Can he be called victor? Brian perhaps, since his armies drove the Northmen to the sea." One more finger down. "Even," she added, "if he too stayed from combat and was hewn like a rooted tree. Consider Sigurd then, who died by the enchantment that made him strong." Another finger marked the tally. "Or Thorstein, who went unwillingly into that slaughter and was overlooked by death. Has he the bearing of a victor?" She laughed. "Will that clumsy remnant of a man stand out in the annals of heroes or compose an epic to commemorate their valor?"

Claudia listened to Aibhall's mirthless laughter and gazed down from Ben Edar at the aftermath of the battle. Some of the graceful ships of war were already underway. Then she saw Thorstein's ship. She shouted, "He's forgotten. He's not waiting for us. Evan, isn't that Thorstein's ship?"

Evan rushed to her side. The ship was tacking slowly out of the harbor, no oarsmen visible. Most of the men she could see inside were lying inert or braced against the rowing benches. Thorstein could barely bring the ship about. There were few to assist him with the awkward tacking boom. In the light airs the ship staggered and limped like one of the wounded. Mostly it was the ebbing tide that carried it on its wavering course toward the open sea.

"Hey," cried Evan. "Wait for us." He turned to Aibhall. "Make him wait. What are we doing here anyway?"

Claudia didn't dare take her eyes off Thorstein's ship,

but she heard Aibhall reply with chilling calm, "He will not wait. He was in haste and bent on picking the wounded from the bay. He is ever trusting. He believes you are there with him beneath the *feth fiada*. When he calls for you, it will be too late."

Claudia froze. Hating Aibhall, she could only agree with her and be furious with Thorstein into the bargain. He spent his life repeating his errors of trust, giving everything away. First with the hilt. Again, before Audna, with the monk. Over and over he trusted, bared his heart's secrets, and always with regret. It wasn't fair. Now she and Evan would be the victims of his foolish trust. Afterward he would blame himself and grieve, but what good would that do them?

"Why?" demanded Evan. "Why are you doing this?" Then panic seized him and he began to call, first to Thorstein, finally, his voice shrill and desperate, to Nessa.

Aibhall made no attempt to raise her voice above his. She merely stated flatly, "For the hilt your sister carries and will carry into the Hill of the Sidh. It belongs to us."

Claudia's heart sank. That impulsive moment when she had looked at it. Safe from Thorstein's eyes, she hadn't given a thought to the Sidh maiden. "Evan," she snapped, "shut up. We have to think." How would they return if they were forced to give up the bronze man?

Evan had yelled himself hoarse. He jumped up and down, waving frantically at the boat.

"And stop all that dancing," Aibhall told him as if she were on Claudia's side. "It is irritating. Besides, no one will see you. No one would suspect or search—"

But Claudia suddenly changed her mind. "Yes, call. Go ahead." For Aibhall, with all her superior powers, had failed to note that Nessa had proved once before that she could see through Aibhall's cloak of invisibility. Not suspecting? Not searching? Claudia saw again the way Nessa had darted toward them on the sand. She had seen. She had probably fathomed Aibhall's evil intent. "Oh, why were we so stupid?" Claudia wondered out loud, and heard Aibhall's exultant laugh.

"Nessa." Evan cupped his hands over his mouth and shouted the name over and over again.

Claudia waited for a sign that Nessa had heard. They never saw her. What they saw was a tiny splash beside the ship, a black dot poking up like the head of a seal looking for its landward bearings. Then the dot disappeared.

"You should not have done that," Aibhall complained. "I'm not taking you to a very roomy grave. Only one king is buried there, and it will be hard enough cramming you in. He is from an older time when burial chambers were not so spacious as your Audna's."

The children were rooted there, staring into the metallic bay. They couldn't judge the distance from their height. They couldn't guess where to set their eyes. Then the dark spot, bigger now, appeared close to the offshore rocks. At least Claudia thought it was Nessa's head that showed; it was ringed with a torc of silver water.

Evan shook his head. "It's just a rock. It's still there. See?"

Then it was gone, the gray water slopping over what he believed to be a weed-covered boulder. Claudia pressed her hands to her eyes and looked once more. The rock was really gone. She knew it was Nessa.

Aibhall said, "That fool Thorstein is trying to go after her. He'll sink them all if he ventures near the rocks."

Claudia shifted her gaze and saw that Thorstein had altered his course. He would be risking the lives of all those wounded if he turned there with the wind pushing him onshore. She clapped her hands to her mouth, a pointless gesture since Thorstein would never hear across the water as Nessa had. All Claudia could think of was that time in the shed when he had asked her if she trusted him and then confided in her.

"Where is she?" Evan moaned. "I can't find her any more."

Aibhall said, "He wears his good intentions like one in chains of his own forging. No wonder they could not be bothered with killing him. Never have I known so weak a man."

Claudia wheeled on her. "You don't even know him. You can't imagine what he thinks." She was ranting at herself, at her own abandonment of trust. In that first moment of panic she had turned on the one person who cared about the children of Audna as children.

Aibhall declared tightly, "Dunlang at least seized glory."

"That's not the way you talked when you were trying to get him to quit," Claudia retorted. She saw Thorstein leave the tiller and limp toward the tacking boom. He stumbled, probably over the legs of the wounded, and pitched forward, disappearing from view. Before she could catch sight of him again, the boat had turned some more and was wallowing close to the froth-fringed rocks under the cliff.

"He will change his course," Aibhall told Claudia.

"He must keep his vessel clear of this headland. The rocks should warn him of the greater hazard, for the death of a king is a time when creatures may pass to and from the spirit world. He would do well to heed the warning of those rocks."

"I think I see her," Evan shouted. "There, Claude. There by that sort of island."

"That's a seal among the rocks," Aibhall told him. "Now you will have to leave your Pictish sister to her fate. It is time we completed our journey. I care not for the Icelander's course."

Thorstein seemed to be setting the ship onto the wind again. The tide held him off from the rocks he skirted. He ducked out of sight and moments later reappeared to fling something high above his head.

"It's his crow," Claudia murmured, excitement buried deep within the wonder that filled her. Then she felt the *feth fiada* sweep her and Evan into its folds.

"I knew I didn't want any crow along," Aibhall grumbled.

The crow in Evan's arms objected to being covered again and squawked with indignation.

Claudia and Evan could only gaze out toward the thing that dipped once toward the waves and then climbed the air currents until it was level with them. High above the bay it took its recognizable shape.

"No," Aibhall shouted at it. She turned inland, dragging the children behind her.

"Why don't you just take the hilt?" Evan cried out.

"I know better. Stolen, it would bring only harm. The maid must bring it."

Their backs to the sea, the children could only guess at the crow's progress. Ahead of them lay Aibhall's destination, giant upright slabs supporting an enormous tablestone that slanted precariously, as if to crush the unwary seeking shelter there. It weighed the darkness with its cold, unfinished fall.

"In there," directed Aibhall, bringing them alongside her and then pushing them toward the yawning entrance. "The other crow pursues us. It will show them our way."

But Thorstein's crow was swifter than the Sidh maiden and her unwieldy captives. Claudia could hear it flapping overhead, could feel the rush of air as it swooped like a bird of prey.

Aibhall screamed, "Set your crow on it." She yanked the crow from Evan's hands. "There." She sounded triumphant. "Crow will fight crow and distract the Icelander. Inside now. Into the Hill."

But the children resisted with all their force, while beside them both crows, like reflections of each other, dove and ripped at the *feth fiada*. In her fury, Aibhall flung the folds in their way; they tore through these as well. The children, suddenly released, stood a moment, uncertain, and then raced seaward to the place from which Aibhall, pointing far below, had made out a solitary seal among the rocks.

They hesitated before descending. They thought they could see Nessa, could not be sure, did not dare to waste a moment. Thorstein's ship was standing off from the rocks. Was the Icelander shouting to them? They could only guess. Their ears filled with the rising wind, with the sea, with the fear that clogged their senses and impelled them on, sometimes falling, sometimes seizing a second to recover, gulping air, splayed out like the rotting gulls that strewed the turf-lined shelves of the cliff.

Toward the sea the cliff dropped away. There were no more shelves where they might bury their faces in the sour, bird-limed grass, not even outcroppings to grab and break their descent. "Dive?" asked Evan in an incredulous whisper. Panting, Claudia could only nod. It wasn't so far now. She dared to look into the water where the crust of land split open. Nessa was there, showing them that they might plunge into this wedge of the bay.

Still they held back. Thorstein's voice reached them now, exhorting them to linger not. As if to confirm his warning, the crows plummeted to them. Evan reached for the smaller crow, swayed, teetered, and grabbing it went straight down. The crow in his grasp set up a terrible squawking that ended abruptly with a splash. Thorstein's crow hovered but a second, peering with cold appraisal into Claudia's tear-stained face. She heard Thorstein shout once to her: "Follow."

She was incapable of anything like a dive. Terrified, she could only push herself backward so that she would not have to look down. She cut through the air like a scythe. She was a blade describing an arc in a hissing void. She opened her eyes on a cold gray mirror and slammed into it.

The breath was knocked out of her, sight and hearing as well. But she could feel the buoyancy, the hand that held her, the body that supported her own. She thought she could hear Evan gasp and splutter beside her. "Give Claudia a chance to rest," she heard. She wasn't sure who spoke those words. It might have been herself.

Then the crow's voice broke through the blur of water, as harsh and solid as the land itself. Its raucous complaint stayed with her until the stippled moonlight drew her and Evan out of that age of darkness and showed them the sleeping islet of Thrumcap on the muttering sea.

thirty-three

THE children slept late. Claudia was half aware that sheep had come nosing around the door of the shack. She heard the plaintive blat of a lamb, waited for its mother's throaty response, and drifted into sleep again. Evan never stirred. Only when Colman's boat chugged into the cove and the crow awoke to hunger and gladness were the children roused.

They were still groggy when Mr. Withorn sprinted up the path to find them. The fact that his expedition had been largely unsuccessful didn't faze him. He had had the time of his life, had seen at least one gray seal in the early morning, as well as countless harbor seals. He'd have some great pictures to show.

Mr. Colman only grunted a kind of welcome to his crow. "Put the other back?" he wanted to know.

"Oh yes," they both assured him. The other one was safe. Fervently they believed this. Thorstein would take Nessa to Eyin Helga. With the other two children lost, he'd take special care. Neither Claudia nor Evan could bring themselves to consider whether Nessa would return, like Thorstein's crow, to the ship. They couldn't bear to think of her left to the sea. So they said, "Yes," emphatically. Everyone and everything was safe.

Mr. Colman looked past them as if he had lost interest in the conversation, then softly remarked, "There's your seal. Followed our boat."

Mr. Withorn, eager to get home and start developing film, was nevertheless distracted enough to charge down to the cove. The seal disappeared. "Never mind," he called up to them. "They never let you near. I should have known. Pack up your things, and I'll begin stowing gear on the boat."

Evan stood there, still a bit groggy, squinting down at the cove. Thoughtfully he stared, one bare foot raised to scratch against the inside of the other leg. He rubbed absently, then turned toward the heart of the island.

Claudia let him go. This was one time she wasn't about to charge him with leaving all the dirty work to her. She followed Mr. Colman into the shack and began haphazardly to throw everything into the sleeping bags. Then she rolled them up.

By now Mr. Colman was swearing affectionately at the crow. From the few words that Claudia could catch, she gathered that he was declaring his unreadiness to set out all night ever again with someone like that camera fellow. She understood that some of this griping was aimed indirectly at her.

"Well," Claudia offered, "we got her back there anyhow." Then she was at a loss. She couldn't tell him that Nessa was in the keeping of Thorstein, who was clumsy and bungled things but sailed a true course and let Memory serve him. She could not bear the idea that

Nessa was still in the rocky reaches of the outer bay below Ben Edar or in the tortured currents of Eyin Helga. "At least . . . ," Claudia stammered, "it wasn't in the grave."

"I'd sooner go to my grave in my own time," the old man declared almost fiercely, "than be drifting . . . drifting. . . ."

Mr. Withorn filled the doorway, blocking out the light, declaring his readiness to be off. He peered in as far as he could. "Where's Evan?"

Claudia handed him one of the sleeping bags and told him that Evan would be back soon. She turned to thank Mr. Colman and found that he was leaning back against the wall, snoring softly. The crow eyed her with suspicion. Then it began to preen itself, drawing from under its wing a single thread of gold. It tugged on the thread till it was pulled free, then dropped it into the filth at her feet. Satisfied, it shook itself and rattled its scraggly feathers.

After waiting nearly an hour, Mr. Withorn insisted on going to look for Evan. Claudia suggested he might be across on the low, rocky side of the island where the seals usually sunned themselves at low water. Dispiritedly she followed Mr. Withorn in that direction.

They saw the seal before they caught sight of Evan, who was crouched so low on a slanting rock that at first he seemed to be made of stone. But they couldn't miss the seal, which had somehow made its way into a tidal inlet and was rolling lazily in the protected water.

Mr. Withorn whispered, "My God, it's a gray. And it doesn't seem to mind Evan at all. Look at that."

Claudia was looking. She took in Evan's deep concentration. It was as though he was lost in conversation.

"Must be the same one," Mr. Withorn exclaimed. "It's either sick or injured, or else someone's pet. You know, an orphan raised by someone so that it trusts—"

"No," Claudia whispered as he started down, stepping cautiously on grass to muffle his tread. "No, it isn't a pet."

"But it's not afraid." Mr. Withorn grinned back at her. "God, I'm glad I have my camera. I almost left it on board."

"Please," Claudia pleaded, scrambling down to him, "don't go there. It's just for Evan."

"Oh, I'll get a shot of Evan with the seal too. It's incredible. He's actually tamed it."

"Mr. Withorn," Claudia said to him, "you don't understand. Evan wouldn't do that." She knew she was floundering. "It's not just that he couldn't. He wouldn't."

Mr. Withorn turned slowly and sent Claudia a penetrating look. "Is this what your secret here was all about? Don't be afraid to tell me. It's marvelous."

Helpless, Claudia returned his gaze. "Please don't go any closer. Evan will come in a minute."

"Don't worry." Mr. Withorn offered her a conspiratorial smile. "I won't horn in on him. I'll just get close enough for a few good shots." Crouching low, he picked his way along the beach boulders, halting now and then to raise his camera. Drift littered the rough shoreline. Claudia hoped he would be stopped by the rotting ribs of a dory, the wharf timbers lying aslant with rusting spikes protruding from them. But one of those spikes merely caught the cuff of his pants.

She had a vision like a double exposure of Thorstein tumbling over the wounded in his ship. Then Mr. Withorn, lurching off balance, stepped with all his weight on a round pot buoy that rolled out from under him. She saw his hand clutch frantically at the sky. He hauled himself up, apologies erupting from him as curses might have burst from another man.

Only Claudia and Evan saw how the seal shot straight up from the water, eyes large with alarm, before it slipped from their sight.

Mr. Withorn rubbed his elbow, shook out his ankle, and praised Evan for his sensitivity and perseverance. "Not many boys your age would be able to pull that off," he declared.

Evan said nothing. His eyes were set toward the rocks that dotted the island's bay.

Claudia thought she saw the head surface for an instant, then submerge. She imagined the eyes, bright and fearful and darkly intense. She listened to Mr. Withorn, his voice full of entreaty; he offered Evan every consolation he could muster. There would be photographs. He'd snapped a few great pictures before he'd tripped and scared the seal away. "That's worth something. Isn't it?" he pleaded to Evan's back.

Evan nodded very slightly.

Claudia began to breathe more easily. Pretty soon Evan would be ready. Pretty soon he'd get up and walk back across the island to the dinghy.

"Wait till you show those pictures to your family," Mr. Withorn declared with desperate elation. "To your friends."

Claudia knew that with only a few words she could spare Evan and at the same time help out Mr. Withorn. Words, like the camera set between himself and the unfathomable, could fend off his glimpses of the infinite,

341

dark cold. If Claudia spoke to him, he would be able to slow down and attend to his bruised elbow, his broken light meter strap. Yet she just sat there.

It was inconvenient, not frightening, to be wordless. She knew that those crusty black crows would not desert her. They could be called, blinking and stubborn, bedraggled and hoarse, into any sunlight.

So she ended up like Evan, staring and silent, waiting for the shadows to wing across the sun and dim the blinding vision.

AUTHOR'S NOTE

WHEN Evan asked Aibhall who really won at Clontarf, he had an idea that winning must have settled something or finished something. But the Battle of Clontarf was as much a beginning as an ending. Of course the Irish and Norse wrote different accounts of the battle; more than nine hundred years later scholars are still sifting through the questions raised by those early accounts. There are studies on every aspect of the battle—from a treatise in the *Proceedings* of the Royal Irish Academy with astronomical computations to establish the exact time of high water in Dublin Bay on April 23, 1014, to A. J. Goedheer's valuable book, *Irish and Norse Traditions About the Battle of Clontarf.*

For centuries the traditional Irish view held that Clontarf was decisive in reversing the heathen tide and freeing Ireland from the stranglehold of the "foreigners." But the Norse settlements did not end with the battle. Sitric Silkenbeard, ruler of the Norse kingdom of Ath Cliath (Dublin), was converted to Christianity and continued to reign until he retired to spend his last years in a monastery. Though the viking raids of the ninth and tenth centuries brought as much terror and destruction to Ireland as they did to Britain and the Continent, the long Norse occupation of strategic river mouths (later to become major Irish cities) was also characterized by development vital to trade and shipping and by a mingling of language and legend as well as of the people themselves.

During those turbulent years the names of places and peoples frequently changed and even overlapped. For example, Brian called himself *Imperator Scotorum* or High King of the Scots (which then meant Irish); at the same time the Norse referred to the joined kingdoms of Dalriada and Pictland as Scotland. The face of Britain changed most rapidly during the eleventh century when its various kingdoms were conquered first by the Danes in 1016 and then, in 1066, by the Normans.

Any map of the period may be misleading because of the frequency of those changes and because names differed according to viewpoints. Most modern place names like Norway (the Northern Way) didn't then exist. Often there was a multiplicity of designations for one geographic area and its people. The Irish or Scots of Erin and Dalriada used many names, few of them polite, in referring to the Scandinavians: "Foreigners," "Outlaws," and "Pagans" are some, though they usually distinguished between the Danes, who were Black Foreigners (*Dubh-Gaill*) and the Norse, who were Fair Foreigners (*Finn-Gaill*), and also Men of Lochlann (*Lochlannaigh*) or Northmen (*Nordmanni*).

Scotland and its islands were occupied from about the first century B.C. through the second century A.D. by a people who constructed the round double-walled and galleried towers known today as brochs. By the sixth century, when Celtic missionaries began to settle in the islands, the Orkneys (Orcades) were occupied by northern Picts. It is likely that the Norse migration into those islands occurred earlier and more gradually than it did farther south where the first raids date from the eighth century.

Byrgisey, a Norse name meaning fortified island, is a gentle tidal islet of about fifty acres off the Orkney mainland; it is known today as the Brough of Birsay. Sigurd the Stout's youngest son, Thorfinn, who was not yet born when Olaf Tryggvason "converted" his father to Christianity, succeeded his older brothers as earl. It was he who had a "splendid minster," dedicated either to Peter or to Colm, built on Byrgisey's green slope. All that is left from that time are the excavated fragments of the church and monastic buildings and some foundations of the Great Hall and other Norse long houses.

There are also ecclesiastical remains on the tiny island of Eynhallow (Norse name: Eyin Helga). As with the Brough of Birsay, where stone fragments with Pictish symbols and an early cross with ogham writing were found, local traditions and place names suggest a pre-Norse occupation by Celtic missionaries.

But though these and many other fragments of the civilizations of the Picts and Celts and Norse abound both in and out of museums, and though chronicles, annals, and sagas may help to fit them into a coherent picture of their time, the Picts elude the historian. The only surviving Pictish record is a partial list of kings; some names and dates of battles are confirmed by other sources. There are also references in Irish annals to the Cruithne, or Irish Picts, including in one of these the assertion that a seventh-century Irish monk named Baitan was related to a Pict called Talorg.

The Picts lived in and around many of the brochs, which they modified into what are called wheel-houses.

The Picts were reputed to be skilled seamen and they became the most serious threat to Roman power in northern Britain. Beyond this, little is known of their history; their long struggle with the Dalriadic Scots ended finally in defeat in the ninth century, by which time the Scandinavians occupied much of what had been Pictish territory in the north.

Though the Picts could not prevail against more vigorous and aggressive peoples, they left the mark of a unique civilization in their vital stone art. But even this art, with its still undeciphered symbols, reminds us that we can never really learn who and what the Picts were. Enslaved, driven off into pockets of isolation, assimilated into cultures which eclipsed theirs entirely, they, like Nessa, remain lost.

There are only hints of them in the folklore of Scotland and Ireland, in tales of little folk who have vanished, or perhaps in the legends of people gone with the seals. Creenie, which derives from Cruithne (Irish Picts), was a term of derision applied to an isolated hill people in Galloway as late as the beginning of the last century. The creenies were reported to be a poor, small, black-haired and ugly people characterized by features reflecting drastic inbreeding and extreme physical and mental degeneration.

It is the winners, or at least the survivors, who write the annals and chronicles of their times. The Picts were among history's losers, and we can only imagine the qualities of this people whose legacy of stone and symbol endures in silence.